THE
TIN ROOF
BLOWDOWN

THE
TIN ROOF
BLOWDOWN

A
Dave Robicheaux Novel

JAMES LEE BURKE

First published in Great Britain in 2007 by Orion Books,
an imprint of The Orion Publishing Group Ltd
Orion House, 5 Upper Saint Martin's Lane
London WC2H 9EA

An Hachette Livre UK Company

1 3 5 7 9 10 8 6 4 2

A CIP catalogue record for this book is
available from the British Library.

ISBN (Hardback) 978 0 7528 8916 0
ISBN (Trade Paperback) 978 0 7528 8917 7

Printed in Great Britain by Mackays of Chatham plc,
Chatham, Kent

The Orion Publishing Group's policy is to use papers that are natural,
renewable and recyclable products and made from wood grown in
sustainable forests. The logging and manufacturing processes are
expected to conform to the environmental regulations of the
country of origin.

www.orionbooks.co.uk

ACKNOWLEDGMENTS

MY THANKS TO GLEN PITRE for his personal account about brown recluse spiders and for his account involving the desperation of the people trying to escape the storm on Highway 23.

For John and Kathy Clark

Before the mountains were settled,
Before the hills, I was brought forth;
While as yet He had not made the earth or the fields,
Or the primal dust of the world.
When He prepared the heavens, I was there,
When He drew a circle on the face of the deep,
When He established the clouds above,
When He strengthened the fountains of the deep,
When He assigned to the sea its limit,
So that the waters would not transgress His command,
When He marked out the foundations of the earth,
Then I was beside Him as a master craftsman;
And I was daily His delight,
Rejoicing always before Him,
Rejoicing in his inhabited world,
And my delight was with the sons of men.

(Proverbs 8:24–31)

CHAPTER 1

My worst dreams have always contained images of brown water and fields of elephant grass and the downdraft of helicopter blades. The dreams are in color but they contain no sound, not of drowned voices in the river or the explosions under the hooches in the village we burned or the thropping of the Jolly Green and the gunships coming low and flat across the canopy, like insects pasted against a molten sun.

In the dream I lie on a poncho liner, dehydrated with blood expander, my upper thigh and side torn by wounds that could have been put there by wolves. I am convinced I will die unless I receive plasma back at battalion aid. Next to me lies a Negro corporal, wearing only his trousers and boots, his skin coal-black, his torso split open like a gaping red zipper from his armpit down to his groin, the damage to his body so grievous, traumatic, and terrible to see or touch he doesn't understand what has happened to him.

"I got the spins, Loot. How I look?" he says.

"We've got the million-dollar ticket, Doo-doo. We're Freedom Bird bound," I reply.

His face is crisscrossed with sweat, his mouth as glossy and bright as freshly applied lipstick when he tries to smile.

The Jolly Green loads up and lifts off, with Doo-doo and twelve other wounded on board. I stare upward at its strange rectangular shape, its blades whirling against a lavender sky, and secretly I resent the fact that I and others are left behind to wait on the slick and the

I

chance that serious numbers of NVA are coming through the grass. Then I witness the most bizarre and cruel and seemingly unfair event of my entire life.

As the Jolly Green climbs above the river and turns toward the China Sea, a solitary RPG streaks at a forty-five-degree angle from the canopy below and explodes inside the bay. The ship shudders once and cracks in half, its fuel tanks blooming into an enormous orange fireball. The wounded on board are coated with flame as they plummet downward toward the water.

Their lives are taken incrementally—by flying shrapnel and bullets, by liquid flame on their skin, and by drowning in a river. In effect, they are forced to die three times. A medieval torturer could not have devised a more diabolic fate.

When I wake from the dream, I have to sit for a long time on the side of the bed, my arms clenched across my chest, as though I've caught a chill or the malarial mosquito is once again having its way with my metabolism. I assure myself that the dream is only a dream, that if it were real I would have heard sounds and not simply seen images that are the stuff of history now and are not considered of interest by those who are determined to re-create them.

I also tell myself that the past is a decaying memory and that I do not have to relive and empower it unless I choose to do so. As a recovering drunk, I know I cannot allow myself the luxury of resenting my government for lying to a whole generation of young men and women who believed they were serving a noble cause. Nor can I resent those who treated us as oddities if not pariahs when we returned home.

When I go back to sleep, I once again tell myself I will never again have to witness the wide-scale suffering of innocent civilians, nor the betrayal and abandonment of our countrymen when they need us most.

But that was before Katrina. That was before a storm with greater impact than the bomb blast that struck Hiroshima peeled the face off southern Louisiana. That was before one of the most beautiful cities in the Western Hemisphere was killed three times, and not just by the forces of nature.

CHAPTER
2

THE CENTERPIECE OF my story involves a likable man by the name of Jude LeBlanc. When I first knew him he was a nice-looking kid who threw the *Daily Iberian,* played baseball at Catholic High, and was a weekly communicant at the same church I attended. Although his mother was poorly educated and worked at menial jobs and his father a casualty of an oil-well blowout, he smiled all the time and was full of self-confidence and never seemed to let misfortune get him down.

I said he smiled. That's not quite right. Jude shined the world on and slipped its worst punches and in a fight knew how to swallow his blood and never let people know he was hurt. He had his Jewish mother's narrow eyes and chestnut hair, and he combed it straight back in a hump, like a character out of a 1930s movie. Somehow he reassured others that the earth was a good place, that the day was a fine one, and that good things were about to happen to all of us. But as I watched Jude grow into manhood, I had to relearn the old lesson that often the best people in our midst are perhaps destined to become sojourners in the Garden of Gethsemane.

Ordinary men and women keep track of time in sequential fashion, by use of clocks and calendars. The residents of Gethsemane do not. Here are a few of their stories, each of them touching, in an improbable way, the life of a New Iberia kid who grew into a

3

good man and did nothing to invite the events fate would impose upon him.

ON FRIDAY, August 26, 2005, Jude LeBlanc wakes in a second-story French Quarter apartment, one that allows him a view of both the courtyard below and the spires of St. Louis Cathedral. It's raining hard now, and he watches the water sluicing down the drainpipes into the beds of hibiscus, banana trees, and hydrangeas below, pooling in the sunken brickwork that is threaded with leaves of wild spearmint.

For just a moment he almost forgets the ball of pain that lives twenty-four hours a day in the base of his spine. The Hispanic woman whose name is Natalia is fixing coffee and warm milk for him in the tiny kitchen off the living room. Her cotton sundress is dark purple and printed with bone-colored flowers that have pink stamens. She's a thin woman whose strong hands and muscular tautness belie the life she leads. She glances at him over her shoulder, her face full of concern and pity for the man who roaches back his hair as Mickey Rooney did in old American movies she has rented from the video store.

When she hooks, she works with a pimp who drives an independent cab. She and her pimp usually find johns in the early a.m. along Bourbon and take them either to a private parking lot behind a burned-out building off Tchoupitoulas or a desiccated frame house owned by the pimp's brother-in-law on North Villere, thereby avoiding complications with their more organized competitors, most of whom enjoy established relationships with both cops and the vestiges of old Mob.

Natalia brings him his coffee and warm milk and a single powdered beignet from the Café du Monde on a tray. She draws the blinds, turns the electric fan on him, and asks, "You want me to do it for you?"

"No, I don't need it right now. I'll wait until later in the day."

"I don't think you got no sleep last night."

He watches the rainwater feathering off the roof and makes no reply. When he sits up on the rollaway bed, tentacles of light wrap around his thighs and probe his groin. Natalia sits down beside him, her dress dropping into a loop between her knees. Her hair is black and thick and she washes it often so it always has a sheen in it, and when she takes it down on her shoulders she is truly lovely to look at. She doesn't smoke or drink, and there's never a hint of the life she leads in her clothes or on her skin, not unless you include the tracks inside her thighs.

Her face is lost in thought, either about him or herself, he's not sure. To her, Jude LeBlanc is a mystery, one she never quite understands, but it's obvious she accepts and loves him for whatever he is or isn't and imposes no judgment upon him.

"Can I do something else for you?"

"Like what?"

"Sometimes I feel I don't ever do you no good, that I can't give you nothing," she says.

"You fixed breakfast for me," he says.

She changes her position and kneels behind him on the rollaway, rubbing his shoulders, clutching him briefly to her, resting her cheek against the back of his head. "They got drugs in Mexico the pharmaceutical companies don't allow on the market here," she says.

"You're my cure," he replies.

She holds him, and for just a moment he wants to release all the desperation and hopelessness and unrelieved sense of loss that have characterized his life. But how do you explain to others that a false Gleason score on a prostate biopsy can result in so much damage to a person's life? Most people don't even understand the terminology. Plus he does not wish to rob others of their faith in the exactitude of medical science. To do so is, in a way, the same as robbing them of the only belief system they have.

The Gleason scale had indicated that the cancer had not spread outside the prostate. As a consequence the surgeon had elected not to take out the erectile nerve. The positive margins left behind went into the lymph nodes and the seminal vessels.

Natalia flattens herself against him, pressing her loins tightly into his back, and he feels desires stirring in him that he tries not to recognize, perhaps secretly hoping they will preempt the problems of conscience that prevent him from ever escaping his own loneliness.

He gets up from the rollaway, trying to hide his erection as he puts on his trousers. His Roman collar has fallen off the nightstand and a tangle of animal hair and floor dirt has stuck to the bottom rim. He goes to the sink and tries to clean it, rubbing the smudge deeper into the collar's whiteness, splashing it with grease from an unwashed pot. He leans heavily on his hands, his sense of futility more than he can hide.

Outside, the velocity of the wind is fanning the rain off the roof in sheets. A flowerpot topples from the balcony and bursts on the bricks below. Across the courtyard, a neighbor's ventilated wood shutters rattle like tack hammers on their hinges.

"You going to the Ninth Ward today?" Natalia asks.

"It's the only place that will have me," he replies.

"Stay with me," she says.

"Are you afraid of the storm?" he asks.

"I'm afraid for you. You need to be here, with me. You can't be without your medicine."

She calls it his "medicine" to protect his feelings, even though she knows he's been arrested twice with stolen prescription forms and once with morphine from an actual heist, that in reality he is no different from her or any other junkie in the Quarter. The irony is that a peasant woman from the Third World, one who works as a prostitute to fuel her own addiction, has a spiritual love and respect for him that few in his own society would be willing to grant.

He feels a sudden tenderness for her that makes his loins turn to water. He puts his mouth on hers, then goes out into the rain, a newspaper over his head, and catches one of the few buses still running down to the lower end of the Ninth Ward.

CHAPTER
3

Otis Baylor proudly calls himself a North Alabama transplant who is at home anyplace in the world, New Orleans or New Iberia or wherever his insurance company cares to send him. He's effusive in manner, generous in his giving, and devoted to his family. If at all possible, he refuses to judge others and to be marked by the prejudices of either his contemporaries or the people of his piney-woods birthplace, where as a boy he witnessed his father and uncle attend cross lightings in full Klan regalia.

In fact, Otis learned the insurance business from the bottom up, working a debit route in the Negro and blue-collar neighborhoods of Birmingham. Where other salesmen had failed, Otis was a shining success. At a convention of salespeople in Mobile, a cynical rival asked him his secret. "Treat folks with respect and you'll be amazed at how they respond," Otis answered.

Today he drives home early in rain and heavy traffic, telling himself that neither he nor his family will be undone by the forces of nature. His house was built in 1856 and was mute witness to Yankee occupation, epidemics of yellow jack, street battles between Union loyalists and White Leaguers, the lynching of Italian immigrants from streetlamps, and tidal surges that left the bodies of drowned clipper ship sailors hanging in trees. The men who built Otis's house had built it right, and with the gasoline-powered generators he has placed in his carriage house, the flashlights and medical supplies and canned food and bottled water he has packed into his pantries and his attic, he is confident he and his family can persevere through the worst of natural calamities.

Have faith in God, but also have faith in yourself. That's what Otis's daddy always said.

But as he stares at the rain sweeping through the live oak trees in his yard, another kind of fear flickers inside him, one that to him is even more unsettling than the prospect of the hurricane that is churning toward the city, sucking the Gulf of Mexico into its maw.

Otis has always believed in the work ethic and taking care of one's self and one's own. In his view, there is no such thing as luck, either good or bad. He believes that victimhood has become a self-sustaining culture, one to which he will never subscribe. When people fall on bad times, it's usually the result of their own actions, he tells himself. The serpent didn't force Eve to pick forbidden fruit, nor did God make Cain slay his brother.

But if Otis's view is correct, why did undeserved suffering come in such a brutal fashion to his homely, sad, overweight daughter, his only child, whose self-esteem was so low she was overjoyed to be invited to the senior prom by a rail of a boy with dandruff on his shoulders and glasses that made his eyes look like a goldfish's?

After the prom, Thelma and her date had headed up Interstate 10 to a party, except the boy, who had moved to New Orleans only two months earlier, got lost and drove them into a neighborhood not far from the Desire Welfare Project. Mindlessly, the boy killed the engine and asked directions of a passerby. When he discovered his battery was dead and he couldn't restart the engine, he walked to a pay phone to call Otis, leaving Thelma by herself.

The three black thugs who stumbled across her were probably ripped on weed and fortified wine. But that alone would not explain the ferocity of their attack on Otis's daughter. They stuffed a red bandana in her mouth and twisted her arms behind her while they forced her between two buildings. Then they took turns raping and sodomizing her while they burned her skin with cigarettes.

Two years have passed since that night and Otis still seeks explanations. Thelma's attackers were never caught, and Otis doubts they ever will be. Psychiatrists and therapists and the minister from Otis's church have done little good in Thelma's recovery, if "recovery" is the word. He wakes in the middle of the night and sits by himself in the den, determined that his wife will not discover the level of torment in his soul.

More important, perhaps, he refuses to be embittered or to join ranks with his neighbors who comprised part of the forty percent of the electorate that voted for the former Klansman and Nazi David Duke in a gubernatorial runoff.

He makes a cheese, lettuce, and mayonnaise sandwich, places it on a tray with a can of soda and a long-stemmed rose, and carries the tray up to Thelma's room. She is bent over her desk, dressed in a black T-shirt and black jeans with big brass brads on them, earphones clamped on her head. He has no idea what she is listening to. Sometimes she is enthralled by recordings of birdsong or waterfalls; other times she listens to heavy-metal bands that make Otis wish he had been born deaf.

"I thought you might want a snack," he says.

Her mouth is painted with purple lipstick, her hair dark and freshly shampooed and clipped in bangs so that it looks like a helmet. Her face wears a perpetual pie-plate expression that makes others feel the problem in communicating with her is theirs, not hers. She vacillates between bouts of anorexia, binge eating, and bulimia. By normal standards, she would not be considered a likable person. But why should she be? Otis asks himself. How many young girls were psychologically prepared to deal with the damage these men had inflicted upon her?

She begins eating the sandwich without removing the earphones or speaking to him. He reaches down and lifts the foam-rubber pads from her head.

"Can't you say hello to your old man?" he asks.

"Hi, Daddy," she says.

"Want to help me latch the shutters when you're finished?"

She looks up at him. An intense thought, like a dark bird with a hooked beak, seems to hide behind her eyes. "A civil defense guy said it's going to be awful."

"It could be. But we're tough guys."

He tries to read her expression. It's not one of fear or apprehension. In fact, he wonders if it isn't one of fulfilled expectation. She's a reader of Nostradamus and is drawn to prophecies of destruction and death, as though she wishes to see the unhappiness in her own life transferred into the lives of others.

"The insurance companies are going to screw the city, aren't they? Does your company write exceptions for water damage?" she says.

"That's silly."

"Not if you're one of the people about to get screwed."

He leaves the room and closes the door behind him, repressing the anger that blooms in his chest.

Downstairs his wife is dropping thirty-pound bags of crushed ice into the Deepfreeze. Her name is Melanie and she insists that he not call her "Mel," even though that was the affectionate nickname he gave her when they first courted.

"Why are you doing that?" he asks.

"So we'll have a way to preserve our food if we have a total outage," she replies, a cloud of escaped cold air rising into her face.

He starts to explain that he's already covered that possibility with his installation of gasoline-operated generators, that in effect she's displacing the room in the freezer that should be used for all the perishables they can pack into it.

But he doesn't argue. He was a widower when he met her five years ago on a beach in the Bahamas. She was a divorcée, deeply tanned and gold-haired and beautiful, much younger than he, a strong woman physically, bold in her look, her brown eyes wide-set and unblinking, her laughter suggesting disregard for convention and perhaps a degree of sexual adventurism. She was the kind of woman who could be a friend as well as a lover.

Otis was fifty-three at the time, prematurely bald but proud of the power in his hands and shoulders and not ashamed of his libido or the profuse way he sweated when he worked or the scent of testosterone his clothes sometimes carried. He was what he was and didn't pretend otherwise. Obviously Melanie, or "Mel," did not find him an unattractive man.

They were opposites in many ways, but each seemed to possess a set of qualities that compensated for a deficiency in the other, she with her urban sophistication and degree in finance from the University of Chicago, he with his work ethic and his common sense in dealing with people.

They said good-bye in the Bahamas without consummating their brief courtship but continued to talk long-distance to each other and exchange presents and e-mails. Two months passed, and on a summer night when the light was high in the sky and he could no longer stand his loneliness, Otis asked Melanie to meet him at the Ritz-Carlton in Atlanta. He was surprised at her aggressiveness in bed and the fact she came three times their first night together, something no other woman had ever done for him. He proposed one week later.

His friends thought he was impetuous and that perhaps he was being taken advantage of by a woman twenty years his junior. But what did he have to lose? he told them. His daughter needed a mother; Otis needed a wife; and let's face it, he said, women with Melanie's looks didn't come his way every day.

After the first year he began to realize he had married a complex if not mercurial woman. Her attitudes were often inflexible, although the issue involved was usually insignificant. She canceled the cable service because the technician tracked mud into the foyer. She accused Otis of overtipping waiters and allowing the gardeners to get by with sloppy work. She seemed to carry a reservoir of anger with her as she would a social bludgeon, and selectively utilized it to cause embarrassment in public places and ultimately get her way.

An acquaintance in Chicago has told him that Melanie's former husband was an alcoholic. The friend's offer of information about Melanie's past has only made Otis more confused. Melanie is rigidly abstemious, and Otis does not understand how her former husband's behavior could account for her unpredictable mood swings today.

But the transformation in Melanie that was most difficult for Otis to accept took place after the attack upon Thelma. Each evening she began to show fatigue and complained of nausea and insisted on talking about nonexistent problems with their finances. He could feel her back constrict when he touched her in bed. On Saturday and Sunday mornings she awoke an hour earlier than he and went downstairs and into her day's schedule, effectively neutralizing any romantic overture on his part.

On one occasion, unbeknown to her, he glimpsed her picking his clothes off the back of a chair, smelling them, then flinging them with disgust into a dirty clothes hamper.

Now, as the worst storm in Louisiana's history approaches the city, he wonders if she blames him for the assault upon his daughter. Is that the reason behind her irritability and her implicit criticism of whatever he does? Does she no longer think of him as protector of his family?

"I'm going to the club for a workout. Want to come?" he says.

"Now? Are you serious?"

"My daddy used to always say, 'Respect Mother Nature, but nail down the shutters and don't let her scare you.'"

She can hardly hide her ennui at his mention of his sawmill-employee father who went to the ninth grade. "Take Thelma with you," she says.

"She doesn't like the club."

Melanie makes no reply and begins pulling dishes from the dishwasher and putting them away loudly in the cabinets.

"What is it? Why do I make you angry?" he says.

She seems to teeter on a direct answer to his question, her eyes charged with light. Then the moment passes. "I'm not angry. I just don't think it's good for Thelma to stay in her room all the time. Maybe she should think about getting a job," she says.

But secretly Otis has always suspected that his wife is like many Northerners. She likes people of color collectively and as an abstraction. But she doesn't feel comfortable with them individually. It's been obvious from the night of the attack that she doesn't want her friends to know her stepdaughter has been the victim of black rapists.

"You think I let Thelma down somehow?" he asks.

She examines her hands over the sink, feeling the bones in them, the joints of her fingers. She has begun to complain of arthritis, although she has not seen a doctor for at least a year. She looks at the rain beating on the philodendron and the banana trees and windmill palms in the side yard.

"Why did you let her go to the prom with an idiot who doesn't know how to wash the dandruff out of his hair, much less protect his date from a bunch of animals?" she says.

"You never made any mistakes when you were that age?" he replies.

"Of that magnitude? No, I had to wait until I was a mature woman to do that," she says.

He slings his workout bag over his shoulder and goes down the covered walk to the carriage house and backs his car under the canopy of oaks and into the street, knocking the trash can into the hedge. Melanie's last statement to him is one he knows he will never be able to scrub out of his memory, no matter what form of amends or atonement, if any, she ever tries to make.

That thought is like a cold vapor wrapped around his heart, and briefly the avenue and windswept neutral ground and the scrolled purple and pink neon tubing on the corner drugstore go out of focus.

THE HEALTH CLUB is almost empty, the basketball court echoing with the sounds of a solitary shooter bouncing shots off a steel rim. The shooter is Otis's neighbor, Tom Claggart, an export-import man who flies in a private plane with business friends to western game farms, where they shoot animals that are released from either cages or penned areas shortly before the hunters' arrival. Tom has told Otis, with a lascivious wink, that he and his friends also land at a private airstrip not far from a brothel outside Vegas.

"Got her battened down?" he says, the basketball grasped between his palms.

"Pretty much," Otis says.

Tom's torso is as solid as a cypress stump, his head bullet-shaped. Each week a barber clips his mustache, which is threaded with white, and lathers his scalp and shaves it with a straight-edged razor.

"I think after landfall we're gonna have monkey shit flying through the fan," Tom says.

"I don't know as I follow you," Otis replies.

"The black Irish get restive after natural disasters." Tom is smiling now, as though the two of them share a private knowledge.

"I guess we'll find out," Otis replies.

Tom flings his basketball down the court and watches it bounce and roll across the maple boards into the shadows. The windows high up on the walls are streaked with rain, whipped by the branches of trees. His face becomes thoughtful. "I've never talked to you about this before, but my sister-in-law told me what happened to your daughter. They ever catch those guys?"

"Not yet."

"That's a shame. If they didn't catch them by now, they probably won't."

"I couldn't say," Otis replies.

"You own a gun?"

"Why?"

"Come Monday, those bastards are gonna be swarming all over the neighborhood. If I were you, I'd stop jerking on my dork and smell the coffee."

"What makes you think you can talk to me like that?"

"Just speaking to you as a neighbor and a friend."

"Don't."

"This isn't like you, Otis."

That's what you think, you idiot, Otis says to himself, and is surprised by the virulence of his own thoughts.

CHAPTER
4

It's Saturday evening and long lines of automobiles are streaming out of New Orleans, northbound on Interstate 10, although rumors have already spread that there is not a motel room available all the way to St. Louis, Missouri.

But for the glad of heart, life goes on full-throttle in the French Quarter. In a corner bar off Ursulines, one in which Christmas lights never come down, Clete Purcel has positioned himself at a window so he can watch a shuttered cottage across the street, in front of which a black male is smoking a cigarette in an illegally parked panel truck. The rain has stopped and the air is unnaturally green and contains the dense, heavy odor of the Gulf. There is even a rip of bone-white light in the clouds, as though the evening sunset is about to resume. The black male in the panel truck is talking on a cell phone and blowing his cigarette smoke out the window, where it seems to hang in the air like damp cotton. Then he twists his head and stares at the bar, and for a moment Clete thinks he has been made.

But the black man is watching a woman in spiked heels and skintight shorts walking rapidly down the sidewalk, her sequined, fringed purse swinging back on her rump. The owner of the bar is opening all the doors, filling the interior with a bloom of fresh air that smells of brine and wet trees. The revelers inside react as though a bad moment in their lives has come and gone.

"You want another drink? It's on the house," the owner says.

"I look like I can't pay for my drinks?" Clete says.

"No, you look like you got the heebie-jeebies. Maybe you ought to get yourself laid."

Clete gives the owner a look, one that makes the owner's eyes shift off Clete's face. The owner is Jimmy Flannigan, an ex–professional wrestler who now wears earrings and has a full-body wax done at a parlor on Airline Highway.

"So don't get laid. But you're making my customers nervous. No one likes to get stepped on by out-of-control circus elephants."

Clete has long ago given up contending with Jimmy's insults. "I got news for you. The Apocalypse could blow through this dump and your clientele wouldn't notice," he says.

Jimmy pours into Clete's glass from a Scotch bottle with a chrome nipple on it. The Scotch swirls inside the milk like marbled ice cream. "What's eatin' you, Purcel? Just off your feed?" he says.

Clete drinks his glass half empty. "Something like that," he says.

How can he explain to Jimmy Flannigan the sense of apprehension and the déjà vu that dries out his mouth and causes his scalp to tighten against his skull? Or describe helicopters lifting off a rooftop into a sky ribbed with strips of blood-red cloud while mobs of terrified Vietnamese civilians fight with one another and plead with United States Marines to let them on board? You learn it soon or you learn it late: There are some kinds of experience you never share with anyone, not even with people who have had their ticket punched by the same conductor you have.

Clete returns to the window and tries to concentrate on the black man parked across the street. The black man is Andre Rochon, a twenty-three-year-old bail skip whose forfeited bond is less consequential than the information he can provide on two other bail skips who are into Clete's employers, Nig Rosewater and Wee Willie Bimstine, for thirty large.

Two drinks later the scene has not changed. And neither has the knot of anxiety in Clete's stomach or the band of tension that keeps tightening like a strand of piano wire wrapped around his head.

Clete is convinced he's watching a meth drop in the making. The two other players are the Melancon brothers, full-time wiseasses with busts on both their sheets for strong-arm robbery, illegal possession of firearms, and intimidation of witnesses. Clete suspects that one or both of the Melancon brothers is about to show up at the shuttered cottage.

But nothing seems to happen either outside or inside the cottage, and the man in the panel truck is becoming restless, turning his radio on and off, starting and restarting his engine.

What to do? Clete asks himself. Take down Rochon as a penny-ante bail skip or gamble that the Melancon brothers will show up? When the storm makes landfall late tomorrow night or early Monday morning, the lowlifes will either go to work looting the city or be blown like flotsam in every direction. Either way, it will be almost impossible to get a net over Rochon and the Melancons.

Clete decides it's Showtime.

He puts an unlit cigarette in his mouth, combs his hair in the mirror behind the bar, and fits on his porkpie hat. His cream-colored slacks are pressed, his oxblood loafers shined, his Hawaiian shirt taut on his massive shoulders. A hideaway .25 is Velcro-strapped to his ankle, a slapjack and penlight in one trouser pocket, a set of cuffs in the other. He wishes he were on a plane, lifting above highways that are clogged with automobiles, buses, and trucks, their headlights all pointing north. Or over in New Iberia, where he has a second office and a room he rents at an old motor court on East Main. But you don't surrender the place of your birth either to evil men or natural calamity, he tells himself, and wonders if he will feel the same in twenty-four hours.

"You decided to meet a lady friend after all?" Jimmy says.

"No, I got an appointment in the street with a piece of shit that should have been a skid mark on the bowl a long time ago," Clete says. "If it gets rough outside in the next few minutes, I don't want NOPD in on it. You with me on that?"

"At this bar, nine-one-one is a historical date."

"You're a beaut, Jimmy. Put a couple of inner tubes on the roof."

"What about you?"

"Ever hear of circus elephants drowning in New Orleans? See, no precedent."

Clete steps out on the sidewalk. The light has gone out of the sky, and clouds are rolling blackly over his head. He can feel the barometer dropping rapidly now and he smells an odor that is like sulfur or rotten eggs or water beetles that have washed into the sewer grates and died there. Andre Rochon stares straight ahead, his wrists resting idly on the steering wheel, but Clete knows that Rochon has either made him for a cop or a bondsman and is deciding whether to brass it out or fire up his truck and bag-ass for North Rampart.

Clete crosses the street and opens his badge holder and hangs it in front of Rochon's face. "Step out of the vehicle and keep your hands where I can see them," he says. "That's not a suggestion. You do it or you go to jail."

His words are all carefully chosen, indicating in advance to Rochon that he has viable choices, that with a little cooperation and finesse he can skate on the nonappearance and have another season to run.

Rochon steps out onto the asphalt and closes the door behind him. He wears tennis shoes without socks and paint-splattered slacks and an LSU T-shirt scissored off at the midriff and armpits. His arms are scrolled with one-color tats. He smells of funk and the decayed food in his teeth. His face is narrow, a grin tugging at one corner of his mouth. He strokes the exposed skin of his stomach, as a narcissist might. He probes his navel with one finger. "You a PI, blood?" he says.

Clete glances at the streetlight on the corner, his eyelashes fluttering. "See, people don't give me nicknames, particularly when they're racial," he says. "Right now you're standing up to your bottom lip in pig shit. In the next minute, one of two things will happen. You'll either give up the Melancon brothers or you'll be on your way to Central Lockup. If you want to be on the bottom floor when the hurricane hits, I'll try to arrange that."

"Eddy and Bertrand already evacuated. I'm just here to see 'bout my nephew. I'm telling the troot', man." Rochon presses his palm against his sternum, his face earnest.

"See, you're doing something else that bothers me. George W. Bush spreads his hand on his chest when he wants to show people he's sincere. You think you're George W. Bush? You think you're the president of the United States?"

Rochon is confused, his eyes darting back and forth. "Why you leanin' on me like this? 'Cause of something Eddy and Bertrand done?"

"No, because you skipped your court appearance and burned Nig and Wee Willie for your bond. You also smell bad. Willie and Nig don't like people who don't shower or brush their teeth and who smell bad. They got to spray the chairs every time you come in their office. Now you've disrespected them on top of it."

"Man, you been drinkin' the wrong stuff."

Clete's hands feel dry and stiff at his sides. He opens and closes his palms and wets his lips. He can feel a dangerous level of anger building inside him, one that has little to do with Andre Rochon.

"Get on your cell and tell Eddy and Bertrand to pull the rag out of their ass and get over here," he says.

"I ain't got their number."

"Really? Well, let's see what you do got."

Clete throws him against the side of the truck and shakes him down. When Rochon tries to turn his head and speak, Clete smashes his face into the paneling, so hard he dents it.

"Shit," Rochon says, blood leaking from his nose across his upper lip. "I ain't did nothing to deserve this."

"What do you have in the truck?"

"Nothing. And you ain't got no warrant to go in there, nohow."

"I work for a bond service. I don't need warrants. I can cross state lines, kick your door in, and rip your house apart. I can arrest and hold you anywhere I want, for as long as I want. Know why that is, Andre? When someone goes your bail, you become his property. And if this country respects anything, it's the ownership of property."

"I ain't holding, man. Do what you want. I ain't did nothing here. When this is over, I'm filing charges."

Clete opens the driver's door and shines his penlight under the front seats and into the back of the truck. The homemade plank floor in back is bare except for a coil of polyethylene rope that rests on a spare tire. A stuffed pink bear with white pads sewn on its paws is wedged between the floor and the truck's metal side.

Clete clicks off the light, then clicks it on again. The images of the rope and the stuffed animal trigger a memory of a newspaper story, one that he read several weeks ago. Did it concern an abduction? In the Ninth Ward? He's almost sure the story was in the *Times-Picayune* but he can't remember the details.

"Who belongs to the stuffed bear?" he says.

"My niece."

"What's the rope for?"

"I was putting up wash lines for my auntie. What's wit' you, man?"

Behind him Clete hears an automobile with a gutted muffler turn the corner. "I'm taking you to Central Lockup. Get that grin off your face."

Then Clete hears the car with the blown-out muffler accelerating, a hubcap detaching itself from one wheel, bouncing up onto a sidewalk. He turns just as the grillwork of a 1970s gas-guzzler explodes the open door of the panel truck off its hinges and drives it into Clete's face and body. For just a moment he sees two black men in the front seat of the gas-guzzler, then he is propelled backward into the street, his skin and hair speckled with broken glass. He lands so hard on the asphalt his breath is vacuumed out of his chest in one long, uncontrollable wheezing rush that leaves him powerless and gasping. The gas-guzzler mashes over his porkpie hat and fishtails around a corner at the end of the block. As Clete tries to shove the door off his chest, Andre Rochon fires up his panel truck and roars away in the opposite direction, his red taillights braking once at the intersection before disappearing into the darkness.

Jimmy Flannigan and Clete's other friends from the bar pick him up and clean the glass off his clothes and touch him all over like he's a piece of bruised fruit, amazed that their friend is still alive. Someone even calls 911 and discovers that every cop and emergency vehicle in Orleans Parish is already overloaded with obligations far beyond their capacity. Clete stands dazed and chagrined in the middle of the street, unable to accept the fact he just got taken down by three dirtbags who couldn't clean bubble gum off their shoes without a diagram.

He tells his friends to go back inside the bar, then opens the door to the cottage. Inside, a boy not more than seventeen is sitting on the floor, watching a cartoon on a television set, a paper bag packed with clothes resting by his foot. The volume on the television is deafening. "Turn that off," Clete says.

The boy does as he is told. He wears the stylized baggy pants and oversized T-shirt of a gangbanger, but his clothes look fresh from the box and his body is so thin it could be made of sticks.

"Where are your folks?" Clete asks.

"My auntie already lined up at the 'Dome to get us cots. My Uncle Andre is taking me there in a li'l bit," the boy replies. "Everybody suppose to bring food for five days. That's what they say."

"Andre Rochon is your uncle?"

"Yes, suh."

"What's your name?"

"Kevin Rochon."

"Your uncle had to take off somewhere. If you're going to the Superdome, you'll have to walk."

"It ain't no big deal," the boy says, and refocuses his attention on the cartoon.

Right, Clete says to himself.

He goes back to the bar and dispenses with Scotch and milk and orders a frosted mug of beer and three shot glasses brimming with Beam. Within an hour, he's as drunk as everyone else in the building, safe inside the sweaty ambiance of jukebox music and manufactured good cheer. His face is oily and hot, his head ringing with nonexistent sounds that are generated by armored vehicles and helicopter blades. Two stranded UCLA co-eds are dancing on the bar, one of them toking on a joint she holds to her lips with roach clips. Jimmy Flannigan fits his hand around the pitted back of Clete's neck and squeezes, as though grasping a fire hydrant. "I just come back from the Superdome. You ought to see the lines. Everybody from the Iberville Project is trying to pack in there," he says.

"Yeah?" Clete replies, unsure of the point.

"Why they sending everybody from the projects to the 'Dome?" Jimmy asks.

"It has stadium seating," Clete says.

"So why do people from the projects got to have stadium seating?"

"When Lake Pontchartrain covers the city, maybe some of the poor bastards can find an air pocket under the roof and not drown," he says.

CHAPTER
5

Oₙ Sᴜɴᴅᴀʏ ᴀꜰᴛᴇʀɴᴏᴏɴ in New Iberia, the clouds are gray, the leaves of the live oaks along Main Street riffling with an occasional gust of wind. The end of summer has arrived with a smell of dust and distant rain and smoke from meatfires across the bayou in City Park but with no hint that south of us a churning white vortex of wind and water so great in magnitude that only a satellite photograph can do it justice is grinding its way toward the Louisiana-Mississippi coast.

As I watch the progress of the storm on the television set I feel like a witness to a holocaust in the making. For two days, the governor of Louisiana, Kathleen Blanco, has been pleading for help to anyone who will listen. A state emergency official in Metairie has become emotionally undone during an CNN interview, waving his arms, his face blotched like a man coming off a drunk. He states unequivocally that sixty-two thousand people will die if the storm maintains its current category 5 strength and hits New Orleans head-on.

My adopted daughter, Alafair, just out of Reed College, answers the telephone in the kitchen. I hope the call is from Clete Purcel, agreeing to evacuate from New Orleans and stay at our house. It's not. The call is from the sheriff of Iberia Parish, Helen Soileau, who has other concerns.

"We just busted Herman Stanga," she says. "We got his meth lab and nailed two of his mules."

"You know how many times we've busted Herman Stanga?"

"That's why I want you to supervise the case, Pops. This time we bury him."

"Dealing with Herman Stanga is like picking up dog feces with your hands. Get someone else, Helen."

"The mules are of more interest to me right now than Stanga. I've got both of them in lockup."

"What's interesting about people who have minus signs in front of their IQs?

"Come on down, check it out."

THE BARRED CELL has no windows and smells of the disinfectant that has been used to scrub all its steel and concrete surfaces. The two men locked inside have taken off their shirts and their shoes and are doing push-ups with their feet propped on a wood bench. Their arms and plated chests are blue with Gothic-letter tats. Their armpits are shaved, their lats as hard-looking as the sides of coopered barrels, tapering into twenty-eight-inch waists and stomachs that are flat from the sternum to the groin. With each pushup, a network of tendons blooms against the tautness of their skin. They have the hands of bricklayers or men who scrub swimming pools clean with muriatic acid or cut and fashion stone in subfreezing weather. The power in their bodies makes you think of a tightly wound steel spring, aching for release, waiting for the slightest of external triggers.

One of them stops his exercise routine, sits on the bench, and breathes in and out through his nose, indifferent to the fact that Helen and I are only two feet from him, watching him as we would an animal at a zoo.

"I dig your tats. Are y'all Eighteenth Streeters?" I say.

He grins and makes no reply. His hair is cut high and tight, his scalp notched with scars.

"Latin Kings?" I ask.

"Who?" he says.

"How about Mara Salvatrucha?" I say.

He pauses before he replies, his fingers splaying stiffly on his knees, the soles of his shoes clicking playfully on the floor. "Why you think that, man?" he asks.

"The 'MS' tattooed on one eyelid and the '13' on the other were clues," I say.

"You nailed me, man," he says. He looks up into my face, grinning. But the black luster in his eyes is the kind that makes one swallow, not smile in return.

"I thought you guys were out on the West Coast or creating new opportunities in northern Virginia," I say.

His eyes are fixed straight ahead, as though he can see meaning inside the cell's shadows. Or perhaps he's staring at images inside his own head, remembering deeds that are testimony to the theory that not all of us descend from the same tree. He bobbles his head back and forth on his shoulders, working out a kink, a prizefighter in the corner awaiting the first-round bell. "When's chow?" he says.

"The caterer will be here at six," Helen says.

The other man gets off the floor and begins touching his toes, a neat crease folding across his navel, his narrow buttocks turned toward us. I glance at the computer printouts attached to the clipboard in my hand. "Your street name is Chula?" I say to the man sitting on the bench.

"Yeah, man, you got it."

"What's your name mean?" I ask.

"'Put it away,' man. Like at jai alai? Before the guy slams the ball into the wall, everybody shouts out, 'Chula! Put it away.'"

"Y'all got impressive sheets. Lewisburg, Pelican Island, Marion," I say. "Why fool with a small-town pimp like Herman Stanga?"

"The black dude? We just stopped and asked for directions. Then cops was all over us," the seated man says.

"Yeah, mistakes like that can happen," I reply. "But here's the deal, Chula. We've got a hurricane blowing in and we don't have time for bullshit from out-of-town guys who haven't paid any local dues. See, Louisiana is not a state, it's a Third World country. That means we really get pissed off when outsiders come in and think they can wipe their feet on us. You guys are mainline, so I won't try to take you over the hurdles. Stacking time at Angola can be a real bitch, particularly if we decide to send you up with a bad jacket. If you want to take the bounce for Herman Stanga, be our guest. But you either get out in front of this or we'll crush your cookie bag."

The man who has been touching his toes stops and faces me. "Watch this, man," he says.

He leaps against the wall with one foot and does a complete somersault, in a wink returning to an upright position. "What you think about that? Learned it in El Sal from the guys who killed my whole family and took turns raping me before they sold me to a carnival. Come on, man, tell me what you think about that."

"To be honest, I think you should have stayed with the carnival," I reply.

The remark isn't intended to sink the hook in. But inadvertently that is what happens. Just when Helen and I are almost out of the corridor, the man street-named Chula rakes a tin cup back and forth on the bars. "Hey, you, the guy with the *maricona,* my sister is fucking a junkie priest from New Iberia. You say we ain't paid no dues here? That ain't local dues, man?"

Helen returns to the cell door, her arms pumped. "What did you call me?" she says.

Chula shrugs and smiles self-effacingly. "It don't mean nothing against you. Your friend there shouldn't have made fun about somebody being sold to a carnival," he says. He leans against the wall, detaching from the world around him, his face striped with the bars' shadows.

BACK HOME, I try to forget the two men in the holding cell. Molly, my wife, is a former nun and once worked with the Maryknolls in Central America. She has freckles on her shoulders and dark red hair that is thick and clipped short on her neck. She and Alafair are picking up the garden tools in the backyard and locking them in a tin shed behind the porte cochere. The air is breathless, cool, rain-scented, the live oak and pecan trees and the bayou as still as images in a painting. "Did Clete call?" I ask.

"No, but I called him. He's not going to evacuate," Molly says. She studies my face. She knows I'm not thinking about Clete. "Did something happen at the jail?"

"A local priest named Jude LeBlanc fell through a hole in the dimension about a year ago. He has terminal cancer and a morphine addiction and three or four warrants out for his arrest."

The truth is, I don't want to talk about it. If age brings wisdom, it lies in the realization that most talk is useless and that you stay out of other people's grief.

"What's that have to do with the jail?" Molly asks.

"A member of an El Salvadoran gang called MS-13 said his sister was in the sack with Jude."

"Did you ask him where your friend was?"

"You never empower the perps, no matter how many aces they're holding," I say.

A hard gust of wind blows down the long corridor of trees that line Bayou Teche, wrinkling the water like old skin, filling the air with the smell of fish roe and leaves that have turned yellow and black in the shade. Katrina will make landfall somewhere around Lake Pontchartrain in the next seven hours.

"Let's fix supper," she says.

"I don't have much of an appetite," I say.

Her face looks dry and empty, her cheeks slightly sunken. She lets out her breath. "God, those poor people," she says.

HURRICANES DO NOT lend themselves to description, no more than do the pyrotechnics of a B-52 raid at ground zero. I have seen the survivors of the latter. Their grief is of a kind you never want to witness. They weep and make mewing sounds. Any words they speak are usually unintelligible. I have always suspected they have joined a group the Bible refers to as Heaven's prisoners, anointed in a fashion most of us would resist even if we recognized God's finger reaching out to touch our brow.

A category 5 hurricane carries an explosive force several times greater than that of the atom bomb dropped on Hiroshima in 1945.

But unlike a man-made weapon of mass destruction, a hurricane creates an environment that preempts our natural laws. Early on the air turns a chemical green and contains a density that you can hold in your palm. The lightning and the thunder arrive almost like predictable friends, then fade into the ether and seem to become little more than a summer squall. Rain rings chain the swells between the whitecaps and the wind smells of salt spray and hard-packed sand that has warmed under the sun. You wonder if all the preparedness and alarm hasn't been much ado about nothing.

Then the tide seems to shrink from the land, as though a giant drainhole has formed in the center of the Gulf. Palm trees straighten in the stillness, their fronds suddenly lifeless. You swallow to stop the popping sound in your ears, with the same sense of impotence you might experience aboard a plane that is dramatically losing altitude. To the south, a long black hump begins to gather itself on the earth's rim, swelling out of the water like an enormous whale, extending itself all across the horizon. You cannot believe what you are watching. The black hump is now rushing toward the coastline, gaining momentum and size, increasing in velocity so rapidly that its own crest is absorbed by the wave before it can crash to the surface in front of it.

It's called a tidal surge. Its force can turn a levee system into serpentine lines of black sand or level a city, particularly when the city has no natural barriers. The barrier islands off the Louisiana coast have long ago eroded away or been dredged up and heaped on barges and sold for shale parking lots. The petrochemical companies have cut roughly ten thousand miles of channels through the wetlands, allowing saline intrusion to poison and kill freshwater marsh areas from Plaquemines Parish to Sabine Pass. The levees along the Mississippi River shotgun hundreds of tons of mud over the edge of the continental shelf, preventing it from flowing westward along the coastline, where it is needed the most. Louisiana's wetlands continue to disappear at a rate of forty-seven square miles a year.

It's 1:00 a.m. and I can hear the wind in the oaks and pecan trees. The ventilated shutters on our house are latched, vibrating slightly against the jambs. The only sign of a weather disturbance is a flicker of lightning in the clouds or a sudden gust of rain that patterns our tin roof with pine needles. Two hours to the east of us the people of New Orleans who have not evacuated are watching their city ripped off the face of the earth. Why is one group spared and one group not? I don't have an answer. But I am determined that two newly arrived members of our community will not enjoy the safety of our jail, at least on their terms, while decent people are drowned in their own homes.

I call the night jailer and tell him to separate the two MS-13 members.

"What if they ax me why?" he says.

"Tell them we have a policy against homosexuals sharing the same cell in Iberia Parish," I reply.

"Tell them *what*?"

A half hour later I drive to my office and read again through the faxes and computer printouts on the two MS-13 members. There are always dials on the perps. It's just a matter of finding them. The perps might be con-wise and they may have the cunning of animals, but when it comes to successfully confronting the system, they're charging uphill into a howitzer.

I check my firearm at the entrance to the lockup area and ask the night jailer to bring Felix "Chula" Ramos to the interrogation room. When Chula arrives, his body is clinking with waist and leg chains. He is wearing only a pair of white boxer undershorts and they look strangely innocuous against his tattooed skin.

"Lose the restraints, Cap?"

The night jailer is old and has gin roses in his face. He is not interested in either the thespian behavior of others or saving them from themselves. "Holler on the gate," he says.

Chula sits at the government-surplus metal table and takes my inventory, one hand relaxed on the tabletop. "I could rip out your throat. Before you could even beg, that fast," he says, snapping his fingers.

I pinch the fatigue out of my eyes. "Your fall partner, what's-his-name, Luis, is an ignoramus, but I think you're even dumber than he is."

The skin twitches under Chula's left eye, as though an insect is walking across it. "Say that again?"

"You guys dissed me and the sheriff because you have outstanding federal warrants on you and you thought you'd be blowing Bumfuck for an upscale federal facility. It's not going to happen."

"You're sending us to 'Gola, you're saying?"

"Eventually, but right now we're transferring you to Central Lockup in New Orleans. Notice I said 'you,' not 'you all.' Orleans Parish has warrants on both you guys. It's chickenshit stuff, but we'll be honoring the protocol and shipping you off before dawn. "

"The whole city is getting blown off the map. Who you kidding, man?"

"With luck the prisoners at Central Lockup won't be deserted by the personnel. But who knows? The salaries of civil servants in Orleans Parish suck. Can you tread water in a flooded room full of other guys doing the same thing?"

"That ain't funny, man."

"The sheriff and I had a big laugh about y'all's jackets. Your fall partner boosted a bank in Pennsylvania, but a dye marker exploded in the bag and queered all the bills. So your idiot of a friend took seventy-five thousand dollars in hot money to a coin laundry and washed the bills over and over until they were pink. Then he tried to buy a forty-thousand-dollar SUV with them. This lamebrain not only outsmarted you, he cluster-fucked you six ways from breakfast. You're going to do double nickels at Angola, half of it for him. If you think I'm lying, call me after you go into lockdown with the Big Stripes. Know what the Midnight Special is up there? Think of a sweaty three-hundred-pound black dude driving a freight train up your ass."

I wink at him. He stares at the opaque whiteness of the door, a shadow-filled crease forming across his brow. I can hear him breathing in the silence. A bolt of lightning crashes outside and the lights in the building flicker momentarily. "What you want, man?"

"You said your sister was in the sack with a junkie priest."

CHAPTER
6

By MIDMORNING NEWSCASTERS all over the country were announcing that Hurricane Katrina had changed direction and had dropped from a category 5 storm to a category 3 just before making landfall, devastating Gulfport but sparing the city that care forgot.

New Iberia's streets were clogged with traffic, as were those of every other town and city in southwest Louisiana, the Wal-Mart parking lot a coordination center for fundamentalist churches that unhesitatingly threw open their doors to anyone in need of help. But the sun was shining, the wind flecked with rain, the flowers blooming along East Main, more like spring than summer. We all took a breath, secure in our belief that we had faced the worst and that the warnings of the doomsayers had been undone by our collective faith.

But the newscasters were wrong and so were we. New Orleans's long night of the soul was just beginning.

During the night hurricane-force winds and a tidal surge had driven oceanic amounts of water up the Mississippi River Gulf Outlet, nicknamed the "Mr. Go" canal, all the way through St. Bernard Parish into Orleans Parish and the low-lying neighborhoods along the Intercoastal Canal. After sunrise, residents in the Lower Ninth Ward said they heard explosions under the levee that held back the waters of Lake Pontchartrain. Rumors quickly spread from house to house—either terrorists or racists were dynamiting the only barrier that prevented the entirety of the lake from drowning the mostly black population in the Lower Nine.

The rumors were of course false. The levees burst because they were structurally weak and had only a marginal chance of surviving a category 3 storm, much less one of category 5 strength. Every state emergency official knew this. The Army Corps of Engineers knew this. The National Hurricane Center in Miami knew this.

But apparently the United States Congress and the current administration in Washington, D.C., did not, since they had dramatically cut funding for repair of the levee system only a few months earlier.

I had been successful in obtaining the address of my friend the junkie priest, Jude LeBlanc, from one of the MS-13 gang members. But at 9:00 a.m. Monday all of my priorities were rearranged for me when Helen Soileau walked into my office, her shield already hung on a lanyard from her neck. "Throw your shit in a bucket, Pops. Half the department is being assigned to the Big Sleazy," she said.

"What's going on?"

"Take your choice," she replied.

WE DIDN'T SEE the first large-scale wind damage until we were well east of Morgan City. The sugarcane was crushed flat in the fields, as though it had been steamrolled and matted into black dirt. Telephone poles were snapped in half, sections blown out of signboards, roofs ripped from stores in rural strip malls. The four-lane highway was patina-ed with leaves and gray mud from the flooded woods that lined each side of the roadway, and thousands of shrieking birds freckled the sky, as though they had no place to land. Helen was driving, her face somber, a dozen more departmental vehicles behind us, their flashers rippling with color. Some of the vehicles were towing boats that were packed to the gunwales with first-aid kits, gasoline-powered generators, donated food, clothing, and bottled water, all of it tarped down and swaying on bumper hitches.

Helen was an attractive, muscular woman whose intelligence and integrity I had always admired. She had started her career as a meter maid at the NOPD, in an era when a female officer had to pay hard dues among her male colleagues. The fact she didn't try to hide her androgynous nature had made her a special target for several members of the department, in particular a plainclothes by the name of Nate Baxter, a degenerate and former vice cop I genuinely believed belonged in a soap dish.

One morning at roll call, just after a sniper had opened fire on pedestrians from a hotel rooftop in the Quarter, Nate took over from the watch commander and addressed all the uniformed patrol personnel in the room.

"I want every swinging dick out there on the firing line, in vests and with maximum ordnance," he said. "We've got one agenda. That guy gets cooled out. Nobody else gets hurt, civilians or cops. Everybody clear on that?"

So far, so good.

Nate turned his gaze on Helen, the skin denting at the corner of his mouth. "Helen, can you tell us whether 'swinging dick' includes you in or leaves you out?" he said.

Several cops laughed. Helen was in the second row, bent forward, her eyes still fixed on the notepad that was propped on her thigh. There was a cough or two, then the room fell silent.

"Glad you brought up the subject of genitalia, Detective," she said. "A couple of weeks ago a transvestite CI told me you made a few cross-dressers cop your stick in the backseat of a cruiser when you were in Vice. Back then, the transvestite was using the name Rachel. But actually Rachel is a man and his real name is Ralph. Ralph said you'd undergone penile enhancement. Since I don't get to use the same restroom as the swinging dicks, I can't really say if Ralph is lying or not. Maybe these other officers know."

She stared thoughtfully into space. Nate Baxter's career never recovered from that moment. He launched a vendetta against Helen through the departmental bureaucracy and as a consequence was always looked upon by his fellow officers as a malicious coward who couldn't cut it on a level playing field.

We were on the bridge over the Mississippi now, the wide brown expanse swollen and breathtaking down below, an upside-down houseboat spinning in the current as it floated out from under the bridge. Helen tore the wrapper on a granola bar with her teeth and spit the paper out on the steering wheel.

"What's bothering you?" I asked.

"Nothing," she replied, one cheek tight with chunks of granola.

I didn't pursue it. We came down the other side of the bridge, swinging out on an elevated exit ramp above flooded woods whose canopy was stripped of leaves and strung with trash.

"We're supposed to coordinate with a half-dozen agencies down here, including NOPD. I say screw that," she said. "I'm going to have a talk with all our people before we go in. We do our job and we maintain our own standards. That means we don't shoot looters. Let the insurance companies take their own losses. But if somebody fires on us, we blow them out of their socks."

She looked at my face. "What's funny?" she asked.

"I wish I had still been with NOPD when you were there."

"Want to elaborate on that?"

"No, ma'am, I really don't," I replied.

She bit down on her granola bar and gave me another look, then drove on into the city. None of us was quite ready for what we would see.

IT WASN'T THE miles of buildings stripped of their shingles and their windows caved in or the streets awash with floating trash or the live oaks that had been punched through people's roofs. It was the literal powerlessness of the city that was overwhelming. The electric grid had been destroyed and the water pressure had died in every faucet in St. Bernard and Orleans parishes. The pumps that should have forced water out of the storm sewers were flooded themselves and totally useless. Gas mains burned underwater or sometimes burst flaming from the earth, filling the sky in seconds with hundreds of leaves singed off an ancient tree. The entire city, within one night, had been reduced to the technological level of the Middle Ages. But as we crossed under the elevated highway and headed toward the Convention Center, I saw one image that will never leave me and that will always remain emblematic of my experience in New Orleans, Louisiana, on Monday, August 29, in the year of Our Lord, 2005. The body of a fat black man was bobbing facedown against a piling. His dress clothes were puffed with air, his arms floating straight out from his sides. A dirty skim of yellow froth from our wake washed over his head. His body would remain there for at least three days.

Any semblance of order at the Convention Center was degenerating into chaos. The thousands of people who had sought shelter there had been told to bring their own food for five days. Many of them were from the projects or the poorest neighborhoods in the city and did not own automobiles and had little money or food at the end of the month. Many of them had brought elderly and sick people with them—diabetics, paraplegics, Alzheimer's patients, and people in need of kidney dialysis. The sun was white overhead, the air hazy and glistening with humidity. The concrete apron outside the Center was teeming with people trying to find shade or potable water. Almost all of them were yelling angrily at police cars and media vehicles.

"You going to set up a command center here?" I said.

I could see Helen biting her lower lip, her hands clenching on the steering wheel. "No, they'll tear us apart," she said. "The streets in the Quarter are supposed to be dry. I'm going to swing down toward Jackson Square—"

"Stop!"

"What is it?"

"I just saw Clete Purcel. There, by the entrance."

Helen rolled down the window and squinted into the haze. The gush of superheated air through the window felt like steam blowing from the back of a commercial laundry. "What's Clete doing?" she said.

It took a moment for both of us to assimilate the scene taking place against the Convention Center wall. A huge, sunburned man, wearing filthy cream-colored slacks and a tropical shirt split at the shoulders, was trying to fit an inverted cardboard box over the body of an elderly white woman who was draped in a wheelchair. Her body was flaccid in death, and Clete could not get the box around her without knocking her out of the chair.

"Hang on, Helen," I said, and got out of the cruiser before she could reply.

Out of the corner of my eye I saw her make a U-turn, pause briefly, and head toward the French Quarter, the rest of the caravan trailing behind her. But Helen was a good soul and she knew I would hook up with her soon, probably with Clete in tow. She also knew you don't leave your friends behind, regardless of what the rest of the world is doing.

I held the old woman upright in the wheelchair while Clete covered her head and upper body with the box. Then I smelled an odor from her clothes that brought back memories of a distant war that I wanted to forget.

"You think that's bad. Go inside the Center. All the plumbing is broken. There're dead people piled in the corners. Street rats are shooting guns in there and raping anybody they want," Clete said. "You got a spare piece?"

"No, where's your hideaway?"

"Lost it on Royal, I think. A whole balcony came down on the street. I got hit with a flying flowerpot." He wiped the sweat out of his eyes with the flat of his hand and stared out at the wreckage of the city and the looters sloshing through the streets, their arms loaded with whatever they could carry. "Who needs terrorists? Look at this shit, will you?"

FOR THOSE WHO do not like to brood upon the possibility of simian ancestry in the human gene pool or who genuinely believe that societal virtue grows from a collective impulse in the human breast, the events of the next few days would offer their sensibilities poor comfort. Helen had been worried she would have to give up command of her department to either NOPD or state or federal authorities. That was the least of our problems. There was no higher command than ourselves. The command structure and communication system of NOPD had been destroyed by the storm. Four hundred to five hundred officers, roughly one third of the department, had bagged ass for higher ground. The command center NOPD had set up in a building off Canal Street had flooded. Much to their credit, the duty officers didn't give up their positions and wandered in chest-deep water outside their building for two days. They had no food and no drinking water, and many were forced to relieve themselves in their clothes, their handheld radios held aloft to keep them dry.

From a boat or any other elevated position, as far as the eye could see, New Orleans looked like a Caribbean city that had collapsed beneath the waves. The sun was merciless in the sky, the humidity like lines of ants crawling inside your clothes. The linear structure of a neighborhood could be recognized only by the green smudge of yard trees that cut the waterline and row upon row of rooftops dotted with people who perched on sloped shingles that scalded their hands.

The smell was like none I ever experienced. The water was chocolate-brown, the surface glistening with a blue-green sheen of oil and industrial chemicals. Raw feces and used toilet paper issued from broken sewer lines. The gray, throat-gagging odor of decomposition permeated not only the air but everything we touched. The bodies of dead animals, including deer, rolled in the wake of our rescue boats. And so did those of human beings, sometimes just a shoulder or an arm or the back of a head, suddenly surfacing, then sinking under the froth.

They drowned in attics and on the second floors of their houses. They drowned along the edges of Highway 23 when they tried to drive out of Plaquemines Parish. They drowned in retirement homes and in trees and on car tops while they waved frantically at helicopters flying by overhead. They died in hospitals and nursing homes of dehydration and heat exhaustion, and they died because an attending nurse could not continue to operate a hand ventilator for hours upon hours without rest.

If by chance you hear a tape of the 911 cell phone calls from those attics, walk away from it as quickly as possible, unless you are willing to live with voices that will come aborning in your sleep for the rest of your life.

The United States Coast Guard flew nonstop, coming in low with the sun at their backs, taking sniper fire, swinging from cables, the downdraft of their choppers cutting a trough across the water. They took the children, the elderly, and the sick first and tried to come back for the others later. They chopped holes in roofs and strapped hoists on terrified people who had never flown in an airplane. They held infants against their breasts and fat women who weighed three hundred pounds, and carried them above the water to higher ground with a grace we associate with angels. They rescued more than thirty-three thousand souls, and no matter what else happens in our history, no group will ever exceed the level of courage and devotion they demonstrated following Katrina's landfall.

After sunset on the first day, August 29, the sky was an ink wash, streaked with smoke from fires vandals had set in the Garden District. There were also electrical moments, flashes of light in the sky, heat lightning or perhaps sometimes the igneous trajectory of tracer rounds fired from automatic weapons. The rule books were going over the gunwales.

Looters were hitting pharmacies and liquor and jewelry stores first, then working their way down the buffet table. A rogue group of NOPD cops had actually set up a thieves headquarters on the tenth floor of a downtown hotel, storing their loot in the rooms, terrorizing the management, and threatening to shoot a reporter who tried to question them. New Orleans cops also drove off with automobiles from the Cadillac agency. Gangbangers had converged on the Garden District and were having a Visigoth holiday, burning homes built before the Civil War, carrying away whatever wasn't bolted down.

Evacuees in the Superdome and Convention Center tried to walk across the bridge into Jefferson Parish. Most of these people were black, some carrying children in their arms, all of them exhausted, hungry, and dehydrated. They were met by armed police officers from Jefferson Parish who fired shotguns over their heads and allowed none of them to leave Orleans Parish.

An NOPD cop shot a black man with a twelve-gauge through the glass window of his cruiser in front of the Convention Center while hundreds of people watched. The cop sped away before the crowd attacked his vehicle. Some witnesses said he ran over the victim's body. The cop claimed the dead man had tried to attack him with a pair of scissors.

A half block from a state medical clinic I counted the bodies of nine black people, all of them floating facedown in a circle, like free-falling parachutists suspended on a cushion of air high above the earth.

We heard stories of gunfire from rooftops and windows. Emergency personnel in rescue boats became afraid of the very people they were supposed to save. Some people airlifted out by the Coast Guard in the Lower Nine said the gunfire was a desperate attempt to signal the boat crews searching in the darkness for survivors. Who was telling the truth? What cop or fireman or volunteer kneeling on the bow of a rescue boat, preparing to throw a rope on a rooftop, wanted to find out? Who wanted to eat a round from an AK-47?

Charity and Baptist Memorial hospitals had become necropolises. The bottom floors were flooded, and gangbangers turned over rescue boats that were trying to evacuate the patients. Without electricity or ice or unspoiled food or running water, hospital personnel were left to care for the most helpless of their wards—trauma victims with fresh gunshot wounds, those whose bodily functions depended entirely upon machines, patients who had just had organs surgically removed, and the most vulnerable group, the aged and the terrified, all of it inside a building that was cooking in its own stink.

But a lot of NOPD cops were loyal to their badge and their oath and worked tirelessly alongside the rest of us for the next seventy-two hours. Among their number were many of Clete's long-time detractors and enemies, but even the most vehement of them had to concede that Clete Purcel was a beautiful man to have on our side—the kind who covers your back, tightens your slack, and humps your pack. He knew every street and rat hole in New Orleans, and he had also fished every bayou and bay and canal from Barataria to Lake Borgne. He was on a first-name basis with hookers, Murphy artists, petty boosters, whiskey priests, junkies, skin bar operators, transvestites, disgraced cops, strippers, second-story creeps, street mutts, bondsmen, journalists, and old-time mobsters who tended their flower gardens in the suburbs. His bravery was a given. His indifference to physical pain or verbal insult was vinegar and gall to his enemies, his loyalty to his friends of such an abiding nature that with conscious forethought he would willingly lay down his life for them.

But even Katrina did not change Clete's penchant for the visceral and the sybaritic. On August 31 he said he was going to check his apartment and office on St. Ann in the Quarter. Two hours passed and no Clete. It was afternoon and Helen and I were in a boat out in Gentilly, surrounded by water and houses that were beginning to smell from the bodies inside. The combination of heat and humidity and lack of wind was almost unbearable, the sun like a wobbling yellow balloon trapped under the water's surface. Helen cut the engine and let us drift on our wake until we were in the shade of an elevated stretch of Interstate 10. Her face and arms were badly sunburned, her shirt stiff with dried salt.

"Go find him," she said.

"Clete can take care of himself," I said.

"We need every swinging dick on the line. Tell him to get his ass back here."

"That's what Nate Baxter used to say."

"Remind me to scrub out my mouth with Ajax," she replied.

I caught a ride on another boat to high ground, then walked the rest of the way into the Quarter. The Quarter had taken a pounding from the wind and the rain, and ventilated shutters had been shattered off their hinges and the planked floors of whole balconies stripped clean from the buildings and sent flying like undulating rows of piano keys down the street. But the Quarter had not flooded and some of the bars, using gasoline-powered generators, had stayed on the full-tilt boogie for three days—their patrons zoned and marinated to the point they looked like waxworks figures that had been left under a heat lamp.

I found Clete in a corner dump two blocks from his office, his tropical shirt and cream-colored slacks black with oil, his skin peeling with sun blisters, his face glowing from the huge mug of draft beer he was drinking and the whiskey jigger rolling around inside it. A brunette woman in a halter and cutoff blue-jean shorts and spiked heels was drinking next to him, her thigh touching his. The tops of her breasts were tattooed with chains of roses, her neck strung with purple and green glass beads, her mascara running like a clown's.

"Time to dee-dee, Cletus," I said.

"Lighten up, big mon. Have a soda and lime. The guy's got cold shrimp on dry ice," he said.

"You're shit-faced."

"So what? This is Dominique. She's an artist from Paris. We're going over to my place for a while. Did you see that big plane that flew over?"

"No, I didn't. Step outside with me."

"It was Air Force One. After three days the Shrubster did a fly-over. Gee, I feel better now."

"Did you hear me?"

He leaned over the counter, filled his mug from the tap, and poured a jigger of Beam into it. He upended the mug, drinking it to the bottom, his eyes fastened on mine. He smiled, his face suffused with warmth. "This is our country, big mon. We fought for it," he said. "I say screw all these cocksuckers. Nobody jacks the Big Sleazy when the Bobbsey Twins from Homicide are on the job."

I had no idea what he was talking about. But in AA you do not try to reason with drunks. In Clete Purcel's case, you did not invade the private cathedral where he sometimes lived.

"I'll tell Helen you'll catch us later," I said.

He laid the full weight of his big arm across my shoulders and walked with me to the door. The cloud of testosterone and beer sweat that rose from his armpit was suffocating.

"Give me an hour. I just need to clean up and fix some supper for me and Dominique," he said.

"Supper?"

"What's wrong with that?"

"That woman isn't from France. She used to work in a massage parlor in Lafayette. She was one of Stevie Giacano's whores."

"Who's perfect? You've got something negative to say about every woman I meet."

"That's a comment on your judgment, not mine."

I saw the hurt flicker in his face before I could take back my words. He took his arm from my shoulders and stepped out on the sidewalk. The street was strewn with plaster, broken glass, chimney bricks, beer cans and red plastic beer cups, roofing shingles, and thousands of water beetles that had been forced up through the sewer grates and that snapped under your feet when you stepped on them. But in the waning of the afternoon, in the pool of shadow made by the building at our back, in the popping of a Mardi Gras flag someone had hung on a staff from a balcony, I felt for just a moment that an older and fonder vision of New Orleans might still be available to us.

"I'm sorry for what I said, Clete."

His eyes crinkled, threading with white lines at the corners. He pulled a slip of paper out of his shirt pocket with two fingers and offered it to me. "Aside from her painting career, Dominique coincidentally knows every working girl in the Quarter. You still want to find that junkie priest who's hooked up with the sister of the MS-13 dude?" he said.

You didn't put the slide or the glide on Clete Purcel.

CHAPTER

7

On our way back to rendezvous with Helen, we stopped at the second-story apartment where Jude LeBlanc lived with the Hispanic woman by the name of Natalia Ramos. But the apartment door was locked and the shutters latched. A neighbor, a Cajun woman who had ridden out the storm, said Jude had left the apartment for the Ninth Ward on Friday afternoon and Natalia had decided to join him. "I heard there's bad t'ings happening down there. Maybe they ain't coming back, no," the neighbor said.

"Do you know where they went in the Ninth?" I asked.

"There's a church down there that don't ax no questions about him. Natalia said it's made of stucco and got a bell tower," she replied.

"Thank you," I said, and started to go.

"Hey, you?" the neighbor said.

"Yes?"

"Maybe he ain't doing right, a priest living wit' a woman and all, but that's a good man, yeah."

That night was one of surreal images that I suspect have their origins more in the unconscious than in the conscious mind. People looked and behaved as they do in our sleep—not quite real, their bodies iridescent with sweat, their clothes in rags, like creatures living out their destinies on moonscape.

I saw a man rowing a boat, vigorously pulling on the oars, his back turned toward two bodies that were piled in the bow, his face set with stoic determination, as though his efforts could undo fate's worst cut.

I saw a black baby hung in the branches of a tree, its tiny hands trailing in the current, its plastic diaper immaculate in the moonlight. I saw people eating from plastic packages of mustard and ketchup they had looted from a café, dividing what they had among themselves. Ten feet from them a dead cow matted with flies lay in the back of a wrecked pickup, a lead rope twisted around its neck.

A gelatinous fat man wearing boxer trunks and mirrored sunglasses floated past us on a bed of inner tubes, a twelve-pack of beer balanced on his stomach, one hand held high in a toast to a passing airboat.

"You want a ride up to high ground?" I said.

"And miss the show? Are you kidding?" he replied, ripping open another beer.

I saw kids running from an antebellum home they had just torched, silhouetted against the flames, like pranksters trick-or-treating on Halloween. When the gas lines exploded, sparks showered down on the entire neighborhood. Two blocks away vigilantes with shotguns and deer rifles prowled the flooded streets in a bass boat powered by an electric motor. One of them wore a headlamp, another a safari hat with a leopard-skin band. They were all sharing drinks from a silver flask and happy as hogs rolling in shit. I don't know if they found their prey or not. In fact, at the time I was too tired to care.

We heard rumors that teams of elite troops, Special Forces or Rangers or Navy SEALs, were taking out snipers under a black flag. We heard that an alligator ate a deer on the second story of a flooded house by the Industrial Canal. Some NOPD cops said the personnel at Orleans Parish Prison had blown town and left the inmates to drown. Others said a downtown mob rushed a command center, thinking food and water were being distributed. A deputy panicked and began firing an automatic weapon into the night sky, quickly adding to the widespread conviction that cops were arbitrarily killing innocent people.

The number of looters and arsonists and dangerous felons in custody was growing by the hour, with no place to put them. We kicked looters loose, only to see them recycled back into a temporary holding area two hours later. Some of those in custody were probably murderers—drug dealers or sociopaths who had taken advantage of the storm to eliminate the competition or settle old grudges. When a chain-link jail was created at the airport, we started packing the worst of the bunch into school buses for the trip up I-10 into Jefferson Parish.

That's when I heard a woman on a wrist chain screaming at an Iberia deputy who was trying to push her up onto the steps of a waiting bus. She sat down heavily on the curb, pulling others down with her.

"What's going on, Top?" I asked the deputy.

"She spit on a fireman and scratched his face. She started yelling about a priest on a church roof," the deputy said. "I think she's nuts. She was also holding a few pharmaceuticals."

The woman looked Hispanic and wore a filthy purple sundress with bone-colored flowers printed on it. Her hair and skin were greasy with oil, her bare feet bloody.

"Who's the priest?" I asked her.

She looked up at me. "Father LeBlanc," she answered.

"Jude LeBlanc?" I asked.

"You know him?" she said.

"I knew a priest by that name in New Iberia. Where is he?"

"In the Lower Nine, at St. Mary Magdalene. He filled in there sometimes because they ain't got no regular priest."

"Can you kick her loose?" I asked the deputy.

"Gladly," the deputy said, leaning down to the chain with his cuff key.

She was off balance when she stood up. I steadied her with one hand and walked her toward a first-aid station. "What happened to your feet?" I said.

"I lost my shoes two days ago. We were on a roof that didn't have no shingles. The nails were sticking out of the boards."

"Where's Jude, Natalia?"

"How you know my name?"

"Your brother is Chula Ramos. He's a member of MS-13. He told me about you and Jude."

She twisted out of my hand and faced me. Her sundress was glued against her skin, her forehead bitten by insects. A helicopter mounted with a searchlight swooped by overhead, chasing looters in the business district.

"Where's my brother? You using him to get to Jude?" she said.

"You want to lose the attitude or go back on the chain?"

Her eyes roved over my face, one tooth biting on the corner of her lip. "He was trying to get people at Mary Magdalene to evacuate. But a lot of them didn't have no cars. So we all went up to the church because it's got a big attic. Jude saw a boat floating by, one with a motor on it. He swam after it, in the dark. That was two nights ago."

I saw Helen waving at me. A fight had broken out on one of the buses and through the windows I could see men in silhouette flailing at one another.

"Go on," I said.

"I saw him start up the boat and drive it back toward the church. I shined a flashlight on him so he could see better. It was a green boat, with a duck painted on the side, and I could see him sitting in the back, driving it straight for the church. He was gonna take everybody out of the attic. He'd got an ax from somebody and was gonna chop a hole in the roof, because the window wasn't big enough for a lot of the people to go through.

"I could hear him chopping up on the roof. The water was rising and I didn't know if he could cut through the boards quick enough. Then the chopping stopped and I heard lots of feet scuffling and somebody cry out. I think maybe it was Jude."

The incessant blast of airboats, the idling diesel engines of buses and trucks, the thropping of helicopter blades were like a dental drill whirring into an exposed nerve. Helen clicked a flashlight on and off in my direction to get my attention, her tolerance waning.

"I have to go now," I said. "After you get your feet treated, I want you to get on that truck over there. In a couple of hours it's going to a shelter in St. Mary Parish. I'm writing my cell phone number on my business card. I want you to call me when you get to the shelter."

"The ones who couldn't get out the window drowned," she said.

"Say again?"

"Almost all the people in the attic drowned. I dropped the children out the window, but I didn't see them again in the water. Most of the others was too old or too big. I left them behind. I just left them behind and swam toward a big tree that was floating past. I could hear them yelling in the dark."

I started to speak, to offer some kind of reassurance to her, but there are times when words are of no value. I walked away and rejoined Helen and the other members of my department, all of whom were dealing with problems that were both tangible and transitory.

When I looked for Clete Purcel, I could not see him in the crowd.

CHAPTER
8

Otis Baylor was proud of the way his home had withstood the storm. Built of oak and cypress, with twin brick chimneys, by a clipper-ship captain who would later fight at the side of the Confederate admiral Raphael Semmes, the house lost no glass behind its latched shutters and developed no leaks in the ceilings, even though oak limbs weighing hundreds of pounds had crashed down on the roof. Otis's neighbors were without power or telephone communication as the hurricane's center plowed northward into Mississippi, but Otis's generators worked beautifully and lit up his home with the soft pink-white radiance of a birthday cake.

By midday Tuesday he was clearing his drive of broken tree limbs, lopping them into segments with his chain saw, preparing to get his car out of the carriage house and make contact with his company's state headquarters in North Louisiana. His street was still flooded, the water way up in his and his neighbors' yards, but Otis was convinced the city's storm-pump system would eventually kick in and drain all of uptown New Orleans. Why wouldn't it? The city had gone under in '65 and had come back better than ever. You just had to keep the right perspective.

But as the piles of sawed limbs grew higher and higher in his backyard, he realized it would take a cherry picker to clear the biggest pieces of debris from his drive and he also realized that probably eighty percent of his neighbors had evacuated, leaving their homes to whoever wished to enter them. He didn't condemn them, but he couldn't understand a man who would give up his home either to the forces of nature or to lawless men.

The sky turned purple at sunset and hundreds of birds descended into his backyard, feeding on the worms that had been flooded to the surface. Otis went into the kitchen and poured a glass of whiskey, put a teaspoon of honey in it, and sipped it slowly while he stared out the back window at the gold strips of sunlight that clung with a kind of fatal beauty to the ruined branches of his trees.

"The toilet won't flush," Thelma, his daughter, said.

"Did you fill the tank from the bathtub?" he asked.

"It won't flush because everything is backing up. It's disgusting," Thelma said.

"The sewer system will be back online in no time. You'll see."

"Why didn't we leave like everybody else? It was stupid to stay here."

"This is one time I agree with her," Melanie, his wife, said from the kitchen doorway. She was smoking a cigarette, her shoulder propped against the doorjamb, every gold hair on her head neatly in place.

"I've fixed a cold supper for us—chicken sandwiches and cucumber salad, with ice cream for dessert," Otis said. "I think we have a lot to be thankful for."

"Like our visitors out there," Melanie said. She nodded toward the front of the house, blowing smoke from the corner of her mouth.

Otis set down his glass of whiskey and went into the living room. Through the front windows and the tangle of downed tree limbs in the yard, he could make out four young black men in a boat farther up the street. They had cut the gas feed and tilted the motor up on the stern of the boat, so the propeller would not catch on the curb as they drifted onto the flooded lawn of a darkened house.

One of them stepped down into the water and pulled the boat by its painter toward the front door.

"Why not give our black mayor a call?" Melanie said.

"That kind of talk doesn't help anything," Otis said.

Melanie was quiet a long time. He heard her mashing out her cigarette, then felt her standing close behind him. "Can you tell if they're armed?" she asked.

"I can't see them well in the shadows." Otis glanced through a side window. "There's Tom Claggart. I suspect if those fellows want trouble, they'll find it with Tom."

"Tom Claggart is a blowhard and an idiot. He's also a whoremonger," Melanie said.

Otis turned and stared at his wife.

"Don't look at me like that. Tom's wife told me he gave her syphilis. He and his buddies go to cathouses on their hunting trips."

Otis didn't want to talk about Tom Claggart. "We can't be responsible for what vandals do down the street. I'll go out and yell at them, but the owners of those houses made a choice and that's the way it is."

"Don't provoke them. Where's your rifle?"

"Our house is well lighted. They can see it's occupied. They won't come here."

"You don't know that."

"Their kind live under rocks, Melanie. They don't do well in daylight."

She was standing even closer to him now, the nicotine in her breath touching his face. Her voice dropped into a whisper. "I'm scared, Otis," she said. She slipped her arm in his. He could feel the point of her breast against him. He couldn't remember when she had been so confessional in her need, so dependent upon his strength. "Put the rifle in our bedroom. I know you have it. I saw you with it the other day."

"I'll keep it close by. I promise."

She let out her breath and rested her cheek against his shoulder. In ten seconds' time the embittered woman he had been living with had disappeared and been replaced by the lovely, intelligent woman he had met on a Bahamian beach, under the stars, years ago.

Otis waited until Melanie and Thelma were setting the dining room table, then removed a pair of binoculars from his desk in the den and focused them on the men who were breaking into homes on the other side of the neutral ground. Tom Claggart tapped on the side window. Otis unlocked the French doors and pulled them open.

"What is it?" he asked.

"The Snoop Dogg fan club is looting the goddamn neighborhood is what," Tom said.

"What do you want me to do about it?"

Tom Claggart's shaved head was pinpointed with sweat in the humidity, his muscle shirt streaked with dirt. "We need to take back our fucking neighborhood. You want in or not?"

"What I want is for you not to use that kind of language around my home."

"Those guys out there file their teeth, Otis. Considering what happened to Thelma, you of all people should know that."

"If they try to come in my home, I'll kill them. So far they haven't tried to do that. Now go back to your family, Tom."

"My family left." Tom's face was flat when he said it, his buckshot eyes round and dead, as though he were announcing a fact he himself had not yet assimilated.

"I'm sorry. I can't help you," Otis said.

Otis closed the French doors and locked them. As he looked at Tom's expression through the glass, he felt a deep sense of sorrow for him, the same way he had once felt toward his uneducated, work-exhausted father whose sense of self-worth was so low he had to put on a Klansman's robes to know who he was.

"Who was that?" Thelma asked.

"A fellow who will never own anything of value," Otis said.

"What's that mean?" Thelma asked.

"It means let's eat," Otis said, patting her fondly on the back.

But a few minutes later Otis Baylor realized he had arrived at one of those intersections in life when a seemingly inconsequential decision or event changes one's direction forever. He had forgotten to return the binoculars to the desk drawer and in the fading twilight Thelma had picked them up and begun scanning the street with them.

She froze and a muted sound rose from her throat, as though she had stepped on a sharp stone.

"What's wrong, kiddo?" he asked.

"Those guys in the boat," she replied.

"They'll take what they want and they'll go away. They won't come here."

"No, it's *them,* Daddy."

He took the binoculars from her and fixed them on the four black males who had now worked their way farther down the street, still on the opposite side of the neutral ground. "Those are the men who attacked you?" he said.

"The one in the front of the boat is for sure. He kept lighting cigarettes and laughing while they did it to me," she said. "The guy behind him, the one with the hammer in his hand, he looks just like the guy who—"

"What?"

Her face was beginning to crumple now. "Who made me put it in my mouth," she said.

Otis cleared his throat slightly, as though a tiny piece of bone were caught in it. He could feel his chest laboring for his next breath, his palms opening and closing at his sides, his mouth drier than he could remember. "You're absolutely certain?"

"You don't believe me? You think I would just pick out some black guys I never saw before and lie about them? Is that what you think of me?"

The pathos in her face was such he could hardly look at it.

He walked out on his front porch and stared down the street at the four men. Their boat was a big aluminum one, painted green, the black men and the green boat almost lost in the shadows of the building. He climbed the stairs to the second floor and in the hallway pulled down the lanyard on the collapsible steps that folded into the attic. His Springfield was propped against a cardboard box packed with his dead mother's clothes, which he could not bring himself to give away. The rifle had been a present from his father on Otis's sixteenth birthday and was the best gift Otis had ever received, primarily because his father had owned very little, not even the clapboard house in which they lived, and the most dear of his possessions had been his Springfield rifle.

It still had its original military dark-grained stock and leather sling and iron sights, but the oiled smoothness of its action and the accuracy with which it fired a round had no peer.

The attic was musty and dry, strangely comfortable and peaceful in the shadowy light of the single electric bulb that hung from a cord overhead. Otis unlocked the bolt and from a box of army-surplus ammunition began pressing one .30-06 shell after another into the rifle's magazine. He felt the spring come tight under his thumb and slid the bolt forward, locking it down, a metal-jacketed, needle-nosed round resting snugly in the chamber.

He climbed back down the folding steps and walked through his bedroom to the glass doors that gave onto the balcony. But the sky was dark now, the stars and moon veiled with smoke, the tangle of downed trees on his neighbors' lawns impossible to see through. He opened the doors onto the balcony and stepped outside, wrapping his left forearm inside the rifle's sling. The warm current of air rising from his flower beds made him think of spring, of new beginnings, of seasonal predictability. But the autumnal gas on the wind was a more realistic indicator of his situation, he thought. It was a season of death, and for Otis it had begun not with the hurricane but with the rape of his daughter.

He had never tried to describe to others the rage he felt when he saw his daughter in the emergency room at Charity Hospital. Her attackers had even burned her breasts. A black policewoman had tried to console him, promising him that NOPD would do everything in its power to catch the men who had harmed Thelma. She said his daughter needed him. She said he should not have the thoughts he was having. She said he was a bystander now and that he must trust others to hunt down his daughter's tormentors, that in effect the legalities of her case were not his business.

The look Otis gave the policewoman made her face twitch. From that moment on he resolved he would never allow anyone access to the level of rage that churned inside him, not until he found the three faceless black men who lived quietly on the edges of his consciousness, twenty-four hours a day.

Otis doubted that many people had any understanding of the

thought processes, the obsession, a father enters into when he wakes each morning with the knowledge that the degenerates and cowards who ruined his daughter's life are probably within a few miles of his house, laughing at what they have done. Perhaps the father's emotions are atavistic in origin, he told himself, just as protection of the cave is. Perhaps those feelings are hardwired into the brain for a reason and are not to be contended with.

After Thelma was arrested for possession of marijuana, Otis attended several Al-Anon meetings in the Garden District. The only other man there as reticent as he was a neatly groomed accountant who worked for a religious foundation. For five meetings the accountant sat politely in a chair and never volunteered a word. One night the group leader asked the accountant if the meetings had helped him or his alcoholic wife. The accountant seemed to consider the question for a moment. "When my daughter was raped by her teacher on a field trip I thought about laundering ten thousand dollars to have him castrated. But I still haven't decided if that's the right thing or not. So, yeah, I guess in a way you could say I've made some progress."

The room was so quiet Otis thought all the air had been sucked out of it. After the meeting, he followed the accountant to his car. It had just rained and the night air was pungent with the smell of magnolia blossoms, pulsing with the sounds of tree frogs.

"Hey?" Otis said.

"Yeah?" the accountant said.

"Have a good one, bud," Otis said.

"You trying to tell me something?" the accountant said.

"I just did," Otis replied.

Now he was walking downstairs with a loaded rifle cradled against his chest. He could hear Thelma talking to Melanie in the kitchen, telling her she was sure that at least two of the men in the green boat were her attackers. Then she began to tell Melanie for the first time, in detail, what they had done to her.

Otis stepped out on the mushiness of the St. Augustine grass that grew like a deep blue-green carpet on his lawn. Four houses down the street, on the opposite side, he could see a flashlight's beam

moving behind the second-story windows of a home where Varina
Davis, the wife of the Confederate president, had once stayed. But
he didn't see the green boat and he wondered if he was watching
the same vandals or a new group. He crossed Tom Claggart's yard,
walking on the dirty rim of water that covered the sidewalk and
extended almost to Tom's gallery. Suddenly he was bathed in white
light from a battery-powered lantern that Tom had chosen, just at
that moment, to carry out on the gallery.

"Turn that thing off!" Otis said.

"You got those guys spotted?" Tom asked.

"I'm not sure. Go back inside, Tom."

"I got some guys coming over. We can close off the block and rip
the whole problem out by its roots. Get my drift?"

"No, I didn't."

Tom clicked off his lantern. "Bang on the door if you need the
cavalry," he said. "My friends don't take prisoners."

Otis sloshed into the street until his foot touched the curbing that
bordered the neutral ground. But even on top of the neutral ground
the water level was above his ankles and he could see the V-shaped
wake of a cottonmouth moccasin swimming toward a mound of oak
limbs that was draped over an automobile.

He positioned himself behind the trunk of a palm tree and stared
at the house from which he could hear glass breaking and furniture
being overturned. In his mind's eye he saw himself crashing through
the front door, advancing up the stairs, and taking them out one by
one, the exit wounds stippling the wallpaper with their blood, the
impact of their bodies hitting the floor like bags of sand.

No, it had to be an eye for an eye, he thought. Thelma had identified only two of the four men as her attackers. He could not kill
arbitrarily, if in fact he was capable of killing at all. It was easier to
think about than to do it. When the test came, could he pull the trigger? Was he willing to join the ranks of men like Tom Claggart and
his friends?

But if the looters threatened him, if they were armed or they refused to halt, that would be another matter, wouldn't it?

A house burst into flame on the next block, orange sparks twisting high in the sky. In the distance he could hear gunfire and he could see a helicopter trying to land on a hospital roof, and he wondered if snipers were shooting at it. His hands were damp on the stock of the rifle, his eyes stinging with sweat. When he swallowed, his saliva tasted as metallic as blood.

He stepped off the far side of the neutral ground and began working his way down the street, past automobiles whose windows had been broken and their stereos ripped from their dashboards. He waded up onto the lawn of the house the looters were ransacking and watched the flashlight beam go from room to upstairs room. Then the light shone down a staircase, its beam bouncing off the downstairs hallway as the person carrying the flashlight descended the stairs. Otis wrapped his left arm in the sling and steadied the rifle's barrel against the trunk of a live oak, waiting for the front door to open.

But the flashlight went out and the inside of the house fell into darkness. The front door did not open.

Where was the boat?

Otis stared into the shadows on both sides of the house and could see nothing of significance. Then, as heat lightning rippled across the clouds, he realized the flooding at the back of the house was even greater than in front. In fact, the alley and the garages along it were filled by a dark, swiftly running river that had created a navigable canal though the entirety of the neighborhood.

Somebody hit the starter button on an outboard motor and Otis saw the bow of the aluminum boat plow down the alley, the dark shapes of four men slouched forward in the seats.

He walked back home, his rifle slung on his shoulder. Tom Claggart and his friends were talking loudly in Claggart's yard, lighting smokes, locking and loading, grinning at Otis. A couple of them wore olive-green T-shirts and camouflage pants with big pockets on them. "You save any for us?" one man asked.

"They cut bait," Otis replied.

"Too bad," the man said.

"Yeah, too bad. There's nothing like hanging black ivory on the wall," Otis said.

He had said it as bitterly and as ironically as possible. But to his listeners his remark was that of a kindred spirit. They roared at the inference. For Otis, that moment would remain like a dirty fingerprint on the mist, one that would come back to haunt him in ways he could not have imagined.

CHAPTER

9

EDDY AND BERTRAND Melancon were not given to complexities. They kept it simple. If a good situation put itself in your road, you made use of it. If it might jam you up, you put it in the ditch. Anything wrong with that?

Eddy and Bertrand saw the storm as a gift from God. White people in New Orleans had been making money on the black man's back for three hundred years. It was time for some payback. The uptown area of the city, from Lee Circle all the way up St. Charles Avenue to the Carrollton District, was like a tree full of ripe peaches waiting to be shook. The Melancon brothers had never been house creeps. They specialized in armed robbery and took down only high-value victims and thought breaking and entering was for chumps who deserved what they got when they walked into a blast from a twelve-gauge shotgun. But when tens of thousands of homes and stores were abandoned and without power, their security systems worthless, the cops either gone or pulling scores themselves, what was a guy supposed to do? Crowd into the stink at the Superdome or the Convention Center and try to find a place on the floor where somebody hadn't already downloaded his bowels?

The boat they had boosted in the Ninth Ward was perfect for the job. It had a wide beam, a shallow draft, cushioned seats, and a seventy-five-horse motor on it. As long as they concentrated on jewelry, coin collections, guns, and silverware, and avoided loading with heavy stuff like television sets and computers, they could possibly amass major five-figure money by dawn. They just had to keep it simple. The only dude between themselves and Central Lockup was that cracker Purcel, a bucket of whale sperm who did scut work for Wee Willie Bimstine and Nig Rosewater, and they'd run over his fat ass with their 'sheen in the Quarter, left that motherfucker not knowing what hit him.

Now they were going house-to-house on a flooded street where every live oak was broken in half on top of the yards, only one house with lights working in it, choppers flying overhead to the hospital roof, not a police boat in sight, Bertrand and Eddy both working the upstairs of a mansion that had beds in it with canopies over them, like the kind in *Gone with the Wind*, Eddy stuffing a woman's fur coat into a drawstring laundry bag along with a handful of necklaces he found buried at the bottom of her panty drawer.

Bertrand shined the light into the top of the closet. "Look what we got here, man," he said.

Eddy paused in his work and stared upward at the panel his brother was prying loose from the closet wall. Both brothers were thick-bodied men, the muscles in their shoulders swollen and hard as iron from shrug-lifting sixty-pound dumbbells in each hand. Both were stripped to the waist and sweating profusely in the superheated interior of the house, Bertrand with a red bandana knotted tightly around his head.

Bertrand reached inside the wall and lifted out a short-barreled blue-black revolver with checkered walnut grips and a Ziploc bag fat with white granular crystals. "Oh mama, Whitey's private stash and a thirty-eight snub. This is gonna be one pissed-off dude," he said. "Wait a minute. That ain't all."

Bertrand stuck the bag of cocaine down the front of his trousers and handed the revolver to his brother. He reached back inside the wall and lifted out five bundles of one-hundred-dollar bills, each of them wrapped with a wide rubber band. He whistled. "Do you believe this shit? This motherfucker's in the life."

"Maybe this ain't the place to take down," Eddy said.

"Hey, man, ain't nobody know we here. This is our night. We ain't blowing it."

"You're right, man. The dagos ain't running things no more, no-how. What you doing?"

Bertrand stuck the bundled bills in the bag, his eyes dancing in the glow of the flashlight. "Don't worry about it."

A third man entered the room. He had pulled off a gold-and-purple T-shirt and wadded it up and was using it to mop the sweat off his chest and out of his armpits. He wore paint-splattered slacks and tennis shoes without socks. Whiskers grew on his chin like strands of black wire. "Kevin thinks he saw a guy out in the street," he said.

"That kid's been wetting his pants all night. I told you not to bring him," Bertrand said.

"He's just saying what he saw, man," the third man said. His eyes dropped to Bertrand's waistline and the Ziploc bag that protruded from his trousers. "Where'd you get the blow?"

"Same place we got the thirty-eight. Now go take care of Kevin. We gonna be right there. I don't want to be hearing about nobody out in the street, either. It's Michael Jackson and *Thriller* out there. This city is a graveyard and we own the shovels and the headstones. Motherfucker come in here, he gonna eat one of these thirty-eights. You hear me, Andre? Get your ass downstairs and bring up the boat. And don't be cranking it till we there."

"What y'all got in the laundry bag?" the third man said.

"Andre, what it take for you to understand?" Bertrand said.

"I'm just axing," the third man replied. "We in this together, ain't we?"

"That's right. So go do what he say," Eddy said.

Andre huffed air out his nostrils and disappeared down the stair-way. Bertrand tapped one fist on top of the other, his gaze roving around the room. "There's more. I can feel it. I can smell money in the walls," he said.

"What you smell is them flowers all over the place. What kind of people put flower vases in every room in the house right before a hurricane?" Eddy said.

The question was a legitimate one. Who could afford to place fresh bowls of roses and orchids and carnations in a dozen rooms every three or four days? Who would want to? Bertrand stared at the water stains in the wallpaper and pushed against the softness of the lathwork underneath, his stomach on fire, rivulets of sweat running out of his bandana. "These walls is busting wit' it, Eddy. It's a drop or something," he said.

"Give it up, man," Eddy said. "It's burning up in here. It must be a hundred and twenty degrees."

Bertrand looked hard at his brother and grimaced as his ulcers flared again. This could be the perfect score. Why did his insides have to betray him now, why was his head always full of broken glass? Why wasn't anything easy?

"All right," he said, drawing a quiet breath.

"That's better," Eddy said. "You're always grieving, man, firing yourself up over things you cain't change. We ain't made the world. Time to enjoy life, not worry so much all the time."

Both of them went downstairs, the flashlight's beam bouncing in front of them. Then Bertrand clicked off the light and the two of them climbed into the boat with Andre and his nephew. The sky was orange from a fire on the next block and inside the smoke and mist and humidity the air smelled like garbage burning on a cold day at the city dump.

Bertrand looked back over his shoulder at the house. For some reason that he couldn't understand, he felt his entry into this deserted, antebellum structure had just changed his life in a fashion that was irreversible. But for good or bad? Why were knives always whirling inside him?

Suddenly, like a camera shutter opening in his mind, he saw a young girl fighting against the polyethylene rope that bound her arms and ankles, thrashing her feet against the floor of a panel truck, her stuffed bear lying beside her. He shook the image out of his head and pointed his face into the wind as their aluminum boat sped down the flooded alleyway, trash cans bobbing in the engine's wake, helicopters flying overhead to airlift the most desperate of the desperate from the hospital in which Bertrand Melancon had been born.

•　•　•

It was close to midnight before Otis dressed for bed. He removed the cartridge from the chamber of the Springfield, pressed it back down in the magazine, and locked down the bolt. He propped the rifle by a dormer window that gave an encompassing view of the front yard, checked all the doors again, and kissed Thelma good night. Then he made an old-fashioned for both himself and Melanie and took them up to the bedroom on a silver tray with three pieces of chocolate on it.

"What's all this for?" she asked.

"We owe ourselves a treat. Tomorrow will be a fine day. I genuinely believe it will."

She wore a pink nightgown and had been reading on top of the sheets. The gasoline-powered generators could not adequately support the air-conditioning system, but the attic fan was on and her bare shoulders looked cool and lovely in the breeze through the window. She placed her book on the floor and bit into a square of French chocolate, pushing little pieces of it back into her mouth with her fingertips. She smiled at him. "Turn out the light," she said.

Later, when Otis fell asleep, his thoughts were peaceful, his body drained of all the rage and turmoil that had beset his life since his daughter was attacked. His home had survived Katrina. His wife was his wife again. And he had gone after his daughter's attackers with both firmness of purpose and a measure of mercy. More important, he had made his house a safe harbor in a time of societal collapse, the front yard and driveway pooled with an apron of light that held back the darkness and the men who prowled it. A man could have done worse.

INSIDE THE BACK of the looted Rite Aid drugstore, Bertrand Melancon felt like fire ants were eating the lining of his stomach. Andre and his nephew still didn't know about the bundled cash in the laundry bag, but it was only a matter of time before they either saw it or figured out why Eddy was acting hinky. Maybe it was better to split the loot fair and square and be done with it, he thought. The Rite Aid had been ripped apart and was in complete darkness, but it was a good place to cool out, do a few lines of the high-grade flake from the house full of flowers, and work things out. Yeah, that was it. Don't stiff nobody and you don't got to be watching your back all the time. But dividing up cold cash that *he* found, that *he* ripped out of the wall, wasn't going to be easy. On several levels, personal and otherwise.

"Look, me and Eddy got a surprise for you. That last house had some money in a wall. We're gonna give y'all your cut now, in case something go sout' and some of us get picked up," Bertrand said.

There was no sound in the room. Andre was seated on a metal desk, drinking from a warm can of Coca-Cola he'd found under a destroyed display rack out front. He had thrown away his soiled LSU T-shirt and in the flashes of heat lightning through the window his skin was the color of dusty leather, his nipples like brown dimes. "How come we just hearing about that now?" he asked.

Bertrand slapped a mosquito on his neck and studied it. "'Cause I didn't want no complications back there," he said. "'Cause I don't be explaining everything as we go. 'Cause you getting cut in on what you ain't found, Andre, wit' an equal share for your young relative here, even though you and him ain't had nothing to do wit' finding the money. If I was you, I'd show some humbleness and be thankful for what I got."

"The split's always been fair, ain't it?" Eddy said.

"If it ain't been fair, I wouldn't have no way of knowing, would I?" Andre said.

But Bertrand no longer cared if Andre believed him and Eddy or not. That house back there on the flooded alley was creaking with cash-ola. Ten more minutes with the ball-peen and the crowbar and he would have had the upstairs walls peeled down to the floor. Bertrand could see stacks of cash tumbling out on his shoe tops.

He looked at his watch. It was one in the morning. He and Eddy could be at the alley in less than a half hour, cut the engine, and hand-pull the boat in from the side street. Nobody would even know they were there. Because they already knew the layout they could probably work inside without flashlights. This was the big score, man. He'd done right by Andre and his nephew and it was time to get back into action. Screw this diplomacy shit.

"Me and Eddy are going back. Y'all stay here," Bertrand said.

Andre pinched his abs, his eyes empty, his mouth pursed. "How come we get left behind?"

"Let me ax you a better question," Bertrand said. "How come you always feeling yourself up?"

"Why don't you lay off me, man? Case you ain't noticed, the buses and the streetcar ain't running," Andre said. "We suppose to carry our loot t'rou town?"

"Andre's right, man. One for all and all for one. We all going back together," Eddy said. He lit a cigarette and blew out smoke without removing the cigarette from his lips. He looked at Andre's nephew. "You up for that, my li'l brother?"

Kevin was seated on the floor, eating a fried pie, his springy hair bright with sweat. He wiped his mouth with his shirt. "I ain't scared," he said.

Bertrand wanted to shove Eddy's head into a commode.

OTIS SLEPT THE sleep of the dead, his wife's hip nestled against him, the attic fan drawing a breeze across their bodies. He dreamed of his parents and the tiny yellow house he had grown up in. In the spring the grass was always cool in the evening and full of clover, and when his father came home from work at the sawmill, they played a game of pitch-and-catch in the front yard. There were cows and horses in a field behind the house, and a big hackberry tree in the side yard that shaded the roof during the hottest hours of the day. Otis had always loved the house he had grown up in and he had loved his family and had always believed he was loved by them in return.

He believed this right up to the Indian-summer afternoon his father discovered his wife's infidelity and shot her lover to death on the steps of the Baptist church where he served as pastor, then came home and was shot down and killed by a volunteer constable who had once been his fishing partner.

Otis sat straight up in bed. Then he went into the bathroom and tried to wash his face in the lavatory. The faucet made a loud, squeaking sound, and a pipe vibrated dryly in the wall.

"What was that?" Melanie said from the bed.

"It's just me. I forgot the water was off."

"I thought I heard something outside."

He walked back into the bedroom, his bare feet padding on the carpet. All he could hear was the steady drone of the attic fan and the wind in the trees on the north side of the house. He looked out on the street. The moon had broken out of the clouds and created a black glaze on the surface of the floodwater. A solitary palm frond rustled against the side of a tree trunk on the neutral ground and a trash can turned in an eddy by a plugged storm drain.

"I had a bad dream. I was probably talking in my sleep," he said.

"Are you sure no one is out there?"

"I never told you how my father died."

She raised herself on her elbow, her face lined from the pillow. "I thought he had leukemia."

"He did. But that's not how he died. He was shot to death by a friend of his, a constable. He was going to kill my mother," Otis said. He was sitting on the edge of the bed, staring into space, his back to his wife, when he said this.

The room was silent a long time. When he lay back down, Melanie took his hand in hers. "Otis?" she said, looking up into the darkness.

"Yes?"

"We mustn't ever tell anyone about this. That is not what happened in your family."

In the glow of moonlight through the window, her face looked as though it had been sculpted in alabaster.

"Say that again?" Otis asked.

"You're a respected insurance executive in New Orleans. That's what you will remain. That story you just told me has no application in our lives today."

"Mel?" he began.

"Please. I've told you not to call me that, Otis. It's not a lot to ask."

Otis went downstairs to the den and lay down on a black leather couch, a cushion over his head, his ears ringing with a sound like wind in seashells.

• • •

BERTRAND COULDN'T give up his resentment toward Eddy all the way back to the house where he'd found the cash and dope and the .38 snub. Eddy loved playing the big shot, handing out favors to people, screwing a cigarette in his mouth, firing it up with a Zippo, snapping the lid back tight, like he was the dude in control. Except Eddy was being generous with what wasn't his to be generous with, in this case the biggest score of their lives. Andre was sitting backward on the bow of the boat, like he was lookout man, scanning the horizon, some kind of commando about to take down Osama bin Laden.

What a pair of jokers. Maybe it was time to cut both of them loose.

But the real reason for Bertrand's resentment of Eddy and Andre had little to do with the score at the house and he knew it. Every time he looked into their faces he saw his own face, and what he saw there set his stomach on fire again.

Maybe he could get away from Andre and Eddy and start over somewhere else. Forget about what they had done when they were stoned. Yeah, maybe he could even make up for it, write those girls a note and mail it to the newspaper from another city. It hadn't been his idea anyway. It was Eddy who always had a thing about young white girls, always saying sick stuff when they pulled up to them next to a red light. Andre had been a sex freak ever since he got turned out in the Lafourche Parish Prison. Bertrand never got off hurting people.

But no matter how many times Bertrand went over the assault on the two victims, he could not escape one conclusion about his participation: He had entered into it willingly, and when he saw revulsion in the face of the girl they had taken out of the car with the dead battery, he had done it to her with greater violence than either his brother or Andre.

In these moments he hated himself and sometimes even wished someone would drive a bullet through his brain and stop the thoughts that kept his stomach on fire.

The street was completely dark, except for one house where the owner obviously had his own generators working. Eddy cut the engine at the end of the block and let the boat drift through mounds of partially submerged oak limbs into the side yard of the house they had creeped three hours earlier.

In minutes the four of them were ripping the Sheetrock and lathwork and plaster off the studs in every room in the house. In fact, it was fun tearing the place apart. The air and carpets were white with dust, the flower vases smashed and the flowers scattered, the kitchen a shambles, electric wiring hanging like spaghetti out of the walls.

"This motherfucker gonna brown his drawers when he come home," Eddy said. "Hey, man, dig Andre in the kitchen."

Bertrand couldn't believe it. Andre had unbuttoned his trousers and was looping a high arc of urine into the sink.

"That's sick, man," Bertrand said.

"You're right," Andre answered. He spun around and hosed down the stove and an opened drawer that was full of seasoning, saving out enough for the icebox.

That was it, Bertrand said to himself. He was splitting.

Then Eddy splintered a chunk of plywood out of the pantry ceiling with his crowbar, and a cascade of bundled fifty- and one-hundred-dollar bills poured down on his head. "Oh man, you was right from the jump, Bertrand, this is a motherfucking bank."

The four of them began scooping up the money, throwing it into a vinyl garbage bag, Bertrand estimating the count as each pack of bills thudded into the bottom of the bag. He ran out of math in the sixty-thousand range.

"We rich," Andre said. "We rich, man. We rich. Ain't nobody gonna believe this."

"That's right, 'cause you ain't gonna tell them," Bertrand said.

"Hey, man, Andre's cool. Don't be talking to a brother like that," Eddy said.

"Eddy, I want you to clean the wax out of your ears and hear this real good. That's the last time you're gonna act like you big shit at my expense," Bertrand said.

"Hey, like Andre say, we all rich. We ain't got time to be fighting among ourselves," Kevin said. "We gonna burn the house? I mean, to get rid of the fingerprints and all?"

The three older men stared at him with their mouths open.

UP THE STREET, on the other side of the neutral ground, Tom Claggart and two friends had nodded off on pallets they had laid out on Claggart's living room floor, hoping to catch the faint breeze that puffed through the doorway and to avoid as much as possible the layers of heat that had mushroomed against the ceilings. Their pistols and shotguns and hunting rifles were oiled and loaded and propped against the divan or hung on the backs of chairs. Their boxes of brass cartridges and shotgun shells were placed neatly on the mantel above the fireplace. All their empty beer cans and bread wrappers and empty containers of corn beef and boneless turkey and mustard and horseradish and dirty paper plates and plastic forks and spoons were wrapped and sealed in odor-proof bags. When one of them had to relieve himself, he did so in the backyard and took an entrenching tool with him.

No hunting camp could have been neater or better regulated. There was only one problem. Tom Claggart and his friends had not been presented with an opportunity to discharge a round all night, even though they and several others had made probes by boat and on foot into two adjoining neighborhoods where sparks from burning houses drifted through the live oaks like fireflies.

It seemed hardly fair.

"DON'T GO BACK by that lighted house, man. Go back the way we come," Bertrand said from the bow of the boat.

"No, man, we're hauling ass. We ain't bothered them people. They ain't gonna bother us," Eddy said, sitting sideways in the stern, opening up the throttle.

"You just don't listen, man," Bertrand said, his words lost in the roar of the engine.

The boat swerved through clumps of broken tree limbs in the

street and raked on the curbing along the neutral ground. Andre was laughing, sticking his hand down in the vinyl bag to feel the tightly packed bundles of cash there, his nephew eating one of the candy bars he'd found in the Rite Aid. The wind had cleared the smoke off the street, and the water was black, stained with a rainbow slick, a busted main pumping a geyser in the air like a fountain in the park. If Bertrand got out of this with his share of the score intact, he was leaving New Orleans forever, starting over in a new place, maybe out on the West Coast, where people lived in regular neighborhoods, with parks and beaches and nice supermarkets close by. Yeah, a place where it was always seventy-five degrees and he could open a restaurant or a car wash with the money from the score and tool down palm-lined avenues in a brand-new convertible, Three 6 Mafia blaring from the speakers.

Yeah, that was the way it was going to be.

The motor coughed once, sputtered, and died. The boat rose on its wake and glided into a fallen oak limb, the branches scratching loudly against the aluminum sides. Bertrand could feel his skin shrink on his face, his ears popping in the silence. "I don't believe it," he said.

"It's out of gas. It ain't my fault," Eddy said.

"You never looked at the gauge?" Bertrand said.

"You didn't look at it, either, man. Get off my case," Eddy said.

"Maybe the line just got something in it," Andre said.

"It's empty, man," Eddy said.

Andre stood up clumsily, rocking the boat. He tugged at the gas can and slammed it back down. "What we gonna do?"

"You gonna shut up. You gonna stop making all that noise," Bertrand said.

"I'm just trying to help, man. We can tow it," Andre said.

"There's water out there that's six feet deep," Bertrand said.

Andre started to speak again.

"Just let me think," Bertrand said.

The four of them sat silently in the darkness, the branches of the downed oak limb sticking them in the eyes and the backs of their necks each time the wind blew against the boat.

Bertrand stepped over the side into the water. "Y'all wait here. Don't do nothing. Don't talk. Don't make no noise. Don't be playing wit' the money in the bag. Keep your ass in the boat and your mout' shut. Y'all got that?"

"What you gonna do?" Eddy said.

"Hear that sound? The man over there got generators in his garage. That means he got gas cans in his garage."

"Why you walking bent over, wit' your hand on your stomach?" Andre asked.

"'Cause y'all give me ulcers," Bertrand replied.

"I ain't meant nothing by it. You a smart man," Andre said.

No, just not as dumb as y'all, Bertrand thought to himself.

He waded across the neutral ground and approached the driveway of the lighted house. A bulb burned on the front gallery and another inside the porte cochere. A light in the kitchen fell through the windows on part of the driveway and the backyard. His heart was hammering against his rib cage, his pulse jumping in his neck. He tripped on a curbstone and almost fell headlong into the water. In the darkness he thought he saw eyes looking at him from the tangles of brush and tree limbs in the yard. He wondered if he was losing his mind. He stopped and stared into the yard, then realized wood rabbits had sought refuge from the floodwater and had climbed into the downed limbs and were perched there like birds, their fur sparkling with moisture.

Bertrand worked his way around the far side of the porte cochere, avoiding the light. He crossed between two huge camellia bushes, the leaves brushing back wetly against his arms, and entered the parking area by what uptown white people called "the carriage house." Why did they call it a carriage house when they didn't own no carriages? he asked himself. 'Cause that's a way of telling everybody Robert E. Lee took a dump in their commode in 1865?

He could hear at least two generators puttering beyond the half-opened door of the "carriage house." Then he detoured through the backyard and crossed into the neighbor's property, looked around, and removed an object from under his shirt. He bent over briefly, then retraced his steps back into Otis Baylor's yard, his ulcers digging their roots deeper into his stomach lining. He stepped inside the carriage house and let his eyes adjust to the darkness. Five jerry cans of gasoline were lined against the wall. He hefted up one in each hand and headed for the street, the St. Augustine grass by the porte cochere squishing under his shoes, the weight of the gas swinging in the cans. He had pulled it off. Right on, Bertrand. Stomp ass and take names, my brother, a voice said inside him.

Then he was past the apron of electrical light that shone into the yard, back into the safety of the street and the warmth of the flood-water that covered his ankles and rose up the calves of his legs like an old friend. Soon he would split from Eddy and the Rochons and be home free and free at last, loaded with money for good doctors and the good life. It would be Adios, all you stupid motherfuckers, Bertrand Melancon is California-bound.

Then he saw Eddy towing the boat from behind the pile of downed limbs, giving up their natural cover, an unlit cigarette hanging from his mouth. Andre and Kevin were outside the boat, too, steering it around obstacles in the water, all them now in full view of the house from which Bertrand had just stolen the jerry cans of gasoline.

"What the fuck you doing, man? Why didn't y'all stay put?" Bertrand said.

"What took you so long? You stop to flog your rod back there? Fill her up and let's go," Eddy said.

He sparked his Zippo, the tiny emery wheel rolling on the flint— once, twice, three times.

"Eddy—" Bertrand heard himself say.

The Zippo's flame flared in the darkness, crisping the end of Eddy's cigarette, lighting an inquisitive smile on his face, as though he had not understood what his brother had said.

Bertrand heard a single report behind him, but he could not coordinate the sound with the event taking place in front of him. A red flower burst from Eddy's throat and a split second later, right behind Eddy, the cap of Kevin Rochon's skull exploded from his head, scattering his brains on the water like freshly cooked oatmeal.

CHAPTER

10

IN ANY AMERICAN slum, two enterprises are never torched by urban rioters: the funeral home and the bondsman's office. From Clete Purcel's perspective, the greatest advantage in chasing down bail skips for bondsmen like Nig Rosewater and Wee Willie Bimstine was the fact their huge clientele of miscreants was sycophantic by nature and always trying to curry favor from those who had control over their lives. Big-stripe Angola graduates who would take a back-alley beating with blackjacks rather than dime a friend would rat-fuck their mothers in order to stay in Nig and Willie's good graces.

From the moment Clete Purcel had been run down in the Quarter, his porkpie hat stenciled with tire tread, the word was out: Bertrand and Eddy Melancon and their asswipe friend Andre Rochon were shark meat.

While the Melancons and Rochon and his nephew Kevin were powerboating all over uptown New Orleans, eating white speed boosted from a pharmacy, drinking warm beer and eating rotisserie chickens courtesy of Winn-Dixie, laughing at the unbelievable amount of loot they were amassing, they were dimed on at least two occasions by fellow lowlifes who had ended up in the chain-link jail at the airport, where Nig and Willie's representatives were doing fire-sale amounts of business.

But ironically it was not betrayal by his colleagues that brought about Bertrand's undoing. For probably the first time in his life he acted with total disregard for his own self-interest and loaded his brother into the boat while Andre bag-assed down the street and Eddy hemorrhaged cups of blood from his throat.

Bertrand's hands were trembling as he fueled the boat engine. He was sure the shooter was still out there, either in one of the yards or inside one of the houses that fronted the street. He was convinced the shooter was taking aim at him, moving the scope or the iron sights across Bertrand's face and chest or perhaps his scrotum, taking his time, enjoying it, softly biting down on his bottom lip as he tightened his finger on the trigger. The image caused a sensation in Bertrand that was like someone stripping off his skin with pliers. His hands were not only slick with Eddy's blood and saliva but shaking so badly his thumb slipped off the starter button when he tried to depress it.

When the engine caught, he twisted the throttle wide open and roared across the floodwater, Kevin's body bobbing in his wake. He thudded over a dead animal at the intersection and heard the propeller whine in the air before it plowed into the water again. He was almost sideswiped by an NOPD boat loaded with heavily armed cops. He slapped across their wake and veered up a cross street into an alley, pausing long enough to wedge the garbage and laundry bags inside a garage rafter. Up ahead, he could see the lights of a helicopter that was descending on a hospital rooftop. He reduced his speed and took a deep breath, exhaling slowly. He and Eddy had found safe harbor, a place where someone would care for his brother and save his life. It was the building in which they were both born. It was almost like coming home.

Bertrand had never heard of Dante's Ninth Circle. But he was about to get the guided tour.

THE FIRST FLOOR of the hospital had three feet of water in it. The corridors were black, except for the beams of flashlights carried by the personnel. The heated smell of medical and human waste in the water made Clete pull his shirt up over his mouth so he could breathe without gagging. Twice he tried to get directions, but the personnel brushed by him as though he were not there. He gave it up and went back outside, sucking in the night air, the sweat on his face suddenly as cool as ice water.

A black NOPD patrolman who must have weighed at least 275 pounds shined a flashlight in Clete's face. In his other hand he held a cut-down twelve-gauge Remington pump propped on his hip. His unshaved jaws looked filmed with black grit, and an odor like moldy clothes and locker-room sweat emanated from his body. His name was Tee Boy Pellerin, and as a state trooper he had once lifted a cruiser with his bare hands off his partner's chest.

"What you looking for, Purcel?" he said.

"A gunshot victim by the name of Eddy Melancon," Clete replied.

"Is he alive or dead?"

"I wouldn't know. The hospital is storing dead people?" Clete said.

"I wish. I got four of them in a boat. I been trying to dump them all over town. Nobody's got any refrigeration. You talking about Eddy Melancon from the Ninth Ward?"

"Yeah, Bertrand Melancon's brother. Nig Rosewater heard Eddy got capped looting a house this side of Claiborne."

"Try the third floor. The trauma victims who made it through the ER are getting warehoused up there. You got a flashlight?"

"I lost it."

"Take this one. I got an extra. You haven't been upstairs?"

"No."

Tee Boy gazed into space, as though a long day and a long night had just caught up with him.

"So what's upstairs?" Clete asked.

"The geriatric ward is on the third floor. If it was me, I wouldn't go in there," Tee Boy said.

"What are you trying to say?"

"There ain't no good stories in that building, Purcel. After tonight, I'm gonna pray every day God don't let me die in bed."

Clete took the stairs to the third floor. The temperature was stifling, like steam from cooked vegetables that had flattened against the ceilings, and broken glass crunched under his shoes. He entered a ward where the elderly had been rolled into the corridors to catch a meager breeze puffing from the windows that had been blown out on the south side of the building. The people on the gurneys wore gowns that were stiff with dried food and their own feces. Their skin seemed to glow with a putrescent shine that he associated with fish that had been stranded by waves on a hot beach. A woman's fingers caught Clete's shirt as he passed her. Her face was bloodless, her eyes the liquid milky-blue of a newly born infant looking upon the world for the first time.

"Is my son coming?" she said.

"Ma'am?" Clete said.

"Are you he? Are you my son?"

"I think he'll be here any minute now," Clete said, and moved quickly down the corridor, a lump in his throat.

The intensive care area looked like a charnel house. Pockets of water had formed in the ceiling and were dripping like giant paint blisters on the patients, most of whom still wore their street clothes. The patients who had been brought up from the ER had been shot, stabbed, cut, beaten, electrocuted, hit by automobiles, and pulled half-dead from storm drains. Some had broken bones that were still unset. A woman with burns on eighty percent of her body was wrapped in a sheet that had become glued to her wounds. A man who had been struck by the propeller of an airboat made sounds that Clete had not heard since he lay in a battalion aid station in the Central Highlands. Almost all of the patients were thirsty. Most of them needed morphine. All of those who were immobile had to relieve themselves inside their clothes.

Clete grabbed an intern by the arm. The intern had the wirelike physique of a long-distance runner, his eyes jittering, his pate glistening with moisture. "Get your hand off me," he said.

Clete raised his palms in the air. "I'm a licensed bail agent. I'm looking for a fugitive by the name of Eddy Melancon. An informant said his brother dropped him off at this hospital."

"Who cares?"

"The victims of his crimes do."

The intern seemed to think it over. "Yeah, Melancon, I worked on him. Third bed over. I don't think you'll find him too talkative."

"Is he alive?"

"If you want to call it that."

"Hey, Doc, I know y'all are having a rough go of it up here, but I'm not exactly having the best day of my life, either. How about getting the mashed potatoes out of your mouth?"

"His spinal cord is cut. If he lives, he'll be a sack of mush the rest of his life. You want to talk to his brother?"

"He's here?" Clete said, dumbfounded.

"Five minutes ago he was." The intern shined his flashlight down the corridor at a man sitting in an open window. "See? Enjoy."

Clete threaded his way between the gurneys and tapped Bertrand Melancon on the shoulder with his flashlight. "Hello, asshole. Remember me? The last time you saw me it was through the front windshield of your car," he said.

"I know who you are. You work for them Jews at the bail bonds office," Bertrand said.

"I also happen to be the guy you ran your car over."

"I don't own a car. Say, you're blocking my breeze, you mind?"

Clete could feel his mouth drying out and tiny stitches beginning to pop loose inside his head. "How would you like to go the rest of the way out that window?"

"Do what you gonna do, man."

For Clete, Bertrand Melancon seemed to personify what he hated most in the clientele he dealt with on a daily basis. They were raised by their grandmothers and didn't have a clue who their fathers were. They got turned out in jail and thought of sexual roles in terms of prey or predator. They lied instinctively, even when there was no reason to. Trying to find a handle on them was impossible. They were inured to insult, indifferent to their own fate, and devoid of guilt or shame. What bothered Clete most about them was his belief that anyone from their background would probably turn out the same.

"Turn around. We going to meet a black cop named Tee Boy Pellerin," Clete said, pulling his cuffs loose from the back of his belt.

"You'll dig this guy. He grew up in the Lower Nine himself. He's got a soft spot for gangbangers who strong-arm rob their own people and sell meth to their children. Just don't step on his shoeshine. He hates guys who step on his shoeshine."

Clete crimped the cuffs tight on both of Bertrand's wrists and spun him back around so he could look him squarely in the face. "Did I hear you laugh?"

"I ain't laughed, man."

"Yeah, you did. I heard you."

"Troot is, I don't care what you do, fat man. You ought to take a bat'. Get this over. I'm tired of listening to you."

Clete wanted to hit him. No, he wanted to tear him apart, seam and joint. But what was the real source of his anger? The reality was he had no power over a man who had tried to do a hit-and-run on him. There was no place to take him. Clete had bummed a ride to the hospital on an airboat full of cops who had continued on down the avenue to the Carrollton District. Central Lockup was underwater, and he had no way to effectively transport Bertrand to the chain-link jail at the airport. With luck he could surrender custody of Bertrand to Tee Boy and collect a bail-skip fee from Nig and Willie, plus collect for finding Eddy Melancon among the living dead at the hospital, but chances were Bertrand would utilize the chaos of Katrina to slip through the system again.

Also, Andre Rochon was still out there, and Clete had a special beef to settle with him.

Clete worked Bertrand down a stairwell and shoved him outside.

"I ain't fighting wit' you, man. Quit pushing me around," Bertrand said.

"Shut up," Clete said, walking him toward Tee Boy, who was sitting on a low wall that separated the parking lot from the hospital. Tee Boy was eating a sandwich partially wrapped in aluminum foil.

"What you got here?" he asked.

"Bertrand Melancon, three bench warrants, strong-arm robbery, intimidating witnesses, and general shit-head behavior since he was first defecated into the world. I'm surrendering custody of Bertrand to you. I already warned him about what happens to people who step on your shoeshine."

"This ain't funny, Purcel."

"You're right, it isn't. Bertrand and his brother Eddy ran me down with their car on Saturday evening. They did this while I was searching the panel truck of their fellow scum wad Andre Rochon. In the back of that panel truck I saw a stuffed animal and a coil of polyethylene rope. Just before shit-breath here ran me over, I remembered an article I saw in the newspaper about three black guys who abducted a fifteen-year-old girl. She was walking back from a street fair in the Lower Nine. She was carrying a stuffed bear. These guys dragged the girl into a panel truck and tied her up and raped her. You still live in the Lower Nine, don't you, Tee Boy?"

"Yeah," Tee Boy replied, brushing crumbs off his face, his eyes settling on Bertrand.

"You think this outstanding example of young manhood could be a possible suspect?" Clete asked.

"What about it, boy?" Tee Boy said.

"What about what?" Bertrand said.

"Are you planning to step on my shoeshine?"

"Are you crazy, man?"

Tee Boy hit him hard in the face with the flat of his hand, the kind of blow that rattles eyeballs in their sockets. "I ax you a question. You gonna answer it?"

"No, suh, I ain't planning to step on your shoeshine."

"You kidnap and rape a girl in the Lower Nine?"

"I brought my brother to the hospital 'cause somebody shot him t'rou the t'roat. A kid wit' us was killed, too. I ain't tried to run away. I come here for help. I missed my court appearance 'cause I was sick. That's all you got on me. You quit hitting me."

"Turn around. Look out there at that boat tied to the car bumper," Clete said. "See those bodies in there? Those bodies belong to dead people. You're going to be cuffed to them. It's a long way to the chain-link jail at the airport. If you were Tee Boy and you got stuck with four corpses and a dog turd like yourself and you had a chance to deep-six the whole collection at a convenient underwater location, what would you do?"

But Clete realized he was firing blanks. Bertrand Melancon had seen a bullet turn his brother's body into yesterday's ice cream, and manufactured horror scenarios from a bail-skip chaser came in a poor second on the shock scale. Clete also realized that Tee Boy Pellerin was not listening to him, either, that his eyes were fastened on Bertrand and that his face was breaking into a grin as he connected dots and information Clete had no knowledge of.

"Want to let me in on it?" Clete said.

"We had a 'shots fired' and a fatality about two or three hours ago. Four looters were working out of a boat back toward Claiborne. A kid took a big one through the head. Guess whose place they'd just hit?"

"I don't know," Clete replied.

"Guy owns a flower store. Also a bunch of escort services. His wife looks like the Bride of Frankenstein." Tee Boy was starting to laugh now.

"Sidney Kovick?" Clete said.

"These pukes ripped off the most dangerous gangster in New Orleans and tore his house apart on top of it. One of our guys went inside and said it looked like somebody had drove a fire truck through the walls." Tee Boy was choking on his sandwich bread now, laughing so hard that tears were rolling down his cheeks. "Hey, kid, if you stole anything from Sidney Kovick, mail it to him COD from Alaska, then buy a gun and shoot yourself. With luck, he won't find your grave."

Tee Boy stood up and coughed into his palm until his knees were buckling.

"Who's this Kovick guy?" Bertrand said to Clete. "Y'all just jerking my stick, right?"

CHAPTER

11

AFTER SEVEN DAYS I was rotated back to New Iberia. I had almost forgotten Natalia Ramos, the companion of Father Jude LeBlanc. In fact, I had deliberately pushed her name out of my mind. I wanted no more of New Orleans and other people's grief. I just wanted to be back on Bayou Teche with my family and Tripod, our raccoon, and our unneutered warrior cat, Snuggs. I wanted to wake in the morning to the smell of coffee and moldy pecan husks in the yard and camellia bushes dripping with dew and the fecund odor of fish spawning in the bayou. I wanted to wake to the great gold-green, sun-spangled promise of the South Louisiana in which I had grown up. I didn't want to be part of the history taking place in our state.

"Phone's ringing, Dave," Alafair said from the kitchen.

"Would you answer it, please?"

Through the doorway I could see her frying eggs and ham slices in a heavy iron skillet, lifting it by its handle without a hot pad, her back to me. It was hard to believe she was the same little El Salvadoran Indian girl I had pulled from a submerged plane out on the salt many years ago. She clanged the skillet on the stove and picked up the phone, resting her rump against the drain board, giving me a look.

"Is Dave Robicheaux here? Wait a minute. I'll check," she said. She lowered the receiver, the mouthpiece uncovered. "Dave, are you here? If you are, a lady would like to speak to you."

That's what you get when your kid goes to Reed College and joins kickboxing clubs.

I took the receiver from her hand. "Hello?" I said.

"This is Natalia Ramos, Mr. Robicheaux. I'm here at the shelter, the one you told me to go to. Have you found out where Jude went? I can't get no information from anybody at the shelter. I thought maybe you had lists of people who was picked up by the Coast Guard."

"No, ma'am, I'm afraid I don't."

"Jude's in pain all the time from his cancer. He went down to the Lower Nine to give his people Communion. He'd always been scared to give people Communion at Mass."

"I'm sorry, Ms. Ramos, but you're not making sense."

"His hands tremble all the time. He thinks he'll drop the chalice. He'd always let another priest give out Communion at Mass. But this time he was gonna say Mass and give people Communion."

In the background I could hear voices echoing in a large area, perhaps inside a gymnasium or a National Guard armory. Alafair was setting my breakfast on the kitchen table, placing the plate and knife and fork and coffee cup and saucer carefully on the surface so as not to make any noise. Her hair was long and black on her shoulders, her figure lovely inside her jeans and pink blouse.

I didn't know what to say to Natalia Ramos. "Where are you?" I asked.

"At the high school in Franklin."

"I'll be there in forty-five minutes."

"Where's Chula at?" she asked.

"Your brother?"

"Yeah, where'd you put him at?"

"In the Iberia Parish Prison, along with his fall partner."

I thought her next statement would be an abrasive one. But I was wrong.

"Maybe he can get some help there. Jail is the only place Chula ever did all right. I'll be waiting for you, Mr. Robicheaux."

I placed the telephone receiver back in the cradle, already regretting that I had taken the call.

"Who was that?" Alafair said.

"A Central American prostitute and junkie who was shacked up with a Catholic priest."

I sat down and began eating. I could feel Alafair behind me, like a shadow breaking against the light. She rested her hand on my shoulder. "Dave, you have the best heart of any man I've ever known," she said.

I could feel the blood tingle in the back of my neck.

THE HIGH SCHOOL gymnasium in Franklin, down the bayou in St. Mary Parish, was lined with row upon row of army-surplus cots. Children were running everywhere, inside and outside, sailing Frisbees that a local merchant had brought from his store. I found Natalia washing clothes by hand in the lee of the building, her arms deep inside an aluminum tub, the tails of her denim shirt tied under her breasts. I asked her to tell me again of her last moments with Jude LeBlanc.

"He brought the boat to the church roof. He was up there chopping a hole with an ax to get everybody out. Then I heard a fight up there. I didn't see him again."

It was warm in the shade, but her face looked cool and dry, her ribs etched against her dusky skin. She wore sandals and baggy men's khakis and looked like a Third World countrywoman who was washing the clothes of children who were not her own. She did not look like a prostitute or a junkie.

"Did you bring any dope into the shelter?" I said.

"You drove here to ask me that?"

"You were holding when you got busted. I got you off the wrist chain and sent you here. That makes you my responsibility. So that's why I'm asking you if you brought any dope into the shelter."

"I been trying to get clean. There's some people in the gym putting together a Narcotics Anonymous group. I'm gonna start going to meetings again."

She had managed to answer my question without answering my question. "Ms. Ramos, if I find out you are using or distributing narcotics in this shelter, I'm going to get you kicked out or put in jail."

She squeezed out a pair of children's blue jeans and laid them on the side of the tub. "I got to go back to New Orleans."

"I think that's a mistake."

"I keep seeing Jude drowning there in the dark, without no one to help him."

"Jude is a stand-up guy. My advice is that you don't treat him as less."

"He used to say a special reconciliation Mass on Saturday afternoon for all the whores and junkies and street people. He gave everybody absolution, all at one time, no matter what they done. Somebody attacked him to get his boat. I think they killed him. I got to find out. I just can't live without knowing what happened to him."

"Ms. Ramos, tens of thousands of people are missing right now. FEMA is trying to—"

"How come nobody came?"

"Pardon?"

"People were drowning all over the neighborhood and nobody came. A big, fat black woman in a purple dress was standing on top of a car, waving at the sky. Her dress was floating out in the water. She was on the car a half hour, waving, while the water kept rising. I saw her fall off the car. It was over her head."

I didn't want to hear more stories about Katrina. The images I had seen during the seven-day period immediately after the storm would never leave me. Nor could I afford the anger they engendered in me. Nor did I wish to deal with the latent racism in our culture that was already beginning to rear its head. According to the *Washington Post,* a state legislator in Baton Rouge had just told a group of lobbyists in Baton Rouge, "We finally cleaned up public housing in New Orleans. We couldn't do it, but God did."

How do you explain a statement like that to people who are victims of the worst natural disaster in American history? The answer is you don't. And you don't try to fix a broken world and you don't try to put Band-Aids on broken people, I told myself.

"I believe Jude would want you to remain at the shelter. You can do a lot of good here. I promise I'll do my best to find out what happened to him," I said.

"I think he talked about you," she said.

"Excuse me?"

"Jude said he used to deliver the newspaper to a policeman who owned a bait shop. He said the policeman was a drunk but he was a good man who tried to help people who didn't have no power. Isn't that you he was talking about?"

She knew how to set the hook.

AFTER LUNCH I drove to the Iberia Parish Sheriff's Department and went upstairs to my office. The contrast between the normalcy of my job in Iberia Parish and the seven days I had just spent in New Orleans was like the difference between the bloom and confidence of youth and the mental condition of a man who has been stricken arbitrarily by a fatal illness. The building's interior was spotless and full of sunshine. Cool air flowed steadily from the wall vents. One of the secretaries had placed flowers on the windowsills. A group of deputies in crisp uniforms and polished gunbelts were drinking coffee and eating doughnuts on the reception counter in front. From my second-story office window I could look out on a canopy of palm and live oak trees that cover a working-class neighborhood, and behind the cathedral I could see a cemetery of whitewashed brick crypts where Confederate dead remind us that Shiloh is not a historical abstraction.

Helen glanced through the glass in my door, then opened the door without knocking. "You look sharp, Pops," she said.

"I hear that a lot," I replied.

She walked to my window and gazed at the Sunset Limited passing down the railroad tracks. She wore a pair of tight slacks and a white shirt with the short sleeves folded in neat cuffs. A four-by-seven yellow notepad was stuffed in her back pocket. She hooked her thumbs in the sides of her gunbelt. "You rested up?"

I squeezed my eyes shut and opened them again. "Say it, Helen."

"I just got off the phone with FEMA and the FBI. The civil service and governmental structure of New Orleans has been destroyed. We're about to get hit with a shitload of casework we don't need."

"Shouldn't you be telling this to the entire department?"

"This particular case involves one of Clete Purcel's bail skips. It also involves a guy you know by the name of Otis Baylor."

"An insurance man?"

"That's the guy. The Feds believe a number of homicides may have been committed by vigilantes who decided they'd have some fun during the storm. They think Otis Baylor may have popped some looters who had just gutted Sidney Kovick's house."

"Home invaders hit Sidney Kovick?"

"Yeah, evidently four of the dumbest shits in New Orleans. One got his head blown off and one will be a quadriplegic the rest of his life. The Feds believe Baylor had a grudge against blacks for raping his daughter and he probably used the opportunity to take a couple of pukes off the board."

"It doesn't sound like him."

"The Feds are taking heat about going after gangbangers and letting white shooters skate. The Baylor investigation will probably be a lawn ornament for them. Anyway, we're supposed to do what we can. You okay with that, bwana?"

"What's Clete Purcel's role in all this?"

She pulled the yellow notepad from her back pocket and looked at it. "The brother of the quadriplegic is named Bertrand Melancon. Clete had him in custody but lost him in the handover at the chain-link jail. Here's the irony in all this, Dave. Clete told the Feds he thinks the Melancon brothers and a friend of theirs named Andre Rochon might actually be rapists."

"Based on what?"

"Clete says Rochon's panel truck contained evidence that might link Rochon and possibly the Melancons to an abduction and rape in the Lower Nine."

"Yeah, he told me about these guys. They're the ones who ran over him right before the storm. You want me to see Baylor?"

"You mind?"

I once knew a door gunner in Vietnam who wouldn't go on R & R out-of-country for fear he would desert and not return to duty. So he stayed stoned in the door of his Huey, stoned in the bush, and stoned in Saigon, and finished his tour without ever leaving the fresh-air mental asylum of Indochina. As Helen waited for my answer, my friend's point of view seemed much more reasonable than I had previously thought.

EARLY THE NEXT MORNING I checked out a cruiser and drove back to New Orleans. The sky over the wetlands was still filled with birds that seemed to have no destination or home. After four days, members of the 82nd Airborne had arrived in the city and most of the looting and violence had stopped. But eighty percent of the city was still underwater, and tens of thousands of people still had nowhere to go.

I turned off St. Charles and threaded my way through piles of downed trees on several side streets in the general direction of Otis Baylor's house. Finally I parked my cruiser and either waded or walked across people's lawns the rest of the way.

The front porch of Otis Baylor's house was rounded, with a half-circle roof on it supported by Doric columns. I raised the brass ring on the door and knocked. The water had receded on his street, exposing the neutral ground. Down the street, on the opposite side, I could see the home of Sidney Kovick. A repair crew was pulling plywood off the picture windows.

Otis Baylor opened the front door. His face was round and empty, like that of a man who had just returned from a funeral. "Yes?" he said.

"I'm Dave Robicheaux, from the Iberia Parish Sheriff's Department, Mr. Baylor," I said. "I've been assigned to help in the investigation of a double shooting that took place in front of your house. You might remember me from New Iberia."

He did not extend his hand. "What can I do for you?"

"I've got a little problem here. A high school kid got his brains blown out in front of your house, and a full-time loser with him took a round through his spinal cord. The Feds think vigilantes may have done it. Frankly, I don't think this investigation is going anywhere, but our department is on lend-lease with the City of New Orleans and we need to do what we can."

There was a beat, a microsecond pause in which his eyes went away from mine.

"Come in," he said, holding open the door. "You're lucky you caught me at home. I'm using the house as my office now, but I'm usually in the field with my adjusters. Would you like some tea? I still have ice in my freezer."

"No, thanks. I'll make this as quick as I can, sir."

He invited me to sit down with him in his den. The books on his shelves were largely referential or encyclopedic in nature, or had been purchased from book clubs that specialize in popular history and biography. His desk was overflowing with paper. Through the side window I could see a bullet-headed man on a ladder trying to free a splintered oak limb from his roof.

"An FBI investigator said you heard a single shot but you don't know where it came from," I said.

"I was asleep. The shot woke me up. I looked out the dormer window and saw a kid floating in the water and another guy lying half inside the front of the boat."

"You own a firearm, Mr. Baylor?"

"It's Otis. Yes, a 1903-model Springfield bolt-action rifle. You want to see it?"

"Not right now. Thanks for offering. After you saw the kid in the water and the one half inside the boat, did you go outside?"

"By the time I got my clothes on, one guy had loaded the wounded one all the way into the boat and was already down to the corner. Another guy was running."

"They were all black?"

"As far as I could tell. It was dark."

"And you saw nobody else on the street or on a porch or in a house window?"

"No, I didn't."

I opened the manila folder in my hand and read from the notes given to me over the phone by an FBI agent working out of Baton Rouge. "The Feds and the guys from NOPD believe the shot had to come from this side of the street."

"Maybe it did. I wouldn't know."

"The only occupied houses in immediate proximity to the shooting were yours and your next-door neighbor's."

"I have no argument with other people's conclusions as to what happened here. I've told you what I heard and what I saw." He looked at his watch. "You want to see the Springfield?"

"If you don't mind."

He went upstairs and returned with the rifle, handing it to me with the bolt open on an empty magazine. "Am I a suspect in the shooting?"

"Right now, we're eliminating suspects."

"Why didn't your friends take my firearm? That's what I would have done."

"Because they didn't have a place to store evidence. Because they didn't have a warrant. Because the system is broken."

But there was another reality at work as well, one I hadn't shared with him. The round that had struck Eddy Melancon's throat and emptied Kevin Rochon's brainpan never slowed down and the metal tracings inside the wounds it inflicted would be of little evidentiary value.

I lifted the rifle to my face and sniffed at the chamber. "You just oiled it?"

"I don't remember exactly when I cleaned it."

"Can I see the ammunition that goes with it?"

"I don't even know if I have any."

"What kind of ammunition do you fire in it?"

"It's a thirty-aught-six-caliber rifle. It fires thirty-aught-six-caliber rounds."

I was sitting in a burgundy-colored soft leather chair, an autumnal green-gold light filtering through the trees outside. But the comfortable ambience did not coincide with the sense of disquiet that was beginning to grow inside me. "That's not my point, sir. This is a military weapon. Do you fire metal-jacketed, needle-nosed rounds in it?"

"I target shoot. I don't hunt. I shoot whatever ammunition is on sale. What is this?"

"It's illegal to hunt with military-type ammunition, because it passes right through the animal and wounds instead of kills. I think the two shooting victims got nailed with a metal-jacketed rather than a soft-nosed round. One other thing. You keep referring to the DOA as a 'kid.' You call the other looters 'guys.'"

"I didn't notice."

"You're correct, the DOA was a teenager. The wounded man and his brother are both adults. The man who fled was probably a guy by the name of Andre Rochon, also an adult. You speak of these guys with a sense of familiarity, as though you saw them up close."

He rolled his eyes. He started to speak, then gave it up. He was sitting in a chair at his desk, his long-sleeved white shirt crinkling. His stolid face and square hands and scrubbed manner made me think of a farmer forced to go to church by his wife. I continued to stare at him in the silence. "Listen, Mr. Robicheaux—"

"It's Dave."

"I've told you what I know. Right now there are thousands of people in Louisiana and Mississippi waiting to hear from their insurance carrier. That's me. I wish you well, but this conversation is over."

"I'm afraid it's not over." I closed the manila folder and set it by my foot, as though its contents were no longer relevant. "Years ago I attended a convention of Louisiana and Mississippi police officers at the Evangeline Hotel in Lafayette. That particular weekend the FBI had dragged the Pearl River in search of a lynching victim. They didn't find the guy they were looking for, but they found three others, one whose body had been sawed in half. I was in the hotel bar when I heard four plainclothesmen laughing in a booth behind me. One of them said, 'Did you hear about the nigger who stole so many chains he couldn't swim across the Pearl?' Another detective said, 'You know how they found him? They waved a welfare check over the water and this burr-headed boy popped to the surface and yelled out, 'Here I is, boss.'

"These guys not only made me ashamed I was a police officer, they made me ashamed I was a white man. I think you're the same kind of guy I am, Mr. Baylor. I don't think you're a racist or a vigilante. I know what happened to your daughter. If my daughter were attacked by degenerates and sadists, I'd be tempted to hand out rough justice, too. In fact, any father who didn't have those feelings is not a father."

His eyes were blue and lidless, his big hands splayed on his knees, the backs as rough as starfish.

"Get out in front of this, partner," I said. "The justice system is emblematic and selective. Don't let some bureaucratic functionaries hang you out to dry."

His eyes stayed locked on mine, his thoughts concealed. Then whatever speculation or conclusion they had contained went out of them and he looked toward the doorway.

"Hi, Melanie. This is Mr. Robicheaux, from New Iberia. He was in the neighborhood and just dropped by to see how we're doing. I told him we're doing just fine," Otis Baylor said.

"Yes, I remember you. It's very nice to see you again," his wife said, extending one hand, an iced drink in the other. "We're doing quite well, considering." She looked at the Springfield rifle that was propped by my chair. "This isn't about the Negroes who were shot, is it? We've already told the authorities everything we know. I can't believe something like that occurred in front of our house."

I WALKED NEXT DOOR and looked up the ladder at the bullet-headed man wrestling with a broken oak limb on his roof. Out in the alley, a forklift was unloading a massive generator from the bed of a truck.

"Could I speak with you, sir?" I called, lifting up my badge holder.

The bullet-headed man climbed down from the ladder, his face ruddy from his work. I told him who I was and why I was in the neighborhood. "Tom Claggart," he said, his meaty hand gripping mine warmly.

"Has the FBI or the city police talked with you?"

"Hang on a minute."

He walked out to the alley and told the forklift operator where to set the generator in his yard. Then he returned, looking back over his shoulder to make sure the generator ended up in the right place, on an old brick patio half sunk in mud.

"Got a friend who's a shipbuilder. He gave me one of his generators," he said. "I should have put one in before the storm, like Otis did. What was that you were saying?"

"Has the FBI or the city police been out?"

"No, I wish they had."

"You heard the shot?"

"I didn't hear anything. I was sound asleep. I'd been chasing those bastards all over the neighborhood."

"I see. Why do you wish the FBI or NOPD had talked with you?"

"To tell them to clean up the goddamn city, that's why."

I nodded, my expression pleasant, my eyes focused on his flower bed. "You own firearms, sir?"

"You bet your ass I do."

"Think any of your neighbors might have gotten sick and tired of being robbed and intimidated the other night?"

"Can you spell that out a little more clearly?"

"People get fed up. Or sometimes fed up and scared. A housewife picks up a thumb-buster and blows an intruder through a glass window. The guy turns out to be a serial rapist. At most police stations, there's usually a round of applause at morning roll call."

He looked at me blankly, his mouth a tight seam.

"The Second Amendment gives us the right to bear arms to protect our homes and our loved ones," I said. "During a time of social anarchy, the good guys sometimes feel a need to use extreme measures. I think their point of view is understandable. You hearing me on this, Mr. Claggart?"

"Otis has had a big cross to carry," he replied.

"I'm aware of that." I kept my eyes fastened on his.

He huffed air out of his nose and looked at Otis Baylor's house. For just a moment I thought I saw a cloud slip across his face, the stain of resentment or envy take hold in his expression. "He said something about hanging black ivory on the wall."

"Mr. Baylor said this?"

"Earlier in the evening, when some guys were breaking into houses on the other side of the street."

"Did others hear him say this?"

"A couple of friends were in the yard with me. Otis had been outside with his rifle. Listen, I don't blame him. We offered to help him, in fact."

"Would you write down the names of your friends and their addresses, please?"

"I hope I'm not getting anybody in trouble. I just want to do the right thing," he said, taking my pen and notepad from my hand.

With neighbors like Tom Claggart, Otis Baylor didn't need enemies.

BUT THERE WAS an ancillary player not far away I could not resist interviewing. Sidney Kovick was an enigmatic man whose personality was that of either a sociopath or a master thespian. He was tall, well built, with dark hair, close-set eyes, and a knurled forehead, and he wore fine clothes and shined oxblood loafers with tassels on them. When he walked he seemed to jingle with the invisible sound of money and power. When he entered a room, most people, even those who did not know who he was, automatically dialed down their voices.

He had grown up on North Villere Street and worked as a UPS driver before he joined the Airborne and went to Vietnam. He came home with a Bronze Star and a Purple Heart but seemed to have no interest in his own heroism. Sidney had liked the army because he understood it and appreciated its consistency and predictability. He also appreciated the number of rackets it afforded him. He lent money at twenty percent interest to fellow enlisted men, had ties with pimps in Saigon's Bring-Cash Alley, and sold truckloads of PX goods on the Vietnamese black market. Sidney didn't believe in setting geographical limits on his talents.

Whenever someone asked Sidney's advice about a problem of any kind, his admonition was always the same: "Don't never let people know what you're thinking."

He owned a flower shop, loved movies, and always wore a carnation in his lapel. His favorite quote was a paraphrase of a line spoken by Rhett Butler in *Gone with the Wind:* "Great fortunes are made during the rise and fall of nations." Sidney was invited to the governor's inauguration ball, rode on the floats during Mardi Gras, and performed once on the wing of a biplane at an aerial show over Lake Pontchartrain. Longtime cops looked upon him as a refreshing change from the street detritus they normally dealt with. The only problem with romanticizing Sidney Kovick was the fact he could snuff your wick and sip a glass of burgundy while he did it.

Workmen were going in and out of his front door. I stepped inside without knocking. The interior looked like an army of Norsemen had marched through it. Sidney stood in his dining room, looking up at a chandelier that someone had shredded into tangled strips with an iron garden rake.

"They hit you pretty hard, huh?" I said.

He stared at me as though he were sorting through faces on a Rolodex wheel. "Yeah, the puke population is definitely out of control. I think we need a massive airdrop of birth-control devices on two thirds of the city. What are you doing here, Dave?"

"Investigating the shooting of the guys who creeped your house."

"House creeps don't piss in your oven and refrigerator."

"You're right," I said, plaster crunching under my shoes. "Looks like they tore out all your walls and part of your ceilings. Think they were after anything in particular?"

"Yeah, the secrets to the Da Vinci Code. You still off the sauce?"

"I'm still in AA, if that's what you mean."

"Get your nose out of the stratosphere. I was going to offer you a couple of fingers of Beam, because that's all I've got. But I didn't want to offend you. I hear one of those black guys was turned into an earth slug."

"That's the word. I haven't interviewed him yet."

"Yeah?"

I wasn't sure if he was listening or if he was asking me to repeat what I had just said. He told a workman to get a ladder and pull down the wrecked chandelier. Then he touched the ruined surface of his dining table and brushed off his fingers. "Which hospital is the human slug in?" he said.

"Why do you ask?"

"I feel sorry for him. Anybody who could do this to people's homes must have a mother who was inseminated by leakage from a colostomy bag."

"You always knew how to say it, Sidney."

"Hey, I was born in New Orleans. This used to be a fine city. Remember the music and the amusement park out at Lake Pontchartrain? How about the sno'ball carts on the street corners and families sitting on their porches? When's the last time you walked down a street at night in New Orleans and felt safe?"

When I didn't answer, he cocked a finger at me. "Got you," he said.

On my way out I saw Sidney's wife in the yard. She came from a fishing hamlet down in Plaquemines Parish, a geological aberration that extends like an umbilical cord into the Gulf of Mexico. She was as tall as her husband and had a lantern face, cavernous eyes, and shoulders like a man. For decades her family had been the political allies of a notorious racist judge who had run Plaquemines Parish as a personal fiefdom, even padlocking a Catholic church when the bishop appointed a black priest to serve as its pastor.

But she appeared to have little in common with her family, at least that I could see. In fact, Eunice Kovick's father once said of his daughter, "The poor girl's face would make a train turn on a dirt road, but she's got a decent heart and feeds every stray dog and nigra in the parish."

Why she had married Sidney Kovick was beyond me.

"How you doing, Eunice?" I said.

"Just fine. How are you, Dave?"

"Sorry about your house. Y'all have pretty good insurance?"

"We'll find out."

"Do you have any idea why those guys would rip your walls and ceilings out?"

"What did Sidney say?"

"He didn't speculate."

"No kidding?"

She had one of the sweetest smiles I ever saw on a woman's face.

"See you, Eunice," I said.

"Anytime," she said.

MY LAST STOP was at the hospital where Bertrand Melancon had dropped his gun-shot brother.

CHAPTER
12

BUT I DISCOVERED that Eddy Melancon had been moved to a hospital in Baton Rouge. I headed up I-10 into heavy traffic, the cruiser's emergency bar flashing. By the time I reached the Baton Rouge city limits, the streets were jammed with automobiles, trucks, buses, and utility repair vehicles. Even with the priority status my cruiser allowed me, I didn't arrive at Our Lady of the Lake Hospital until midafternoon.

I almost wished I hadn't. I suspected that Eddy Melancon had probably caused irreparable injury to many people in his brief life-span, but if such a thing as karma exists, it had landed on him with the impact of a spiked wrecking ball.

He looked weightless in the bed, raccoon-eyed, as though the skin around the sockets had been rubbed with coal dust. His body was strung with wires and tubes, his arms dead at his sides. I opened my badge holder and told him who I was. "Do you know who popped you?" I asked.

He focused his gaze on my face but didn't respond.

"Can you talk, Eddy?"

He pursed his lips but didn't speak.

"Did the shot come from in front of you?" I said.

His voice made a wet click and a sound that was like air leaking from the ruptured bladder inside a football. "Yeah," he whispered.

"You saw the muzzle flash?"

"No."

"You heard the shot but you saw no flash?"

"Yeah. Ain't seen it."

"Are you aware you guys ripped off Sidney Kovick's house?"

"Ain't been in no house."

"Right," I said. I pulled my chair closer to his bed. "Listen to me, Eddy. If people you don't know come to see you, make sure they're cops. Don't let anybody you don't recognize check you out of this hospital."

His eyes looked at me quizzically.

"If you made a big score at Sidney's, he's going to take it back from you," I said. "He'll use whatever method that works."

Eddy tried to speak, then choked on his saliva. I leaned over him, my ear close to his mouth. His breath smelled like the grave, his words breaking damply against my cheek.

"Say that again."

"We took a boat. That's all," he said.

"From Sidney Kovick?"

"In the Lower Nine. We just wanted to stay alive. Ain't been in no house uptown."

I placed my business card on his chest. "Good luck to you, partner. I think you'll need it," I said.

When I got back home that night, I slept like the dead.

AT SUNRISE I ate a bowl of Grape-Nuts and sliced bananas and drank coffee and hot milk on the back steps. The mist was gray in the live oaks and pecan trees, and both Tripod, our three-legged raccoon, and Snuggs, our cat, ate sardines out of a can by my foot. Molly opened the screen door and sat down beside me. She was still wearing her house robe. She ticked her nails on the back of my neck. "Alafair spent the night at the Munsons'," she said.

"Really?" I said.

She gazed down the slope at the bayou. The gold and red four-o'clocks were still open in the shadows at the base of the tree trunks. Out in the mist I could hear a heavy fish flopping in the lily pads. "Got time to go inside?" I asked.

AT 10:00 A.M. Helen Soileau came into my office. "How'd you make out yesterday?" she said.

"I wrote up everything I found and faxed it to the FBI in Baton Rouge. There's a copy in your box. I also talked to an NOPD guy on the phone. I don't think this one has legs on it."

"You don't think Otis Baylor shot these guys?"

"His neighbor seemed willing to finger him, but I had the sense the neighbor had some frontal-lobe damage himself. I think bodies are going to be showing up under the rubble and mud for months. Who's going to be losing sleep over a couple of looters who caught a high-powered round while they were destroying people's homes?"

"All right, let's move on. The Rec Center at City Park is full of evacuees. We need to get some of them to Houston if we can. Iberia General and Dauterive Hospital are busting at the seams. It's worse in Lafayette. I tell you, Streak, I've seen some shit in my life, but nothing like this."

I couldn't argue with her. In fact, I didn't even want to comment.

"What did you think of Lyndon Johnson?" she asked.

"Before or after I got to Vietnam?"

"When Hurricane Betsy hit New Orleans in '65, Johnson flew into town and went to a shelter full of people who had been evacuated from Algiers. It was dark inside and people were scared and didn't know what was going to happen to them. He shined a flashlight in his face and said, 'My name is Lyndon Baines Johnson. I'm your goddamn president and I'm here to tell you my office and the people of the United States are behind you.' Not bad, huh?"

But I wasn't listening. There was a detail about the Otis Baylor investigation I hadn't mentioned to Helen, because she didn't like complexities and in particular she didn't like them when they fell outside our jurisdiction.

"I stopped by Sidney Kovick's house yesterday and had an informal chat with him. The looters ripped the Sheetrock and lathwork and plaster from most of his walls and ceilings."

"Score one for the pukes."

"I think they took Sidney down in a major way. Sidney has never had an IRS beef. It wouldn't surprise me if his walls had been loaded with cash."

"So what?"

"He was trying to find out which hospital the quadriplegic looter is in."

"And?"

"The quadriplegic is at Our Lady of the Lake in Baton Rouge. I tried to warn him, but he's not a listener."

Helen pulled at an earlobe. "Bwana?"

"What is it?"

"Whatever happens to that bunch is on them. Got it?"

"I wouldn't have it any other way."

CLETE PURCEL did not lose custody of Bertrand Melancon during the handover at the chain-link jail at the airport. Bertrand got loose farther up the road, by Gonzales, when the prison bus he was riding in pulled into a soaked field that had been created as a holding area during the height of the storm. Hundreds of inmates from jails in two parishes had huddled in the field, along with their guards, while lightning exploded over their heads and the rain almost tore the clothes from their bodies. Many of them, I suspect, went through the most religious moments of their lives. But when Bertrand Melancon arrived and was told to line up at a Porta Potti, the drama that his peers had experienced had already slipped into history and the field was simply a churned and trash-strewn piece of farm acreage where egrets and displaced seagulls competed for litter.

"How long we got to be here, man?" Bertrand asked a guard.

"The Four Seasons is kind of backed up right now. But we told the maids y'all were coming and to prepare your rooms as quick as possible," the guard replied.

Most of the inmates on the buses had no desire to run. Most were tired, mosquito-bitten, sunburned, and sick from bad food. Most of them wanted to be watching television in an air-conditioned main-line prison that provided clean beds and served hot meals. If most of them had their choice, they would be housed in a building with six-foot-thick walls and a foundation that Noah's deluge couldn't disturb.

Bertrand had other plans. At twilight, when the bus pulled out on the highway, he pried the grillwork off a back window and dropped into a rain ditch. His absence was not noticed until the bus was half-way to Shreveport.

Nig Rosewater personally came to Clete's upstairs apartment on St. Ann to give him the news. Nig could not be described as having a neck like a fireplug. He had no neck. His jowls and chin seem to grow straight down into his shoulders. His starched shirt and gold collar pin did not help his appearance, either. In fact, with his gold necktie, he looked like a hog eating an upright ear of buttered corn.

"Nig, I deliver the freight. I got a signed receipt for transfer of custody. At that point Bertrand Melancon became the property of Orleans Parish," Clete said. "The other half of your thirty-grand skip is in Our Lady of the Lake. You owe me three grand."

"You didn't have nothing to do with catching the vegetable in the hospital. So that makes your fee fifteen hundred at best," Nig replied. "And that's not why I'm here, either. I had two of Sidney Kovick's people banging on my door at seven this morning. I told them I don't know where Bertrand Melancon and Andre Rochon are, because if I knew that kind of information, I wouldn't be out over fifteen large right now. So they want to know which hospital the vegetable is in. I tell them I don't know that, either, since the government don't consult with me when it's shipping people all over the country.

"One of these guys says, 'Your fifteen large is toilet paper. You deliver up the boons who broke into Mr. Kovick's house or Mr. Kovick is gonna figure whatever they done or they took is on you.'"

Clete's apartment was located above his office. The day was bright and sunny outside, and the bodies of birds that had been driven by storm wind against the side of his building were piled on his balcony, their feathers fluttering in the wind.

"I don't see how any of this falls on me, particularly when you're already trying to stiff me on my recovery fee," Clete said.

"Buy yourself a better brand of wax removal, Purcel. These guys took Sidney down for something he can't claim as an insurance or business loss. His guys said my fifteen large is toilet paper. What's that tell you? These morons blundered into a big score, maybe something they can't unload. What if it's bearer bonds or high-tech military stuff? Whose interest would it be in to let a couple of street pukes skate on the bail? Who would have the connections to fence or launder whatever the pukes took from Sidney?"

Clete honked his nose into a handkerchief, concealing his expression. "I say brass it out and tell them to screw themselves. Don't let Sidney push you around."

"You're pissing me off."

"Gee, I'm sorry about that."

The power was off in the apartment and Nig was sweating inside his sports coat. "Why don't you clean the dead birds off your balcony? It stinks in here," Nig said, the sheen of fear in his eyes unmistakable.

BEFORE THE HURRICANE, Clete had filled his bathtub, lavatory, and sink with tap water. Now he was using it on a daily basis to sponge-bathe, shave, brush his teeth, and to refill his toilet tank. After Nig was gone, Clete put on fresh clothes, combed his hair, and slipped on his nylon shoulder holster and blue-black Smith & Wesson revolver. He went downstairs to the courtyard and fired up his latest Cadillac acquisition, a powder-blue vintage convertible that was pocked with paint blisters, the top spotted with mold. As soon as the engine caught, a huge cloud of oil smoke exploded from the tailpipe. His porkpie hat canted on his head, Clete swung out onto the street, chewing on the corner of his lip, wondering how far to push a man whose potential no one in either the New Orleans underworld or New Orleans law enforcement ever accurately assessed.

Across the river in Algiers, whole neighborhoods had survived the storm with no flooding and only a temporary loss of power. From the bridge, with his convertible top down, Clete could look back and see the glassy shine of brown water that still covered most of New Orleans and the miles of roofless houses and the rivers of mud that had filled automobiles like concrete. The image was so stark and irrevocably sad he involuntarily mashed on the accelerator and almost rear-ended a gasoline truck.

In Algiers, he parked in front of a flower shop that was tucked neatly inside a purple-brick building on a residential street. Two of Sidney Kovick's employees were playing gin rummy at a table in the shade of a green-and-white-striped canopy that extended from the top of the display window. The two men were leftovers from the old Giacano crime family and for a brief time had thought their day in the sun had come and gone, until 9/11 landed on them like a gift from heaven and the governmental bête noire shifted from pukes dealing crack in the projects to Mideastern young males loading up with cell phones at the local Wal-Mart.

Clete got out on the sidewalk, opened his coat, and lifted his .38 from his shoulder holster with the ends of his fingers. He held it up in the air so the two men could see it, then dropped it on the passenger seat of the Caddy. "Keep an eye on that for me, will you, Marco?" he said.

"No problem," Marco said.

"Hey, Purcel, your convertible looks like it's got herpes," the other man said.

"Yeah, I know. I told your sister not to sit on it. But what are you gonna do?" Clete replied as he entered the shop, a bell ringing over his head.

The temperature inside was frigid, the glass lockers smoky with cold. The tall man behind the counter was dressed in seersucker slacks and a long-sleeved blue shirt open at the collar, exposing the thick curls of black hair on his chest.

"What's the haps, Sidney?" Clete said.

Sidney began placing roses a stem at a time into a green vase. "Nig Rosewater sent you here?"

"Nig says you want the pukes who took you down. That's understandable. But that makes four of us—you, me, Nig, and Wee Willie Bimstine. What I need to explain to you is we got no idea where these guys are."

"Don't lie to me. You already found one guy at the hospital. But he's not there anymore."

"That's right, I did find him and he got moved to 'whereabouts unknown.' So don't be telling me I'm lying."

"So why are you here?"

"Because your messengers evidently made an implied threat when they visited Nig this morning. I thought that showed a lack of class."

"Lack of class?"

"Is there an echo in your store?"

Sidney nodded toward a table that was set against a side wall. "Sit down. I'm about to eat. You want a coffee?"

"I wouldn't touch a chair that Charlie Weiss or Marco Scarlotti sat in unless it was sprayed for crab lice."

Sidney put his hand inside his shirt and scratched an insect bite on his shoulder and looked at the tips of his fingers. "It's true you smoked a federal informant when you were with NOPD? A guy who never saw it coming?" he said.

"What about it?" Clete said, his eyes slipping off Sidney's face.

"Nothing. You're just an unusual guy, Purcel."

Clete cleared an obstruction in his throat and let the moment pass. "Here's what it is. One way or another, I'm going to put Andre Rochon and Bertrand Melancon back in the system. That's because I have a personal beef with these guys and it doesn't have anything to do with you. But that doesn't mean we can't do business. If I recover cash or goods from your house, you pay me a twenty percent finder's fee. If that's not cool, see what you can get from your insurance carrier.

"In the meantime, you leave Nig and Willie and me alone. I know all about that chain-saw story and the guy in Metairie. Personally I think it's Mafia bullshit. Regardless, I take care of the pukes, and Heckle and Jeckle out there stay out of it. Sound reasonable, Sidney?"

"Ten percent on the recovery."

"Fifteen."

"I'll get back to you."

"Screw you," Clete said.

Sidney's gaze drifted out the front window, where his two men were playing cards in the shade. "What makes you think you can deliver?"

"It's like prayer, what do you got to lose?"

One at a time, Sidney placed three more rose stems in the vase. "Don't mess it up," he said. He fixed his eyes on Clete's, a blade of sunlight slicing like a knife across his face.

"ARE YOU CRAZY?" I said to Clete after he telephoned and told me what he had done.

"What was I supposed to do? Let an animal like Kovick threaten me and my employer?" he said.

In the background I could hear a sound like a rack of bowling pins exploding. "Why don't you just sprinkle broken glass in your breakfast food? Save yourself the time and effort of fooling with Kovick?" I said.

"What's that line in Machiavelli about keeping your friends close but your enemies closer?"

"Yeah, it's Machiavelli and it's crap," I replied.

"Look, I need a place to stay. My power is still off and something with black tendrils on it is growing out my drains."

"What about your room at the motor court?"

"It got rented to some evacuees."

"Stay with us," I said, trying to keep my voice flat, imagining any number of nightmarish events associated with Clete as houseguest.

"Molly won't mind?"

"No, she'll be happy."

"I'm at the bowling alley on East Main. I'll motor on over. Tell Molly not to fix anything. I've got it covered. Everything is copacetic, big mon."

And motor over he did, at 6:00 p.m. sharp, with a bucket of Popeyes fried chicken and buttermilk biscuits and a big carton of fried oysters and dirty rice. He also brought a separate bag of paper plates, plastic forks and knives, paper napkins, and a six-pack of Dr Pepper. He went about setting the table while Molly and Alafair tried to hide their smiles.

"Clete, we have plates and silverware," I said.

"No need to dirty things up," he said.

Molly shook her head behind his back to stop me from admonishing him. Alafair wasn't as diplomatic. "You have any salad in there, Clete?" she said.

"You bet," he replied, and proudly lifted a quart of potato salad from the sack.

But Clete's gay mood was often an indicator of worries and memories that he shared with few people. To the world he was the trickster and irresponsible hedonist, sowing mayhem and destruction wherever he went. But in his sleep he still dreamed of two adults fighting in their bedroom late at night and of kneeling in short pants on grains of rice his father sprinkled on the floor, and of liquid flame arching into a village of straw hooches. If sometimes he looked disconcerted, he would never admit he had just glanced out a window into the darkness and had seen a dead mamasan staring back at him.

After we ate, he took a long walk into City Park by himself, then returned to the house and went to bed early in our guest bedroom. Shortly after 4:00 a.m., I heard Tripod running up and down on the clothesline where we hooked his chain. I put on my khakis without waking Molly and opened the back door. Clete was sitting at our redwood table in his skivvies, his skin netted with moonlight. When he heard the screen open, he removed a pint bottle of bourbon from the tabletop and set it by his thigh.

"You don't have to hide that," I said.

"I couldn't sleep. I thought I heard thunder. But the sky is clear."

I sat down next to him. "What's eating you, podna?"

"I went back to my old neighborhood in the Irish Channel. I always hated the house where I grew up. I hated my old man. But I went back there and saw what the storm had done, and I had feelings I've never had before. I missed my old man and the rattling sounds his milk truck made when he drove off at four in the morning. I missed my mom cooking pancakes in the kitchen. It was like everything in my childhood was finally over, but I didn't want it to be over. It was like I had died and nobody had told me about it."

He picked up the pint bottle from the bench and unscrewed the cap. The bottle was wrapped in a brown paper bag and the moonlight glinted on the neck. He lifted the bottle to his mouth and tilted it up to drink. I could smell the bourbon as it rolled back over his tongue. I envisioned its amber color inside the yellow staves of the curing barrel, the bead it made inside the bottle's neck when it was air-locked under the cork, the splash it made when it was released again and poured over ice and mint leaves inside a glass. Unconsciously I swallowed and touched at my brow as though a vein were tightening in my head.

"It's called a vision of mortality," I said.

"What is?"

"The feelings you experienced when you went back to your old house."

"I'm afraid I'm going to die?"

"You saw the Big Sleazy die, Clete. It's like having an affair with the Great Whore of Babylon. When you finally come to your senses and get her out of your life, you find out she was the only woman you ever loved."

Clete upended the bottle again, his throat working rhythmically, watching me with one eye, as though someone had spoken to him from one of his dreams.

BUT CLETE WAS not the only friend or acquaintance from New Orleans seeking refuge in Iberia Parish. Two weeks after I had been sent to help investigate the shooting death of Kevin Rochon and the crippling of Eddy Melancon, Helen Soileau called me into her office. She spit a piece of her thumbnail off her tongue. "Otis Baylor just moved back to town with his family. Evidently they still own a home on Old Jeanerette Road," she said.

I waited for her to go on.

"You think he dropped those two looters or not?" she said.

"You mean is he that kind of guy? No, I don't think he is. But—"

"What?"

"His daughter had a terrible experience at the hands of three street pukes. I don't know what I would do if I were in his shoes."

"I didn't hear that last sentence."

"Maybe Baylor thought they were going to break into his house. Maybe his nerves were fried."

"If this guy is dirty on a homicide, he's not going to use our parish as a sanctuary. Talk to his wife and daughter."

"I'd rather drop this one."

"I'd rather not be present at my own death. Get out of here."

Baylor's home was a dark green nineteenth-century one-story house with tall windows and high ceilings and a peaked tin roof streaked with rust that had a purple cast in the shadows, not unlike my own. It had a wide screened-in gallery and was set back from Bayou Teche under pecan and palm trees and a solitary live oak dripping with Spanish moss. A glider hung on chains from one of the oak limbs, and a tan Honda was parked in the shale driveway, its paint spotted with bird droppings. A girl of about nineteen answered the door.

"I'm Dave Robicheaux, from the sheriff's department," I said, opening my badge. "Is Mr. Baylor here?"

"He's at work," she said.

She wore black sweatpants and a white T-shirt that was flecked with tiny pieces of leaves. "I was cleaning up the backyard when you rang the bell."

"Are you Otis Baylor's daughter?"

"I'm Thelma Baylor."

"Is your mother here?"

"My stepmother is at the grocery store."

"Could I talk with you? I'm investigating the shooting of the looters in front of your home in New Orleans. We have a lead or two, but I still can't quite picture where these guys were when they were shot."

"What does it matter? They were shot."

"That's true, isn't it? Could I come in?"

"You can watch me rake leaves if you want."

I followed her through the kitchen into the backyard. On both sides of her simple house were antebellum plantation homes of the kind one normally sees only on postcards. One hundred yards farther down the bayou, across the drawbridge, was a trailer slum where every form of social decay imaginable was a way of life. "You like New Iberia?" I asked.

"Are there always traffic jams at the Wal-Mart, or is that just because of the storm?" she said, drawing a bamboo rake through leaves that were black with mold.

I figured this one was going to be a long haul. I sat down on the back steps. "Did you hear the shots?"

Her eyes looked into neutral space, her rake missing a beat. "I heard a shot. It woke me up."

"Just one shot?"

"Yes."

"Where were you sleeping?"

Her face looked pale and round in the shade, devoid of expression, her lipstick glossy and unnatural, her bangs as precise as a nun's wimple. "In my room."

"Upstairs?"

"Yes, my room is upstairs. Do you want to talk to my father? I don't see how any of this is helpful."

"Do you think your next-door neighbor, Tom Claggart, is capable of popping a couple of looters?"

"Mr. Claggart is an upended penis with arms and legs and a face drawn on it. I don't know what he's capable of."

Time to take a chance, I told myself. "I know about the attack on your person two years ago, Miss Thelma. I have a daughter a little older than you. If I thought she was in danger, particularly from the kind of men who hurt you, I'd take them off at the neck."

Her rake slowed in the leaves, her chest rising and falling.

"I lost my mother and a wife to violent men," I continued. "I think men who abuse women are invariably physical and moral cowards. I think a man who rapes a woman should be first in line at the injection table."

She became motionless. Grains of dirt were stuck to the side of her mouth.

"I think you saw and know more than you're telling me," I said.

"I saw a guy floating facedown in the water. Another guy was wounded. A third guy started running through the water. A fourth guy was trying to hold the wounded guy in the boat."

"That's very detailed. I appreciate it." I made a note on a pad and put away my pen, as though we were finished. "Where was your father?"

"In his bedroom."

"Where was your mother?"

"She's my stepmother. My real mother is dead."

"Where was your stepmother?"

"In the bedroom with my father."

"Did your old man shoot those guys?"

"If you won't believe him, you won't believe me. Why bother asking?"

"I think you carry a big burden, Miss Thelma. I'm not here to add to it."

"You need to shut up, Mr. Robicheaux."

"Pardon me?"

"Why do you assume you know what happened to me? Why do you assume my family wants revenge on people we have nothing against? I can't stand people like you. You don't have any idea of what it's like to be a rape victim. If you did, you wouldn't be patronizing and trying to manipulate me."

"I apologize if I gave that impression."

"It's not an impression."

I stood up from the steps and brushed off the seat of my trousers. "I'm sorry just the same."

"Fuck you."

As I left the yard, I glanced back over my shoulder. Her body seemed to float inside a nimbus of light particles and dust and smoke and bits of desiccated leaves. For just a moment, as she resumed her work, stroking the rake hard across the ground, the bamboo tines splintering on the root system of a cypress tree, the intensity of her concentration and anger gave her a kind of integrity that I always associated with Alafair.

THE FOLLOWING DAY I called the Baylor house and asked Mrs. Baylor to come into the department for an interview.

"More about the looters who were shot?" she said.

"That's correct."

"Is this absolutely necessary?"

"Yes, ma'am, it is," I said.

"We're out on Old Jeanerette Road, just past Alice Plantation. Why don't you come here if you want to talk?"

I realized Thelma had not told her stepmother of my visit. "I'd be happy to."

"Mr. Robicheaux, let's do this on another basis. I seriously believe you're wasting your time with us, but nonetheless we'd like to be your friend. Can we take you and your family to dinner? I think you'll see we're truthful people and want to assist you in any way we can. But the reality is we're bystanders who have no idea who shot those men."

"That's kind of you. But there's a protocol I have to pursue. Will you be home in the next half hour?"

"No, I have a doctor's appointment."

"How about tomorrow?"

"I'm not sure. May I call you?"

"I need to make an appointment with you right now, Mrs. Baylor."

"Unfortunately that's not possible. I've tried to be cooperative, Mr. Robicheaux. But this is starting to get a little tiresome. I'd better say good-bye now. I wish you success in your investigation."

The line went dead.

Wrong move, Mrs. Baylor.

• • •

I WENT INTO Helen's office. "I interviewed Otis Baylor's daughter yesterday and just got an Academy Award nose-in-the-air performance from his wife," I said.

"Slow it down, Pops," she said, leaning back in her swivel chair.

"They're lying," I said, spreading my notes on Helen's desk. "Look, both Otis and his daughter say they heard a single shot. Both use the same language. They say 'It woke me up.' When I mentioned multiple shots to the daughter, she even corrected me. I was bothered from the get-go by Baylor's statement that he heard a single shot. That's not what people say when they're awakened by gunfire. All they know is that a frightening sound shook them out of their sleep. They don't count shots."

I saw Helen's attention sharpen.

"Both Otis and Thelma described what they saw in the same sequence. Each of them began by mentioning a man floating in the water. There were four guys in or around the boat. But Otis and Thelma mention the kid who was floating in the water first. Why not the guy hemorrhaging blood out of his mouth? I think they had their story prepackaged."

Helen rubbed at the back of her neck. Whenever she was pensive, her face always went through an androgynous transformation that was both lovely and mysterious to watch. I believed that several different people lived inside her, but I never told her that. Her lovers had included many men and women over the years, including Clete Purcel. Sometimes she looked at me in a way that made me feel sexually uncomfortable, as though one of the women who lived inside her had decided to stray.

"Have you heard any more from the Feds or NOPD?" she asked.

"Nope."

"Write up what you just told me and fax it to Baton Rouge. Tell them to clean up their own shit while you're at it. I want this stuff out of our hair."

"Why the change in attitude?"

"Have you looked at The Weather Channel?"

"No," I said.

"That new hurricane, what's-its-name, the one that was supposed to smack Texas?"

"Rita?"

"It's not."

IS THERE A DESIGN in the events of our lives? Or do things just happen, much like a junkyard falling down a staircase? If it's the latter, how do you deal with it?

If you have ever invested with regularity in the pari-mutuel arts, or shot craps in a game that made your hand sweat on the dice, or allowed yourself to believe you had the psychic power to intuit the next card out of the shoe at a blackjack table, you have probably crossed the wrong Rubicon on many occasions and are familiar with the following experience:

There is magic in your hands and your walk. The magenta sky above the track and the flamingos lifting out of a grassy pond in the center ground are indicators that your perfecta wheel cannot lose. Inside the casino, the dice are as hard-edged and solid as rubies in your palm, and you double your bets on the pass line each time you bounce the dice down the felt into the backboard. The plunging neckline of the young woman dealing out of the shoe at the black-jack table cannot compare in its allure to the thrill of receiving a low number on the fifth card of a five-card Johnny.

You know that you cannot lose, that it is God's will that you not lose. Others draw close to you in the same way that candle moths surround an incandescent light burning inside a crystal container. They gasp in awe at both your recklessness and the vindication of your faith in yourself. They want to brush against you and absorb your power into their bodies.

Then things start to go south. Your horse is disqualified because the jockey has bumped another rider's horse on the far turn. The dice turn to lumps of lead in your hand and come up treys, boxcars, and snake eyes. The young female dealer blackjacks on you and deals you every high card in the deck, busting you again and again, stifling a yawn, her cleavage hovering like a withdrawn invitation only inches from your face.

Welcome to "the dead zone." It's a special place that, unbeknown to himself, every degenerate gambler seeks. Check out the bar at the track after the seventh race. The people there are as happy as satiated hogs. They have lost the grocery money, the rent, the mortgage and car payment, even the vig they owe a Shylock. But they're safe now because they have nothing else to lose. They also have the empirical evidence to prove once and for all time that the universe has conspired to cheat and injure them. Their personal failure is God's, not theirs. The soul is packed in dry ice now, the battle over.

When I went into the coffee room at the department, several uniformed deputies were watching CNN. Their collective expression and posture reminded me of helicopter pilots I had seen many years ago in a predawn briefing room backdropped by the China Sea. Most of these pilots were warrant officers not over twenty years in age. But I could never forget the suppressed tension in their faces, the deliberate restraint in their voices, the self-imposed solipsism in their eyes that told you the dawn was indeed about to come up like thunder from China across the bay.

Hurricane Rita contained winds of 185 miles an hour and originally had been projected to make landfall somewhere around Matagorda Bay, northeast of Corpus Christi. Then its direction shifted farther to the east. Officials in Houston, fearing a repeat of Katrina in their own city, effected a massive evacuation, choking highways all the way to San Antonio and Dallas. Then the hurricane shifted direction again, this time almost certainly zeroing in on Beaumont and Port Arthur.

Texas was going to take the hit. Our exposure would be marginal, nothing more than minor wind damage, trees knocked down, a temporary power outage. We breathed a sigh of relief. Providence had given us a free pass.

Then the National Hurricane Center in Miami disabused us of our hubris. In fact, the forecast was unbelievable. Louisiana was about to get pounded full-force, with twenty-foot tidal surges and

wind that would rip off roofs from Sabine Pass to the other side of
the Atchafalaya River. More unbelievably, we were being told the
storm would probably make landfall in Cameron Parish, just south
of Lake Charles, the same place the eye of Audrey swept through in
1957. The tidal wave that preceded the '57 storm curled over the
courthouse and downtown area like a giant hammer and crushed it
into rubble, killing close to five hundred people.

"Weren't you around when Audrey hit?" a deputy asked as I
stared up at the television screen.

"Yeah, I was," I replied.

"On an oil rig?"

"On a seismograph barge," I said.

"It was pretty bad, huh?"

"We got through it okay," I said.

He was a crew-cut, martial-looking man, with too much starch in
his uniform and a toothpick in the corner of his mouth. He removed
the toothpick and dropped it in a waste can and focused his attention on the television screen. I could hear a wet sound in his throat
when he swallowed.

No one wants to go to the same war twice. You pay your dues in
order to enter the dead zone and you're supposed to be safe. Unfortunately, that's not the way it works.

CHAPTER
13

NEW IBERIA AND LAFAYETTE were now filled with evacuees fleeing Hurricane Rita as well as those who had fled Katrina. Firearm
and ammunition sales were booming. The original sympathy for the
evacuees from New Orleans was incurring a strange transformation.
Right-wing talk shows abounded with callers viscerally enraged
at the fact evacuees were receiving a onetime two-thousand-dollar
payment to help them buy food and find lodging. The old southern
nemesis was back, naked and raw and dripping—absolute hatred for
the poorest of the poor.

AT SUNSET Friday evening the air was as gold as pollen, as though
Indian summer were upon us. The decrease in barometric pressure
seemed to signal little more than a shower. What appeared to be rain
rings were bream dimpling the surface on the edge of the lily pads.
I could hear my elderly neighbor playing the piano behind an open
window. Then the air grew cool and moist, and leaves began stripping
from the trees in the yard, whirling in vortexes down the slope to the
water. As the sky filled with dust, a shadow spread over the yards and
gardens of the homes along East Main, and the bayou was suddenly
wrinkled by a hard wind blowing from the southeast. My neighbor
got up from her piano and began slamming down windows.

From my back steps I saw the aluminum roof of a picnic shelter in

City Park peel away like the top of a sardine can and tumble end over end across the grass. I saw a man continue fishing when lightning struck an oak tree in the center of the park. I saw a man stripped to the waist in an airboat roar past our property, smiling serenely at the heavens. I heard a civil defense siren blowing at City Hall.

I went on duty at midnight and was given the opportunity to meditate once again on the biblical admonition that the sun is made to rise upon both the evil and the good, and the rain is sent to fall upon the just and unjust alike. Except for ripped shingles or tree limbs crashing on telephone or power lines, East Main was spared. But in south Iberia Parish, twelve feet of water surged into trailers and low-lying homes. That was nothing compared to the fate of the coastal parishes.

A tidal wave of salt water, mud, dead fish, oil sludge, and organic debris literally effaced the southern rim of Louisiana. Farther inland, what it did not efface, it ruined. Throughout the wetlands, almost every home was made uninhabitable, every telephone pole broken at ground level, every road made impassable. The rice and sugarcane fields were encrusted with saline, the farm machinery buried in mud, the settlements down by the Gulf reduced to twisted pieces of plumbing sticking out of grit that looked like emery paper.

The greatest suffering was incurred by animals. An estimated hundred thousand cattle drowned in Vermilion and Cameron parishes alone. They crowded onto galleries, tried to climb onto tractors and cane wagons, and even ended up on rooftops. But they drowned just the same.

I stood on top of a hay baler with a pair of binoculars and, facing south, made a one-hundred-eighty-degree sweep from east to west and back again. I could not see a living creature. Not a dog or a cat, not even a bird. The trees had been stripped to the bark and looked like gnarled fingers. Brick houses were blown into birdshot. Fifty-foot shrimp boats lay upside down a hundred yards from water. Drowned sheep were stacked inside the floodgate of an irrigation lock, like zoo animals crowding against the bars of their cage. Cemetery crypts were obliterated, and the coffins washed into residential yards and in one instance through the broken front window of a country store. I saw at least thirty head of Herefords tangled in a barbed-wire fence, their stomachs bloated in the heat, swarms of gnats hovering above them.

By Monday morning I was used up.

"Go home, Streak," Helen said.

"Nope," I said.

"Why not?"

"I'll go home when you do," I said.

"I went home last night and came back. I ate supper and put on fresh clothes. I also took a nap. I put you in charge while I was gone."

I stared at her emptily.

"Go home, bwana," she said.

As I drove into New Iberia, the streets were drying in the sunshine, the sidewalks plastered with wet leaves. I parked my truck in my driveway and went inside the house. But Alafair and Molly and Clete were gone. I stripped off my clothes in the emptiness of the house and got in the shower, like the war veteran returning from a place that is still locked in his head but which he will never tell anyone about. Then I sat in the bottom of the stall, the water splaying on my back, and fell sound asleep.

WHILE RITA WAS shredding the coast of Louisiana, Eddy Melancon lay propped up in a bed close by a fourth-floor window at Our Lady of the Lake in Baton Rouge. He had a fine view of the night sky and the elevated interstate highway and the sheets of rain sweeping across the lines of cars entering and leaving the city. But Eddy cared little about the view or the fact a nurse had gone out of her way to move his bed and prop him up so he could look out upon the city and the light show in the sky. The truth was, Eddy Melancon could not stop thinking about his own person. It lay there, in the bed, as though dropped from ten thousand feet, disconnected from all motor controls, insentient, flaccid, and fed by tubes whose needles punctured his veins without Eddy's feeling them.

It was like being buried alive inside his own body. Each time he fell asleep, he saw broken images in his head leading up to the moment somebody had locked down on him with a high-powered rifle. He heard the sound of the tiny emery wheel striking dryly on his cigarette lighter, then he both heard and smelled the flare of lighter fluid inside the flame guard. Just as he sucked the smoke deep into his lungs, he saw a needle-nosed projectile zipping over the floodwater, flying through the fire, making a thropping sound as it entered and exited his body, splintering his spinal cord like it was dried tuber.

In the dream, he wanted to wrap his arms over his face or dive into the water. But he couldn't move or run or even drop the burning lighter from his hand. When he would wake, he would believe for just a moment that his terror was the result of a nightmare and that his motor control was now restored, that he could walk to a bathroom and urinate into a bowl while the day and the world adjusted to his needs. But his paralysis encased him like concrete. He would push out his tongue on his lips and close and open his eyes in the dark, waiting for either movement or sensation to find its way back into his body. He would drop his eyes to where his hands lay on the sheet and wait for them to obey his mental commands. That's when he would hear a scream inside his head that was louder than any voice he had ever heard in the actual world.

Eddy studied the curtains of rain sliding down his window and the patterns of shadow they made on his skin. When the two men in hospital greens entered his room, he thought they were going to check his catheter or sponge-bathe him or hold a glass drinking straw to his mouth. Or maybe they would talk to him. His voice box had been spared. As long as he could talk, he still possessed a measure of control in his life. He could talk to these guys about his recovery. There must be ways to repair spinal breaks, he thought. Yeah, it was just a matter of getting to a better hospital in Houston or Boston or New York, places like that. Bertrand must have stashed the money from the house score. There would be plenty for good doctors and rehab programs. Yeah, let these local motherfuckers go play wit' their bedpans, he told himself.

One of the men in greens stared down at Eddy, his face floating above him like a white balloon. "How you feeling?" he asked.

"I'm feeling okay," Eddy whispered.

Why had he answered like that? Like some kid spitting watermelon seeds and tap-dancing for Mr. Charlie. That's not the way he had talked to the hospital personnel before. What was different about this guy?

"Because we want you to be comfortable for the ride down to the OR," the same man said.

"It's the middle of the night," Eddy said.

"Everything is haywire, Eddy. This storm really screwed us up," the man said. He yawned and looked at his watch. "Let's get you down the hall. I got to get home to my kids."

The second man positioned a gurney next to Eddy's bed. When a tree of lightning printed itself against a backdrop of black sky, Eddy saw the man's face clearly. It was concave, the eyes recessed, the head elongated and bald, the lips the pink shade of an eraser on a pencil. The second man began disconnecting the wires and tubes that only moments earlier Eddy had looked upon as an annoyance.

"What you doin', man?" he said.

The man with the concave face smiled down at him. "Relax. You're in good hands," he said.

Then the two men in greens lifted him as though he were weightless and set him gently on the gurney. As they pushed him through the corridor toward the elevator, they kept glancing down at him with benevolent expressions, their hands patting him reassuringly whenever he started to speak. On the first floor he heard the elevator doors open, then he felt the gurney's wheels rumbling through a passageway. A moment later there was a whoosh of air and the sound of doors sliding again, and he could smell rain and engine exhaust and hear sirens pealing through the streets.

The two men lifted the gurney and loaded it into the back of an ambulance.

"Who y'all? What y'all doin' to me?" Eddy said. "Help!"

The man with the concave face and recessed eyes got inside with him and shut the door. Eddy's weight shifted on the gurney as the ambulance pulled out onto the street and drove away at high speed.

"Scared?" the man said.

"Ain't scared of nothing," Eddy replied. "Not of no peckerwoods, not of nothing."

"You ought to be," the man said, inserting a chocolate bar into his mouth. He smiled as he chewed on the chocolate.

CLETE PURCEL worked out of his secondary office on Main and stayed at our house, but he returned to New Orleans three times in his pursuit of the Melancon brothers and Andre Rochon. He used a city map to re-create the possible routes Bertrand Melancon could have used in his escape from Otis Baylor's neighborhood immediately following the shooting. He walked through backyards and alleys and at a residential intersection found a woman throwing the remnants of her kitchen onto her terrace, smashing dishes and glassware on the flagstones.

"Can I help you?" she said when she saw him watching her. Sweat was leaking out of her hair band.

He showed her his PI badge and told her about the shooting down the street. He gave her the date and the approximate time the shooting took place.

"I know all about it. I think they got what they deserved," she said. She wore a halter and shorts and flip-flops, and she had chestnut hair that hung in strands on her brow. Her skin was unnaturally white and dotted with moles. Clete doubted if she was the type who would be seen in halter and shorts were it not for the intense heat inside her house.

"Two of those guys are still on the loose. I'd like to find them. They were in a green aluminum boat, with an outboard motor on it."

"What, you think they're parked somewhere on the street waiting for you?"

"No, I think they dumped some stolen property around here. I'd like to recover it for my client."

She walked out on the edge of her lawn. She put her hands on her hips and stared at the intersection. There were blue veins in the tops of her breasts. "I saw an outboard like that almost hit an airboat full of cops. A black man was in the stern. It looked like another guy was slumped down in the bilge. They swung around behind my house and went up the alley. Were they the ones you're after?"

"It sounds like them. Did they stop?"

"I wish they had."

"Pardon?"

"If looters broke into my house, I was going to serve them ham sandwiches I'd filled with rat poison. I mixed the poison with mustard so they couldn't taste it. I made a dozen of them."

Clete finished jotting down her words about the boat in his notebook. "Mind if I ask you a personal question?"

"What is it?" she said, her left eye wrinkling at the corner.

"Why are you smashing your dishware?"

"Because the goddamn insurance company just told me my policy doesn't cover water damage. Because I thought I'd give their worthless asses breakage they could understand. Because they just fucked me out of every cent I got from my divorce."

Clete looked down the street, suppressing a smile. "Sorry, I didn't get your name. Like to take a break, get something to eat?" he said.

IT WAS NOON, Wednesday, and I was in Clete's New Iberia office, located in a refurbished brick building on Main Street, listening to his account of his most recent trip to New Orleans. The nineteenth-century tin ceiling was stamped with a fleur-de-lis design and the walls were decorated with antique firearms. Outside the rear window was a brick-paved patio, shaded by potted palm and banana trees, where Clete often ate his lunch. But today he couldn't stop talking about the Melancon brothers and Andre Rochon and the new woman he had met down the street from Otis Baylor's house.

I believed Clete was still wired from Katrina and was now giving himself over to an obsession, one that allowed him to believe if he nailed the guys who had run over him with their automobile, he could somehow revise all the events that had turned a gingerbread Caribbean city into food for every kind of jackal in the book.

"I got it figured, big mon," he said. "Bertrand Melancon almost collided into an airboat full of NOPD guys, so he swerved down this alley behind Courtney's house—"

"Whose house?"

"The gal I told you about, the one breaking dishes all over her terrace. Bertrand bagged it down the alley and hid Sidney Kovick's goods somewhere along the way. The hospital is only three blocks from Courtney's. I think I even found his boat. It was wedged under a pile of trees. The motor was gone, but it's a green, aluminum job. *Ducks Unlimited* is painted on the hull. I bet they boosted it from a rescue operation."

"I think you're spending more time on these guys than you should," I said.

"How'd you arrive at that brilliant idea?"

"Twisting these guys won't bring back New Orleans, Clete. It's gone. Just like our youth. The place we knew will be a place we look at in books that feature historical photography."

He got up from behind his desk and stared out the window. He was wearing a short-sleeved green shirt with bluebirds and flowers printed on it. The back of his neck was pitted, his hair lightly oiled and clipped. I could see the color rising in his neck. "Don't say that about New Orleans."

"All right, I won't. The guys who let people drown for two days are going to pour billions into rebuilding poor neighborhoods."

He turned and faced me. The flattened scar that ran through one eyebrow and across his nose was the dull color and shape of an elongated tire patch. "The shield I carry could have come out of a cereal box. The only credibility I have is the degree of respect I instill in scum like the Melancons. I wish it was different. I wish I was still with NOPD. But I flushed my legitimate career a long time ago. Don't be lecturing at me, Streak."

The room was silent a long time.

"I got a call this morning on my cell from Bertrand Melancon," he said.

"The Melancons have your number?" I replied, glad to have something else to talk about.

"Nig gave it to Bertrand. He says his brother was kidnapped out of Our Lady of the Lake. He wants me to get him back. That's what I was trying to tell you, but you kept interrupting me."

"Who kidnapped him?"

"Bertrand thinks it was Sidney Kovick's people."

"What did you tell him?"

"That I don't work for street pukes, particularly ones I think are rapists."

"What's the rest of it?"

"I made a mistake. I should have figured out a way to bring him in. Bertrand must have found something in that house he can't fence. In fact, I got the impression he's not sure what he's holding."

"You're not making sense."

"That's what I told Bertrand. He wants to cut a deal with Sidney to get his brother back, but he thinks whatever it is he's holding is so hot Sidney is going to kill him and Eddy and Andre Rochon once he gets it back."

"Don't get any deeper in this."

"You haven't heard the half of it. Bertrand started talking about bodies under the water in the Lower Nine. He said they glowed under his boat. He said he's going to Hell for something he did. I told him to take his bullshit to a priest and to lose my cell number. You know what he said?"

I didn't want to hear more of it. Clete's face was spotted with color, the way it got when his liver was aching for a drink.

"Bertrand said the last person he wanted to see was a priest. He said it was a priest who caused the bodies in the water to glow."

"I'm gone," I said.

"See what happens when I'm straight up with you?" he yelled at my back.

I WENT BACK to the department, my head pounding. The enormous loss of life in New Orleans kept the media focus on Katrina, but Hurricane Rita had hurt us bad, too, and had also flattened or flooded thousands of homes along the southeast Texas coast. In Lake Charles and Orange, Texas, there were blocks of houses that looked like a lumberyard after a tornado has gone through it. My desk and cell phones rang constantly. My intake basket was overflowing, my mailbox stuffed with pink message slips. Every cop, firefighter, and paramedic in the parish was getting by on a few hours' sleep a night, sometimes on a desktop. Cops and firefighters from other states were on lend-lease to us, but the workload was staggering. I didn't have time to worry about people who had made bad choices for themselves or whom I couldn't help, including Father Jude LeBlanc.

Wasted words, wasted words.

In his office Clete had mentioned a detail about the green aluminum boat that I couldn't get out of my head. I picked up the phone on my desk and punched in his number. "You said you found the boat Bertrand Melancon was using?"

"Yeah, it was upside down under a pile of tree limbs and trash by the emergency room entrance," he replied. "It looked like it had blood smears on the bow."

"The words *Ducks Unlimited* were painted on the hull?"

"Yeah, what about it?"

"Was there anything else on the hull?"

He thought for a second. "A mallard, with its wings outstretched. What's the deal?"

"Jude LeBlanc's girlfriend said Jude had found a boat to evacuate his parishioners from the church attic. She said it had a duck painted on it. Jude was chopping a hole in the attic when somebody attacked him. She never saw him again."

He didn't reply, and I knew Clete had done something else he wasn't eager to tell me about.

"What are you hiding?" I said.

"Bertrand Melancon called me again, about three minutes ago. He wants help, but he won't come in. He thinks I'll either stomp his ass or turn him over to Sidney Kovick. So I gave him your cell and office numbers. If you don't want to talk to the guy, just hang up on him."

"You made the right move."

"I don't believe it. Are you feeling okay?" he asked.

THAT EVENING Molly and I ate by ourselves at the kitchen table. Clete had gotten his old room back at the motor court up the street from the Winn-Dixie, and Alafair was working as a volunteer at the evacuee shelter in City Park.

"I thought you'd like smothered steak for a change. You don't like it?" she said.

I couldn't focus on her question. "I think Jude LeBlanc probably drowned in the Lower Nine. But maybe his death was a homicide," I said.

I saw a quiet sense of exasperation take hold in her face, like a bad memory from her sleep that the daylight hours would not dispel. "Dave, nobody can ever change what happened in New Orleans. I remember Jude. I liked him. But he was a sick man."

"I may have knowledge of a murder. I'm a police officer. I can't just say, 'Sorry, sonofabitch, I've got my own problems.'"

She looked through the window at the shadows in the pecan trees and live oaks and the wide expanse of Bayou Teche, now twenty feet up in the yard. She set her fork down on her plate. Her thumb ticked at a callus on her palm. "Maybe you should take a nap and rest up before you go back on duty."

"A street puke by the name of Bertrand Melancon told Clete he saw the bodies of drowned people glowing under his boat in the Lower Nine. I think he and some lowlifes like him attacked Jude and took his boat. I think it cost Jude his life and the lives of people who were waiting in a church attic for Jude to rescue them. That's hard to blow off."

Her plate was only half empty. She picked it up and walked outside, peering down the slope as though she wanted to witness the gloaming of the day. I thought perhaps she was going to finish her supper at the picnic table in solitude. But she scraped her smothered steak and rice and brown gravy and creamed corn on the ground for Tripod and Snuggs. When she came back in, she washed her dishes and knife and fork in the sink, set them in the dry rack, and let out her breath. "I think I'll take a walk. Do you want to come?" she said.

"Not right now, thanks."

"Then I'll see you later."

"I like the food real good, Molly. I can't get all those dead people off my mind. I think about them and I want to kill somebody. That's just the way it is."

I heard the front door shut behind her. Through the side window I could see my neighbor's rotund, feminine, middle-aged son up-ending a longneck beer in his backyard, his throat working smoothly, a band of late sunlight sparkling inside the bottle.

Fifteen minutes later, a tan Honda stopped at the curb. Alafair got out and thanked the young woman driving, then came inside. "Where's Molly?" she said.

"Taking a walk. Who was that?"

"Thelma Baylor. She's helping out at the shelter."

"Really?" I said.

"She says you were out to her house."

"That's right."

"She says you think her dad shot some black guys."

"It's a possibility."

"I don't think Mr. Baylor is that kind of man."

"Maybe he's not, Alf."

"Don't call me that stupid name."

"Mr. Baylor's daughter was raped and sodomized and burned with cigarettes by three black degenerates. If that happened to you, maybe I would not be the same kind of person you think I am."

"Don't talk like that, Dave."

"I don't want to tell you whom to associate with, but I'd lose the connection with Thelma Baylor."

"That's as judgmental as it is unfair."

"So is killing people."

"What are you talking about?"

"Like you said, Mr. Baylor doesn't seem like the kind of guy who gets off dumping a seventeen-year-old kid's brainpan into the water. But how about his daughter? You think she might be a candidate?"

"I come home from the shelter and I feel like I just walked through cobweb."

"Did you eat yet?"

"God!" she said.

I walked across the railroad tracks in the drone of cicadas to an AA meeting that was held twice a week in a cottage opposite the old high school I attended many years ago. After the meeting, I walked to the office and began sorting out the piles of paperwork in my intake basket. At 10:14 p.m. my cell phone rang.

"You Mr. Robicheaux?" a voice said.

"I am."

"These motherfuckers in Baton Rouge ain't gonna do nothing 'bout my brother."

"Would you watch your language?"

"*What,* my brother been kidnapped and you bothered 'bout my motherfucking language?"

"I'm going to take a guess. You're Bertrand Melancon."

"Look, man, I don't know if them stones got blood on them or what, I just want my brother back."

"Stones with blood on them?"

"You got a hearing problem?"

My wiring was frayed, my batteries on zero. The behavior of violent and stupid people never varies. The problem in attitude and frame of reference is yours, not theirs. If you're a pro, you become laconic and impassive and turn their own energies against them. But I wasn't up for it. "You listen, you idiot, your brother was shot because he asked for it. I don't know what 'stones' you're talking about and I'm not your brother's keeper or yours, either."

"I tried to tell that fat cracker Purcel, but he wouldn't listen. I want to wash this city off me, man. I want to take my brother out of here. I want to make up for what we done. I ain't blowing gas, Jack. You gonna help me or not? If you ain't, say it now."

"Where are you?"

"I got to have your word, man."

"You're not in my jurisdiction. The warrants on you are in Orleans Parish. That's as good as it's going to get."

I could hear him breathing into the phone's mouthpiece. "You know your way around Jeanerette? I see a cruiser, I see a uniform, I'm a rocket."

CHAPTER
14

THE CLUB WAS constructed of cinder block, with a flat tin roof salvaged from a barn, and was located on a back street in Jeanerette not far from a drawbridge over the Teche. The sky was black, but floodlights illuminated the signs advertising the drive-by window where the owner sold frozen daiquiris to the happy-motoring crowd at five bucks a pop. The outside lights also lit the iron framework of the bridge and the bayou's surface, which was running high up on the pilings and looked like yellow rust. When I got out of my pickup, the night air was throbbing with the sounds of tree frogs, the wind blowing through a sugarcane field out in the darkness. I didn't want to enter the club. I didn't want to breathe the cigarette smoke and bathroom disinfectant and refrigerated sweat, and revisit the world in which I had lived a large part of my teenage and adult life. But that's what I did.

The only light inside came from the neon beer signs over the bar and the partially opened doors to the restrooms. The booths were made of wood and red vinyl and were nicked, split, gouged, and cigarette-burned, and reminded me of a row of darkened caves along the wall. Most of the people drinking in the club were either African-American or blue-collar, hard-core coonasses or people who called themselves Creoles and lived on both sides of the color line. It was a place marked by neither joy nor despair and seldom by violence or as a place of inception for romantic trysts. It was a place people went when they wished to set their lives into abeyance, where clocks didn't matter, and where Fox News assured them the problems in their lives were of other people's manufacture.

In a booth at the back of the club I saw a young black man sitting by himself, a beer and a length of microwave white boudin unwrapped from its wax paper in front of him. He was wearing a short-brim fedora, with a tiny red feather in the band, one like John Lee Hooker used to wear. But he had the same haunted, jailhouse look as the kid whose mug shot was in a manila folder in my office file cabinet. His eyes lifted into mine. "You Robicheaux?"

I sat down across from him. "You called me 'mister' on the phone. You can call me 'mister' now or 'Detective' now."

"Whatever."

"I've got a long night ahead of me. What is it you have that might be of interest to us?"

"Man, you're reeking of hostility. What's your fucking problem?"

"You are."

"Me? What I ever done to you?"

"I have it on fairly good authority you and your brother and your friends are probably rapists."

"How about lowering your voice, man?"

I could feel a tuning fork start to tremble inside me. I once saw American troops who had been hung in trees and skinned alive. The anger I experienced then was of a kind that destroys our humanity and gives false justification for the evil we in turn perpetrate upon others. I had these same feelings toward Bertrand Melancon now.

I went to the bar and bought a bottle of carbonated water and sat back down. I drank from the bottle and screwed the cap tight. "What did you take out of Sidney Kovick's house?"

He kept trying to read my face, as though he were watching a dangerous animal through the bars of a cage. "A thirty-eight and some cash and silverware and shit. Lookie here, man, before I say anything else—"

"What are these 'stones' you keep talking about?"

"No, man, you got to clear up this rumor I'm hearing. About this guy Kovick. He cut off somebody's legs with a chain saw?"

"Sidney and his wife used to live in Metairie. They had a little boy who was five years old. He was playing on his three-wheeler in the next-door neighbor's drive. The neighbor came home drunk and drove over him with his car and killed him. About six months later the neighbor disappeared. No one knows what happened to him. But some people say Sidney put on a raincoat and rubber gloves and went down in a basement in Shreveport and committed an awful deed. I don't know if I'd put a lot of credence in that or not."

Bertrand's face looked stricken and seemed to actually turn gray with fear. He clenched his hands between his thighs and drew air through his teeth. "Man, I don't want to hear stuff like that."

"You mess with Sidney, that's the way it flushes. Tell me about the stones you took from Sidney's house."

"No fence is gonna touch them. The word's out. The guy holding these rocks is gonna get hung up in a meat locker, a piece at a time. That ain't a shuck, man. Three different guys tole me that. That's why they took Eddy. While we're sitting here, they're sweating Eddy. I cain't stand thinking about it."

His breath was sour with funk, his face coated with an oily sheen. He gripped his stomach and shut his eyes.

"You okay?" I said.

"I got ulcers."

"And you're eating boudin and drinking alcohol?"

"Lookie, what if I leave most everything for you in a bag, maybe I just hold back a li'l, and you give it to Mr. Kovick?"

"Where did the shot come from?"

He swallowed, disconcerted, angry over his powerlessness and the fact that I kept redirecting the conversation. "I ain't seen it. I just heard it and saw Eddy go down."

"You know what bothers me here, Bertrand? You make no mention of Kevin Rochon. He was seventeen. He was the only one among y'all without a sheet. He got his brains blown out and all you can talk about is yourself and your brother."

"We tole Andre not to bring him. It ain't our fault. Why you keep getting on my case?"

"You boosted a boat in the Lower Nine, didn't you?"

I saw his fingers splay on his stomach again, his mouth hang open as a rush of pain flared into his bowels and rectum. "I cain't take this. I wish it had been me instead of Kevin or Eddy. I just want to get my brother back. I just want out."

He wasn't acting. I genuinely believed that Bertrand Melancon had taken up residence in a place that does not have geographical boundaries, one that we associate with mythology and outmoded religions.

"If I were you, I'd ship Kovick's goods to his flower store in Algiers. With luck, he'll turn your brother loose and he won't come after you."

I tried to hold my eyes on his and not blink, but he read the lie in them.

"I'm dead, ain't I?"

"Tell me what you did to the priest in the Lower Nine."

"That fat cracker said you was straight up. But you ain't no different from me. You working the angle, running the con, trying to make me sick and afraid so you can get what you want. The people glowed under the water. That's what happened out there, man. Won't nobody believe that. But I seen it. I hope I end up wit' them. Maybe you gonna feel like that one day, too, motherfucker."

He clutched his boudin inside the wax paper it had been heated in and took it with him out the door. I unscrewed the cap from the bottle of carbonated water and drank from the neck. I wondered at the ease with which I had just gone about dismembering an impaired man. The club was stone-quiet. I could hear the carbonation bubbling inside the bottle in my hand.

MOLLY WAS ASLEEP when I got home, her face turned toward the wall, her hip rounded under the sheet. I laid my shirt and trousers across the back of a chair, but I didn't get in bed. Instead, I sat on the floor, in my skivvies, inside a box of slatted moonlight, my spine against the bed frame. I sat there for a long time, but I cannot tell you exactly why. Outside, I could hear the drawbridge clanking at Burke Street and the droning of a deep-draft workboat laboring down the bayou.

"What are you doing down there?" Molly said above me.

"I didn't want to wake you up."

I could hear her moving herself across the mattress so she could see me better. "You're not going crazy on me, are you?"

She meant it as a joke.

"I have memories I can't get rid of, no matter what I do," I replied. "It's like trying to self-exorcise a succubus. I don't have your degree of spiritual conviction, Molly. I remember events that happened either yesterday or years ago, and I remember the bastards who caused them, and I want to go back in time and do them great injury. That's not honest. I want to paint the wall with them."

She lay on her stomach, propped on her elbows, her head hanging down close to mine. "You can't confide in me? You don't think we're a partnership in dealing with whatever problems come down the road? Is that where we are in our marriage?"

She tapped a finger on my neck. "I asked you a question, trooper."

"I just put the screws to a black kid in Jeanerette. He's a street puke and meth dealer and maybe a rapist. But you don't rip out their spokes when their wheels are already broken."

Her face hovered on the side of my vision. I could smell the shampoo in her hair. She put one hand on my shoulder and squeezed it. "You never deliberately hurt an innocent person in your life, Dave," she said. "You take on other people's suffering without their ever asking. Your greatest virtue is your greatest weakness."

I turned my head and looked into her face. Her mouth was pink, her skin shiny in the moonlight. She'd had her hair cut short so that it was thick and even on the ends where it hung down on her cheeks. One of her nightgown straps had pulled loose and I could see the spray of freckles on her shoulder. She walked her fingers through my hair. "Will you get off the floor, please?" she said.

I lay down beside her and pulled her against me. I could feel her breath against my ear. Her hands pressed me hard in the small of my back. She hooked a thumb in the elastic of my underwear and began to work the fabric down on my hip. Then she gave it up and let me undress by myself while she pulled off her panties and nightgown. I started to get on top of her, but she pushed me back and sat on my thighs, her arms propped by my shoulders. She stared down at me in a way I didn't understand. "I don't know what I would do if anything happened to you, Dave. I never thought I would feel that way about a man. But I do about you," she said.

"Molly—" I began.

"No, that's the way it is. Anyone who tries to hurt you will have to kill me first."

She lowered her hand and pressed me inside her. When it was over, I placed my head against the dampness of her breast and could hear her heart beating as loud and full as a drum.

THE NEXT DAY, Thursday, a homeless man was rooting in a Dumpster behind a Baton Rouge veterinary clinic, spearing cans out of it with a stick that he had mounted a nail on. All the animals had been removed from the clinic in advance of Hurricane Rita and the veterinary had not returned to reopen his business. The bar next door had opened at 7:00 a.m., but the only movement inside was the swamper airing out the building and sweeping trash through the back door into the alley. The homeless man filled his vinyl bag with cans and was tying the top when he heard a sound that did not fit into the normal routine of his morning.

He set his bag down gingerly on the asphalt and let the cans settle inside the vinyl. He listened for the sound to repeat itself but heard nothing except the wind blowing through the trees in the cemetery at the end of the block. He walked down to one end of the alley and looked both ways, then went to the other end and did the same. The swamper, a black man, paused in his work. "Something wrong?" he said.

"You ain't heard that sound?" the homeless man asked.

"What sound?" the swamper said.

"A sound like an animal trapped in the wall or something."

"There ain't no animals in that building. Owners came and got 'em all. Lightning burned out the air-conditioning. Ain't no animal in the wall, either."

The swamper went back in the bar, but the homeless man continued to stand in the middle of the alley, turning his head one way, then another, as the wind gusted and died. He picked up his bag of cans and flung it over his shoulder, the heavy load of it hitting him solidly in the back. Then he heard the sound again. This time there was no doubt where it came from. The homeless man set down his bag and pulled open a heavy metal door that gave onto a foyer and the delivery entrance to the clinic.

Deep inside the gloom, he could make out a gurney that had been left by the clinic door. On top of it was an oblong shape someone had wrapped with a sheet and strapped down against a rubber pad that smelled of urine. The homeless man lifted up the sheet, revealing the crown of a black man's head. He peeled back the sheet farther and saw the black man's eyes and unshaved jaws and a bandaged wound in his throat. But it was the eyes and the expression in the black man's face that caused the homeless man's hands to shake.

"I'll get help. I'm coming back. I promise," he said.

He tripped over his bag of cans as he ran for the back door of the bar, waving his arms.

THAT SAME AFTERNOON I received a call from Special Agent Betsy Mossbacher in Baton Rouge. She had grown up in Chugwater, Wyoming, and wore jeans and boots and on one occasion tracked horseshit into Helen Soileau's office and to Helen's face referred to her as a member of "the tongue-and-groove club." Oddly, they became the best of friends.

"How's it going, Dave? I'm taking over the shooting of Eddy Melancon and Kevin Rochon. I thought I should update you."

Betsy Mossbacher was an in-your-face cowgirl, probably the most socially inept federal law officer at the Bureau, and the worst nondrunk automobile driver I ever worked with. But her level of integrity and courage was unquestionable. I had previously thought that the investigation into the shooting of Melancon and Rochon would either die as a result of investigative dead ends or simple bureaucratic inertia. Betsy's assignment as the new case officer was not good news for whoever had pulled the trigger.

"I'm only involved in the Melancon-Rochon investigation in a tangential way," I said.

"I love your vocabulary. But cut the crap. A homeless guy found Eddy Melancon behind an animal hospital early this morning."

"Melancon is dead?"

"That would be one way of describing him. He has sensation from the neck up, but there's no way to know about his brain. There were adhesive traces over his mouth and nose. I suspect he was tortured in some fashion involving air deprivation. My guess is he didn't have anything to give up and it took a long time for his abductors to accept that."

She paused to let the implications sink in. "What have you got on your end?"

"Not much. It started as a lend-lease investigation following Katrina," I said. "I talked with Bertrand Melancon in a bar in Jeanerette last night. I think he's holding goods he stole from Sidney Kovick's house and is afraid to keep them and even more afraid to give them back."

"You were with Bertrand Melancon and didn't bust him?"

"Our Ritz-Carlton is full-up. How about yours?"

I could hear her frustration building. "Listen, Dave, this case would go away except for the fact somebody put a bullet through the brain of a seventeen-year-old black kid with no record. Too many white swinging dicks were having a fine time shooting black ass in uptown New Orleans. Or at least that's what my boss thinks. Secondly, Sidney Kovick is a person of ongoing great interest to the Bureau. When you interview perps who are in my caseload, I want to know about it."

"Bertrand told me he's holding stones of some kind from Kovick's house. He was talking about stones that have blood on them."

This time it was my turn to let the implications sink in.

"Blood diamonds?" she said.

"That's what it sounds like."

"You mean a street puke may have scored millions on a simple B and E?"

"I think right now Bertrand would trade them for a bus ticket to Saskatoon."

I WANTED TO forget about the Melancon brothers and the Rochons and Sidney Kovick, but I couldn't get Father Jude LeBlanc off my mind. Regardless, I hadn't brought up his name with Betsy Mossbacher. Why? Because the honest-to-God truth is law enforcement is not even law "enforcement." We deal with problems after the fact. We catch criminals by chance and accident, either during the commission of crimes or through snitches. Because of forensic and evidentiary problems, most of the crimes recidivists commit are not even prosecutable. Most inmates currently in the slams spend lifetimes figuring out ways to come to the attention of the system. Ultimately, jail is the only place they feel safe from their own failure.

Unfortunately, the last people on our minds are the victims of crime. They become an addendum to both the investigation and the prosecution of the case, adverbs instead of nouns. Ask rape victims or people who have been beaten with gun butts or metal pipes or tied to chairs and tortured how they felt toward the system after they learned that their assailants were released on bond without the victims being notified.

I don't believe in capital punishment, but I don't argue with the prosecutors who support it. The mouths of the people they represent are stopped with dust. What kind of advocate would not try to give them voice? But what could I possibly do for Jude LeBlanc? He had volunteered for the Garden of Gethsemane, hadn't he? Everybody takes his own bounce.

Those were the kinds of thoughts I walked around with in the middle of the day.

THAT EVENING, at sunset, the sky directly overhead was absolutely blue, the trees in our yard dark with shadow and pulsing with robins who were returning from the North. As we were clearing the dishes from the kitchen table, Alafair happened to glance out the window. "Clete Purcel is in our backyard," she said.

He was sitting at the redwood table, watching a tugboat pass on the bayou. Tripod and Snuggs were both on the tabletop, enjoying the evening. Tripod was sniffing the breeze while Snuggs paced up and down, his stiffened tail bouncing off Clete's face.

Clete lit a cigarette, something I hadn't seen him do in months. I went outside and sat down next to him. His face was red, but I couldn't smell booze on his breath or weed on his clothes. He read my eyes. "I drove back to the Big Sleazy with the top down," he said.

"You in the dumps about something?"

"Courtney and I got a little greedy."

"Wait a minute, who's Courtney again?"

"Courtney Degravelle, the gal who lives up the street from Otis Baylor's house, the one who saw Bertrand Melancon almost side-swipe an NOPD airboat."

I took the cigarette from Clete's hand, dropped it on the ground, and mashed it out.

"Dave, cut me some slack, will you?"

"Got greedy how?"

He lifted up Snuggs by his tail and bounced him up and down on his back paws. Snuggs was thick-necked and had short white hair and muscles that rippled when he walked. His ears were chewed and bent, his fur threaded with pink scars. He was profligate in his romantic life and proprietary about his yard. He fought ferocious battles to safeguard Tripod and often slept on the roof at night to make sure no interlopers violated his and Tripod's turf. Clete was the only person he would allow to take liberties with him, I suspect because Snuggs knew a brother in arms when he saw one.

"Courtney says she saw a young black guy prowling in the alley behind her house a couple of weeks ago. He was pulling something out of a rafter in a garage. She didn't think a lot about it until I told her I believed Bertrand Melancon stashed Kovick's goods somewhere in that alley before he took his brother to the hospital."

"You told her all this?"

"Hey, she's trying to help. She called me yesterday and says she found some soaked bills in her hedge. Not just a few, bundles of them. I think Bertrand dropped them in the water and they floated down to Courtney's."

"How much are we talking about?"

"Seventeen grand and change."

"You and Courtney were going to keep it?"

"I thought about it. What was I going to do, take it to Sidney? What if it wasn't his? Think he was going to admit that? 'Not mine, Purcel. You keep it because you're a great guy.'"

"So what did you do?"

"I had a funny feeling about the bills. If they were Sidney's, why would he keep them in his house? Even if the money was hot, he could launder it through a South American bank. So I took a few bills to Fat Tommy Whalen, remember him, Tommy Orca, used to fence smash-and-grab jewelry and watches for the Carlucci crew? Tommy started going over the bills with a magnifying glass, making all these bubbling sounds of approval, until finally I say, 'You turning queer for dead presidents?'

"'Yeah, "queer" is the word, Purcel,' he says. 'The work is beautiful, but it's queer. Who did it?'

"Can you believe that? The street pukes not only had the bad luck to rob and destroy Sidney Kovick's house, the money they got out of it is counterfeit."

His account had been long and circuitous, which was always Clete's method of avoiding an admission of some kind.

"Back to the subject," I said.

"I want to take a bath in lye water. Ever since Katrina hit, I've been hearing the sound of little piggy feet running for the trough. Washington insiders are down here by the shitload. Now I'm as dirty as they are."

I tapped him between the shoulder blades with the flat of my fist. "You're the best of the best, Cletus. Give the bills back to Courtney Degravelle and tell her to turn them over to the FBI. Stay away from Sidney. End of story."

Snuggs did a U-turn, bumping his tail across Clete's face, waiting for Clete to scratch him between the ears.

IN THE MORNING I called Betsy Mossbacher's extension at the FBI office in Baton Rouge and got her voice mail.

"Sidney Kovick may have had counterfeit money stashed in his house. Some bills washed up in an alley down the street. Again, I'm not sure they're his. Good luck," I said.

I hoped I would not hear from Betsy for a while. She rang back three minutes later. "How do you know about these bills?" she asked.

"Confidential informant," I replied.

"Right."

Then I broached the subject that had preyed on my mind since Natalia Ramos had first told me of Jude LeBlanc's probable fate. "You hear anything about a priest drowning in the Lower Nine?"

"No."

"His name is Father Jude LeBlanc. He was trying to chop a hole in the attic of a church when his boat was stolen from him. Maybe the Melancon brothers and the two Rochons were the guys who took the boat."

"A lot of people were washed out to sea," she said. "I think there're still hundreds of people under the debris. Some state troopers believe there're over thirty-five people buried under one building alone. The smell is awful."

"There's more to the story, Betsy. Bertrand Melancon says he saw luminescent bodies under the water in the Lower Nine. You hear of anything like that?"

"I'd better let you go."

"Don't blow me off. Melancon said Jude LeBlanc caused the bodies to glow. The guy's got the Furies after him. He saw or did something out there. Maybe he committed a homicide."

"These are bad times. Why carry a load that will break your back and not make the load lighter for anybody else? Take care of yourself, Dave."

• • •

MANY YEARS AGO, United States Senator Huey P. Long, also known as the Kingfish, made a gift of our state to Frank Costello. In turn, Costello subcontracted the vice in Louisiana to a crime family in New Orleans. NOPD and the Mob coexisted in much the same way the Mob had coexisted with legal authority in Chicago and New York. The French Quarter was Elsie the cash cow, and no one was allowed to mess with her. The model was the Baths of Caracalla. Conventioneers from Omaha and Meridian could watch bottomless strip shows on Bourbon. They could spit whiskey and soda on each other in hotel bedrooms and get laid by hookers who looked like movie stars. At Mardi Gras they could frolic with transvestites and twirl their phalluses on the balcony of Tony Bacino's gay nightclub. If the bill was a little high, few complained. The operational rule was simple: Everyone had a grand time and went home happy. Sin City was safe and all sins committed there were forgiven, courtesy of NOPD and the local chapter of the New Orleans Mafia.

"Law and order" and "family values" were not abstractions. Murphy artists got thrown off roofs, and jack-rollers and street dips got escorted to the parish line and had their bone structure remodeled. Anyone who stuck up a restaurant or bar frequented either by New Orleans cops or wiseguys got smoked on the spot. No one was sure what happened to child molesters. I always suspected some of them started new incarnations as fish chum.

Cultural symbiosis was a way of life. The Mob's leadership was amoral and ruthless, but they always operated in pragmatic fashion. They were family men and adhered to certain rules, one of which was not to attract attention. As businessmen, they understood the importance of public church attendance, ceremonial patriotism, and the appearance of decency. Most of them kept their word, particularly when they dealt with NOPD. In fact, it was the only currency that allowed them to remain functional.

This all changed when crack cocaine hit the city. Within two or three years' time, the walking dead were all over the downtown area. Black teenagers who looked like they had baked their mush in the microwave that morning were wandering around with nine-millimeters, totally disconnected from the suffering and death they sometimes inflicted. New Orleans's long and happy relationship with the Great Whore of Babylon was over. A kid with the IQ of tapioca pudding might rob you of your money in the St. Louis Cemetery and as an afterthought, for no reason he would ever be able to explain, splatter your brains all over a brick crypt.

John Dillinger, while being booked at the Crown Point, Indiana, jail, was asked by a newsman what he thought of Bonnie Parker and Clyde Barrow. He grinned lopsidedly and replied, "They're a pair of punks. They're giving bank robbery a bad name." In New Orleans the respectable criminal infrastructure of the city was being replaced by pipeheads and street pukes. They were the new "punks" and they were ruining the fun for everyone.

But some members of the old order clung to the old ways and re-fused to accept the fact they were dinosaurs. One of these was a 585-pound pile of whale sperm by the name of Fat Tommy Whalen, also know as Tommy Orca and Tommy Fins. He wore ice-cream linen suits and had slits for eyes. His neighborhood country club revoked his membership after he cannonballed off the diving board and sent a tidal wave into a wedding party and knocked the bride into a flower bed. His family vehicle was an SUV whose undercarriage was supported by tank springs. The youngest of his five children, his daughter, weighed over three hundred pounds. Years ago, every Wednesday and Saturday night, Tommy took the entire Whalen family to an all-you-can-eat, six-dollar buffet in Metairie and drove the owner out of business. He was a Damon Runyon character I had shared a box with at the racetrack, a gelatinous cartoon of a human being who smelled of baby power and lilac water and mouth spray. But the dope culture had been the bane of respectable illegal enter-prise in New Orleans, and Tommy's personal code had gone down the toilet with the city's.

The shorter version? Clete Purcel had managed to walk into an airplane propeller.

The general story made the *Times-Picayune;* the particulars came to me from a New Iberia paramedic who had gone to work in New Orleans right after the storm.

Tommy Fins arrived at Sidney Kovick's flower store in Algiers in fine style, resplendent in white slacks that would fit a rhino and sky-blue silk shirt and flowing polka-dot necktie. One of Sidney's hired help, Marco Scarlotti, opened the door of the SUV for him, as though royalty were arriving, and walked with him to the entrance of the store. The morning was still cool, the green-and-white-striped canopy above the display window filling with the breeze off the river. Marco opened the door wide for Fat Tommy to enter. "Sidney is running a few minutes late. Have some coffee and chocolate doughnuts. We got a shitpile of them," he said.

"Yeah, I could use a snack. Thanks, Marco."

"You got it, Tommy. You're looking good. Looks like you lost a few pounds."

But while Tommy Orca had been talking to Marco, he had not kept his attention focused on the width of the doorway. Before he realized it, he had wedged himself inside the door frame, his buttocks splayed on one jamb, his stomach and scrotum crushed into the other. "You got to give me a push, Marco," he wheezed.

Marco began shoving from behind, squatting down, pushing with his shoulder as though loading a horse onto a trailer. Then his fellow bodyguard Charlie Weiss came from the back of the shop and began pulling on Tommy's arm, twisting it in the socket.

"Your face don't look too good. You okay?" Marco said. "Get him a glass of water, Charlie."

"He weighs enough as it is. Christ, his legs are giving out. Stand up, Tommy. This is not the place to sit down. Oh shit," Charlie said.

By the time the paramedics arrived at the store, Tommy's enormous girth had settled into the door frame like a partially deflated blimp. His lips were filmed with spittle, his breath an agonized gasp.

"Hang on, buddy. We're going to knock out the wall," a paramedic said.

But Tommy wasn't listening. His face was pouring sweat, his eyes focused on Marco's. "I'm fucked," he said.

"No, we're getting you out, Tommy. Just hang on, man," Marco said.

Tommy breathed in and out, as though deliberately oxygenating his blood. "Listen, tell Sidney that Clete Purcel has got his queer. Tell Sidney to take care of my family."

Then Tommy the Whale closed his eyes and swam out to sea, leaving Clete with a millstone hung around his neck.

CHAPTER

15

O TIS BAYLOR CAME into my office early Monday. He wore slacks
and suspenders, a long-sleeved white shirt and a tie, and seemed to
radiate the freshness of the morning. But obviously he did not want
me to misinterpret the purpose of his visit. "I have a question that
needs to be resolved," he said.

"Sit down."

"A man named Ronald Bledsoe came by my house Saturday, un-
announced and uninvited. He said he's a private investigator working for the state. He showed me a gold badge and an ID card with
his photograph on it. Is this something the state is doing?"

"I'm not sure. What did this fellow want?"

"He said he's investigating the shooting of those black kids. He
asked me if one of them had gone up my driveway. I told him I
didn't know. He asked me if I'd found any items on my property
that might have been stolen from other people's homes."

"What did you tell him?"

"That if I'd found stolen goods anywhere, I would have turned
them over to the authorities. He said my neighbor had seen one of
the looters in my driveway."

"Which neighbor?"

"At first he didn't want to tell me. Then he said it was Tom Claggart. I didn't like this man's manner, Mr. Robicheaux."

"It's Dave."

He ignored my correction. "I think this man is a fraud. He's a strange-looking fellow. He has strange eyes."

I took a yellow legal pad out of my desk. "Did he leave a business card?"

"No. I didn't ask for one, either."

"Would you describe him, please?"

"He's a tall white man, bald, with a long face that's sunken in the middle. His mouth is a funny color, like it has rouge on it, or it doesn't go with his skin. He's got a soft voice and accent, the kind people from the Carolinas have. His eyes are green. My daughter was working in the yard. He kept looking at her. I don't want this guy around my house again."

"If he comes back, tell him to leave. If he doesn't, call us."

"You'll come out?"

"Yes, sir."

"That's all I needed to know." He started to rise from his chair.

"I wanted to ask you a question on another subject," I said, pushing aside my legal pad as though our official business were over. "In the army the first military weapon I fired was the '03 Springfield."

He was standing up now, waiting for me to pull the string.

"It's a fine rifle. Did you leave yours behind in New Orleans?" I said.

"No, it's in my house in New Iberia. You want to see it?"

"I thought maybe I could shoot it sometime."

"Be my guest. You must have a lot of time on your hands," he said.

After he was gone, I stirred my pen in a circle on my ink blotter. Otis Baylor was either an innocent man or a very smart one. If he or a member of his family had shot the two looters, the temptation would have been to lose the probable murder weapon in the event the round was found embedded in a house or tree trunk across the street. But I suspected Otis did not get where he was by doing the predictable.

I pulled the file on the shooting from my metal cabinet and looked back at the notes on my interview with the next-door neighbor, Tom Claggart. Claggart had said he had been sound asleep and had not heard the shot that crippled Eddy Melancon and killed Kevin Rochon. But the man calling himself a private investigator claimed Claggart had told him he saw one of the looters emerge from Otis Baylor's driveway. If the PI was telling the truth, Claggart had lied to either me or the PI.

Why?

I didn't know.

Early Tuesday morning Clete Purcel woke to the sound of bird-song in his cottage at the motor court. In its shabby way, his home away from home was a grand place, straight out of another era, with no telephones in the rooms, shaded by live oaks, the slope down to the bayou spangled with autumnal sunshine. He fixed coffee and dropped a ham steak and three eggs in a frying pan and brushed his teeth and shaved while his food cooked. Then he opened the blinds and looked out upon his Caddy, its top spotted with bird droppings. It sat where he had parked it the previous night, under a spreading live oak. A tall man whose waxed bald head seemed unnaturally elongated was studying it, a knuckle poised on his chin. He leaned down and looked at the wire wheels and the rusted chrome on the back bumper and the Louisiana tag filmed with dried mud. He wiped the film from one number on the tag with his thumb, then dusted off his fingers.

"Can I help you with something?" Clete said from his doorway.

"I was admiring your vehicle. I restore vintage cars as a hobby," the man replied. He had heavy eyebrows, like half-moon strips of animal fur that had been glued onto an expressionless face. "I own a Rolls-Royce. But I love Cadillacs, too. Where'd you get yours?"

"A movie company was making a film in New Iberia. They sold off all their vehicles when they left town."

"I wish I could have gotten in on that," the man said. "My name is Ronald Bledsoe. What's yours?"

"You'll have to excuse me. I'm eating breakfast right now," Clete said. He started to close the door.

"I just moved in across the way and wanted to introduce myself."

"That's funny. A family that got blown out of Cameron Parish was staying there."

"My agency helped them relocate. I'm a private investigator."

"Is that why you were checking out my tag?"

"No, it's just a habit I have. I see dirt and I wipe it off. Early up-bringing, I guess."

"Maybe you can recommend a place that restores old Caddies."

The man who called himself Ronald Bledsoe stared thoughtfully at the bayou. "As a matter of fact, I do know a local gentleman. Let me write his name down for you on my business card." He wrote on the back of a card and handed it to Clete. "Tell him I sent you."

"Thanks a lot. I appreciate this," Clete said, holding up the card, sticking it into his shirt pocket.

CLETE FINISHED HIS BREAKFAST, then called me on his cell phone. "A guy with a hush-puppy accent and the name Ronald Bledsoe was messing around my Caddy. He's hinky as a corkscrew. Can you run him through the NCIC?"

"I already did."

"What'd you get back on him?"

"The same guy was out to Otis Baylor's house. Baylor thought he was weird, too. The National Crime Information Center has nothing on him."

"Why was this guy talking to Baylor?"

"He seemed to think Bertrand Melancon might have stashed stolen goods on Baylor's property. He claims to be working for the state."

"His business card says he's out of Key West. I called the number, but the phone is disconnected. He also referred me to a car detailer in Lafayette. The guy didn't recognize the name. You think he's working for Sidney?"

"Maybe."

"This guy is a real creep, Dave."

"How many PIs are normal people?"

"I can't believe you just said that."

"You know what I mean."

"I'm glad you explained that. Otherwise I would think you're insulting as hell."

CLETE HAD SAID that since Katrina he had heard the sounds of little piggy feet clattering to the trough. I think his image was kind. I think the reality was far worse. The players were much bigger than the homegrown parasites that have sucked the life out of Louisiana for generations. The new bunch was educated and groomed and had global experience in avarice and venality and made the hair-oil and polyester crowd in our state legislature look like the Ecclesiastical College of Cardinals. Think of an inverted pyramid. Staggering sums of money were given to insider corporations who subcontracted the jobs to small outfits that used only nonunion labor. A $500 million contract for debris removal was given to a company in Miami that did not own a single truck, then the work was subcontracted to people who actually load debris and haul it away. Emergency roof repairs, what are called "blue roof jobs," involved little more than taking down rolls of blue plastic tarp on plywood. FEMA provided the tarp free. Insider contractors got the jobs for one hundred dollars a square foot and paid the subs two dollars a square foot. In the meantime, fifty thousand nonunion workers were brought into the city, most of them from the Caribbean, and were paid an average of eight to nine dollars an hour to do the work.

Why dwell on it? It's unavoidable. It became obvious right after Katrina that the destruction of New Orleans was an ongoing national tragedy and probably an American watershed in the history of political cynicism. I knew early on that the events taking place in New Orleans now would lay large claim on the rest of my career if not my life. If I had been able to convince myself otherwise, the call I was about to receive from Special Agent Betsy Mossbacher would have quickly disillusioned me.

"Sorry to bother you again, but I've got some conflicting information here regarding a Felix Ramos, street name Chula Ramos. This guy and his buddy were supposed to be transferred from the Iberia Parish Prison into our custody," she said.

"That's right. He and his fall partner got nailed at a meth lab. I interviewed both of them. That was right before Katrina. You guys were supposed to pick them up."

"Two informants, independently of each other, say Chula is working as an electrician and plumber in New Orleans. I've talked to five different people in Iberia Parish, including your jailer. No one seems to know where Ramos is or what happened to him or if he ever existed. Can you explain that?"

"How about his partner?"

"His partner is in the stockade. There's no problem with his partner. Not unless you guys lose him before we can get down there."

"I'll get back to you."

I called the parish prison and the district attorney. Then I went into Helen's office. "The FBI thinks we've lost Felix Ramos, one of those guys who—"

"Yeah, the one who called me a queer in Spanish."

"Yeah, that one," I said, my eyes slipping off hers. "The ADA who caught the case says he was marked for transfer to federal custody, so she put everything on hold. In fact, she thought the FBI had already picked him up."

"Maybe they did. Maybe they lost him in their own system."

"Betsy Mossbacher isn't one to screw up like that. She says Ramos may be drawing paychecks in New Orleans. A lot of MS-13 guys are in the trades."

"Give me a few minutes," she said.

I went back to my office. It was almost quitting time. I felt like I was in a bad dream, unable to extract myself from New Orleans and the Melancon-Rochon shooting and the probable homicide of Jude LeBlanc. I wanted to go home and eat a hot supper with my family and perhaps walk down Main Street with them in the twilight and have a dessert on the terrace behind Clementine's restaurant. I wanted to have a normal life again.

My extension buzzed. "Ramos's name got misspelled on the arrest report," Helen said. "The misspelling went into the computer. We have three other inmates in custody who have similar names. One of them finished his sentence during Rita. The day he was supposed to get out he was at Iberia General for treatment of a venereal infection. Felix Ramos walked out in his stead. To top it off, the ADA says the bust probably won't hold anyway. Ramos was a hundred feet from the lab when it was raided and there's no evidence or witness statements to put him inside it. Nothing like drinkin' rum and Coca-Cola on the bayou, huh, boss?"

IN THE MORNING I decided the only way to deal with the Melancon-Rochon file was to hit it head-on and to stop giving a free pass to people who had lied to me. There was no conventional telephone service in New Orleans and I doubted there would be any for a long time. I called Otis Baylor and asked if he had a cell number for his next-door neighbor, Tom Claggart. "There might be one in my Rolodex," he said.

"Do you mind looking it up?"

After a pause, he said, "Just a minute."

He came back to the phone and gave me the number, but he did not hide his impatience well. "Does your call to Tom Claggart concern us?"

"I'm not sure. But it's a police matter, Mr. Baylor. We're not obligated to inform the public about the content of an investigation or the procedures we follow. I think it's important we all understand that."

He eased the telephone back into the cradle, breaking the connection.

I punched in Claggart's cell number. He answered on the third ring. "Tom Claggart," he said.

"This is Dave Robicheaux again. I need to check a discrepancy between—"

"How'd you get this number?"

"That's not the issue, Mr. Claggart."

"It is to me. My cell number is private."

"Would you like to conduct this interview in handcuffs?"

"I'm sorry. We're under a lot of pressure here. I should have gone with Otis Baylor. He can be a pain in the ass, but at least he's honest."

"Say again?"

"I should have bought my insurance policy from Otis. My carrier is sticking it to me. I hear Otis has been approving his clients' water-damage claims on the spot. I bet his company is shitting their pants."

I tried to get the conversation back on track. "There's a discrepancy between your statement to me and the account you gave a private investigator regarding the shooting of the looters. You told me you were asleep and you heard and saw nothing. Do you stand by that statement?"

"I had a few drinks that night. Things got kind of mixed up."

"Did you tell the private investigator one of the looters was in the Baylor driveway, that maybe he left stolen goods there?"

"I don't remember saying that. I mean, I don't remember saying that last part."

"The investigator's name is Ronald Bledsoe. Do you remember that name?"

"I think so."

"Can you come into my office?"

"No, I can't do that. I'm all tied up here. I don't know what all this is about."

Why had he lied? Was it because he had done nothing to stop the looters? Was he simply trying to hide the fact he was a blowhard? People lie over less.

"You told Bledsoe the truth?"

"Maybe I saw one of those black guys in the shadows. But I didn't see the shooting. Look, I just want out of this."

"Out of what?"

"Everything. I didn't hurt anyone. Leave me alone."

I could almost smell his fear on the other side of the connection. "Mr. Claggart?"

He clicked off his cell.

In my mind's eye I saw a man whose eyes were tightly shut, his hand clenched around his cell phone as he tried to rethink every misstep he had just made. I saw a man who despised himself for his own weakness and who now carried the extra burden of knowing that through his own volition he had revealed himself to others as a liar and a fraud if not a coward. Also he had blurted out that he had not "hurt anyone," when in fact no one had accused him of doing so. There was a very good chance Tom Claggart was speaking of another incident, perhaps another crime, of which I had no knowledge. For whatever reason, he had done all these things to himself, without external provocation. I believe that Tom Claggart had just discovered that stacking time on the hard road is a matter of definition and not geography.

AFTER I HUNG UP, I assembled three photo lineups. A photo lineup is composed of six mug shots inserted in a cardboard holder. Among the six photos only one is of the suspect. Ideally the other photos should be of people in the same age range and of the same race as the suspect. The photo lineup has several advantages. The viewer, who is often a victim of a violent crime, is spared public embarrassment and is less fearful of retaliation from the suspect's friends and relatives and hence less apt to be influenced by the presence of either prosecutors or defense attorneys in a police station environment. Secondly, jailhouse photography indicates by its nature that the suspect has been put away previously and hence can be put away again.

I inserted mug shots of Andre Rochon, Eddy Melancon, and Bertrand Melancon among their peers, dropped all three lineups in a brown envelope, and drove up Old Jeanerette Road to Otis Baylor's house while a sun shower chained the bayou with rain rings.

I cannot say what I thought I would accomplish. I was tired of people lying to me, that was obvious, but I wanted to confront Otis Baylor for another reason. As Americans we are a peculiar breed. We believe in law and order, but we also believe that real crimes are committed by a separate class of people, one that has nothing to do with our own lives or the world of reasonable behavior and mutual respect to which we belong. As a consequence, many people, particularly in higher income brackets, think of police officers as suburban maintenance personnel who should be treated politely but whose social importance is one cut above that of their gardeners.

Ever watch reality cop shows? Check out the guys who are always streaking through wash lines and across darkened yards, their tennis shoes flopping on their feet, their crime of the day possession of a dime bag. What conclusion does the viewer arrive at? Crimes are committed by shirtless pukes. Slumlords and politicians on a pad get no play.

It was time that someone put a human face on the men who ate a high-velocity round directly opposite Otis's front door.

I had assumed Otis Baylor would still be home. But he wasn't. "Can you tell me where he is?" I asked his daughter on the gallery.

"He's probably down in Vermilion Parish, down by the coast. His company covered a lot of the houses down there."

"I understand your old man is standing up for his clients."

"Standing up, like?" she replied, her eyelids fluttering as though she could barely deal with my impaired abilities.

"Your dad is making good on his clients' water-damage claims. I hear a lot of people aren't that lucky."

"Maybe my father will end up working as a route manager for the newspaper, too."

"Could we sit down somewhere?"

"I have a class at one."

"Is your mother home?"

"I told you, she's my stepmother. And no, she's not here."

"I don't want to be rude, Miss Thelma, but I'm pretty tired of your bad manners. Step out in the light, please."

"What for?"

"We'd like to make sure we have a positive ID on the men who were looting your neighborhood. One of these guys is dead and one is a vegetable who was kidnapped and possibly tortured because he knows where some stolen property is hidden. I don't want any more sarcastic remarks from you. In truth, I think your family is about to drown in its own shit. Maybe you can do them a favor by being honest for a change."

We were standing in the yard now. She was trying to blow off the lecture she had just gotten, but her face was white inside the black rectangle of her hair, her bottom lip twitching. I seemed to tower over her and I didn't like the feeling it gave me.

"Here," I said, putting the lineup holders in her hand. "Do any of these guys look like the ones you saw in front of your house the night of the shooting?"

She began sifting the holders, sliding one stiffly against the other, perfunctorily, her eyes not quite focused, as though she already knew she would not recognize any of the men. But I did not expect what happened next. She widened her eyes, not in surprise but in an attempt to control the water welling into them.

"Look, kiddo, I was a little hard on you there. Sit down in the glider and take your time. You and your family are decent people. Y'all got hit by a wrecking ball, but eventually you'll get this behind you."

She sat down heavily in the glider and I realized that something far more serious was on her mind than seeing again the faces of men who had been looting her neighborhood.

"What is it?" I said.

"What is what? I've never seen any of these people. It was dark. I was still half asleep. How could I recognize these people?"

Her fingers were pinched tightly on the photo holders. Then, almost as an afterthought, she pushed them at me. I didn't offer to take them. "You don't recognize anybody in those mug shots?" I said.

"No, I just told you. I don't know who they are."

I sat down next to her. I could hear the chains on the glider biting into the oak bark overhead. "Look at me, Thelma."

"I don't want to look at you. Please go, Mr. Robicheaux. I have an anthropology class. I have to get ready."

I took the photos from her hands. "Why do you want to lie? Why not admit you recognize someone in these photos? Was it you who fired the rifle?"

"No. I've never fired a gun in my life. I hate guns."

Then she pressed the palm of her hand over her mouth and began to gag. I placed my hand on her back. Her shirt was damp with perspiration and it flattened and stuck against her skin. I could feel her muscles constricting with each breath she drew. A tremor rippled through her body and she began to sob and shake all over.

Suddenly I knew her secret. Only one kind of injury produces the level of injury and misery she was experiencing. It's of a kind that never goes away, that carries with it an unearned sense of shame and dishonor and humiliation and rage that the worst of my own memories cannot compete with.

"These are the guys who raped you, aren't they?"

"No," she said, swallowing, drawing it back inside herself, wiping the tears off her cheeks with her fingers.

"Yes, they are, Thelma."

"No, you mustn't say that."

"Somehow they blundered into your life again. You recognized them and you told your old man. You won't admit that because you're afraid you'll provide us with the motivation for his shooting them."

"Don't do this to us, Mr. Robicheaux."

"You're a stand-up kid. But you're not thinking clearly. As soon as you told your father these were the guys who attacked you, he had every right to use violent force to protect his home and family. Get a good lawyer and tell him the truth, then come into our office and do the same."

But she was already running for the inside of her house, like a little girl who has just been tricked into betraying the only friend she has.

CHAPTER
16

CLETE PURCEL'S ADVICE on dealing with mainline perps and full-time dirtbags was simple: When they deal the play, you bust them or dust them. But what about a guy who didn't have a category? Or worse, one who operated without handles?

Early Saturday morning, Alafair went to City Park with Clete, jogging with him down a serpentine asphalt path that led through live oaks still deep in shadow. Somehow she had convinced herself she could wean him from his diet of booze and fried food and the self-delusion that clanking iron three times a week while he drank a pitcher of vodka Collins would control his weight and reduce his blood pressure.

Rain clouds had sealed the sky and inside the trees the air was warm and almost luminescent with humidity. Clete and Alafair jogged past the old brick firehouse, then across close-cropped St. Augustine grass that was emerald green from the rains, past camellia bushes and islands of hyacinths floating in the bayou and a cypress pond set in the center of the park. They thumped across a wood pedestrian bridge and caught the asphalt again, their eyes stinging with sweat, the smell of burning leaves clinging to their skin. Up ahead they saw a man sitting in a picnic shelter, tying his tennis shoe, his mouth twisted in a self-amused smile. He was overdressed for the morning, his navy blue workout pants dark with sweat below his waist, his matching windbreaker open on a T-shirt that was glued to his breastbone.

"See that dude with the caved-in face?" Clete said, panting with the effort.

"What about him?" Alafair said.

"He's bad news. Cut across the grass."

Alafair followed Clete as he angled back toward the bayou, running through shade trees again, down into depressions sprinkled with leaves, tannic with the smell of gas. Then she made a mistake. She looked back over her shoulder at the man with an elongated head and a face that seemed to have melted and been remolded to resemble the back of a thumb.

A moment later she heard a man's feet pounding the sod behind her, his breath coming hard in his throat.

"Thought that was you," the man said to Clete. "Who's your young friend?"

Clete slowed, working hard to catch his wind. "We're on our run, here," he said.

"Watch this," the man said. He sprang onto a picnic bench and caught a limb with both hands, grinning from ear to ear, his exposed stomach fish-belly white, splayed with black hair. He dropped to the ground with a thump. He wiped his hands on the front of his windbreaker, his smile still in place. His eyes were green and recessed, playful as marbles. "I'm Ronald," he said to Alafair.

"How do you do?" she said.

"You didn't tell me your name," he said.

"She didn't give it. We need to finish our regimen, here, Mr. Bledsoe. I'll chat you up some other time," Clete said.

"You're all out of breath, there. I've got cold drinks in my cooler. I have some po'boy sandwiches as well." His eyes shifted to Alafair, lighting with curiosity or perhaps a proprietary sense that he knew and had claim on her. "Are you Mr. Purcel's daughter?"

"No, I'm not."

Clete placed both of his hands against a tree trunk, breathing through his nose, his heart rate starting to drop, his head spinning. "I don't know how else to say this to you, podjo, but you seriously need to dee-dee. That means beat feet down the road. No insult intended."

"You from South Ca'lina?" Bledsoe asked, ignoring Clete, stiffening an index finger playfully at Alafair.

She looked at her watch and rubbed the glass clean with her wrist. She tapped on it with a fingernail, as though the second hand were stuck. In the silence the man named Bledsoe shifted his weight, his shoe crunching a pecan husk.

"I knew a girl 'cross the line in Savannah, looked just like you," he said. "She was part Indian and had the same kind of coloring. She had long legs and wore an ankle bracelet, the kind with little charms all over it. You could hear her jingling when she walked. I always got a kick out of her."

"Go on without me for a minute," Clete said to Alafair.

"Dave and Molly are expecting us, Clete," she replied, squeezing his upper arm. "Let's go."

He put his car keys in her hand. "Bring the Caddy around. I blew my circuits. I'll be all right in a minute." He winked. "Believe me, I'm copacetic here."

The keys felt heavy and hard inside her palm, foreign and reductive somehow, as though their presentation to her had relegated her to the level of an object, one that required protection. The sun came out and she saw motes of desiccated leaves swimming in the shafts of light that fell through the tree overhead. The air was damp and stained with the septic odor of a public restroom a few feet away. She wiped a cloud of mosquitoes out of her face and felt a surge of anger like a bubble rising in her chest. A fox squirrel clattered across a limb above her head and involuntarily she looked up at it. When she lowered her gaze, the man named Ronald Bledsoe was staring at her, intrigued, his eyes roving over her features and the broken lines of sweat trickling into her sports bra.

"I'm going to get my friend's car and come back for him," she said. "If you bother my friend or me in this park again, I'll have you arrested."

"I wouldn't offend you for the world," Bledsoe said, placing his hand on his heart. "But you still haven't told me your name, little darlin'."

She walked back to the parking area by the concrete boat ramp and started up Clete's Caddy, the exhaust pipe coughing a cloud of oil smoke into the air. As she drove back toward the clump of oak trees, she saw Clete talking heatedly to Bledsoe, like a third-base coach angry at an umpire, his arms pumped. All the while, Bledsoe continued to look back at Clete without speaking, nodding occasionally, his mouth forming a smile that made her think of earthworms constricting on a hand-rolled piece of pie dough. She drove out onto the grass and stopped the car a few feet from them. The top of the Caddy was down and leaves drifted out of the trees onto the leather seats. "Time to boogie, Cletus," she said.

"You got it," he said, pulling open the passenger door, looking back over his shoulder, his face as hot as a slap.

Alafair turned the convertible around and headed out of the park. She looked in the rearview mirror. "What'd that guy say?" she said.

"Nothing. He's just one of those guys who's a couple of quarts down."

But wheels were turning in Clete's head all the way back to the house, his sweat drying in a glaze on his skin. She pulled the Caddy to the curb in front of the house and got out. "Tell me what he said, Clete."

"The guy's a meltdown. Just stay away from him." He slid behind the wheel and rubbed his palms along its surface and clicked the radio on and off.

"Stop acting like a dope and tell me what he said."

Clete blew out his breath and lifted his eyes up to hers. "How about I take y'all to dinner tonight?" he replied.

DOWN THE STREET, Clete got stuck behind a tourist bus in front of an antebellum home called the Shadows. He turned out of the traffic at the red light and headed down St. Peter's Street toward his motor court, punching in my number on his cell.

"Dave?"

"Hey, Clete."

"We ran into this character Ronald Bledsoe in the park," he said. "He was coming on wise to Alafair."

"In what way?" I asked.

"Innuendos mostly. But . . ."

"But what?"

"The guy gives me the chills. His eyes were all over Alafair's body. The guy's a sadist. You can smell it on him. Can Alafair hear you now?"

"She's not here."

"What do you mean? I just dropped her off."

I put down the phone and looked out the front door and through the side window. "She's not here, Clete. What did this guy say?"

"I sent her to get the car. He watched her walk away, then he said, 'Old enough to bleed, old enough to butcher. That's what country people say back in South Ca'lina.'"

"I'll call you back," I said.

I knocked the garbage can into an oak tree getting out of the driveway.

ALAFAIR HAD JOGGED back down East Main and crossed the drawbridge at Burke Street, taking long strides, breathing evenly, the bottoms of her running shoes ringing on the bridge's steel grid. The sun was well above the trees now, the bayou's surface bladed with mirrorlike reflections that made her eyes water. Up ahead, inside the park, she saw the man who called himself Ronald Bledsoe standing under a picnic shelter, gazing across the bayou in the direction of her house.

She jogged down the asphalt path, then slowed to a walk, studying the ground as she did, Bledsoe's silhouetted image hovering on the edge of her vision. Dave would have told her not to confront a defective man, not to empower those whose destructive energies always turned against them if you left them alone. But Clete had treated her as he would a child and then had tried to conceal information from her, as though she were incapable of dealing with the world. And Bledsoe had violated her with his eyes and his language and the lascivious curl of his mouth, and had gotten away with it.

She walked down to the bayou's edge, perhaps thirty feet from the picnic shelter. She tossed a stick into the current. The wind wrinkled the water's surface and carried with it the smell of charcoal starter flaring on a grill.

"I knew you'd be back," Bledsoe said from the edge of her vision.

"Is that right?" she replied.

He was sitting on the picnic table now, one foot resting on a bench, his smile like a slit upturned at the corners. "Know how I knew that?"

"No, but why don't you tell me?" she said.

"'Cause you don't let people push you around."

"Really?"

"You have sharp edges. That means people cain't get over on you. That means you don't let an older man boss you around."

The stick she had tossed into the water spun on the edge of the current, a green horsefly resting on top of it. "I didn't want you to have a wrong impression back there," she said.

"I know that. I know what you gonna think before you think it, darlin'."

"You see, I am Indian. I was born in a village in El Salvador. A Catholic priest tried to fly my mother and me into the United States, but we crashed off Southwest Pass. My mother drowned in the plane. I think she was a brave woman."

"You have quite a history. It seems you're educated, too. But you got something else on your mind, too, don't you, little sweetheart? You weren't gonna let Mr. Purcel treat you like you don't know your own mind about things."

He reached into a cooler and removed a dark bottle of beer with a silver and gold label on it. He made a ring with his thumb and forefinger and wiped the crushed ice from the surface, then cracked off the cap. He stepped out into the sunlight and approached her, his hand cupped around the bottle's coldness. "Here," he said. "Put this in your mouth and tell me how you like it."

"I told you about my mother because I wanted you to understand I couldn't care less about the racist and sexist remarks of a peckerwood degenerate. Because of your impoverished background and your cultural ignorance, we're going to let you slide with a C minus as a human being and hope you go away someplace where the standards are minimal. But that's a one-time-only exception. You shouldn't presume you'll be treated as generously in the future. Are you able to follow what you have just heard?"

"Darlin', I've cut it all over the country—black and white girls, Indians, Hispanics, an Eskimo girl once. I think of them all with respect. But it's not the saddle that counts. It's the man who climbs in it." He stepped between her and the sun, his face dropping into shadow. She could smell his deodorant and the peppermint mouthwash on his breath. His hand was moist when he fitted it on her bicep. His fingers began to massage her muscle. "Want to take a ride? In my car, I mean. Down to the bay?"

"Let go of me."

He leaned forward and began to whisper. She felt his spittle touch her skin and his breath probe her ear. The next moment was one she remembered only in terms of images and sensations rather than in a linear fashion. She stepped backward, spinning and pulling loose from his grasp simultaneously. Her left leg came up so quickly from the ground, he never saw it coming. His feet must have been set solidly because he took the blow full on the mouth, his nose and lips bursting under the sole of her shoe.

The beer bottle rolled down the embankment into the water. Bledsoe cupped both his hands to his face and walked half crouched to the picnic shelter, sitting down like a man who was holding his brains inside his head. I braked my truck by the shelter and got out, unsure of what I was seeing. Bledsoe picked a broken tooth off the heel of his right hand and stared at it. Then he grinned at me, his lips bright red. "Bet I know who you are. You're her daddy, Mr. Purcel's friend. My name is Ronald. What's yours?"

THAT AFTERNOON, the sky was glistening with humidity when I parked my pickup truck in front of Sidney Kovick's flower shop in Algiers. Across the river, New Orleans was sweltering in mold and receding pools of sewage, and from a distance looked deserted of automobiles and people. Clete stared at the city of his birth for a long time, then he and I went inside the shop. Sidney came out of the back, a full-length clean apron hung from his neck and tied around his waist. As always, his face showed no expression. Behind him, his wife Eunice said hello by jiggling the fingers of one hand at us.

"I'll make it quick, Sidney," Clete said. "I found some money that was probably washed out of a garage up the street from your house. I took it to Tommy the Whale for his opinion on it. He told me it was queer, so I put it in an envelope, marked it 'FBI,' and dumped it in a mailbox. I don't know if it was your queer or not, but I would have dumped it in a mailbox just the same. That doesn't give you the right to sic this Bledsoe fuck on me."

"Watch your language," Sidney said.

"What Clete is saying to you, Sidney, is you've probably placed a dangerous man in our midst," I said. "This morning he made some nasty remarks to my daughter. She kicked his teeth in, but I suspect he'll be back around. If that happens, I'm going to punch his ticket. But I'm going to punch yours first."

Sidney drew in his cheeks, as though he were gathering the spittle in his mouth, his nostrils swelling slightly as he breathed in and out. He closed the door to the back of the shop and faced us again. "The pukes started this, not me. Two of them got what they deserved. The other two give me back what's mine, all these other problems go away. You guys are screwing with something that's way over your heads."

"Oh yeah? Check this out, Sidney. I was in Saigon when pogey bait such as yourself were funneling PX goods to the VC, so clean the mashed potatoes out of your mouth."

Below the level of the counter, I touched Clete's upper thigh to shut him up.

"You've always had two problems, Purcel. You're ninety-proof most of the time and you never learned how to keep that fat dick in your pants. It cost you your career and your marriage, and everybody in New Orleans knows it except you, so they tolerate you the same way they do a child. But don't never come around here acting disrespectfully in front of my wife again."

"We're losing the thread here, Sidney," I said.

"No, let him talk," Clete said.

I kept my eyes focused on Sidney's, trying to keep an invisible wall between me and Clete and the obvious injury Sidney had done to him. "My daughter is not a player in this. This man Bledsoe insulted her without provocation. You want respect for your own family, but you're not giving it to mine. What do you think we should do about that?"

"Who says this guy Bledsoe works for me?"

"We're talking as family men, Sidney. If you want to blow smoke at us, we're through here. I thought more of you."

His face was opaque, impossible to read. "I got no say in what happens over in New Iberia."

"I'm sorry to hear you take that attitude," I said.

"The pair of you walk in here like your shit don't stink and threaten me in my own store, and it's me who's got the problem? I know what loss is, Dave. You say you're gonna punch my ticket? I got news for you. I paid my dues a long time ago."

Our visit was pointless. Sidney was now using the accidental death of his son as a shield against his own criminality. I cannot say if this was because of his narcissism or a genuine belief that the gods had wronged him and had thereby made him unaccountable for the damage he did to others. But either way, Sidney knew how to wrap himself inside the role of victim.

I hit Clete on the shoulder. "Let's go, podna," I said.

"This isn't over, Sidney. I kicked your ass all over Magazine when we were kids. I can do it again," Clete said.

I opened the door for Clete, the bell ringing over my head. But he remained stationary in front of the counter, the blood in the back of his neck climbing into his hairline, his fists balled, the accusation of drunk and womanizer and disgraced cop embedded in him like a rusty fishhook. Sidney began pulling dead flowers from a vase, shaking the water off the stems before he dropped them in a wastebasket. He glanced up at Clete. "You still here?" he said.

I waited for Clete in the truck. When he came out of the flower shop, his expression was somber, his tropical shirt damp on his skin, his porkpie hat tilted at an angle on his forehead. He made me think of a haystack. Even in the Marine Corps his fellow jarheads had called him "the Heap," out of sync, consumed by his own appetites, instantly recognized as a troublemaker by authority figures. But his greatest vulnerability always lay in the power he gave away to others, in this case to Sidney Kovick.

He got into the truck and eased the door shut, restraining his energies so as not to show his anger and sense of defeat.

"Blow it off, Clete. You've cut Kovick slack when he deserved a bullet in the mouth," I said.

"I let him wipe his feet on me."

"No, you didn't. Sidney Kovick is a pimp. Anyone who has a conversation with him wants to take a shower afterward."

But Clete wasn't buying it. I started up the truck and drove to the end of the block, then turned up the street that led past the alley behind Sidney's shop. I glanced down the alley as we passed. Amid the trash cans and the clusters of banana trees between the garages, I could see a floral delivery van parked at the back door of Sidney's shop. Sidney's wife was helping a Hispanic man load flowers in the side of the van. I stepped on the brake and shoved the transmission into reverse.

"What's going on?" Clete said.

"The guy in the alley with the Gothic-letter tats. He looks just like Chula Ramos," I said.

"Who?"

"The MS-13 dude, Natalia Ramos's brother. He was released from the Iberia stockade by mistake."

"The brother of the hooker who was shacked up with the priest?"

"Yeah, that one."

"You really want to mess with this, Dave?"

"Yeah, I do."

I bounced into the alley and headed toward the van. An elderly woman backed a gas-guzzler out of a garage, wedging her vehicle at an angle between the garage and a cast-iron Dumpster. When I blew my horn at her, she responded by staring at me aghast, then taking off her glasses and wiping them with a Kleenex so she could see me more clearly. I hung my badge out the window and waved for her to pull her car out of the way. She stepped on the accelerator and smashed her taillight into the Dumpster.

I got out of my truck and started walking toward the delivery van. "Hold on there, bubba," I called, not sure if I was actually looking at Ramos.

The Hispanic man slammed the driver's door behind him and drove away.

"What's the trouble, Dave?" Eunice said.

"Who's your delivery man?"

"It's Chula something-or-other. Did he do something?"

I heard Clete walk up behind me. "How'd you come to know this guy, Eunice?" I asked.

"Sidney gave him a job. Chula's sister used to clean Sidney's office in the Quarter."

"Natalia was Sidney's maid?" I said.

"Yes, they're Central American refugees, I think. Sidney wanted to help them. Why?"

I looked at her face. It was clear of guile or deception. Even though Eunice was a big-boned countrywoman and the butt of jokes among NOPD cops, she seemed possessed of an inner beauty. I tried to keep my eyes and face empty. I did not want Eunice to learn of her husband's lies from me.

"Do you have an address or phone number for Chula? I think he might have some information that could be helpful to a federal agent I know."

"I doubt it. Chula comes and goes in his spare time. I think he's working on a FEMA job and living in a bunkhouse. He'll bring the van back about eight. You want to come back or leave him a message?"

"No, that's all right. I'll catch him another time. In fact, forget I was here, will you?"

"If that's what you want."

"It's nice seeing you again, Eunice."

"Same here, Dave." When she smiled, I was convinced, as always, that she had become the most beautiful woman in New Orleans.

I walked back to the truck with Clete. As I started the engine he took off his hat and combed his hair. He slipped his comb in his shirt pocket and put his hat back on. "Sidney was porking the girl from El Sal?" he said.

"That's what it sounds like."

"Why would Eunice want to marry a bucket of shit like that?"

I shrugged and looked at him. I could almost hear the wheels turning in his head. "Pull around in front of the shop," he said.

"You're going to bring him down in front of his wife?"

"Don't worry about it. Just stay in the truck."

"That's no good, Clete."

He opened the passenger door while the truck was moving and got out. He slammed the door and looked back through the window. "You quit judging me, Streak."

Kovick was still behind the counter when Clete reentered the store. "Hey, Sidney, I got something to tell you," he said.

"What's that, Purcel?"

"It's going to surprise you. But try to live with it and adjust and come out on the sunny side of things. Diggez-vous?"

"No, I don't diggez-vous. And I'm not really interested, either."

"I bounced your head off a sidewalk when we were kids. I'm sorry I did that. Just keep Bledsoe away from Dave's daughter. I got no personal beef with you."

"That's the big news flash?"

"Yeah, that's it. Lock your flopper in a vault while you're at it."

Sidney stuck a matchstick in his mouth and rolled it across his teeth, searching for the design in Clete's words.

When Clete got back in the truck, his expression was serene. He clicked the door shut and smiled at me with his eyes.

"What happened in there?" I said.

"Nothing."

"What do you mean 'nothing'?"

"Nothing. That's the point," he said. "Come on, let's motor, big mon."

CHAPTER
17

On Monday morning I called Betsy Mossbacher at the FBI and told her that Chula Ramos was probably working part-time as a delivery man for Sidney Kovick.

"Delivering what?" she said.

"Maybe just flowers. Look, Clete Purcel and I told Sidney we knew he had been stashing counterfeit in his house. He said something to the effect Clete and I were in over our heads."

"What does Purcel have to do with this?"

"Not a lot."

"Some counterfeit money showed up in a Morgan City mailbox. The engraving and paper are impressive. Is this the money we're talking about?"

"It could be."

"You tell Purcel to stay out of federal business."

The purpose of my call was slipping away, and I think that's the way Betsy wanted it. I didn't take the bait. "Why would Kovick tell us we're in over our heads?" I asked.

"I think he's convinced himself he's a patriot defending his homeland. Personally I think he's psychotic. An agent in Mississippi believes Kovick's goons poured the body of Kovick's neighbor into the foundation of a casino in Biloxi."

"You're losing me, Betsy."

"The Taliban funds al Qaeda with the sale of heroin. You don't think they're capable of other criminal enterprises?"

I still didn't know what she was talking about and I wasn't going to guess. "I need a favor from you," I said. "A guy named Ronald Bledsoe may try to harm my daughter. He claims to be a PI out of Key West, but Tallahassee has almost nothing on him, except the fact he got a license through a bail-bonds office about ten years back. Neither does the NCIC. I'm convinced he's a dangerous and depraved man, the kind who leaves shit-prints somewhere. But so far I haven't found them."

"Have you run him through AFIS?"

"Not yet."

"Give it a try. In the meantime, I'll do what I can. What did your daughter do to this guy?"

"Busted his nose and lips and knocked out one of his teeth."

"He's pissed over that?"

But jokes about Ronald Bledsoe weren't funny.

THREE DAYS EARLIER a Guatemalan illegal had been stripping cypress planks off a wall inside the entranceway of a historic New Orleans home. The workman made eight dollars an hour and feared civil authority in this country and his own. But he feared losing his job even more. The contractor who had hired him specialized in the restoration of historical properties. The contractor also made a sizable income by salvaging colonial-era brick, heart-pine floors, brass hinges and door knockers, square-head nails, milk-glass doorknobs, claw-foot bathtubs, iron wall hooks for cook pots, and grapeshot and .58-caliber minié balls embedded in housefronts during the White League takeover of New Orleans in 1874. Every item with possible resale value at a teardown or refurbish job went into a pile.

The workman from Guatemala sank his crowbar into a strip of rotten cypress and peeled it and a shower of Formosa termites onto the floor. Amid the sawdust and insects and spongelike wood he saw a blunted and bent metal-jacketed bullet, no bigger than half the size of his little finger. He blew the dust off it and examined its torn surfaces. "Hey, boss, what you wanta do wit' dis?" he asked.

• • •

Helen called me into her office just before quitting time. Raindrops had started to fall on her window and I could see trees bending in the wind by the cemetery. She was leaning forward on her desk, her chin propped on her fist. It was the kind of body English and opaque manner she used when she was preparing to tell me something I didn't want to hear.

"I just got off the phone with Betsy Mossbacher. She'll be here in an hour and a half," she said. "She has a federal warrant on Otis Baylor's house."

"I talked to her this morning. She didn't say anything about coming to New Iberia."

"She just got the warrant. Last week some repairmen working across the street from Baylor's house in New Orleans dug a rifle slug out of a wall. The contractor had heard about the Melancon-Rochon shooting and called NOPD. They passed it on to the FBI. The round is a thirty-aught-six. It came through a ventilated shutter and a glass pane behind it and embedded between two planks. She says it's in real good shape, considering the fact it may have gone through two people. Anyway, the Feds are jumping on it before word gets back to Baylor."

"So?"

"You need to be there when they serve the warrant."

"They don't need me to serve a search warrant."

"This is our parish. We cooperate with outside agencies, but we don't abandon our own jurisdiction to them. Get with the program, Streak."

I ate a sandwich in my office and met Betsy and another agent in the parking lot at 7:00 p.m. The sky was bright with rain in the west, the live oaks along Main a dark green as we drove out of town toward Jeanerette. I was sitting in the back of their vehicle, feeling like a hangnail, a perfunctory witness to the scapegoating of a man who had been caught up in events that were either beyond his control or his ability to bear them.

Betsy was quiet most of the way. I had the feeling she was not comfortable with her assignment that evening, either. Betsy was always the odd piece in the puzzle box, a straight arrow whose clumsiness and cowgirl manners gave her an unjustified reputation as an eccentric. As in the case of Helen Soileau, her male colleagues often made jokes about her behind her back. The truth was most of them weren't worth the parings of her fingernails.

"You say he's still got the Springfield?" the man behind the wheel said.

"That was the last indication he gave me," I replied.

The agent driving wore his hair boxed on his neck. He kept his hands in the ten-two position on the wheel, his eyes always on the road, never glancing in the rearview mirror when he spoke to me.

"Why wouldn't he dump the Springfield?" he said.

"Because he knows that's the first thing a guilty man would do."

"You're saying he's dirty for this?"

"No, I'm saying Otis is smart. I'm also saying he's probably taking somebody else's weight," I replied.

"Oh yeah? How did you arrive at that?" he asked.

"Hundreds if not thousands of New Orleans residents drowned who didn't have to. I suspect that's because some of the guys in Washington you work for couldn't care less. So a guy who sells insurance gets a chain saw up his ass. That's the way it shakes out sometimes."

This time his eyes shifted into the rearview mirror. "You guys down here have issues about something?"

"Not us. We're happy as clams," I replied.

Betsy gave me a look that would scald the paint off a battleship.

The grounds and trees outside Otis's house were dark with shadow when we arrived, the inside brightly lit, the air cool and filled with a fragrance of flowers and freshly baked bread in the kitchen and rainwater leaching out of the oaks into the leaves. His home was the picture of a family at peace with the world. But nothing could have been further from the truth, particularly after our arrival.

Betsy walked up on the screened-in gallery and knocked hard on the door, her mouth crimped, her ID in her hand. In the gloaming of the day, her hair had the bright yellow color of straw. She glanced at her watch and hit on the door again, this time harder, with the flat of her fist.

Otis answered, wearing a white shirt and tie, a piece of fried chicken in his hand.

"Are you Mr. Baylor?" she asked.

"Yes," he replied, his eyes going from Betsy to me, as though somehow I were his betrayer.

"I'm Special Agent Betsy Mossbacher. We have a warrant to search your house. I want you and your family to sit in the living room while we do. Where is your rifle, Mr. Baylor?"

"I'll get it for you," Otis replied.

"No, you won't. You and your wife and daughter and anyone else who is in the house will sit down in the living room, then you'll tell me where it is," she said.

"What the hell is this?" he said.

"Do what she says, Mr. Baylor," I told him.

He went back in the kitchen and returned with Thelma and Mrs. Baylor. After they sat down, the three of them looked up at us expectantly, as children might, caught between their inveterate American desire to obey the law and the fact that strangers who were basically no different or more powerful than themselves could walk into their home, during dinner, and treat them like livestock.

"The rifle is in the closet of the master bedroom," Otis said. "A box of shells is on the shelf. That's the only firearm in the house."

"Why are you doing this now? I thought all this was settled," Mrs. Baylor said. She had brought her drink from the table. It was tea-colored but had no ice in it. She was trying to appear poised, her back straight, her drink resting on her knee, but somehow she made me think of a china plate threaded with hairline cracks. "Is this being given to the media? Do you know what that will do to my husband's business?"

"No, ma'am, we don't report to the media," Betsy said. "We try to treat you in a respectful fashion. We try to be as unobtrusive as possible."

"Then why do you keep bothering us? This is where our tax money goes? For God's sakes, Otis, say something."

"The men who were shot in front of your house were shot in cold blood, Ms. Baylor. By anyone's definition, that's capital murder," Betsy said. "The seventeen-year-old had no criminal record and lost his life for committing a burglary. Vigilantes were hunting people of color in uptown New Orleans. My boss isn't going to let that stand."

"I'd like to contact my attorney. At this point I don't think we should have any further conversation with you," Otis said.

"That's your right, sir. But we're not your enemies," Betsy said.

"Stop lying," Thelma said.

"Say that again?" Betsy replied.

"You're here to put my father in prison. Stop pretending you're his friend. My father never hurt anybody in his life. You're scum, all of you," Thelma said.

"That's enough, Thelma," Otis said.

Betsy's colleague came from the back of the house with the Springfield looped upside down over his shoulder, the bolt open on the magazine. He carried a carton of .30-06 shells in his left hand. "The marine sniper's dream," he said.

Betsy looked down at Thelma. "Did you see the faces of those black dudes?" she said.

"Yes," Thelma said.

"Where?" Betsy said, surprised.

"Mr. Robicheaux showed me pictures of them the other day."

"Did you ever see them before the night they came to your house?" Betsy asked.

"No."

"Nobody in your family would have any reason to shoot them, huh?" Betsy said.

Thelma's mind was working fast now, her eyes locked on Betsy's, her expression as flat as paint on canvas. "You know that I was raped by black men, don't you? You're using what happened to me to build a case against my father."

"From what I know of your father, he wouldn't arbitrarily shoot someone. What about that, Thelma?" Betsy said.

"That's it. You have what you came for. Now please leave our home," Otis said.

"Give it some thought, Mr. Baylor. You're an intelligent man. We have a reason for taking your rifle. By noon tomorrow we may have evidence that can send you or a member of your family away for the rest of your life. Is that what you want?"

His eyes were glistening, his jaws locked tight.

Outside, I got in the back of the vehicle, glad to be gone from the Baylor home and the fear and angst we had just sowed inside it. The sky was dark now, the lights of houses reflecting off the surface of Bayou Teche. I could see Betsy's face in the glow of the dashboard. "You were pretty quiet inside, Dave," she said.

"It's like using a speargun on fish in a swimming pool," I said.

"Funny attitude for a cop," the man behind the wheel said.

Betsy was half turned in her seat, her eyes searching my face. "You know something you're not telling me," she said.

"Maybe."

"We're on the same side, aren't we, buddy? How about losing the role of the laconic man from Shitsville?" the driver said, looking in the rearview.

"Thelma Baylor looked stricken when I showed her mug shots of the looters. I think they're the guys who raped and tortured her. I think she wanted to conceal that fact from me because it would drive the nail in her dad's coffin."

"You just now decided to tell us that?" the driver said.

I leaned forward against my safety restraint. There were small pits in the back of the driver's neck, just below his boxed hairline. His jowls had a wrinkled sag in them, like those of a man whose face doesn't belong on his youthful body. "My conclusions are speculative in nature. In fact, they're based entirely on personal perception and have no prosecutorial value," I said.

The moon was bright overhead and the cane in the fields that had been mashed flat by Rita looked dry and hard on the ground, like thousands of discarded broom handles. The driver glanced at a row of Negro shacks speeding past us. Several of them had lost their tin roofs, and plywood and blue tarp had been nailed across the exposed joists. Up ahead, a drunk man was walking unsteadily along the side of the road, his body silhouetted by the neon beer sign on a rusted house trailer that served as a bar. "This is quite a place," the driver said. "A person needs to visit it to get the full bouquet."

THE NEXT MORNING a technician from the Acadiana Crime Lab lifted a print off Clete's car tag in the spot where Ronald Bledsoe had rubbed off the mud to see a number more clearly. We ran the print through the Automated Fingerprint Identification System and came up with nothing.

"I don't get it," I said to Helen. "Guys like this get in trouble."

"Maybe he's slicker than we think he is," she said. "Maybe that neurotic personality is manufactured. Maybe he works for the G."

"How about I figure a way to bring him in?"

"I don't want to step on your feelings, but legally Bledsoe is the victim, not the perpetrator. Your daughter remodeled his face with her foot. He could have her up on an A and B and sue y'all cross-eyed for good measure. Count your blessings, Pops."

"I don't see it that way."

"I didn't think you would," she replied.

I WENT HOME for lunch. Alafair was in her room, working on her first attempt at a novel, tapping away on a computer she had bought at a yard sale. I had offered to buy her a better one, but she had said a more expensive computer would not help her write better. She kept a notebook on her nightstand and wrote in it before going to sleep. She had already filled two hundred pages with notes and experimental lines for her book. Sometimes she awoke in the middle of the night and wrote down the dreams she had just had. When she awoke in the morning two scenes had already written themselves in her imagination and during the next few hours she would translate them into one thousand words of double-spaced typescript.

She often wrote out her paragraphs in longhand, then edited each paragraph before typing it on manuscript paper. She edited each typed page with a blue pencil and placed it facedown in a wire basket and began composing another one. If she caught me reading over her shoulder, she would hit me in the stomach with her elbow. The next morning she would revise everything she had written the previous day and then start in on the one thousand words she required of herself for the present day. I was amazed at how much fine work her system produced.

In high school she had been given special permission to enroll in a creative writing class taught by Ernest Gaines at the University of Louisiana at Lafayette. Gaines believed she had an exceptional talent. So did the admissions boards at Reed College in Portland. She was given an academic scholarship and received a degree in English literature last spring. She also earned a graduate fellowship at Stanford University, which she would enter this coming spring. The fact that she had gotten herself into a conflict with an aberration like Ronald Bledsoe was a source of frustration I could barely constrain, particularly when I needed to discuss it with her in a forthright fashion.

"Got a second, Alf?" I said.

She rested her hands in her lap, staring straight ahead, trying to conceal her vexation at being disturbed while she was writing. "Sure, what's going on?" she said.

I pulled up a chair by her desk. "We've run Bledsoe through AFIS and the National Crime Information Center, but he's a complete blank. In some ways that's more disturbing than finding a sheet on him. He's obviously a geek and geeks leave shit-prints. But this guy is the exception."

"So what's that tell you?" she asked.

"That he's slick or he has some juice behind him."

"He got what he deserved. I say fuck him."

"Do you have to talk that way?"

"He put his hand on me. I could feel his spittle in my ear. Want me to tell you what he said?"

"No."

"I didn't think so."

"Okay, Alf."

"Will you stop calling me that stupid name?"

"Look, one other thing, I may end up putting Otis Baylor in jail. I know you and Thelma are friends, so—"

"I got the message. How about giving me credit for having more than two brain cells?"

The years have not brought me much in the way of wisdom. But I have learned that the father of a young woman has to remember only two lessons in caring for his daughter: He must be by her side unreservedly when she needs him, and he must disengage when she doesn't. The latter, at least for me, has been more difficult than the former.

"You have more than two brain cells?" I said.

"Have you ever been hit in the head with a basketful of manuscript paper?" she said.

I WENT BACK to the department at 1:00 p.m. Wally, our hypertensive, elephantine dispatcher and full-time departmental comedian, stopped me on the way to my office. "I was just about to put these messages in your box," he said.

"Thanks, Wally," I said, taking three pink memo slips from his hand.

"His first name is Bertrand. He don't like to give his last name. He also don't have any manners."

"Was this a black kid?"

"Hard to tell. When a guy says, 'Pull the Q-tips out of your nose 'cause I cain't understand what you saying, you honky motherfucker,' does that mean the guy's got racial issues?"

"Could be. Thanks for taking the message, Wally."

"Glad to help out. I love this job. T'anks for introducing me to your friends."

I went to my office and punched in the cell number that Wally had written down on all three message slips. "Bertrand?" I said.

"Is that you, Mr. Dave?" a voice said.

Mr. Dave?

"Yeah, it is, Bertrand. What's up?"

"There's something weird going on. Somebody's handing out free cell phones to people that's in the life. Even people in the shelters, anybody who might know something about them stones. A phone number comes wit' the cell. I seen Andre wit' one. They come from Wal-Mart. Andre's attitude ain't making me feel real comfortable."

"What do you want from me?"

"What you said about me being a rapist was the troot'. I done it wit' Eddy and Andre—twice. We done it to a young girl in the Lower Nine. I been all over down there looking for her. I been in the shelters, too. Maybe she died in the storm."

I didn't want to be his confessor. In fact, my stomach turned at the image of three grown men sexually assaulting a helpless fifteen-year-old girl who'd had the bad luck to walk home from a street fair by herself.

"You still there?" Bertrand asked.

"Yeah, I'm here. You did the crime, stack the time."

But he wasn't listening. "The other girl was sitting in a car that was broke down by the Desire. She was white. She said she'd been at a high school prom. Eddy got pissed off at her and burned her with his cigarette. He burned her on her breasts."

"If you're looking for Valium for your sins, you called up the wrong guy."

"Who else I'm gonna tell, man? People all over the city got cell phones waiting to dime me. They say you call this certain number and a guy wit' this cracker voice tells them he gonna make them rich if they give me up. I walked past a guy in the shelter yesterday and he made these sounds like a chain saw starting up. Everybody t'ought it was funny."

"What happened to Father Jude LeBlanc?"

He paused, then I heard him take a breath. "We'd been at my auntie's house. A wave smashed right t'rou the picture window and washed us out the back. We swam up on this trash pile, but it was full of them brown recluse spiders, the kind that eat into your tissue and mess you up later. A woman was in the water wit' them brown spiders all over her face and in her hair. They was biting her and she was screaming and swatting at them and swallowing water at the same time. That's when we seen the priest pull his boat up to the church roof and start chopping a hole in it wit' an ax. That's when

Eddy said, 'It's that motherfucker or us.' We all went in the water and headed for him, wit' them spiders still in our clothes.

"I was the first one on the roof. I said, 'We need the boat. There's four of us and ain't but one of you. You can come wit' us, maybe, but we taking the boat.'

"He stops chopping and says, 'The attic is full of people. They gonna drown. You guys got to help me.'

"Help him? How I'm gonna help him, wit' Eddy and Andre and Kevin all looking at me to do something, like it's on me, like ain't nobody shooting off their mouth now, like *I* gotta do something, Eddy ain't such big shit no more? So I grabbed the ax. What was I suppose to do? Maybe he was gonna hit me wit' it. I seen a man shove a boy off an air mattress, just stuck his hand out and shoved him in the face, a boy wasn't more than ten years old. That's what it was like down there, man. You wasn't there."

"What did you do to Father LeBlanc?" I said, my heart beating, my palm clammy on the phone receiver.

"He wouldn't give up the ax. He was standing between me and the boat, on the edge of the roof. I went toward him and he just stood there and wouldn't get out of the way. I say, 'Man, we gonna get that boat one way or the other. Don't get fucked up for something you cain't change.'

"He says, 'You don't know what you're doing.' What'd he mean by that? I knowed what I was doing. I was saving my life. I was saving Eddy and Kevin and Andre's life. I knowed what I was doing. I ain't had no choice. How come he said that to me?"

"What did you do, Bertrand?"

"He started fighting wit' me. He wasn't strong at all. His arms was like sticks. He had tracks on them. I couldn't believe it, man, he was a priest and he was a junkie. I could see his teet' and smell his breath and he was clawing at my eyes. That's when I hit him, man, hard, wit' my fist, right in the face. He went over backward in the water and I heard Eddy say, 'Hit that motherfucker wit' the ax. Don't let him get into the boat.'

"But I ain't seen him again. The water was dark and it was like he went straight down the wall of the church into the darkness, like a stone statue sinking. How come he said them words to me? I knowed what I was doing, man. I was saving lives in my own way."

"Are you that stupid? Most of the people in that church attic died because of you. What do you think he meant?" I said.

Bertrand Melancon began to weep, uncontrollably. "I'm going to Hell, ain't I?"

You're wrong, kid. You're already there, I thought to myself.

CHAPTER
18

THE ARREST WARRANT with Otis Baylor's name on it was federal, but eventually the storm-impaired processes of the Orleans Parish DA's office would kick into gear and state charges would be filed against him as well. Ironically, the Feds were busting Otis under a Reconstruction statute that defined murder as a deprivation of a person's civil rights by the taking of his life, the same kind of Orwellian application of law that had been used to prosecute the Klansmen who lynched three civil rights workers in Neshoba County, Mississippi, in 1964. Otis had caught his necktie in the garbage grinder. I suspected that when the judicial system was finished with him, he would have to be washed off the grinder with a hose.

On Friday morning I accompanied Betsy Mossbacher's male colleague and a uniformed state trooper to Otis's temporary office on Main Street to serve the warrant. The FBI agent was the same agent who had retrieved the Springfield rifle from Otis's closet. His name was Tisdale and he was all business. We had parked our vehicles by the bayou, directly opposite Victor's Cafeteria, and were walking down Main under a colonnade when he said, "I've got to be back in Baton Rouge in less than ninety minutes. We've done all the paperwork on our end. All you've got to do is print him and get him into a cell. The transfer of custody will take place in two or three weeks. Don't fuck it up."

"Say that last part again?" I said.

"He's getting warehoused. It's not nuclear science. Feed him, give him a shower every three days, and don't lose him in the system like you did Chula Ramos. You got a question about anything, call Mossbacher. Don't do anything on your own. You got a problem, call us. That's the key. We're renting space in your gray-bar hotel. All you got to do is make sure the toilets flush."

I saw the state trooper look at me from the corner of his eye.

"Tell you what, bub, we'll arrest Otis for you and you can head back for Baton Rouge," I said. "Or, if you like, you can stand around as though you're part of the procedure, but you need to keep your mouth shut and stay out of the way."

"You like Lou'sana?" the trooper said to Tisdale, smiling broadly.

We busted Otis and took him out of his office in handcuffs, his long-sleeved white shirt crinkling, his tie blowing in the wind, his big arms pulled tightly behind him.

For most middle-class people, the word "jail" suggests punishment by means of confinement. To a degree, they're correct. Jails separate miscreants from the rest of us. But "confinement" doesn't come close to the realities of life inside any kind of serious can. The word "violation" is much more accurate.

It starts in the booking room. Your fingertips are rolled on an ink pad by someone you never saw before. Then you are told to clean your skin with a petroleum gel that looks like a glandular excretion. You are placed against a wall and told to hold a brace of numbers against your chest while you're photographed front and sideways. Then a polyethylene-gloved screw does a digital probe of your rectum and sprays you for crab lice. Your physical person belongs to people who do not want to know your name or make eye contact with you or have any level of communication with you. Most of them do not like what they do for a living and they do not like you.

You soon discover that jail is not a place but a condition. You defecate in full view of others. Your fellow inmates urinate all over the toilet seat you must use. The food you eat is prepared and served by people who wouldn't wash their hands at gunpoint. You take showers with men whose eyes linger on your genitalia and others who will shank you from your liver to your lights and that night sleep without dreaming.

As the twelve-string guitarist Huddie Ledbetter cautioned, you don't study your "great long time."

The recidivists of years ago have been replaced by a new breed of criminals, eighty-five percent of whom owe their lifestyle to narcotics, either the sale of it or the use of it or both. Some of them got their first hit of cocaine or morphine derivatives through the umbilical cord. Some of them were subjected to forms of child abuse that I will not discuss with anyone, not even fellow officers. Almost all of them will pay out their lives to the state on the installment system.

Otis Baylor thought he would call his lawyer or a bondsman and be back out on the street within a few hours. "That's right, isn't it?" he said to me in the booking room. "I get a phone call and then I post bond?"

"I don't think you understand your situation," I said. "You're actually in federal custody, charged with a civil rights violation. In effect, we're acting as friends of the federal court. That's because the legal system in southern Louisiana has been in meltdown since Rita and Katrina. My guess is you're going to be indicted by a state grand jury and prosecuted for murder. I wish I could tell you otherwise, but I don't think you're going anywhere for a long time."

"I'm not a flight risk. I own two houses here. I have a family. I've been with the same insurance company for over two decades."

"You'll be going to court eventually. Explain your situation to the judge."

He still had cleansing cream on his hands and he didn't want to touch his clothes with them. He began looking around for something to wipe his hands on.

"There's a roll of paper towels on the shelf," I said.

"I want my phone call," he said.

"You're going into a holding cell right now, Mr. Baylor. A deputy will escort you to a phone later," I said.

He couldn't seem to think. He squeezed at his temples and looked around the booking room, disoriented. "Where did you say the paper towels were?" he asked.

"Behind you, sir."

But he forgot what he was looking for. "My daughter is home by herself. She meets me for coffee and a doughnut each morning. She shouldn't be by herself for long periods of time," he said.

I've had prouder moments in my career.

MOLLY WORKED FOR a Catholic mutual-help center on the bayou that assisted poor people in starting up businesses and building their own homes. The charity had been founded by a group of Catholic Worker nuns who had come to southern Louisiana in the 1970s to organize the sugarcane workers. You can take a wild guess as to how they were received. But since that time, they had earned the respect and even the affection of most people in the area. After the death of my wife Bootsie, I met Molly by chance at the center and a short while later we were married. We were an incongruous couple, an Irish-American blue-collar nun who demonstrated regularly at the School of the Americas and a sheriff's detective with a history of violence and alcoholism. Friends who wanted to be kind wished us well, but I always saw the lights of pity and caution in their eyes.

But we surprised them. Sister Molly Boyle was my grail and I loved her in the same way I loved my church community.

On the Friday I busted Otis Baylor I called her at the center and asked her to meet me for lunch at the Patio Restaurant on Loreauville Road. We sat under a fan, in a corner, away from the crowd near the buffet table. I could feel her eyes on my face. "Bad day at Black Rock?" she said.

"I had to help the Feds serve an arrest warrant on Otis Baylor," I said. "He just got moved to the parish prison."

"Otis?"

"The FBI matched a bullet to a rifle in his house. The bullet has DNA on it from two gunshot victims."

"That's too bad. He's a nice man. I don't know how many people have told me he approved their insurance claims on the spot and put them up in motels. Some of these companies are sticking it to their clients with a cattle prod."

"Otis may have killed a seventeen-year-old kid and turned another one into a quadriplegic."

"I know," she said.

"I tried to warn him about his legal jeopardy."

She inched her hand forward and touched my fingertips. "I know that, Dave. This isn't your fault. Don't treat this personally."

"You want to get the buffet?" I said.

"Sure," she said. "Dave?"

"Yes?"

I could see the uncertainty in her face, like that of a person about to light a candle in a storage room that smells of gasoline. "Ronald Bledsoe came to the center this morning. He asked the reception-ist if we were operating any shelters in St. Mary Parish. He said he was working for the state and looking for two black fugitives. He showed her photos of them."

"What'd she tell him?"

"She lied. She actually had seen one of them. In a shelter in Morgan City. But she lied. I was standing right behind him. He turned around and asked me my name. Bledsoe is scary, Dave."

THAT NIGHT I couldn't sleep. I dreamed of Ronald Bledsoe and Father Jude LeBlanc and the confession of Bertrand Melancon. I dreamed of dark water closing over Jude's head and I dreamed of people in an attic fitting their fingers through the ax gashes in the roof Jude had started when he had been attacked by Bertrand. I heard the people in the attic calling for help on their cell phones and I heard the sound of a motorboat disappearing in the distance, the Melancon brothers and the Rochons snugly on board.

I hated what they had done to Jude LeBlanc and his parishioners. Personally they filled me with disgust and loathing. But I couldn't allow myself the luxury of hate. I couldn't allow it as a lawman or as a recovering alcoholic. AA teaches that those who vex us most are sick, not totally unlike ourselves. Sometimes that's a hard precept to buy into. Unfortunately, recovering drunks are not allowed latitude with their emotions. My favorite passage from Ernest Hemingway will always remain his suggestion in *Death in the Afternoon* that the world's ills could be corrected by a three-day open season on people. Less heartening is his addendum that the first group he would wipe out would be police officers everywhere.

I went into the kitchen and drank a glass of milk in the dark. The oak trees were black-green in the moonlight, the bayou swollen and yellow from the massive amounts of rain in the last few weeks. I tried to sort out all the images from my dreams, to somehow compartmentalize and rid myself of them, but one element in them would not go away: Bertrand Melancon not only kept calling me, trying to justify or expiate his sins, but he had not fled the area. The last part didn't make sense.

The Kovick score had been the realization of the house creep's wet dream. Was he so attached to his brother Eddy that he would run from shelter to shelter or rat hole to rat hole in the vain hope that he could spirit Eddy away from the hospital and take over his personal care, a man whose brain for all practical purposes was now as life-less as his body?

Why not just disappear into the urban vastness of Los Angeles and start over? People did it every day. Bertrand could fence the blood stones there and wash the queer in Vegas and Reno. Unless he wasn't actually in possession of either one of them.

Clete and his girlfriend had found over seventeen grand of coun-terfeit that had probably floated out of a garage in the alley. The rest of it may have gone down storm drains or been picked up from hedges and flower beds by neighbors who didn't bother to report the find to NOPD. But how about the blood stones? Their worth was incalculable. Bertrand could unload one or two of them, buy a storm-damaged or hot car for chump change, and catch a flight out of Dallas or Jackson. Why didn't he do that?

Because he's a thief, I thought, and like all thieves he decided at one point that he deserved more than his fellow house creeps. He hid the stones and he hasn't been able to get back to them.

Where?

I tried to reconstruct his flight from Sidney's house after he and Eddy and the Rochons had torn it apart. What if he had found the stones while looting the house and had decided not to tell the others? What if he had decided, while stealing gasoline from Otis's garage, to hide the stones rather than risk having them discovered by Eddy and the Rochons? He realized he was probably in possession of hundreds of thousands if not millions of dollars in hot jewels. It was the score of a lifetime. Why let his lamebrain companions screw it up?

But ultimately Bertrand had screwed himself. He had stashed the stones a few houses down the street from the most dangerous gangster in New Orleans, a man whose house they had not only robbed but systematically demolished, even ripping the chandeliers from the ceiling with an iron garden rake and urinating on the stove and in the seasoning drawers and the icebox.

I went back to bed and lay on top of the sheet, my arm across my eyes. I could hear the easy sweep of the trees across our tin roof and occasionally the *ping* of a pecan striking the metal. I said a silent prayer for Father Jude LeBlanc, and when I fell asleep I thought I heard his voice rise inside a bubble and burst on the surface of a black lake that was splintered with light.

I LIKE TO REMEMBER the era in which I grew up as one of duck-hunting dawns and summer-afternoon crab boils in a shady pavilion and college dances on Spanish Lake under oak trees that were strung with Japanese lanterns. The springtime of our lives seemed eternal, the coming of fall a mild interlude before flowers bloomed again. But there was a harsh side to the Louisiana of my youth, too, one that isn't always convenient to remember. The majority of people were poor, and for generations the oligarchy that ruled the state exerted every effort in its power to ensure they stayed that way. The Negro was the scapegoat for our problems, the trade unions the agents of northern troublemakers. With the coming of integration, every demagogue in the state could not wait to stoke up the fires of racial fear and hatred. Many of their constituents rose to the occasion.

Nigger-knocking became a Saturday-night sport that local police departments generally ignored. White high school kids shot people of color with BB guns and threw firecrackers at them at bus stops. Most of the kids who did this came from homes where the morning sunlight filtered through the dust like the ugly stain of failure. One of those kids was my college roommate at Southwestern Louisiana Institute, James Boyd "Bo Diddley" Wiggins.

His father had been a deputy sheriff in a North Louisiana parish and was forced to resign after he was arrested in a prostitution sting in New Orleans. The father died in penury, and his wife and children moved onto a corporate plantation, where they picked cotton and broke corn alongside people of color. But Bo Diddley possessed a talent his siblings did not. High school football may have been a sport to others; for Bo it was a magic doorway that opened onto a world his family would never enter.

He attended SLI on an athletic scholarship, tore holes in the opposing team's defensive line with a ferocity that bothered even his coach, and refused to sit near Negro students in his classes. He got into serious barroom fights out on the highway and would come back to the dorm stinking of whiskey and cigarettes, his clothes torn, his mowed head lacerated with broken glass, his nostrils clotted with blood. I genuinely believed Bo was at peace only when he inflicted so much pain on himself he could not hear his own thoughts.

He was expelled from college and given a BCD from the army for busting up a couple of MPs in Honolulu. But the army had done something for Bo Diddley no one else had—they taught him arc welding and gave him a trade. He burned stringer-bead rods on pipelines all over Louisiana and Texas, then opened his own welding shop in Lake Charles and within five years was operating a dozen more in three states.

But Bo was just getting started. He entered the twenty-first century as the owner of six shipyards located along the southern rim of the United States. He also managed to reinvent himself. He got reborn at the Assembly of God Church and posed for Christmas card photographs with evangelical television preachers in front of Third World orphanages. Immediately following 9/11, he was among a Louisiana political delegation that flew to New York City to attend a memorial ceremony at the Twin Towers with the president of the United

States. He was still jug-eared and flat-topped, with recessed buckshot eyes and half-moon scars on his knuckles and a voice that sounded like he had swallowed a clot of Red Man, but he and his bovine wife appeared regularly in the society pages of the Baton Rouge and Lafayette newspapers and each year hosted a charity golf tournament and entertained aging television celebrities.

For reasons I never quite understood, he had kept in touch with me over the years. Maybe, like me, Bo Diddley heard time's winged chariot at his door. Maybe he wanted to revise his youth and pretend that he, too, had been part of the innocence that seemed to have characterized our era. I couldn't say. Bo Diddley had paid hard dues. His tragedy, I think, lay in the fact he had learned nothing from them.

He was waiting by my office door when I came to work Monday morning, his rough hand extended, the square tautness of his face glowing with aftershave. "I know you're busy. I won't take up your time," he said. "I got a lot of resources, Dave. I think I can hep you with a case you're on."

My intake basket was overflowing, my caseload more than I could handle, my own troubles with Ronald Bledsoe without apparent solution. It was not a good time to deal with someone who believes his destiny is to meddle in police business. He followed me into my office.

"Is that fat boy in the dispatcher's cage your local funny man?" he said.

"Wally?"

"He asked me if I bought my cigar in a tire factory. He said he wanted to get some that smelled just like it."

I glanced at my watch and tried to shine him on. "I have a meeting with the sheriff in a few minutes. You mentioned something about a case I'm working on."

"About a priest who went missing in the Lower Ninth Ward, a guy from New Iberia."

"That's Jude LeBlanc. How'd you know I was looking for him?"

"My wife and I been doing some volunteer work in the shelters. We met this El Salvadoran woman, Natalia something-or-other. I guess she was getting it on with this priest just before New Orleans went into the shitter."

Bo may have acquired the trappings of a reborn and successful businessman, but his language and his mind-set still bore the sharp edges of the boy I had known years ago. For Bo, nuance did not exist. The world and the people in it were one-dimensional. Imposing complexity on them was the pastime of a group he called "pointy-headed professors."

"You know something about Father Jude's fate, Bo?"

"I've got a clean-up contract for the Lower Nine. I'm also setting up FEMA trailer villages anywhere we can house these poor devils. But I tell you, the real challenge is making these sonsofbitches go to work."

"Excuse me?" I said.

The grin died on his mouth. "Don't turn serious on me, son. A lot of those boys would choke to death on their own spit unless you swabbed their throats out for them. Dave, I sent emissaries to shelters all over the country, offering good jobs at good pay in the rebuilding of New Orleans. I didn't get one goddamn taker."

"I heard you say that in a television interview. I thought it was bullshit then. I think it's bullshit now," I said.

He shook his head. "I ain't knocking nobody, just telling you what happened. There's a big difference between telling the truth and knocking somebody."

I glanced again at my watch. "It's always good seeing you, Bo."

He raised his eyebrows and I thought his latent aggression and his desire to control those around him was about to surface. But I was wrong. "My secretary is waiting on me, so I gotta haul ass. I didn't mean to be a busybody. I just thought I'd hep out if I could," he said.

Maybe I hadn't given Bo the credit he deserved, I thought.

Through my window, I saw him walk toward a Lexus parked across the street from St. Peter's Cemetery. The day was still cool, the automobile blanketed with shade. A statuesque woman with white-gold hair, wearing sunglasses, a brief skirt, and a tight blouse, was smoking a cigarette outside the passenger door. When Bo Diddley clicked his door opener, she exhaled cigarette smoke at an upward angle and got inside, dropping her cigarette into the gutter, her skirt drawing up on her thigh.

I didn't know what his secretary's talents might be, but I doubted if they had ever included breaking corn or picking cotton.

AFTER LUNCH I drove out to the parish prison to talk with Otis Baylor, whose obstinacy, in my opinion, was becoming more symptomatic of pride than virtue.

Most jailhouse or mainline inmates don't want trouble. They do their time and avoid the wolves and stay out of racial beefs. They don't sass hacks and they don't wise off to guys with tear-duct tats. Like the Japanese, they create their own space and don't violate the space of others. But unfortunately the genes of our simian progenitors are alive and well inside those walls, and the strong prey on the weak, nakedly, and with relish.

Consensual jailhouse romance is a given and so is jailhouse dope, raisin-jack, prune-o, and white slavery. Yard bitches are treated with the same contempt as snitches and survive only by attaching themselves to a powerful caretaker, one who in turn requires complete obedience and loyalty. A juvenile offender thrown in with the general population is usually cannibalized. If you're con-wise, you develop tunnel vision, particularly when it comes to sexual conduct or the in-house drug trade. Defending your own person is imperative, but defending the weak is the province of fools and those seeking martyrdom.

The shift supervisor gave me an account of Otis Baylor's first three days in the can. At first he was treated as an oddity, a man who didn't belong, the kind who gets drunk and plows his car through a pedestrian crosswalk and cannot believe the grief he has brought upon himself and others.

Wiseasses told him to sign up for the nightly movies or off-grounds church services a hack would escort him to. Then they looked into his face and decided there were other places in the jail they wanted to be. Otis ate by himself and refused to speak to others, even to ask a question. He moved about like a silent behemoth whose eyes were always turned inward. When he went into the shower, the breadth of his shoulders, the thickness of his upper arms, and the soft patina of body hair on his skin exuded warning signs that all primitive people are immediately aware of.

Saturday afternoon a mulatto kid by the name of Ciro Goula from St. Martin Parish was stoned on a pipeload of Afghan skunk his "old man" had given him. Ciro was one of those damaged human beings who was not a criminal by nature but who would always be in the company of criminals and inside a criminal environment, because he could not function anywhere else. He was registered with the state health department as a carrier of venereal diseases and had been confined in a state mental hospital once and Angola twice. He was a prostitute and an addict, vain about his person, neurotic as a corkscrew, and indifferent about his ultimate fate. He was doing six months for possession, and during his first week in the main population he had attached himself to Walter Lantier, a white man with two homicides in his jacket. Walter rented Ciro out for dope, cash, or decks of smokes.

But Saturday afternoon Ciro got stoned and in Walter's face because Walter had sold him for an extra dessert to a retarded man who had the worst body odor in the stockade.

"You don't like it, you? You t'ink you better than other people? You t'ink you got a say in what I do?" Walter said. "Tell me how you feel about that in a couple of days, you li'l bitch."

Walter put out the word. For the next twenty-four hours, Ciro was anybody's punch.

On Sunday evening an inmate in the Aryan Brotherhood picked up Ciro in a bear hug and carried him into a shower room. There, he was made to put on panties and a bra and perform in front of three other men tattooed with SS lightning bolts and blue teardrops at the corners of their eyes. Inside the AB, tear-duct tats indicate the bearer has canceled someone's ticket. Membership in the Brotherhood is for life. In terms of effectiveness, their cruelty and violence have no peer. Ciro Goula had always believed, in a bizarre fashion, that his profligacy would protect him from wolves. But Walter Lantier had just volunteered him for duty inside a concrete mixer.

The four AB members in the shower room laughed at him, then sodomized him and plunged his head in a toilet bowl. When he screamed for help, they plunged his head into the water again and flushed the toilet. That's when Otis Baylor strayed into their midst.

"What the hell is the matter with you fellows? What kind of men are you?" he said, gathering up Ciro from a puddle of water on the floor. "Shame on the bunch of you."

"Where do you think you are, Jack?" one of the inmates said.

"You watch your manners, my friend. Or I'll be back for you," Otis said.

The inmate who had addressed Otis looked at him in disbelief, a matchstick frozen in the corner of his mouth. He tried to hold Otis's stare but his eyes broke and he lowered his head. His friends remained motionless, as cave dwellers might if a stranger entered their cave and kicked their food into a communal fire. Otis hefted Ciro to his feet and half carried him down a corridor, past a row of cells, to a barred security gate, on the other side of which two uniformed guards looked at him openmouthed.

"This man needs to be in a hospital. Y'all have a serious discipline problem in here," he said.

OTIS WAS WEARING jailhouse denims and a waist chain when the turnkey brought him to the interview room. Through the window I could see the coils of razor wire on the security fence outside and empty fields in the distance and a rural road that was lined with trash. I asked the turnkey if he could remove the chains. He shook his head and closed the door behind him.

"They got you in segregation?" I said.

"Is that what they call it?" Otis replied.

"Believe it or not, it's for your own protection."

"Then why am I in chains?"

Because a jail is not an adjustable institution, I thought. But Otis was a hardhead and I knew my words would be wasted on him. "I need your permission to go on your property in New Orleans," I said.

"What for?"

"I think Bertrand Melancon may have stashed stolen goods in your carriage house or your yard."

"Why would he do that?"

"The day you understand why these guys do anything is the day you stick a gun in your mouth," I replied.

I thought he might lighten up. But he didn't. "Get a warrant. That's how you guys do it, don't you?"

I leaned forward on the table. His wrists were cuffed to the chain that cinched his waist, and made me think of fins on the sides of a beached fish. "Listen to me. The stolen property I'm talking about belongs to your neighbor Sidney Kovick. You know what kind of man he is. If I'm correct, namely that Bertrand Melancon did stash Sidney's goods on your property, how long do you think it will take Sidney to come to the same conclusion? Furthermore, ask yourself what Sidney is capable of if he thinks you or a member of your family found them."

He looked out the window at the sun shining on the spools of razor wire above the fence. "Do whatever you want, Mr. Robicheaux."

"I admire your standing up for Ciro Goula. But he chose the life he lives and you can't take his weight."

"Have you ever been locked up in a place like this?"

"What if I have?"

"Then you know you don't give an inch."

"George Patton once told his men that wars are not won by giving your life for your country. You win wars by making the other poor bastard give his life for his."

"I'm ready to go back to lockdown."

"You got it," I said. Then I opened the door and yelled down the corridor at the turnkey, "On the gate, here!"

CHAPTER
19

Early Tuesday I collected Clete Purcel at his motor court and headed for New Orleans. When we drove down I-10 into Orleans Parish, the city was little changed, the ecological and structural wreckage so great and pervasive that it was hard to believe all of this destruction could come to pass in a twenty-four-hour period. I had been on the water when Audrey hit the Louisiana coast in 1957 and in the eye of Hilda in 1964 when the water tower in Delcambre toppled onto City Hall and killed all the Civil Defense volunteers inside. But the damage in New Orleans was of a kind we associate with apocalyptical images from the Bible, or at least it was for me.

Perhaps I carried too many memories of the way the city used to be. Maybe I should not have returned. Maybe I expected to see the streets clean, the power back on, crews of carpenters repairing ruined homes. But the sense of loss I felt while driving down St. Charles was worse than I had experienced right after the storm. New Orleans had been a song, not a city. Like San Francisco, it didn't belong to a state; it belonged to a people.

When Clete and I walked a beat on Canal, music was everywhere. Sam Butera and Louis Prima played in the Quarter. Old black men knocked out "The Tin Roof Blues" in Preservation Hall. Brass-band funerals on Magazine shook the glass in storefront windows. When the sun rose on Jackson Square, the mist hung like cotton candy in the oak trees behind the St. Louis Cathedral. The dawn smelled of ponded water, lichen-stained stone, flowers that bloomed only at night, coffee and freshly baked beignets in the Café du Monde. Every day was a party, and everyone was invited and the admission was free.

The grandest ride in America was the St. Charles streetcar. You could catch the old green-painted, lumbering iron car under the colonnade in front of the Pearl and for pocket change travel on the neutral ground down arguably the most beautiful street in the Western world. The canopy of live oaks over the neutral ground created a green-gold tunnel as far as the eye could see. On the corners, black men sold ice cream and sno'balls from carts with parasols on them, and in winter the pink and maroon neon on the Katz & Besthoff drugstores glowed like electrified smoke inside the fog.

Every writer, every artist who visited New Orleans fell in love with it. The city might have been the Great Whore of Babylon, but few ever forgot or regretted her embrace.

What was its future?

I looked through my windshield and saw fallen trees everywhere, power and phone lines hanging from utility poles, dead traffic lights, gutted downtown buildings so badly damaged the owners had not bothered to cover the blown-out windows with plywood. The job ahead was Herculean and it was compounded by a level of corporate theft and governmental incompetence and cynicism that probably has no equal outside the Third World. I wasn't sure New Orleans had a future.

I turned off St. Charles and drove into Otis's old neighborhood. The sun was up in the sky now, and the lawns along the street were stacked with debris and hazed with patches of bright green where blades of St. Augustine grass had grown through the netlike film of dead matter left behind by the receding water. Clete wanted to stop by the home of his new girlfriend. I waited while he knocked on the door. When no one answered, he wrote a note and stuck it in the jamb.

"You told her to meet us?" I said.

"No, I told her I'd call her later. I want to keep her separate from this stuff."

I pulled away from the curb and continued toward Otis's house.

"I've been giving this guy Bledsoe some thought," Clete said. "I think he needs a Bobbsey Twins invitation to leave the area."

"I think that's a bad idea."

"The guy doesn't sleep. His lights are on all night. He had a hooker in Saturday night. She left ten minutes later, looking like somebody had scared the shit out of her."

"Leave him alone, Clete. Helen and I will handle it."

"The guy's got ice water in his veins. He's a psychopath and he's got a grudge against Alafair. I say we break his wheels before he gets into gear."

"Why tell me this now?"

"Because this guy bothers me. Because I don't want Alafair hurt. Because you didn't see that hooker hauling ass."

"Were you drinking last night?"

He paused before he spoke again, this time without heat. "I came back to the Big Sleazy to help you look for the stones. But I think this is a mistake. Those are Sidney's goods. If he thinks you know where they are . . . Christ, Dave, use your imagination. Even the greaseballs kiss his ring."

I had told Otis Baylor almost the same thing but had not followed my own advice. I hoped Clete did not read my face. "I finally hit home with something?" he said.

We probed Otis's flower beds with sticks and pried up the flagstones in the backyard. We searched the garage rafters and under his back porch and used a ladder to climb on top of the porte cochere in case Bertrand had thrown the stones up there. We shoveled up the bricking in the patio and dismantled the chimney on the stone barbecue pit, broke apart birdhouses, raked out an ancient compost dump thatched with morning glory vine, crunched through the remnants of a greenhouse that had been flattened by a pecan tree, and dumped the impacted dirt in three huge iron sugar kettles that had been used as flower planters.

Nothing.

"What are you all doing over there?" a voice called from next door.

Tom Claggart stood on his back porch, straining to get a clear look through the border of broken bamboo that separated his property from Otis Baylor's.

"It's Dave Robicheaux, Mr. Claggart," I said.

"Where's Otis?"

"If you need to contact him, you can call his home in New Iberia," I replied.

"I was just wondering if you had permission to be here," Claggart said.

"This is police business. Go back inside your house," Clete said.

"You don't have to take that attitude," Claggart said.

"Ease up," I whispered to Clete.

"Did you catch those guys?" Claggart asked.

"Which guys?" I asked.

"The ones who got away. The ones who should be in a cage. You should be here at night. They're like rats crawling out of a trash dump."

"Who is?" I said.

"Who do you think? What's wrong with you people? This is a tragedy. No one is safe," he said. "All I did was ask a question and that man with you ordered me back in my house. This isn't the United States anymore." He went inside and slammed the door behind him.

"I think I've seen that guy before," Clete said.

"Where?"

"I don't remember."

A few minutes later, when we were getting back in my truck, I saw Claggart watching us from the upstairs window. When he saw me look back at him, he pulled the shade.

"What's with that dude?" Clete said.

"He's a gun nut with loose wiring."

"This was a mistake coming here, Streak. But you won't listen to your old podjo, will you? No sirree, that's not going to happen."

"I want to go down to the Lower Nine."

"Never think of me as the voice of reason. I couldn't stand it," he said.

He pulled a silver flask from the pocket of his slacks and unscrewed the cap and let it swing from its tiny chain. He took a sip, then another. I could see the warmth of the brandy spreading through his system, the tension going out of his face. He screwed the cap back on the flask and slipped the flask back into his pocket. He brushed at his nose and grinned.

"You're not mad at me?" I said.

"Wouldn't do any good. One day our luck is going to run out. I think you're pushing that day closer to us than it should be, Dave. But that's the way it is. You won't ever change."

It wasn't the individual destruction of the homes in the Lower Ninth Ward that seemed unreal. It was the disconnection of them from their environment that was hard for the eye to accept. They had been lifted from their foundations, twisted from the plumbing that held them to the ground, and redeposited upside down or piled against one another as though they had been dropped from the sky. Some were half buried in hardened rivers of mud that flowed out the windows and the doors. The insides of all of them were black-green with sludge and mold, their exteriors spray-painted with code numbers to indicate they had already been searched for bodies.

But every day more dead were discovered, either by search dogs or returning family members. The bodies were sheathed like mummies in dried nets of organic matter, compacted inside air ducts, and wedged between the rafters of roofs that had filled to the apexes. Sometimes when the wind shifted, an odor would strike the nostrils and cause a person to clear his throat and spit.

Feral dogs prowled the wreckage and so did the few people who were being allowed back into their neighborhoods. Clete and I found the church where Father Jude LeBlanc had probably died. It was made of tan stucco and had a small bell tower and an apse on it and looked like a Spanish mission in the Southwest. Before the storm, bougainvillea had bloomed like drops of blood on the south wall and a life-size replica of Jesus on the Cross had hung in a breezeway that joined the church to an elementary school. But the bougainvillea was gone and the replica of Jesus had floated out to sea.

I could find no one who had any knowledge of Jude LeBlanc's fate. It was almost evening now, and the sky was purple and threaded with smoke that smelled like burning garbage. On a house lot behind the church I saw an elderly black man pulling boards from what used to be his house. I made my way across a chain-link fence that had been twisted into a corkscrew, my shoes breaking through an oily green crust that had dried on top of mud and untreated sewage.

I opened my badge holder. "I'm a friend of Father Jude LeBlanc," I said. "He was at this church when the storm hit."

"I know he was. I was on the roof yonder. I seen a woman dropping children out the attic window into the water," he said. He had stopped his work to talk with me, one hand grasped on a weathered plank flanged with nails. His face was work-seamed, his eyes an indistinct blue, as though the sun had leached most of the color from them.

"You saw Father LeBlanc? You know what happened to him?"

"Mister, I ain't had time to do nothing except get my wife out of my house. I ain't pulled it off, either."

"Sir?"

"I ain't never found her. Whole house caved in under us. Water come squirting right out of the chimney, boiling up around us just like we was on a ship going down."

"I'm sorry."

"I come back looking for our t'ings. Po-lice said I ain't s'ppose to be back here. If I ain't s'ppose to be back here, who is? Two t'ings I don't understand. How come nobody come for us and what was them lights in the water?"

"Pardon?"

"It was dark and a helicopter went by, high up. I seen the lights in the water and at first I t'ought it was a searchlight from the helicopter and the blades of the helicopters was blowing the water. But that wasn't it. The lights was swimming around, like fish that could glow in the dark, except it was much brighter and these wasn't no fish. I t'ink maybe my wife was down there."

He stared into my face, waiting, as though somehow I possessed knowledge that he did not.

AT NOON WEDNESDAY Clete came by the office and asked me to have lunch with him. But something besides lunch was obviously on his mind. I asked him what it was.

"It's Courtney," he said.

"Who?"

"Come in, Earth. Courtney Degravelle, the lady who lives down the street from Otis Baylor. The lady whose house I left a note at yesterday."

"Maybe she didn't see it."

"I left her three voice mails."

"I'll ask NOPD to send somebody by her place."

"I already did that. They don't even know where a third of their department is. Come on, let's go to Victor's."

I wasn't looking forward to the experience. My intuitions proved correct. At the cafeteria, Clete remained agitated and distracted and hardly touched his food.

"Better eat up," I said.

"Last night Ronald Bledsoe came to my cottage and asked me to split a six-pack with him. This morning he invited me to breakfast. He said PIs need to network because Google is driving us out of business. I told him I didn't have that problem, also that I lived in the motor court because of the privacy it gave me."

"What do you think he's up to?"

"He wanted me to know he was at the motor court late last night and early this morning. I tell you, Dave, we need to take this cocksucker out in a swamp and smoke him. That's not a metaphor, either."

The people at the next table stopped eating and looked at one another.

"I'll get a box to go," I said.

• • •

BUT MY CONCERNS with Clete's use of profanity in a hometown restaurant should have been the least of my worries. The next morning, at sunrise, a game warden trying to save a stranded cow in a marshy area not far from the Gulf saw the bodies of two people lying on the edge of a sandbar in the middle of a deepwater lake. Cinder blocks were roped around their waists, and waves rippled across their legs and backs. Both bodies should have sunk to the bottom of the lake, but whoever threw them into the water probably did so in the dark, assuming his boat was in a deepwater channel. The game warden cut the motor of his outboard and let the keel scrape onto the sand.

He jumped into the shallows and grabbed the rope that held both bodies together and pulled them onto the sand. His hands were shaking when he called 911. "I've got two homicide victims here," he said. "One is gunshot, one looks to have died from suffocation. Wait a minute. Jesus Christ, one of them is alive."

FORTY-EIGHT HOURS EARLIER, Andre Rochon had awakened in his latest girlfriend's FEMA trailer outside Baton Rouge, the free cell phone a man had given him resting on his sternum. All he had to do was punch in the number the man had written on a slip of paper for him. What had the dude said? "Provide a li'l information and make yourself rich, my brother." What did Andre owe Bertrand, anyway? If Bertrand hadn't gone into that garage after gas, if they had all just climbed out of the boat and waded back to St. Charles Avenue, Kevin and Eddy never would have been shot.

But Bertrand had to show he was in charge, that the rest of them were punks, while all the time he was ripping off their share of the loot.

Andre got up from the small bed on which he had been sleeping and sat down across the breakfast table from his girlfriend. He wore only a pair of slacks and flip-flops, and he kept fingering his navel, pinching his abs and love handles, staring out the window at the rows of tiny white trailers in the FEMA park.

"You fixing to call somebody about a job?" his girlfriend said.

"There ain't no jobs, girl," he replied.

"I thought that's why the man give you the phone. He was gonna give you a job. That's what you tole me last night."

Actually, Andre couldn't remember what he had said the previous night. He'd drunk some wine and smoked a lot of weed, and at some point in the middle of a conversation a switch had clicked off in his head, then had clicked back on about nine this morning. "You ever dime a sister?" he asked.

"I ain't never dimed nobody, Andre. I don't like it when you talk like a criminal, either."

The diapered infant who slept on his stomach in the bassinet on the far side of the tiny bathroom began to make gurgling sounds. This was bad timing for Andre, who wanted his girlfriend back in the sack, not changing diapers and feeding a baby.

"Give him a bottle. That'll keep him quiet for a while," he said. "Here, I'll do it. Come on, lie down and get a li'l more sleep."

"Cain't you never think of anybody but yourself?" she said.

He stared reflectively into space, his fingers glazing the tautness of his stomach muscles. Andre's new girlfriend was getting to be a drag. "Think I'll go outside and make a phone call, check out a couple of sit'ations. Get some coffee started, will you, baby? Maybe some eggs and li'l toast, too," he said.

The man who answered Andre's call told him to walk down to the highway and wait for an automobile to pick him up. One hour later, Andre Rochon was swallowed up by a black SUV with charcoal-tinted windows and deep leather seats and a destination finder that would take him to a place and an experience he never could have imagined.

His newly acquired friends did not waste time. They taped him to a chair that was bolted to the floor, gave him ten seconds to answer their first question, then drove their fists directly into his face. The blows seemed delivered with more force and energy than he thought human beings were capable of and were like red fire inside his head. In minutes, his mouth and eyes were filled with blood, the expanse of sawgrass and lagoons and saltwater channels outside the window part of a dreamscape that had nothing to do with Andre Rochon or the person who had been Andre Rochon only that morning.

Somehow he had thought betrayal of his friend would be all that was required of him. How could he know where the stones were? Bertrand had ripped him off as well as Sidney Kovick. *He* was a victim, just as these guys were. No, he didn't know where Bertrand was, but he could find out. They were all working together, right?

When he passed out, they poured a bucket of water over his head. Then they wrapped his face in a towel, stretched his head back, and poured water in his nose and mouth.

After dark, he heard them drive away on the shale road atop the levee. When they returned, they smelled of hamburger and onions and coffee. Then they did things to him they had not done before. When he wept, they went outside and talked among themselves. Their voices were devoid of emotion, like football coaches discussing a game plan. Finally one of them said, "It can't hurt. We put too much time into this guy just to throw him away."

What did they mean? He had already told them everything he knew about Bertrand and the shooting and the looting at Kovick's house. He had even told them he was a rapist and a meth dealer and a strong-arm robber, that he had too much on his own sheet to ever turn his abductors in. Maybe they were going to keep him around, use him in some way, give him a job as an inside man. Yeah, that was it. Just stay cool, he told himself. They'd send him after Bertrand, find the motherfucker who'd started all this, fix his black ass for bringing all this grief down on everybody.

They allowed him to use the privy in back, then taped him to the chair again. One of them tied the wet towel around his eyes. "Take it easy, kid," he said. "We'll be done pretty soon."

Done with what?

Through the screen windows he could hear the wind in the saw-grass and fish flopping in the lagoons and the drone of a workboat out on the bay. Then car doors slammed and he heard the muffled voice of a woman as she was dragged into the room and thrown into a chair.

"Lady, we got no beef with you," one of the men said. "But you found some money that wasn't yours and didn't return it. So we want to know what else you found. Don't lie. That's the worst thing you can do, worse than anything you've ever done. You hearing me on this, Ms. Degravelle? Just nod your head. Okay, we got that out of the way.

"You see this black kid here? By his own admission, he's a rapist and a seller of narcotics to his own people. But worse than that, he lied to us after he promised to tell us the truth. So he's got to pay the price. If he don't, he's making liars out of us, too. What's about to happen isn't cruel, it's not undeserved. It's just part of the deal. Don't look away, Ms. Degravelle. You keep your eyes on him."

There was a pause and a silence of no more than three seconds, but those three seconds were the longest in Andre Rochon's life.

The pistol shots were loud and sharp inside the room, like shots fired from a .22 revolver. Andre took one round in the neck and two in the head, both of them as hot as wasp strings.

Later that night, his body roped to another person's and a chain of cinder blocks, he awoke to starlight just as someone rolled him over a gunwale into water that smelled of diesel fuel and fish spawn. When he rose from the darkness of the water and walked up the slope of the sandbar, dragging the cinder blocks and the body of the woman with him, he remembered a priest chopping a hole in a church roof and he wondered why he would recall such a bizarre image at this particular moment in his life.

FRIDAY AFTERNOON Betsy Mossbacher finished her account about Andre Rochon in my office. "He lived about six hours," she said. "The woman was dead when she went into the water. She still had the plastic bag over her head. Our pathologist says she died of a coronary probably brought on by near suffocation."

"Clete knows all this?"

"Yes. But he dummied up on us. How close were he and the woman?"

"They were seeing each other."

"Too bad. Ronald Bledsoe is using Purcel as his alibi. That must be hard to take. Can you explain to me how Purcel can insert himself into every problem in this area?"

"Lay off him, Betsy."

"That woman went through hell before she died. Save your brother-in-arms stuff for somebody else," she replied.

I could hear the traffic out on the street. Betsy formed a pocket of air in one jaw, then got up from her chair and walked to the window. She was wearing jeans, a cotton shirt, cowboy boots, and a wide belt. One of the qualities I admired most in Betsy was the fact her eyes were always clear and she focused them on yours when she spoke. She turned around and looked at me. "Interpol thinks Sidney Kovick may have taken both the blood stones and the counterfeit currency off some al Qaeda operatives in South America. The fact is we're not that interested in the blood stones. But we are interested in how Sidney Kovick got inside al Qaeda."

"What does Sidney say?"

"Nothing. I tried to appeal to his patriotism. You knew he was in the 173rd Airborne Brigade?"

"John Ehrlichman was a recipient of the Distinguished Flying Cross. Who cares?"

"You haven't talked to Purcel?"

"No."

"He was handling it okay."

"You don't know Clete. He doesn't handle anything okay."

"Regardless, he needs to stay out of this investigation. Your friend has a serious problem about minding his own business."

"His neighbor is Ronald Bledsoe. His girlfriend was tortured to death. His city drowned while the most powerful politicians in the country sat on their asses. If these things aren't his business, what is?"

On her way out of the office, she trailed a finger across the back of my neck. "People use me for a dartboard only once, Dave."

THAT EVENING I went to Clete's cottage at the motor court, but he was not there and he didn't return my calls to his cell phone. I stopped in the bar at Clementine's and at an outdoor place on Bayou Teche where he sometimes drank, but no one had seen him.

Perhaps I had been rude to Betsy Mossbacher. But few people understood the complexity of Clete Purcel. He didn't show pain or injury; he absorbed it in the way I imagine an elephant absorbs a rock splinter in its foot. While the wound heals and scars over on the surface, the splinter works its way deeper into the tissue, until infection forms and the inflammation swells upward through the joints into the chest and shoulders and spine, until the elephant's entire connective system throbs with the lightest of burdens placed on its back. Perhaps the latter was not true of an elephant. But it was of Clete.

I stood on the drawbridge overlooking the bayou at Burke Street and thought about the account Betsy had given me of Andre Rochon and Courtney Degravelle's ordeal. I suppose a person could say Rochon had invited his fate, but certainly Ms. Degravelle had not. I thought about the kind of men who would bind and torture their fellow human beings for money or for any other reason. Over the years I had known a few. Some hid in a uniform, some did not. But all of them sought causes and all of them needed banners over their heads. None of them, except those who were obviously psychopathic, ever acted alone or without sanction.

In the twilight Bayou Teche was swollen and wide between its tree-shrouded banks, the backs of garfish roiling the surface next to the lily pads. The sun had burned into a tiny red cinder. The air was suddenly cool, the lawns along the bayou lit by gas-fed lanterns and sometimes by chains of white lights in the oak trees. William Blake described evil as an electrified tiger prowling the forests of the night. I wondered if Blake's tiger was out there now, burning brightly in the trees, the pads of its feet walking softly across a lawn, its slattern breath and the quickness of its step only seconds away from the place where children played and our loved ones dwelled.

I walked home and began baking an apple pie in the kitchen oven, insisting that Molly and Alafair sit with me and talk while I did.

CHAPTER
20

B<small>Y</small> S<small>UNDAY</small> <small>MORNING</small> Clete had still not shown up. I heard the pet flap on the door swing back and forth, then saw Snuggs walk into the kitchen, jump up on the windowsill, and look back outside. I walked out on the porch. Bo Diddley Wiggins was in my backyard, admiring the bayou, wearing a pair of slacks and a short-sleeved print shirt unbuttoned at the top, the lapels ironed out on his shoulders.

"Didn't know if y'all were still sleeping," he said. "How old is that coon?"

"He's old. Like me," I said.

"He took a wet dump all over his papers. That's what I fear most in life. Sitting in a wheelchair, my pecker shriveled up, downloading in adult Pampers while a nigra woman sticks gruel in my mouth."

I heard Molly close the kitchen window. Bo looked at the trees overhead, the sunlight breaking through the branches, a squirrel swinging on a bird feeder. He waited for me to invite him in.

"We're about to head out to Lafayette, Bo. Otherwise I'd offer you coffee," I said.

"I don't have time, anyway. Look, I don't like to meddle. But we go back and I couldn't just blow off your friend's situation. What's-his-name, the rhino who's always getting into trouble around here?"

"Clete Purcel?"

"A couple of my employees are taking care of him right now. They don't want to see him hurt. But the guy went ape-shit out by an old oil platform on my lease and shot at somebody. If it hadn't been for my superintendent, your friend would be in the Lafourche Parish Jail."

"Where is he now?"

"Shit-faced in a bar, with a thirty-eight in a holster strapped on his chest. Why you looking at me like that?"

"Why are your employees going out of their way for Clete Purcel?"

"Because he fishes down there and they know him. Because one of my employees was in Vietnam, just like your friend. Excuse me, Dave, but did I do something wrong in coming here, because I'm definitely getting that feeling."

"No, you didn't, Bo. I appreciate it. If you'll give me directions, I'll go get him."

"I'll take you. Get in my truck. Wait till you see what this baby can do in four-wheel drive on a board road."

Bo drove his vehicle just like he did everything else—full-throttle, not taking prisoners, as though the rest of the world had become his enemy simply because it was on the other side of his windshield. We passed through miles of sawgrass, all of it yellowed by submersion, water and mud splashing above the hood, Bo driving with one hand on a road that was hardly a road, the frame bouncing on the springs.

The bar was at a rural intersection where the stoplight and the cable it hung on had been wrapped by storm winds around a telephone pole. Most of the bar's metal roof was gone and had been replaced with plywood and canvas and blue tarp. The rain ditches along the two intersecting roads were compacted with dead trees and detritus from a tidal surge that had wiped the coastal end of the parish off the map.

The inside of the club was dark, creaking with heat, the only power from a gas-operated generator chugging in back. Clete sat at a round table in the corner, his shoulder-holstered .38 strapped in plain sight across a Hawaiian shirt that stuck to his skin like wet Kleenex. A bottle of tequila, a salt shaker, a shot glass, and a saucer of sliced limes were on the table. So was a sweating can of Bud, which he picked up and sipped from without expression when he saw me and Bo Diddley enter the club.

Two sun-browned men in khaki clothes were drinking coffee at the bar. They nodded at Bo, then returned to their conversation.

"Trying to stoke up the locals?" I said to Clete.

"Who's he?" he said, indicating Bo.

"Bo Wiggins," Bo said, extending his hand.

"Those guys at the bar work for you?" Clete replied, either ignoring or not seeing Bo's hand.

"They said you had some trouble at an old drill location on my lease. They said they heard a couple of pops in the wind and saw a guy roaring down the canal in a boat. They thought maybe this guy tried to rob you. So I called Dave and we drove out."

Clete's face was oily and dilated, his eyes bleary with fatigue and early-morning booze. "See, that's not what happened. The guy in the boat is a guy I've been chasing through three parishes. See, he's a guy who maybe tortured a lady friend of mine to death. They tortured her for a long time, and they put a plastic bag over her head and dumped her over the gunnels down by the salt. They did this because that's the kind of guys they are, guys who get off working out their fantasies on a woman who can't fight back.

"But right now the problem I got is your friends moved my Caddy somewhere and they don't want to tell me where it is. So it would be really good if you would ask them to bring my Caddy around and to put the keys in my hand. Because if they don't, it's really going to mess up my day." Clete held up the face of his watch for Bo to look at. "See, I'm already late for church."

Bo listened with a half-smile on his face, his forearm on the table, his buzz haircut and jug ears silhouetted against a window. The back of his neck was red and pocked with acne scars and greasy with sweat. "No problem, Mr. Purcel. Your car will be here in five minutes," he said.

Bo went to the bar and spoke to his employees, who kept their attention on him and did not look again in Clete's direction.

"You don't know those two guys?" I said.

"No, why?"

"You didn't know one of them served in Vietnam?"

"No, I never saw either one of them. Who's that guy with you?"

"Forget about him. You actually shot at somebody?"

"It's a long story, but three separate people told me they saw that boat in the bay where Courtney's body was found. I hired an airboat and chased the guy all along the coastline. I gave up, then a guy at a dock told me he'd seen the boat down by an oil platform. I drove my car down the levee and almost had him. When he took off, I figured he had to be dirty. I let off two rounds at the waterline. Then those two dudes at the bar showed up and said I was trespassing."

"When's the last time you slept?"

"I think sleep is highly overrated."

"You never saw those guys at the bar?"

He blew out his breath. "I melted my head. I identified Courtney's body from a photograph. The facial shot was taken close up. The plastic bag was only part of it. I'm going to cool those guys out, Dave. Don't try to stop me. It's a done deal."

He picked up his jigger of tequila and drank it half empty, his eyes never leaving mine.

THAT EVENING I put Clete to bed in his cottage at the motor court, and in the morning I brought him a boxed breakfast from Victor's.

"Is there any chance you hit the guy you shot at?" I asked.

"I didn't see any feathers fly, if that's what you mean."

"What'd the guy look like?"

"He looked guilty."

He got into the shower, the water drumming on the tin walls. I couldn't take any more of his booze-soaked craziness.

I went to the office and told Helen what had happened, her face clouding as she listened, her hand opening and closing on a wadded-up piece of paper. "You give this to the FBI," she said.

"I don't think that's the way to go."

"You do it and you do it now, Dave. Now, get out of here."

I couldn't blame her.

•   •   •

OTIS BAYLOR got out of jail on bond and was promptly fired by his insurance company. On the same day he was fired, he became a self-appointed peripatetic counselor to anyone filing a storm-damage claim against his former employer or, for that matter, against any insurance company. He held meetings with home owners in a coffee shop and taught them how to phrase the language in their claims and how to file suit when their claims were unfairly denied. Trees were blown down by wind, not floated against a house by a tidal surge. Structural collapse was caused by twisters, not by flooding. Mold was caused by driving rain after wind had blown out the windows. Lightning exploded the electrical system and curled the walls and split the foundation, not water.

The words "water," "flood," "tidal," and "surge" did not exist.

On Wednesday I saw him on the street, down by Clete's office, his manner strangely composed for a man whose life was hanging in shreds. His shirt pocket was full of ballpoint pens, his upper torso broad and solid inside his clothes. "You find what you were looking for at my house?" he asked.

We were in the shade of a live oak that grew out of the sidewalk, and the wind was blowing leaves along the concrete. "No, *we* didn't, but other people may give it a try," I said.

"They can have at it," he said.

"Courtney Degravelle probably had the same kind of casual attitude."

"The lady down the street?"

"You don't know?"

"Know what?"

"She was murdered. So was Andre Rochon. They were both abducted, tortured, and murdered."

He was absolutely still, his tie fluttering slightly against the pin that held it to his shirt.

"Who did it?"

"Maybe Sidney Kovick's people. Maybe some international guys. Whoever they are, they're well organized."

He looked ashen. "I knew Ms. Degravelle. She was a nice lady. She was tortured to death?"

"She died of a coronary. But, yes, she was tortured terribly."

"My family is at risk, isn't it?"

"I can't say that for sure."

"I've seen this man Bledsoe, the private investigator, around town. He's involved in this, isn't he?"

"You've seen him in the last few days?"

"I saw him on the street before I was arrested. You think he's involved in Ms. Degravelle's death?"

"We're not sure."

"This never ends, does it?"

"I'm going to say something of a personal nature to you, Mr. Baylor. You're a believer. As such, you know it's us against them. The contest is never over, the field never quite ours."

I guess my statement was grandiloquent, perhaps foolish. He looked at me with an expression that was as flat as a painting on a signboard. Then he walked away without saying good-bye, crossing the street through traffic that had to swerve around him.

But unbeknown to Otis, he had just done something that convinced me he was not a killer. He had shown no interest in the death of Andre Rochon, a man who had probably raped his daughter. Those who seek vengeance will accept the state's invitation to witness the execution of their tormentors, in the old days by electrocution, today by lethal injection, but they get no rest and to the end of their days are haunted by the specter of an enemy who is ironically now safe and beyond their grasp.

For good or bad, Otis Baylor was not one of these.

IN A NUMBER of well-written movie scripts, a forensic psychologist undoes the maniacal workings of a serial killer by somehow placing himself inside the killer's head. As a consequence, the forensic psychologist goes a bit mad himself.

This makes for great entertainment. But I don't think it has anything to do with reality. What goes on in the mind of a sociopath? No one knows. Without exception, they take their secrets to the grave and lie about their deeds and the whereabouts of their victims, even when they have nothing to gain. The only group I know to be as secretive are conjurors or, in South Louisiana, what we call "traiteurs." They claim to be healers who receive their power from the forces of good. If you press them on the question, they'll add that a traiteur can pass on his power at the hour of his death to a member of the opposite sex and only to a member of the opposite sex. Press them further and you will probably get a lesson in buried hostility. Why are they defensive? They never say. And that is what's most disturbing about them.

On Thursday morning Alafair walked to her volunteer job at the evacuee shelter in City Park and Molly drove to her job at the Catholic self-help foundation on the bayou, and because the day was such a fine one, I walked the few blocks from my house to the sheriff's department. At noon I checked out a cruiser and drove it home for lunch. As I pulled into the driveway behind Molly's car, I saw Molly come around the back side of the house. She had just gotten home.

"Dave, come look at this," she said.

I got out of the cruiser and followed her into the backyard. "What's up?"

She pointed at the screen door. We usually latched it when we were gone to prevent Snuggs or Tripod from pawing it open and entering the house through the pet flap in the hard door. The screen had been cut and the latch unhooked from the eyelet screwed into the jamb. The lock on the hard door had been pried loose with a flat-bladed screwdriver.

"Have you been inside?" I asked.

She shook her head.

"Wait here," I said, and unsnapped the leather strap on my .45.

I went through the kitchen into the living room and main bedroom, the .45 still holstered, my palm resting on the butt. Then I looked into the bathroom and walked down the hall and into Alafair's room.

Her manuscript had been torn into long strips and scattered on the floor and on her bedspread. The screen on the monitor had been broken in the center with what I suspected was a ball-peen hammer.

The keyboard hung in two pieces by its connection wire on the back of her chair. The metal housing on the computer had been punched with holes, peeled back from the frame, and the innards torn out and stomped into the wood floor. Her laser printer, which she had bought in Portland with money she had made working in the college bookstore, had been crushed flat, probably by someone standing on top of it.

Her backup floppy disks had been scissored into small pieces. Her two notebooks and the hundreds of pages of blue calligraphy on them floated in a half inch of dark yellow urine at the bottom of a waste can. I opened my cell and punched in 911. When I finished the call, Molly was standing in the doorway.

"Ronald Bledsoe?" she said.

"Take it to the bank," I replied.

I PARKED UNDER the live oaks in front of the recreation building in City Park and went inside. The floor of the basketball court was lined with cots, many of them piled with personal belongings, as though the cot itself had become a residence. Alafair was reading a book to a group of children who were sitting in a circle on the floor. I tried to seem relaxed as I walked toward her.

"Got a minute?" I said.

She put a marker in her book and went outside with me. I told her what had happened, my hand touching her arm. While I spoke, she stared down the slope at our house on the far side of the bayou, her face never changing expression.

"He destroyed everything?" she said.

"That's the way it looks," I replied.

"But there's no evidence it's Bledsoe? Nobody saw him?"

"I talked with the neighbors. Nobody saw anything."

"He urinated on my notebooks?"

"He's a sick man. Why even talk about him?"

"You don't have to tell me what he is."

"We're going to Lafayette this evening and buy a new computer and printer. In the meantime, the crime lab is at the house."

"This guy's a jerk, Dave. I send my work-in-progress file every day to a friend in Portland. I also send one to Ernest Gaines. My notebooks are in a floppy disk on top of my bookshelf. Did he get into my bookshelf?"

"No."

"Like I said, he's a jerk."

"You're quite a gal, Alf."

"Don't call me that name. Seriously, I hate that name," she replied.

A TECHNICIAN FROM the Acadiana Crime Lab lifted full and partial prints from Alafair's desk and computer but found none that matched the thumbprint Bledsoe had left on Clete's license tag. Just before quitting time, Clete called me at the office.

"You won't believe this. Bledsoe is back at his cottage," he said.

"I believe it. Did you talk to him?"

"He invited me to dinner. He's barbecuing on a grill under the trees. Jesus Christ, he just waved at me."

I heard Clete pull the curtains.

"Somebody broke in our house today and tore up Alafair's computer," I said. "The perp also destroyed her work materials and put her notebooks in a waste can and urinated on them."

"This guy is overdue for a home call."

"I'll think about it."

I heard him fooling with the cell phone, as though he had walked from the window and was trying to organize his thoughts. "I got something real bad on my conscience, Streak. It's eating my lunch," he said.

"Courtney Degravelle's death is not your fault, partner."

"There's something I didn't tell you. We put all the insurance money in a mailbox like you suggested. I mean, almost all of it."

He paused, waiting for my reaction. But this time I refused to fill in the blanks for him.

"See, Courtney was broke. Her insurance company was screwing her on her claim. She was already two months behind on her mortgage. She wanted to hold back a grand and wash it at a casino in Shreveport. I didn't see the harm."

I rubbed one temple and stared wanly out the window, stupefied by his lack of judgment.

"So that's what she did. She and her sister drove up to Shreveport and unloaded the grand and won about seven hundred on top of it," he said.

I didn't want to hear it. Also, I didn't want to fall into my old role as Clete's enabler, either. But what do you do when your best friend is bleeding inside?

"Tommy the Whale dimed you with Sidney Kovick. Then Sidney's goons found out you and Courtney were an item. It was easier to take her down than come after you. Washing the money didn't have anything to do with it," I said.

"We both know better."

I let it go. Courtney Degravelle had fallen into the hands of men who of their own volition dwell in the Abyss. Perhaps Clete had contributed to her fate. I was his friend. She was dead and so was Andre Rochon. With luck, we or someone else would nail the guys who killed them. What else was there to say?

I HAD OTHER problems to deal with, and choices to make that no cop on the square wants to make. Ronald Bledsoe had remained untouchable. Now he had invaded my home and left his ugly stain on my daughter's life. We could roust and threaten him, but our best efforts would be of no value. Bledsoe was in our midst for the long haul, taunting us, pressing the stone deeper into the bruise with each passing day. Is it dishonorable to fight a war under a black flag in defense of those who cannot protect themselves? I thought not. Or at least that's what I told myself as I considered my options regarding Ronald Bledsoe.

CHAPTER
21

I<small>T WAS RAINING</small> Friday night and Alafair and Molly were at a movie when Otis Baylor parked his car in front of our house and knocked on my door.

"You busy, Mr. Robicheaux?" he said.

"No, sir, come in," I said.

He sat down in a stuffed chair in our living room and looked out the window at the rain falling in the light on top of our philodendron. "I've given some thought to a few things I've said to you. My manner has been abrasive and uncalled for. I think you were trying to be as forthright as you could. I should have given you a little more credit."

"You were under pressure—" I said.

He interrupted me. "Your daughter told Thelma about the scrape she had with this fellow Bledsoe. She also told Thelma about the break-in at your house. It was him, wasn't it?"

"That's my belief."

"Alafair says you can't do much about it."

"No, so far I haven't been able to."

"I've been in your shoes and I know the kind of thoughts you're having."

"I was never that good on going into other people's heads, Mr. Baylor, so in turn I ask that they not tell me what my own thoughts are."

"My family has a violent history. My father and his brother did things I'm ashamed of. Some of their violent tendencies have lived on in me. That means I can recognize it when I see it in others. I think you and I are cut out of the same burlap. If you go after Bledsoe on your own, you'll be playing his game."

"Oh?"

"In the insurance business all policies are written in terms of risk and percentages. It's not guesswork, either. The only other industry as good at calculating profit and loss is the gambling industry. That's why it's not a 'gambling' industry. The player loses, the house wins. There's no exception to the rule. You following me?"

"No."

"Bledsoe didn't file charges against Alafair, did he?"

"Nope."

"Why not?"

"Because he put his hand on her person. Because he made offensive sexual remarks to her."

"That's right. And in a local court his potential for a successful prosecution would be at about thirty percent. But what happens if Alafair's father decides to take the law in his own hands? My guess is Bledsoe's chances for prevailing in court go up to about eighty percent. His chances of winning a civil suit would probably be over ninety."

I was sitting across the coffee table from him. The windows were open and through the screen I could hear the rain clicking on the plants in the flower bed.

"Who shot the looters, Mr. Baylor?"

"Put it this way. The DNA evidence from my daughter's rape kit was lost in the storm, so I'll never know for sure those guys were the ones who attacked her. But if they were, they got what was coming to them and I'm glad they're not around to hurt anyone else. I hope the one on the loose gets his comeuppance, too."

"That might be poor consolation for an innocent man hoeing soybeans in the shadow of a mounted gunbull," I said.

"Don't let me regret I came here, Mr. Robicheaux."

And don't argue with people who are uneducable, I thought to myself. "Not for the world, sir. Thanks for coming by," I said.

Most people who stack time make a series of decisions that ensure their eventual confinement, just like dry drunks finding ways to get back inside saloons. I wondered what tragedy or violent event or reservoir of anger was compelling a good-hearted Rotary Club man to wend his way into the belly of the beast.

As I watched his car drive away, his back tires spinning on a layer of blackened leaves in the gutter, I said a brief prayer for Otis Baylor. I had a feeling he would need all the help he could get.

BERTRAND MELANCON could not remember a time when he was not afraid. He feared his mother for the men she brought home and he feared even more her unpredictable mood changes. She would strike him in the face as easily as she would place a bowl of breakfast cereal in front of him, or perhaps do both within a ten-second time frame. Conversely, most of the men were not mean or violent and in fact would sometimes take him to ball games or give him money to pick up cigarettes or beer for them at the corner package store. But often his mother and the man with her would tell him and Eddy to stay out in the yard until they were called in for dinner. As Bertrand watched them drop the blinds, he knew his house did not belong to him and neither did his mother, and the realization of that fact was worse than his mother's hand across his face.

Bertrand woke each morning with a nameless fear that was like a hungry animal eating a hole through his stomach. The images from his dreams followed him into the day, ill defined, without origin, like the reflection at night of faces in a streetcar window that told him he was of no value.

Eddy said he worried too much. But Eddy started getting drunk on short-dogs in the fourth grade, sometimes on the school bus at 7:30 a.m. Eddy got wiped out on glue in the boys' bathroom and set fire to a girl's locker. When he was twelve he was carrying a shank and claimed he had used it on a kid who had tried to take his tennis shoes at the park.

Bertrand and Eddy pulled their first armed robbery when they were in middle school. An old Vietnamese man was closing up his register in the tiny grocery store he operated when Eddy shot him in the face with a paintball gun. Not only did they clean out the register, Eddy threw canned goods through the glass windows in the wall coolers. Later Bertrand asked his brother why he had taken time to start throwing cans at the coolers when the old man was about to punch in numbers on the telephone. Eddy frowned and said, "Don't know. Just felt like it."

They never planned their scores or their strong-arm takedowns. The events seemed to present themselves of their own accord and were not of anyone's manufacture, in the same way a storm can blow through a house or a match can turn a pool of gasoline into a whoosh of flame under a parked car. Stuff happened, that's all. The hands trembling on the money drawer, the averted eyes, the broken mouth, the gashed scalp, these were images that receded into memory, like tiny bits of paper drifting to the bottom of a well, unplanned, undirected, ultimately inconsequential.

Eddy was never bothered by what they did. In the St. John the Baptist Parish jail it was Eddy who paid a cook four decks of smokes to put roach paste in the food of a wolf who bragged he was going to turn out both Eddy and his brother. It was Eddy who got Andre to pull the van up to the curb and talk to the young girl who was walking home from a street fair with a stuffed animal clutched to her breast. It was Eddy who tied her up in back. It was always Eddy who started it but who somehow got Bertrand to finish it or clean it up. Eddy thrived. Bertrand's stomach stayed on fire. The two of them were joined at the hip, one incomplete without the other, each serving compulsions and insatiable desires neither could explain to himself.

Now, in the wake of Katrina, Bertrand's nameless fear had a face on it. In a shelter in Des Allemands, someone had left a copy of the *Times-Picayune* scattered on the floor of a toilet stall. On the society page was a photograph of Mr. and Mrs. Sidney Kovick repairing the damage done to their historical home by both looters and the hurricane. The cutline contained no mention of the bullet that plowed through Eddy's throat and Kevin's skull.

Bertrand could not take his eyes off Sidney Kovick's face. It made something shrivel inside him. Silently it told him of his insignificance, his failure, the disdain in his mother's eyes, the loathing and disgust in the face of the white girl he had raped and tormented.

When he left the toilet stall, he was convinced there was only one way to end the fear and self-hatred that roiled his stomach and poisoned his blood: He had to destroy the face that hid like a reflection in a darkened window glass wherever he went. He had to kill Sidney Kovick.

SIDNEY LOVED GOING to work at his flower store. The interior of the shop was snug and full of color and fragrance, and the people who came into the shop respected him for his knowledge of flowers and his ability to select or create the right bouquet for the occasion. He always dressed formally when he went to the shop, and he always stood while he worked and only sat down at lunchtime or when he had to use his desk. He believed a good salesman was a good listener, and usually it did not take him long to divine what his customers needed. Few seemed to care about his reputation outside the shop. When a customer wrote a check, Sidney never asked for ID. His product and his prices were good, and so were his customers. Sidney was a gentleman.

Sidney also loved his wife, Eunice. When they first began dating, he showed her his home in Metairie, his yacht at Des Allemands, and his fishing camp in the Florida Keys. He told her he was in the life, but he didn't deal in dope or pornography. When Eunice asked what he did deal in, he replied, "Anything that's consensual and that makes money. End of story." Eunice had grown up in a culture of corruption. Sidney's explanation about his business affairs was enough.

Then their little boy was run over and killed by a drunken neighbor. Through use of an attorney, the neighbor managed to avoid a sobriety test until the next day. He pleaded no contest to reckless endangerment and was required to drive with a restricted license for one year. He did not attend the little boy's funeral and he did not apologize for running over and killing him. Some said he was afraid; others said he believed the problem was legal in nature and had been resolved in the court. But everyone agreed that the neighbor's decision to do nothing was a bad choice.

When the neighbor disappeared six months later, his wife put her house on the market and moved to Omaha. She had not been a person of means, but she bought a condo with cash and lived comfortably on the money she realized from the sale of her house in Metairie. She never complained to either the FBI or local authorities about their inability to find her husband.

Eunice never asked Sidney if the rumors about the neighbor's fate were true. But sometimes when they were alone in the darkness, after making love in their upstairs bedroom, she would raise herself up on one elbow and look directly into his eyes.

"What is it?" he would say.

"Tell me," she would say.

"Tell you what?"

"Tell me you're the good man I know you are."

"I'm a good man at the shop. Other times maybe I'm not so good. It's just the way I am, Eunice."

But maybe she should not ask for more, she told herself, her arm resting on the broadness of his chest, his big heart beating under the palm of her hand.

She helped him at the store and took as much pleasure and pride as he in the quality of flowers they sold. On Saturday morning she fixed coffee and put out cups and saucers and chocolates wrapped in gold foil for their customers. Eunice's smile lit up the day and the shop, and hardly a customer came in who was not made better by it. Sidney Kovick was not big on theology, but if ever there was proof of God's existence, to Sidney it was the presence of Eunice in his life.

BERTRAND HAD STASHED the .38 from Sidney Kovick's house behind the Rite Aid where they had holed up to do a few lines of flake before returning to finish the takedown at the house. The car he drove was a new Toyota a friend had boosted from a Winn-Dixie parking lot in Houma. The interior still smelled of coconut-scented air freshener from a car wash. The friend had even given Bertrand a tape of Three 6 Mafia to play for the drive into New Orleans. "Just drop my 'sheen at my brother's house when you're done wit' it," the friend said. But the friend did not know the nature of Bertrand's mission nor did he know Bertrand's larger plan, namely, to murder the man who had brought him all this grief and then blow Dodge with a bagful of blood diamonds, whatever blood diamonds were, which Bertrand had still not figured out.

As he drove into New Orleans, he was amazed at how much of the city was still without power and how many buildings were without roofs and windows, the yards covered with ruined furniture the owners had piled outside. An NOPD cruiser passed him, the cop behind the wheel glancing once in the rearview mirror. Bertrand turned off the avenue and parked behind a pile of downed tree limbs, his ulcers kicking into operatic mode.

When he was sure the cruiser was gone, he circled the block and slowed his car next to a fat black woman who was pushing a shopping cart across the intersection. The cart was packed solid with mounds of moldy clothes that protruded through the wire basket. "Know where the Rite Aid is at?" he asked.

"It's probably under that sign yonder that say 'Rite Aid,'" she replied.

"Sure 'nuff, it is. You want to make five dollars?"

The woman released the cart and fitted her big hands on top of the windowsill. The skin of her forearms was dark and shiny, notched with pink scars, as thick as elephant hide. "What you after, boy?" she asked.

"Hurt my leg and cain't walk too good. Maybe you can pick up something for me behind the Rite Aid, there."

She looked in the direction of the drugstore. Her breasts were like watermelons hung in cloth sacks, her neck beaded with dirt rings. "You know you ain't got no license plate on your car?"

"Sure 'nuff, again. You got a good eye. Must have bounced off."

"Load my clothes in the back. Then drive me where it's at. Then you pay me fifty dol'ars and drive me home," she said.

"I can work wit' that," he said.

"You scared shitless, boy. You smell like it, too. Whatever you doin', you better start doin' less of it," she said.

He drove the woman to a spot fifty yards from the parking lot behind the Rite Aid. He left the engine running as she waddled to a section of sidewalk that had been wedged up by the roots of an enormous oak tree. The tree had been split by either lightning or its own weight, and the crack in the trunk filled with concrete. But the concrete had deteriorated and created an opening behind which Bertrand had stashed the .38 and the bag of blow inside a wadded-up shirt. The fat woman was wheezing for breath and sweating heavily when she got back inside the car. She set the wadded-up shirt on the seat.

"There's a gun in there," she said.

"That's just tools for my car."

"Give me my fifty dol'ars and take me back to the basket. I don't need no ride home," she said.

She got out at the intersection, the bills crimped in her palm, and pushed her cart down the street, the wheels twisting on the asphalt, fighting against one another. As Bertrand watched her struggling with the balance and weight of the basket, her rear end as big as a washtub inside her green stretch pants, he felt diminished, alone, like someone left behind on a beach, but he did not know why.

He stuck the blow down in his pants and the .38 under the seat, and headed for Algiers, across the wide sweep of the Mississippi. The windows were down, the wind blowing as he crossed the river, but sweat ran down his chest and a stench rose from his armpits. He pulled the bag of blow from his pants, dipped a finger inside, and rubbed the crystals in his nostrils and on his gums.

But Kovick's flake wasn't working for him, either because it had been stepped on too many times or because Bertrand was so wired he could slam a gram and still not extinguish the fire in his stomach or stop the racing in his heart. When he came down the exit ramp into Algiers, he felt like he had stepped into an elevator shaft. A truck swerved around him, blowing its horn. A stop sign flew by him as though it had been suddenly planted on the edge of his vision. He reached again into the bag of blow and knocked it on the floor. Up ahead, a cop was waving cars past an accident scene. By the time he reached the street where Kovick's flower shop was located, he was hyperventilating and thought he was going to pass out.

He parked at the end of the block. He could not remember when he had been this afraid. He tried to think of credible reasons for not going into the store. Two guys who looked like greaseballs were eating lunch at a table under an awning that extended out from the display window. How could he be expected to take on guys who killed people for a living? He could catch Kovick somewhere else, on an even playing field. It didn't have to be here, it didn't have to be today. There wasn't any shame in using his head.

Secretly he knew the real enemy in his life was not Kovick but the fear that had been his companion in the darkness of his room and at every sunrise and at the breakfast table with his mother and on the school bus and in the school yard and in the crack house where he first got seriously wiped out and on the mattresses where he had screwed girls and performed acts that made him wonder if he was a degenerate. Fear was a gray balloon that floated from place to place, object to object, and each time he tried to confront it, it moved someplace else, transforming the most innocuous of situations into dilemmas that he would never confess to anyone else, lest they know him for the frightened man he was.

Now he was trying to run from the guy who had turned his life into a nightmare. Which was worse? he asked himself. To die here or to be chased and laughed at until Kovick's people finally caught him and taped his mouth and carried him into a basement where Kovick would be waiting for him in a raincoat and rubber boots.

But the greaseballs stuffing their faces with sandwiches under the awning weren't products of his imagination, he told himself. He'd never get past them. Even trying was like spitting in the lion's mouth.

When he had almost convinced himself he had a legitimate reason for postponing his appointment in Samarra, the greaseballs finished eating, put their lunch trash in a paper sack, and drove away in a convertible.

Bertrand drove around the block twice, hoping a flood of customers would enter the shop, giving him a viable reason to head back to Houma. Instead, the sidewalk remained empty and no cars pulled to the curb. In fact, the flower shop seemed to have been created brick by brick without any tangential association to the world around it, like an island where Bertrand Melancon was destined to confront the face that had looked upon him with disdain and contempt all his life.

He stuck the .38 snub down in his belt, pulled his shirt over the checkered grips, and got out of the car. He thought he could feel the earth tilt sideways.

Then he realized he had no plan. All the time he had been driving from Houma, his mind had been on recovering the .38 and the flake. When that was out of the way, he had immediately started figuring out ways to avoid confronting Kovick. Now he was in front of Kovick's shop with his pud in his hand and no plan. What was he supposed to do? Go through the front door shooting? What if he missed? What if Kovick had a gun under the counter?

He walked to the end of the block and entered the alleyway that led behind the shop. Garbage cans lay on their sides on the asphalt and clusters of untrimmed banana trees rustled in the wind. The back door to the flower store was ajar. Bertrand could feel his chest constricting, his lungs burning as though someone had poured battery acid in them. He kept his right hand on his shirtfront so the wind wouldn't expose the .38 and used his other hand to wipe the sweat out of his eyes. He never thought anyone could be this afraid.

He pulled back the metal door and looked into the rear of the shop. A tall woman was standing at a worktable, talking on the phone. She smiled at him and motioned him inside by cupping her fingers at him.

He stared at her, befuddled. She must have thought he was a delivery man. Then another realization started to dawn on him: She was Kovick's wife. She had been in the photograph with him in the *Times-Picayune.*

What better way to get even with Kovick than to cap his wife, he thought. That's what Eddy would say, at least if Eddy had a mind to think with, if Eddy wasn't just a sack of viscera attached to a feeding tube.

The woman replaced the phone receiver in the cradle. She was wearing a sundress and had broad shoulders that were tanned and strong-looking, like a countrywoman's. "Are you here to pull the tile in the bathroom?"

"Ma'am?" he said.

"You're not with the plumber?"

"I was looking for an address. I ain't sure I got the right one."

"What's the address?"

He couldn't think. The sound of his own blood roared in his ears. "The address where Mr. Kovick is at," he said.

God, what had he just said?

"He's out front. I'll tell him you're here. What's your name?"

"You ain't got to bother him. I'll get my tools. They're in the truck."

"Wait just a minute," she said. Then she was gone into the front of the shop.

He couldn't decide whether to flee or to pull the .38 from his belt before Kovick came through the heavy felt curtain that separated the front of the shop from the back. A truck rattled past the back door onto the side street, and he almost jumped out of his skin. Then, like an apparition in a dream, Kovick pulled back the curtain and stared into his face. Kovick looked like the biggest man Bertrand had ever seen. "What's the problem?" he said.

Bertrand's mouth was so dry he almost swallowed his tongue when he tried to speak. "Ain't no problem, suh," he said, frozen in place, the thumb of his right hand hitched in his trouser pocket.

Kovick wore a beige suit with pale purple stripes in it and a lavender shirt and a tie that was the color of a pomegranate. His eyes contained a dark light, like obsidian, the focus in them unrelenting. "You here about the bathroom? Some of the pipes are right under the tiles, so you got to be careful how you pry them up. They're old and it won't take much to bust them."

"I ain't here about no bat'room," Bertrand said.

"Then what do you want?" Sidney looked at him sideways as he lifted an empty vase out of a carton on the floor and partially filled it from a wall tap. He set the vase on the worktable and began sorting through an order book. "Did you hear me? What do you want, kid?"

Nothing, except your life, motherfucker, Bertrand heard a voice inside him say.

"What'd you just say?" Sidney asked.

"Nothing. I ain't said nothing."

"You called me a motherfucker?"

"No, suh, I ain't said that."

"I think you did." Sidney's eyes dropped to Bertrand's belt. "What have you got there?"

"Nothing," Bertrand said, backing away.

"Yeah?" Sidney said. He slapped Bertrand across the face, hard, coming around with his shoulder when he did it. "I asked you a question. What's down there?"

"Suh, I ain't did nothing. I'll go away. You ain't never gonna see me again. I promise."

Sidney reached down and jerked the .38 from Bertrand's belt, the steel sight tearing Bertrand's skin. "You little shit," he said. "You came in here packing, with my wife in the store?"

"No, suh. I was just lost."

"Don't lie," Sidney said. He slapped Bertrand full in the face again, knocking spittle from his mouth.

"I thought it was an easy score, man," Bertrand said, his nose full of needles, his eyes brimming with water.

"I got the reputation as an easy score? I got the reputation as anybody's punch? That's what you're telling me in my own shop?"

Bertrand opened his mouth to speak, but no words came out. Sidney flipped open the cylinder of the .38 and dumped the shells in his palm. "Where you from?" he asked.

"Shreveport," Bertrand said.

Sidney dropped the .38 in his coat pocket and fitted his hand inside Bertrand's shorts and pulled them and his trousers out from his stomach. He poured the six rounds down into Bertrand's genitalia, then walked him to the door. "This is what it is, kid. You made a mistake. Come around again and I'll tear up your whole ticket."

Sidney pushed him into the alley and kicked him so hard between his buttocks that Bertrand felt like glass had been shoved up his rectum. He limped to the end of the alley, convinced that blood was running down his thighs. When he got out to the street, when he did not think any more humiliation or misery could come into his life, he saw a wrecker hoisting the front end of his Toyota into the air.

LATER THAT AFTERNOON, the phone rang on my kitchen counter. "Either you or Purcel are behind this, Dave," a voice said.

"Sidney?" I said.

"You surprised I'm alive?"

"You lost me."

"I'm holding a thirty-eight one-inch in my hand. Guess where it came from? It was stolen from my own house. I just took it off a black kid with breath like somebody broke wind. The black kid came in my shop with my own gun and was going to cap me with it. You think that's just coincidence?"

"Where's the black kid now?"

"I don't know. I kicked his ass down the alley before I realized he was one of the guys who tore my house apart. But if I get my hands on him, I'm going to pull all his parts off and bring them to you."

"Bad statement to make to a cop, Sidney."

"Fuck you."

"I'm glad you're all right."

He paused, evaluating my response. "You're saying you didn't sic that kid on me?"

"No, and neither did Clete Purcel."

"Don't give me that crap. Purcel has got a long-standing beef with me. There was a rumble at the bottom of Magazine when we were kids. He thinks I was behind the guy who bashed him across the eye with a pipe. He's a dumb mick. You know how you can tell a dumb mick? They think and act and look like Purcel."

"Lay off Clete. He cut you slack when he could have destroyed you in front of your wife."

"I got no idea what you're talking about."

I had waded out into deep water, but I figured Sidney had asked for it. "Clete knew you had gotten it on with Natalia Ramos. He could have shown you up for the sorry-ass sack of shit you are, but he's too much of a gentleman to do something like that."

"I guess the lesson here is wet-brains hang together. Let me try to line it out for you. I met Natalia Ramos at the video store. She loves movies, like I do. I gave her a job cleaning my office. I also tried to help the junkie priest she was shacked up with. He was a good man, but his cancer kept him on the spike. Tell Purcel he's even dumber than I thought he was."

"You knew Father Jude LeBlanc?"

"You and Dumbo flap your ears down to the state mental hygiene clinic and see if they do brain transplants."

"Ronald Bledsoe broke into my house. That's on you, Sidney."

But he hung up while the words were only half out of my mouth.

The tops of the oak trees in the backyard were denting in the wind, and leaves were tumbling onto the surface of the bayou. I could see children playing with a Frisbee on the green slope of City Park and hear their voices carrying across the water. It was a fine evening, one that should not have been stained by thoughts about men like Ronald Bledsoe. But evil is evil, and it does not depart from our lives because we wish for it to leave. Otis Baylor's advice about not empowering Bledsoe was right on target, but that did not mean I had to play Bledsoe's game.

I called Clete on his cell phone. "Bledsoe doesn't sleep at night?" I said.

"No."

"What does he do?"

"Scares the hell out of hookers or plays card games."

"Cards?"

"On his laptop. There's a bumper sticker from the casino on his car. Maybe that's his jones. All these guys got one. Why?"

CHAPTER
22

I DROVE TO CLETE'S motor court at two o'clock Sunday morning. The sky was dark, the trees alive with wind, the lights burning inside Ronald Bledsoe's cottage. When I knocked, he pulled aside the blinds and looked outside, then dropped the night chain and opened the door. He was dressed in a navy blue robe and fluffy white slippers. He was smiling, his missing tooth replaced by a bridge.

"Sorry to bother you, Mr. Bledsoe. But I saw your light and didn't think you'd mind," I said.

"Not in the least. What a treat." He looked at his watch. "You're just like me. A night owl is what you are. Come in."

The interior of his cottage was immaculate, the bed still made, an open laptop on the breakfast table. "Bet I know what you're gonna ask me," he said.

"Bet you don't," I said.

"You want to know if I'm gonna file charges against your little girl."

"Are you?"

"No, sir, that's not my way."

"That's good of you. Can I call you Ronald?"

"Everybody does, 'cause that's my name." His elongated, waxed head gleamed under the electric light. He lifted a coffeepot off the stove and began filling two cups, glancing sideways at me. "You want sugar and cream?"

"No, nothing," I said, temporarily distracted by the images on his computer screen.

"I run different kinds of games on my laptop," he said. "You like to play cards, Mr. Robicheaux?"

"Call me Dave. I used to go to the track a bit. In fact, it became a problem for me, along with a bigger one I already had."

"That so?"

He handed me a demitasse and a saucer with a tiny spoon on it. But I set it on the table without drinking from it. Electronic playing cards were flipping out of a dealer's shoe and floating across the screen of his laptop. "I thought I could beat the odds, but eventually I got shellacked," I said.

"That so?" he repeated.

"It's every gambler's weakness, kind of like a drunk's. He thinks he can intuit and control the future, but his real mission is to lose."

"Why would a man want to lose?"

"So he can blame the universe for all his problems."

"I never thought of it that way. You a smart man, Mr. Robicheaux. This is an impressive town. Southern people are the smartest there is. Your daughter is highly educated and cultured. A man knows that as a natural fact soon as he lays eyes on her."

"Thanks, Ronald. Look, I wonder if you can help me with a problem. Somebody broke into our home and vandalized her bedroom. You hear about that?"

"No, sir, I didn't."

"So my boss would like to exclude you as a suspect. Could we get a swab from you?"

"Isn't that a form of search, Mr. Robicheaux? Requiring what they call 'probable cause'?" His smile never left his face.

"You're dead-on right about that."

"Well, you got a warrant?" he asked playfully.

"I'm afraid I don't."

"Then you just hold on a minute," he said. He went into the bath and returned with a Q-tip. He stuck one end deep into his jaw and wet it down, then dropped it into a Ziploc bag and handed it to me.

"I don't want you having trouble with your boss lady on my account. No, sir, that won't slide down the pipe."

"You had a partner when you broke into my house?"

He clasped the back of his neck and shook his head. "That offends me. Wish you wouldn't say that." His eyes went up and down my person. "You carrying a firearm, Mr. Robicheaux?"

All the while we had spoken, he had allowed me to call him by his first name but had continued to address me formally, in his way both patronizing and outwitting me.

I pulled back the right side of my sports coat. "Actually I'm supposed to, but this is just a friendly visit. Tell me, do you really believe you can come into a small southern town and wipe your feet on people and go back home without incurring some serious attrition? Do you really believe the South has changed that much?"

He stepped close to me, still smiling, his teeth shiny with his saliva. "I've done every kind of work there is, in every kind of place there is. Love of money is the root of all evil. The Bible says it. People were for sale back then, people are for sale today. This whole town would be a Wal-Mart parking lot if the money was right."

"You're wrong."

"Like hell I am," he replied.

"You know what blood stones are, don't you, Bledsoe?"

"In the civilized world, gentlemen don't address one another by their last names, Mr. Robicheaux. But in answer to your question, no, I don't know much about blood stones."

"Children's arms were lopped off because of those stones. I think they'll bring you to grief."

"I was brought to grief the day I was born. What do you think about that?"

He was so close to me now I could smell the dried soap on his skin. My gaze broke and I stepped away from him. Then I opened the door to let myself out, my breath short, the Ziploc bag in my hand.

"You not gonna drink your coffee, Mr. Robicheaux?"

Outside, his odor seemed to cling to my face. When I started my truck, he was standing in the doorway, his hands in the pockets of his robe, electronic cards flipping into a black satin hat on the screen of his laptop. He was backlit by the interior of the cottage, casting his face in shadow, but there was enough light from a streetlamp to show his teeth shining behind his smile. I backed down the driveway between the two rows of cottages, straight onto Main, the gearshift knob shaking inside my palm.

BACK HOME, I undressed and got in bed beside Molly. When she felt my weight on the mattress, she woke and rolled against me, her body hot to my touch. Before leaving for the motor court, I had told her I had to go to the office to take care of a situation for the dispatcher. Now I lay on my back and looked at the ceiling. She propped herself up on one elbow and looked down at me.

"Everything is okay. Go back to sleep," I said.

She brought her knee sharply into my thigh. "Don't try to put the slide on me, troop," she said.

"I confronted Bledsoe."

"By yourself?"

"Clete was close by. I was okay."

She placed her hand on my chest. "Your heart is pounding."

"I couldn't be in the same room with him. It's hard to explain. I had to get away from him."

"He admitted he broke into our house? He threatened you?"

"That's not the way he operates. The Prince of Darkness is always a gentleman. So are his acolytes."

"Don't talk like that, Dave."

"I'm going to nail him. One way or another, I'm going to tack him to the side of the barn."

She lay back down, the back of her head cupped by the pillow, her eyes fixed on the ceiling. Then she said something I never believed I would hear her say. "I want to buy a pistol."

IN THE MORNING, while I was still off the clock, I drove down to the south end of Lafourche Parish and parked in front of the crossroads bar where Bo Diddley Wiggins and I had gone to pick up Clete after

Clete had shot at a man fleeing down a canal in an outboard boat. The bartender was alone in the bar, in a strap undershirt, sitting in front of a fan, trying to read a newspaper in the half-light. I opened my badge holder on the bar and asked him about the two men who had been there when I had come to collect Clete. There was a pad of body hair on the bartender's shoulders and his eyebrows were laced with scar tissue, pinching his eyes at the corners so that they looked Asian rather than occidental.

"You know the guys who brought my friend in here?"

"They work for Mr. Wiggins. They drink beer here sometimes," he said.

"I knew that when I came in. I need to know where they are now."

"On Sunday, it's hard to say."

"I'm investigating a double torture-homicide. Would you like to answer my questions at the parish jail?"

He folded his newspaper over on itself and pushed it away. "There's a fuel dock four miles down the road. You might find one of them there."

"Thank you," I said, scooping my badge holder off the bar.

"Hey!" he said when I was almost out the door.

"Yes?" I said.

"I drive thirty-four miles on bad roads to get to this job. I make six bucks an hour and tips. FEMA says in another mont' I may get a trailer. How far you drive to work? Your house got a roof on it?"

I drove south to a fuel dock that was located at the junction of a brackish bay and a freshwater canal an oil company had cut into living marsh. Disintegrating pools of diesel oil floated on the water. A rusted barge lay half submerged in the sawgrass. I could see a man in khaki clothes moving about in a small office that had been built on the end of the dock. He was watching an airboat roaring across the bay and he did not hear me walk up behind him.

"Whoa, you scared me!" he said when he turned around. Then he recognized me and reintroduced himself. He said his name was Tolliver and that he was originally from Arkansas and had worked for Bo Wiggins for thirteen years.

"Your friend had a snootful, didn't he?" he said. "Did he get home okay?"

"Did you see him shoot at somebody, Mr. Tolliver?"

"No, I heard a couple of distant pops, the way a shotgun sounds in the wind. A guy was taking off in an outboard and I thought this guy Purcel maybe was a robbery victim. That's the only reason I got involved."

He was a pleasant-looking man, his stomach and love handles protruding over his belt. His forearms were big and brown and on the tops they were covered with reddish hair. He smiled a lot. In fact, he was too pleasant and smiled much more than he should have.

"You don't know who the man in the boat was?"

"No, sir."

"How long have you been working on this dock?"

"A couple of years, maybe."

"A lot of strangers come through here?"

"I just fuel up Mr. Wiggins's boats. I don't pay much mind to what-all goes on around here, I mean, folks fishing and that sort of thing."

"You ever hear of a guy named Ronald Bledsoe?"

"I can't say that I have."

"He's a strange-looking guy. His head and face look like the end of a dildo."

He coughed out a laugh and looked sideways onto the bay. He removed a pair of yellow-tinted aviator glasses from his shirt pocket and put them on, even though the sun had gone behind clouds and the marshland surrounding us had dropped into shadow. He spread his arms on the dock railing behind him and kept shaking his head, as though mulling over a question, although I had not asked one.

"Can you look at me, Mr. Tolliver?"

"I'm telling you all I can, Mr. Robicheaux. I don't know any more."

I kept my eyes fixed on his face until he had to look at me. "Ronald Bledsoe is an unforgettable person, Mr. Tolliver. I also think he's a man of great cruelty. If you shake his hand, you'll feel a piece of black electricity go right up your arm. Tell me again you don't know this man."

"I'm not familiar with the gentleman. No, sir," he said, shaking his head. But I saw the tic under his left eye, just like a bee had walked across the skin.

I took a business card from my wallet and handed it to him. "You look like a man of some wisdom. Be forewarned, Mr. Tolliver. Ronald Bledsoe is an evil man. Serve his cause and he'll consume you."

Tolliver tried to keep his face blank, but when he swallowed he looked like he had a walnut in his throat.

THAT EVENING I dug out an old .22 Ruger semiautomatic from my trunk and took Molly to the police firing range and showed her how to thumb-load the individual cartridges into the magazine and how to chamber a round. Then I taught her the use of the safety and how to dump the magazine from the gun butt and to pull back the slide to ensure a round was not still in the chamber. I did these things methodically and without joy. I did them with both reservation and a sense of depression.

The sky was mauve-colored, the trees along the state road dark with shadows and pulsing with birds. It felt strange watching Molly take a shooting position, her arms extended, one eye closed, the foam-rubber ear guards clamped on her head. It was hard to accept the fact that my wife, a former nun and a member of Pax Christi, was popping away at a paper target with a human silhouette printed on it. When she fired the last round in the magazine, the slide locked open and a tiny tongue of smoke rose from the empty chamber.

"You look unhappy," she said.

"It's been a long day, that's all."

"Are you disappointed in me?"

"No," I said.

"You believe we're giving power away to Ronald Bledsoe, don't you?"

"No," I said.

"You're good at lots of things, Dave, but lying isn't one of them."

I took the Ruger from her hand and dropped it in the canvas

rucksack in which I kept all my shooting equipment. I put my arm over her shoulders and we walked to where my truck was parked in the trees. Hundreds of birds were throbbing in the shadows, and in the west the sun had become a red pool tucked inside a bank of rain clouds. I had the same heavy feeling in my chest that I experienced as a child when my parents set about destroying their home and family. The feeling is related to what psychiatrists call a "world destruction fantasy." I lived with it in my dreams before I went to Vietnam and long after I returned. I addressed it with both Jim Beam and VA dope, and when they didn't work, I addressed it with the heart-pounding adrenaline that comes with the recoil of a pistol in your palm and the smell of gunpowder in your nostrils and the whirring sound that a tumbling round makes when it flies past your ear.

I felt that something irreplaceable was about to go out of my life, but I could not tell you why. Was it just the pull of the earth that you feel at a certain age? There are times when the scrape of a shovel pushed deep into dirt can become a sliver of glass in the ear. Was I more afraid of death than I was willing to admit? Or was Ronald Bledsoe causing my family to remake itself in his image?

When we got home, Molly oiled and cleaned the Ruger and did not return it to me.

AT 9:17 MONDAY MORNING my desk phone rang. "Mr. Robicheaux?" a familiar voice said.

"What do you want, Bertrand?" I replied.

"I come here for some help. I cain't take it no more."

"You've come where?"

"I rode a boxcar to New Iberia. I ain't had no sleep."

"You're in New Iberia?"

"Yeah, I cain't take it anymore."

"You can't take what anymore?"

"Everything. People hunting me. People treating me like I'm the stink on shit. Kovick fixed it so everybody in the FEMA camps know who I am. I ain't got no place to hide. I was gonna cap him. Or I was gonna cap his wife. But I couldn't do nothing except stand there shaking."

"You tried to clip Sidney Kovick?"

"I ain't no killer. I learned that Saturday. I might be a coward, but I ain't no killer."

He described the scene in the flower shop, the fear that fed like weevil worms at his heart, the bitch slaps across the face, the .38 cartridges poured on his genitals, the vicious kick that drew blood from his rectum. His self-pity and victimhood were hard to listen to. But I didn't doubt the level of his emotional pain. I suspected that, under it all, Bertrand Melancon was probably about seven years old.

"Give me your location."

There was a beat. "That ain't why I called. You got to explain something. I went to the evacuee shelter in the park 'cause I ain't had nothing to eat since yesterday. The white girl I seen in the car wit' the dead batt'ry by the Desire was there."

"You mean the white girl you raped?"

"Yeah, that one, she was there, man, serving meals at the shelter. I tole myself that wasn't possible. I axed a guy who she was and he said she was from New Orleans, her name is Thelma Baylor. That's the name of the people in the house where the shot come from, the one that hit Eddy and killed Kevin."

I realized what had happened. Thelma had probably gone to the shelter with Alafair to help out, and Bertrand had blundered inside and had seen her. I tried to concentrate, to prevent his accidental discovery from becoming a catalyst for events I didn't even want to think about.

"She lost weight, she look a li'l older, but it's her, ain't it?"

The idea that he was taking the physical inventory of a young woman he had assaulted and asking me to confirm it seemed to invade the moral senses on more levels than I could count. "She's not your business, partner."

"I got to make it right."

"You stay away from the Baylors."

"I got a plan. I'll get back to you."

He broke the connection.

I checked out a cruiser and drove to the recreation building in City Park. Alafair was stacking the cots of a family that was relocating to Dallas. She seemed preoccupied, not quite focused. A kid was dribbling a basketball in the background, smacking it loudly on the floor.

"Where's Thelma?" I asked.

"Her father picked her up. I think they were going home," she replied. She hefted a load of folded bedclothes and looked at me.

"Was a black guy in his early twenties hanging around? Somebody you haven't seen before?"

"If he was, I didn't notice."

"His name is Bertrand Melancon. He's one of the guys who raped Thelma."

"Why is he here?"

"Guilt, fear, opportunism. I doubt if even he knows. Maybe he's nuts."

"Is this related to Ronald Bledsoe?"

"Yeah, it is. It's related to blood diamonds, too. We need to get Melancon into a cage, for his own good as well as everyone else's."

"I'm sick of this."

"Of what?"

"Ronald Bledsoe was here this morning. He told the room supervisor he'd like to be a volunteer. But his eyes were on me the whole time. He had that sick grin on his face."

Outside the front door, children were playing on swing sets and seesaws under the oak trees. I could remember when Alafair was their age and doing the same kinds of things. "Have lunch with me," I said.

"What are we going to do about this asshole, Dave?" she replied.

I returned to the department and knocked on Helen's door. She wasn't happy to hear the latest on Bertrand Melancon.

"Tell me if I missed anything? He raped the Baylor girl and another girl in the Lower Nine and tried to kill Sidney Kovick, and he's in New Iberia, calling you with his problems of conscience."

"I guess that about says it."

"Where is he now?"

"I don't know."

"Get ahold of Otis Baylor and his daughter. Tell them Melancon is in the area and that we plan on picking him up. But make sure Baylor understands that Melancon belongs to us."

"Got it."

She stood up from the desk and put her hands on her hips. She was wearing western-cut tan slacks and a braided belt and tight shirt. Then unexpectedly she looked me straight-on in the face and her eyes and manner took on that peculiar androgynous cast that had a way of turning her into a lovely mystery, one that was both arousing and unsettling at the same time.

"I should have never sent you back to New Orleans," she said.

"Why's that?

"Because the Feds have money to clean up their own messes and we don't. Because you're a good cop and you never shut the drawer on your cases. Everybody in your caseload stays in your head. If you weren't a cop, you'd have a Roman collar on." Her eyes were violet-colored, warmer than they should have been.

"Can I have a raise?"

She jiggled her fingers at me. "Bwana go now."

I SKIPPED LUNCH and drove out to Otis Baylor's house on Old Jeanerette Road. He was in his yard, inside deep shade, a four-gallon tank of insect spray on his back. He worked his way along the side of the house, spraying the flower beds and the foundation. It was cool inside the shade, but the canvas loops of his spray tank had formed sweat rings on his shirt. I had a feeling Otis Baylor was pinching every dollar he could.

I sat on his front steps without invitation, as a neighbor might. Down the long green slope of his property, the bayou wrinkled in the wind and elephant ears grew thickly along the banks. Otis's nineteenth-century house, with its rusted screens, tin roof, deep shade, and green mold on the foundation, was a humble setting. But inside the trees the air was cool-smelling and filled with the sounds of wind in the bamboo and the drift of pine needles across the roof. It was the kind of place where a man could be at peace with himself and his family and set aside the ambitions that never allow the soul to rest. But I doubted that Otis would ever find that kind of peace, no matter where he chose to live.

"I took your advice," I said.

"About what?"

"Not to play Ronald Bledsoe's game."

He continued to spray along the bottom of the house, as though I hadn't spoken. "These Formosa termites will flat eat your house up, won't they?" he said. "If you don't stay after them, they'll eat right through the concrete."

"One of the guys who attacked Thelma is in town," I said. "He called me on a cell phone. His name is Bertrand Melancon. He's the brother of the guy who took one through the throat."

Otis nodded, his eyes flat, his spray wand hissing across the latticework at the base of the gallery. "Why would he call you?"

"He's scared. I also think he's remorseful for what he's done."

Otis pumped the handle that pressurized his tank, his eyes looking at nothing. "He should be."

Should be scared or remorseful, which? Or both? I pulled on my earlobe. "My boss wants you to know that Bertrand Melancon belongs to us."

"Now, you listen, Mr. Robicheaux—"

This time it was I who interrupted. "You know what kimberlite diamonds are?"

"No."

"A few years back, warlords in Africa were selling them illegally to fuel their war machines. To harvest these diamonds, these warlords massacred large numbers of defenseless people and chopped off the arms of children. That's why they're called blood diamonds. Somehow Sidney got his hands on a bunch of them. The guys who looted Sidney's house accidentally stumbled into the biggest score of their lives. Can you imagine what Sidney or his business partners will do to get them back?"

Otis paused in his work and seemed to stare into the shadows. He slipped the tank off his back and, holding it by one loop, set it gently on the grass, the insecticide sloshing inside. He sat down on the step in front of me, rubbing the backs of his hands, his coarse skin making a whispering sound.

"Those men think we're between them and their diamonds?" he said.

"I'm not sure," I replied.

"Where's this black kid now?"

"I don't know that, either."

"All this is about those diamonds, huh? It doesn't have squat to do with me or my family, does it?"

"I wouldn't say that."

He stood up and shook my hand, then walked into his backyard without saying good-bye.

THAT EVENING ALAFAIR went to a book signing at Barnes & Noble in Lafayette, with plans to stay over at a friend's. Molly and I hooked up my boat and trailer, and drove up to Henderson Swamp. It was a fine evening to fish for big-mouth bass. The wind had died, and the islands of willows and cypress trees had taken on a gold cast against the sunset. Clouds of insects gathered in the lee of the islands, and you could see bream popping the surface and occasionally the slick, black-green roll of a bass's dorsal fin on the edge of lily pads.

Molly had fixed fried-oyster po'boy sandwiches for us and packed several cans of Dr Pepper with crushed ice in a cooler, but I had no appetite and could not concentrate on the perfection of the evening or the fish that were feeding in the shadows of trees that were now etched like pyro-fountains against the sun.

I didn't want revenge against Ronald Bledsoe. I wanted to kill him. I wanted to do it close up, with a .45, one loaded with 230-grain brass-jacketed hollow-points. I wanted to empty the whole magazine into him. I wanted to smell the good, clean, head-reeling odor of burnt gunpowder and feel the jackhammer recoil of the steel frame in my wrist. I wanted to see Ronald Bledsoe translated into wallpaper.

"Why so quiet?" Molly asked.

"No reason," I replied.

Had I confessed the nature of my thoughts to Molly, I would not have only frightened or perhaps even repelled her, I would have also revealed my inability to find a legal solution for dealing with Bledsoe and those like him.

Supposedly we are a Christian society, or at least one founded by Christians. According to our self-manufactured mythos, we revere Jesus and Mother Teresa and Saint Francis of Assisi. But I think the truth is otherwise. When we feel collectively threatened, or when we are collectively injured, we want the Earp brothers and Doc Holliday on the job and we want the bad guys smoked, dried, fried, and plowed under with bulldozers.

For that reason, I no longer feel guilt and shame over my own inclinations. But I don't talk about them, either.

Just as the sun seemed to descend like a molten ball beyond the causeway that spanned the swamp, I cast a Mepps spinner into a cut between two willow islands. There was a current between the islands, and insects that fell from the trees onto the surface were carried into a narrow channel flanged on each side with lily pads. The water was dark and deep and undisturbed. The Mepps arched over the channel and made a tiny splash by a cluster of blooming hyacinths. Just as I began to rotate the handle on my reel, taking the slack from the line, I saw the water swell under the hyacinths as though a pillow of air were rising from the bottom. Then a dorsal fin cut the surface and something hit the Mepps so hard my rod smacked down on the gunwale like a broom handle.

In Louisiana, in freshwater areas, only large-mouth bass hit with that kind of power and force. I socked him hard, setting the treble hook, and tried to lift the rod and keep the tension and weight of the fish off the monofilament. But the tip of my rod arched to the water, bowing so severely I thought it would break, beads of water shining on the line. Then he began stripping the drag, sawing the line under the boat, trying to find a stump or log to wind it around.

Molly used the oars to turn us in a half circle, freeing the line from under the boat and allowing the bass to head up the channel. He came up once, rattling the Mepps at the corner of his mouth, then went deep again and tried to pull the boat. He fought for ten minutes, and when he finally began to swim with the pressure of the line and the hook in his mouth, I knew he was done. It was the kind of victory a fisherman doesn't necessarily take pride in.

I slipped the net under him and lifted him into the boat. He was heavy and wet and thick-bodied inside the netting, the barbs of the treble hook protruding from the webbed skin at the corner of his mouth. I wet one hand in the water and lifted him, still inside the net, onto the boat seat and worked the hook out of his mouth. Then I cupped him under the belly and eased him back into the water. I could see his gills working, then he dropped away into the current like a green-gold bubble going in the wrong direction.

"Giving dispensations these days?" Molly said.

"Only to warriors and other guys who deserve them," I said.

She laughed and opened a can of Dr Pepper and drank it in silence. Then a peculiar phenomenon occurred. Maybe it was because the sun had died and we were deeper into the fall. Maybe it was because the stars were out early and the moon was rising. Maybe car lights on the causeway or the evening glow of Lafayette were reflected off the clouds. But in the cut between the two willow islands, in the darkness of the water where I had just placed the valiant bass, I saw lights that were like pieces of a broken mirror swimming about. I saw them as surely as I had caught that fish and felt it fat and heavy and dripping in my palm.

CHAPTER
23

How do you nail the perps when they have no handles?

Tuesday afternoon, just before quitting time, Clete called me at the office. "A guy who's a regular at the casino just went in Bledsoe's cottage," he said. "This dude is a Texas Hold 'Em player. I saw him reading the back of a package of rubbers in the restroom, in front of about six guys who'd seen him with his girlfriend outside the door."

"You think he can be a lead?"

"He's Bledsoe's kind of guy. Bledsoe has left no trail, but how many of his friends can have the same kind of luck? Doing anything tonight?"

"Not a thing," I replied.

"Let's use two vehicles. I'll stay with them for now. Leave your cell on," he said.

I was about to hang up when he added, "You won't believe the jugs on the broad who's sitting in his convertible. I'm getting a boner just looking through the blinds."

"Will you act your age and stop talking like that?"

"You're right. There's nothing funny about this bunch. Somebody is going to pay for what they did to Courtney. It's been a while since the Bobbsey Twins from Homicide were under a black flag."

I wished I hadn't said anything.

An hour and a half later, while Molly and I were washing the dishes, Clete called again. "I'm about a quarter of a mile behind

Bledsoe and his friend and the broad with Elsie-the-Cow bongos. I think they're headed for the casino. Unless I call you back, we ROA there," he said.

Roger that, I thought, more casually than I should have.

"Where are you going?" Molly asked.

"Clete has a lead on Bledsoe."

"I want to go with you."

"It's just surveillance. It's pretty boring stuff."

"That doesn't matter. He broke in our home. He urinated in Alafair's bedroom. My stomach turns when I think about it. She told me he tried to get on as a volunteer at the shelter."

"He's going off the board, Molly. It's a matter of time."

She stepped closer to me. "You think I have to be protected from reality? I had Maryknoll friends who were raped and murdered in El Salvador. Our government didn't do a goddamn thing about it. Dave, I'm not going to sit around while this man brings his evil into our lives."

"I understand how you feel."

"Do you?"

I looked at the earnestness in her face and wanted to hold her. I put my arms around her back, cupping one hand on her neck. She was wearing a sundress and her skin felt cool and warm at the same time under the wood-bladed ceiling fan. I rubbed my cheek against her hair and squeezed her tighter. "I promise I won't let him hurt us again," I said.

She lowered her head and I felt her hands slide off my back. "Why do you think it's all up to you? Why is it only about you?"

"It isn't," I said. "You have to trust me when I say that. For once, just trust me."

I went outside and started the truck, my face hot, my ears ringing with the harshness of our exchange. The yard had fallen into shadow and cicadas were droning in the trees, like a bad headache that won't go away. Just as I was backing into the street, regretting my words, trying to accept Molly's anger and hurt feelings, she came out on the gallery and waved good-bye.

That's what happens when you marry nuns.

• • •

THE CASINO WAS located on reservation land, down Bayou Teche, in what used to be a rural slum. Now the reservation is prosperous and the people there live in neat homes not far from the confluence of the Teche and another waterway which together form into a bay. The house lots have no fences and contain persimmon and pecan trees, live oaks and slash pines. It's a lovely piece of topography that hides certain economic realities that few care to dwell on.

The patrons of the casino are the working poor, the uneducated, the compulsive, and the addicted. The booze is free as long as the patron continues to gamble. The interior glitters and charms; the restaurant is first-rate. The bands that play there do Cajun and zydeco and shitkicker, too. Inside the hermetically sealed environment, one that has no clocks or windows, all the problems of the outside world disappear.

After Katrina and Rita, the profits at Louisiana's casinos soared to all-time highs. If you have already lost most of the ranch, what does it matter if you lose the basement?

Clete was standing by his car in the parking lot, smoking a Lucky Strike, his features taut with anticipation. A thermos rested on his car hood. I parked next to him, took the cigarette from his mouth, and flipped it sparking on the asphalt. "They're inside?" I said.

"Yeah, they put in their names for a Texas Hold 'Em table. They're at the buffet table now." He unscrewed the top of the thermos and drank from it but offered me none.

"Did you get anything on Bledsoe's bud?"

"Joe Dupree at Lafayette PD ran his tag for me. The car is registered to a Bobby Mack Rydel in Morgan City. Joe's description of the ID photo fits the guy driving the car. I don't know who the broad is. How do you want to play it?"

"What are you drinking?" I asked.

"Vodka Collins. You mind?"

"How big a gambler is Rydel?"

"The Hold 'Em table is a hundred-dollar buy-in. I've seen him buy a grand's worth with the bills in his shirt pocket."

"What about Bledsoe?"

"I haven't seen him in action. There's one thing about creeps, though. They want to be treated like they're normal. Particularly in public."

I thought about it. "Let's spit in the punch bowl. Where's their car?"

"It's the Saab ragtop a couple of rows over."

"Think it might have a vehicle violation or two?"

"I'll check it out," he replied.

Clete walked through the parked cars and looked down at the rear tag on a black Saab. Then he removed his Swiss Army knife from his pants pocket and squatted down below eye level. He was gone from sight longer than I expected. When he returned he was folding a knife blade back into the knife's casing. "You were right. The guy's tag is missing. A couple of his tire valves are busted, too. What a shame," he said.

We entered the casino and walked past banks of slot machines that rippled with color and rang with the sound of coins cascading into metal trays. Hard by the rows of slots were dozens of Hold 'Em card tables, each seating nine players. The game was so popular the players had to get on a waiting list in order to buy a hundred-dollar chair. While the players waited for a vacancy, they fed the slots. When they got tired of waiting, they had another drink on the house and fed the slots some more.

Clete nodded in the direction of two men and a statuesque woman with white-gold hair who were being seated at one of the far tables. Bledsoe was wearing powder-blue slacks, a matching vest, a bolo tie, and a long-sleeved shirt with silver stripes in it. His elongated, polished head and the vacuous smile painted on his face seemed to float like a glistening white balloon above the people around him. His friend, Bobby Mack Rydel, if that was his name, was a heavy, swayback man dressed in brown jeans with big brads on them. He also wore a wide cowboy belt, maroon suede boots, and a dark red shirt with pearl snap buttons. He had long sideburns that flared on his cheeks and a fleshy sag under his chin. He wore an Australian bush hat, the brim turned down all around the crown, the leather chin cord flopping loose on his throat. While he was being seated, he kept his hand in the small of the woman's back.

A security guard was drinking a cup of coffee at the end of the bar, glancing at his watch, occasionally yawning. "What's happenin', Dave?" he said.

"On the job, you know how it is," I replied.

"Overtime is overtime," he said.

Clete put a mint in his mouth and snapped it between his molars. "See that dude in the Digger hat?" he said.

"The what?" the guard asked.

"The guy in the Australian flop hat. You might check your Griffin book," Clete said.

"He's a regular," the guard said.

"All griffins are regulars. That's how they end up in the Griffin book," Clete said.

The guard looked at me for confirmation. I raised my eyebrows and shrugged.

"Thanks for the tip," the guard said.

"No problem, noble mon," Clete said.

We worked our way closer to the table where Bledsoe and Bobby Mack Rydel and the woman with white-gold hair were playing Texas Hold 'Em. Bledsoe had just received his second hole card and was peeling it up with his thumb to peek at it.

"Hey, Dave, look, it's Ronnie Bledsoe, you know, Ole Ronald McDonald from the motor court," Clete said. "Ronnie, how's your hammer hanging?"

Bledsoe turned in his chair, his face uplifted, his mouth puckered, like a guppy at the top of a tank. His eyes seemed to radiate serenity and goodwill. He continued to look up into Clete's face without speaking.

"Sorry, you're busy. Catch you later," Clete said. He pointed at the top of Bledsoe's hole cards. "Stomp ass with that hand." He gave him a knowing wink that everyone at the table could see.

Then he went to the bar and ordered a double Jack straight up and a beer back.

"Slow it down, Cletus," I said.

"No, no, big mon. We take it to them with tongs," he said. "We need Rydel in custody. Just go with the flow."

He knocked back the rest of his Jack and finished his glass of beer. He touched at his mouth with a paper napkin, his face blooming, his eyes lit with a dangerous alcoholic shine.

He went into the men's room and minutes later came back out, a paper towel folded in his right hand. He located himself behind Bobby Mack Rydel and the woman with white-gold hair. While the dealer put down the flop, Clete placed the folded paper towel between Rydel and his girlfriend, deliberately dropping the two shiny purple-and-black square packets it contained on the floor.

"Oh, gee, I'm sorry," he said. He bent over and picked up the packets, then replaced them under the paper towel, first making sure that everyone saw them. "I think they're what you wanted—those hard-ribbed ones, right?"

Rydel used his elbow to rake the two packs of condoms off the table, back onto the floor, never even looking at Clete. Even more dumbfounding was the fact that hardly anyone else at the table paid attention to Clete's behavior.

Clete shifted gears and went into another mode. He studied the three communal cards that were faceup on the felt, his thumb and forefinger on his chin. "That's too bad. You should have gotten out before the flop. Looks like you're screwed, Bobby Mack," he said.

That did it. Rydel removed his hat and hung it by its leather chin cord on the back of his chair. Then he twisted around so he could see Clete more clearly. His eyes were lead-gray, his sideburns neatly etched, the skin around his mouth drained of blood. "Who are you?" he asked.

"You don't remember me?" Clete said.

"No, I never saw you before in my life."

"You remember Courtney Degravelle?"

"No, I don't. You got me mixed up with someone else."

The head of security had walked up behind Clete. He was a re-tired St. Mary Parish sheriff's detective by the name of Tim Romero. He had salt-and-pepper hair and was dressed in a blue sports coat, knife-crease gray slacks, and shined loafers. "Is there a problem here?" he said.

"Not with me," Clete said. "But this guy here is on the grift. I already reported him at the door. If he hasn't switched out cards on you yet, he will."

"Do you mind stepping over to the bar with me?" Romero asked.

"No, I don't mind. But that guy is a griffin and his partner there, the guy with the waxed head, is a pervert."

"That's it, Mr. Purcel, you either come with me or you'll be escorted from the casino."

Clete raised his palms. "You want creeps at your tables, that's your choice. Tell you what, call your colleagues in Atlantic City or Vegas about these two guys and see what kind of feedback you get."

I cupped one hand on Clete's shoulder and looked at Romero. "He's okay. We're going to get a cup of coffee," I said.

"If you say so, Dave. But don't make me regret I took this job," Romero said.

Clete and I went to the bar and immediately he ordered a Jack and a beer back.

"Clete—"

"Trust me," he said. "We're going to nail those guys. We just need to twist the screw a little tighter."

"I think we're firing in the well," I said.

"Wrong," he said.

He sipped from the shot glass and touched at his mouth with the back of his wrist, his stare riveted on Rydel's face. Rydel glanced up at him, then back at his cards. Then he looked up again. Clete's stare stayed on his face. Rydel fitted his hat back on and slanted the brim down like a man keeping the sun's glare out of his eyes.

I got out my cell phone and walked to a quiet place at the end of the bar. I scrolled down to Betsy Mossbacher's cell number and punched the "call" button.

Please pick up, Betsy, I thought.

"Dave?" she said.

"Can you run a dude by the name of Bobby Mack Rydel? I need it right now."

"What's going on?"

"Come on, Betsy, help me out. I think I've got a house fire here."

I don't know how she did it but she did. My suspicion was she or a colleague dipped into an intelligence file. By my watch, it took less than four minutes for her to call back.

"You've got a live one," she said. "Rydel was in Force Recon in the Marine Corps, attended jump school at Benning, and was kicked out with a dishonorable discharge after he was charged with rape in Japan."

Clete had walked over to the slot machines, not far from the card tables, and had positioned himself where he could look directly into Rydel's face. Each time Rydel looked up, Clete was grinning at him, smacking his gum, his big arms folded on his chest.

"He ran a training school for mercenaries in the Florida Panhandle and was probably mixed up with mercs in Mozambique in the eighties," Betsy said. "He has a seventh-degree belt in karate. He beat a man to death in Miami and got off because the victim was armed and Rydel was not. Are you getting this?"

"Yeah, I'm right here," I said.

Rydel had just bet heavily into a large pot, trying to ignore Clete and keep his eyes focused on the game, waiting for the final cards to be turned up by the dealer.

"Rydel is on a watch list in France. Interpol thinks he may be involved with arms smuggling. He may have been with the Contras briefly, but for sure he's worked all over Africa," Betsy said.

Rydel raised the bet, pushing three stacks of chips into the center of the felt. A black man in a purple suit with rings on all his fingers called and raised. Rydel called and raised again, pushing out the last of his chips. The black man shrugged and called the raise, yawning either out of confidence or perhaps acceptance that he had gotten in over his head.

"Here's the last of it," Betsy said. "He's been a contract security employee for several companies operating in the Mideast. His specialty is thought to be interrogation. Don't ask me to do this again."

The communal cards the dealer had dealt faceup in the center of the felt included an ace of spades and an ace, king, and jack of hearts. Rydel turned over his hole cards, an ace of diamonds and an ace of clubs. The two aces from the flop gave him four of a kind, an almost guaranteed winner.

The black man grimaced as though he had just bitten down on an abscessed tooth.

"I catch a hand like that about once every six months," Rydel said.

"Yeah, I know what you mean. Me, too," the black man said.

He turned over his hole cards, a ten and queen of hearts. With the ace, jack, and king from the communal cards, he was holding a royal flush, the best hand in poker.

Clete began wheezing with laughter, his folded arms bouncing up and down on his chest. He passed by Rydel's chair, slapping him hard on the back. "Tough luck," he said. "If you need a credit line, forget it. This is a class joint. They don't take food stamps."

You could hear him laughing all the way to the men's room.

Rydel sat for about thirty seconds staring into space, his hands splayed on his thighs, perhaps counting up the number of instances his attention had been distracted from the game by Clete's ridicule.

He said something in the ear of the woman with the white-gold hair. She wore a white knit dress full of eyelets and her breasts hung as heavy as cantaloupes in her bra. Her eyes were lifted toward the ceiling, fluttering as Rydel spoke. I had a feeling this was not the kind of evening she had bargained for. I also realized I had seen her before.

Rydel got up from the table and followed Clete into the men's room.

"Hello? Are you still there?" Betsy said.

"I'm here," I said.

"Where?" she asked.

"In deep shit," I replied.

CLETE WAS READY for Bobby Mack Rydel when he came through the door. Or thought he was.

"What's your name, Gordo?" Rydel asked.

"Clete Purcel, the friend of Courtney Degravelle, the woman you and your friends tortured to death."

"No, your name is Gordo Defecado, a guy who's both nuts and seriously in need of a tune-up. Think of me as your Mr. Goodwrench."

"I can see it in your eyes. I can smell it on your skin. You did it to her, you bastard."

For a heavy man, Rydel was surprisingly agile. He spun on one foot and nailed Clete in the throat with the other one. Then he kicked Clete in the face and knocked him down in front of the urinals. The men who had been inside the stalls or at the lavatories or about to use the urinals began pushing through the door into the concourse. Clete tried to get up and Rydel kicked him in the ribs, then against the side of the head. He stomped Clete's hand and raised his foot to drive a blow into the back of Clete's neck.

That was his mistake.

Clete locked his hands behind Rydel's knees, then came up off the floor, lifting as he did, toppling Rydel backward so that the back of Rydel's head split on the edge of a lavatory as he went down.

Images that Clete believed he had dealt with long ago seemed to release themselves like red blisters popping on a black screen in his head. He heard a razor strop whooshing down on his naked buttocks. He saw a grass hooch shrink to nothing inside the flame of a Zippo track. He saw a black woman clutching a baby to her breast, standing on top of a flooded church bus, screaming for help that didn't come. He saw a white woman taped in a chair, a plastic bag cinched over her head, her eyes terrified, her lungs sucking the plastic into her mouth.

He pulled Rydel to his feet and drove his fist into Rydel's stomach. Then he caught him full in the face, putting all his weight into it, smashing his head into the mirror, poking a hole in the center of it. When Rydel bounced off the mirror, Clete hit him again, breaking his lips against his teeth. Then he knocked him backward into a stall, holding on to the sides himself, stomping Rydel in the face and head, gashing open his scalp.

I grabbed the back of Clete's shirt collar and tried to pull him out of the stall. He turned on me, his face blotched with color, his eyes lustrous.

"This is one time you don't want to get in my way, Streak," he said. His finger trembled as he pointed it at me.

He kicked Rydel again and again in the face, his breath wheezing, his tropical shirt split down the back. Then he wrenched the toilet seat off the commode and hung it around Rydel's neck.

"How's it feel, motherfucker? How's it feel?" he said.

THE DETECTIVES FROM the St. Mary Parish Sheriff's Department did a good job and found two witnesses who stated the first blows in the fight had been delivered by Bobby Mack Rydel. Clete was told by the casino management he was permanently eighty-sixed, but he got to go home that night, whereas Rydel was eighty-sixed and went to the hospital on top of it.

In the morning Clete was in my office, remorseful, hungover, his face swollen on one side, a bruise in the shape of a frog on his throat. "I screwed it up," he said.

"No, you didn't. You mopped up the floor with him," I said.

"Dave, when I pulled off Rydel's tag and sliced his tire valves, I had another plan. It didn't include you. If he called for a tow truck, I was going to offer him a ride and try to get him alone. I had my own agenda from the jump. I just wanted to get even. I didn't care how I did it. I tried to convince myself he looked like the guy I shot at in the boat. I've been treating these guys like street mutts. It was a mistake. They're a lot smarter than that."

I didn't reply and tried to hide my concern about his admission of a private agenda.

"If I hadn't beaten the crap out of Rydel and turned him into a victim, we could have had him under arrest. I blew our chance to squeeze him. "

"We've got someone else," I said.

"Who?"

"Rydel's girlfriend. I couldn't remember where I had seen her."

He lifted his face, indicating for me to go on.

"I saw her with Bo Diddley Wiggins. It was from my office window, at a distance, but I'm sure it was her."

"Think he's connected with Rydel and Bledsoe?"

"We'll find out. Say, Helen wanted to see me in her office. How about I check with you later?"

Actually Helen did want to see me, but the real issue was to get Clete out of the office before he factored himself into my workday and brought more trouble down on both our heads.

"Call me on my cell," he said.

"Ten-four, partner."

He walked out into the hallway, cocking his porkpie hat on his head, his upper arms like cured hams, the mayhem of yesterday already fading in memory. The deputies he passed in the hallway kept their gaze straight ahead. None of them spoke. If Clete noticed their aversion, he didn't show it. He had been genuinely contrite, but I had no doubt my best friend would always be out of sync with the rest of the world. That said, our excursion to the casino had been a disaster.

Helen had just gotten off the phone when I went into her office. She had been in and out of New Orleans repeatedly, flying in the departmental single-engine plane, returning each time more depressed. She, like others, had difficulty assimilating the magnitude of the damage and even greater difficulty in expressing it to others. This weekend she had agreed to accept back four prisoners who had been transferred from our stockade to Orleans Parish right before Katrina hit. The prisoners had been deserted by their jailers and left to wade in their own body waste for three days. They became so frightened they tore the side walls out of their cells and created a corridor all the way to the outside wall. But they couldn't break through to the outside and remained trapped behind the cell bars until cops from Iberia Parish rescued them.

One of the Iberia cops was a narc street-named Dog Face. When the Iberia transferees realized who one of their rescuers was, they began whistling and giving him the thumbs-up and shouting at him:

"Hey, Dog Face, it's me, Li'l Willie, you busted me on Ann Street."

"What it be, Big Dog Face? You kick ass, man."

"You the Man, Face. You bring any eats wit' you?"

But humorous stories about events that occurred in Katrina's wake were not on Helen's mind. The St. Mary Parish sheriff had just faxed her his investigators' report on last night's incident at the casino.

She placed her fingers on each side of her head and rubbed at her temples, massaging them slowly, as though interdicting a large migraine in the making. "Here's the way I see it, Pops. Ronald Bledsoe may have broken into your house and vandalized Alafair's room. But we have no evidence to prove that. To our knowledge, he has never been charged with a crime anywhere. His friend, this man Rydel, has no warrant on him and to our knowledge is not involved in any form of unlawful activity. But the resources and time of the department are being committed to investigating and surveilling these people. How do I justify that to the taxpayers?"

"I was off the clock last night," I said disingenuously.

She glanced down at the fax sheets on her desk. "One of the St. Mary detectives said Rydel's car tag was stolen and his tires slashed in the parking lot. If the tires were slashed by a vandal, why would he bother to take the tag?"

"Maybe his tag fell off somewhere else."

"The Phillips screws were on the ground. The tag was stolen in the parking lot, obviously by the same guy who cut the tires. If that's Clete's work, doesn't it seem just a little bit adolescent to you?"

I gave her the background on Bobby Mack Rydel I had gotten from Betsy Mossbacher. I put in every detail I could remember, including the fact he had been charged with rape in Japan and had beaten a man to death in Miami. I also mentioned his specialty was interrogation, which often in the bureaucratic language of governmental agencies is a synonym for torture. I also mentioned that his girlfriend was Bo Wiggins's secretary.

"So that means Rydel is connected with a guy who builds steel ships?"

"Maybe."

It was obvious I was overloading her with information that she didn't have time for.

"Look, the guy is a seven-degree black belt," I said. "Alafair took out one of Bledsoe's front teeth with a karate kick. Maybe Bledsoe hooked up with Rydel for a specific purpose."

"To hurt Alafair?"

"The possibility crossed my mind."

She let my tone pass. "I think we need to have an understanding—"

I interrupted her. "I'll be up-front with you. I'm glad Clete busted up Rydel. I hope he stays in the hospital for a long time. If either Rydel or Bledsoe comes after my daughter, I'll do much worse to him."

"Finish your statement," she said.

"I'll kill either one of them or I'll kill both of them."

She folded her hands on her desk blotter. There was a wan look in her eyes, the kind people get when they know their best words are of no value. "A conversation like this will never occur in this office again. You'd better get back to work, Dave."

I started to speak.

"Don't tempt me," she said.

CHAPTER
24

Bertrand Melancon had moved in with his grandmother in what was called the Loreauville "Quarters," up Bayou Teche, nine miles from New Iberia. Tucked between sugarcane acreage and mist-shrouded horse farms, the Quarters was a neighborhood of nineteenth-century tenant cabins that looked like yellow boxcars with peaked tin roofs and small galleries nailed on to them as an afterthought. Some of them were deserted and boarded up with plywood, but his grandmother's place was neat and clean and had fresh paint on it, and she kept tin cans planted with begonias and geraniums on the front gallery and on the windowsills.

Bertrand's grandmother fixed good meals, but her talents were wasted on her grandson. He could not eat anything with cayenne or black pepper or gumbo filet in it. Once or twice, when he was spitting off the gallery, he had noticed a pink tinge in his saliva but had dismissed it. Then this morning he had gotten the dry heaves. When he looked into the toilet bowl, there was no question about what he saw there. Bertrand was fairly certain his insides were coming apart, like wet cardboard, one piece at a time.

He was also fairly certain he was going to die unless he did something to rid himself of the guilt that waited for him each dawn like a carrion bird perched on the foot of his bed. He couldn't undo what he had done to the priest on the church house roof, and he couldn't find the young black girl he and Eddy and Andre had raped in the

Lower Nine. But somehow Fate had caused his path to intersect with Thelma Baylor's, not once but twice, in New Orleans and now in New Iberia.

Making it up to Thelma Baylor and her family was the way out, he told himself. He had the power to make her family rich. Maybe they would never forgive him and still despise him, but they would be rich just the same and he would be free and the pain would go out of his stomach and he could start over again in California.

Fate was giving Bertrand a second chance. At least that was what he told himself. If his intuitions were not true, he knew he would die soon. That thought caused him a spasm of pain that made him grip his stomach muscles and close his eyes.

There was only one hitch in his desire to redeem himself: How was he supposed to do it?

He could write a letter of apology and tell the Baylors where to find the stones and leave it in their mailbox or under a door. But even as he started composing the sentences in his mind, he knew his prescription for his own redemption was too easy. He was going to have to look Thelma Baylor and her family in the face. That image, particularly when it came to looking the father in the face, made sweat break on his brow.

Why was everything so hard?

His first morning in the Loreauville Quarters he borrowed his grandmother's car, a rusted-out hulk that oozed oil smoke from under the frame, and headed down the bayou toward New Iberia. The cane fields were wet and fog rolled off the bayou on the horse barns and spacious homes and oak-lined driveways of the people who were actually his neighbors, although they would never look upon him as such. He continued on down the state road into New Iberia and turned toward Jeanerette and the house where Thelma Baylor lived. He passed through both rural slums and immaculate acreage owned by the Louisiana State University agricultural school. He drove alongside rain ditches that were layered with trash and clumps of simple homes inside pecan trees. He passed a graveyard filled with crypts that reminded him of the cemeteries across from the New Orleans French Quarter.

But no matter what he looked at, he could not escape the fear that was like a cancerous tuber rooted in his chest. He tried every way possible to rationalize not confronting Thelma or her family directly. Wasn't it enough simply to give them an amount of money that was probably beyond their wildest dreams? Wasn't it enough that he was sorry, that his own health had been ruined, perhaps even his life made forfeit? How much was one guy supposed to suffer?

But besides his guilt over Thelma Baylor and the priest on the church roof and the young girl in the Lower Nine, he had another burden to carry. He had not only been slapped in Sidney Kovick's flower store and had his pistol taken away from him by an unarmed man, he had proved himself a coward and had been treated as such, kicked between the buttocks, like a punk or a yard bitch, in view of passersby at the end of the alley.

He passed an eighteenth-century plantation home built of brick and saw a modest green house with a screened-in gallery ensconced inside shade trees. The numbers on the mailbox were the same as the ones he had gotten out of his grandmother's directory. He drove to the drawbridge over the bayou, looking straight ahead in case anyone was watching. He rumbled across the bridge and turned his car around so he could have a full view of the Baylor house without anyone taking note of his interest. A light was on in the kitchen and steam was rising from the tin roof where the sunlight touched it. What if he just knocked on the door and announced who he was? If they wanted to shoot him, they could shoot him. If they wanted to have him busted, they could dial 911. What could be worse than watching his insides transformed into dissolving red clots in the toilet bowl?

He stayed parked for perhaps five minutes on the road's shoulder, just on the other side of the bridge, blue oil smoke seeping through the floorboards. There was little traffic across the bridge this time of day. But when he glanced in the rearview mirror, he saw a white man who had an elongated, waxed head and indented face standing in front of a café, looking about innocuously, as a tourist might. When Bertrand glanced in the mirror a second time, the man was gone.

He shifted his grandmother's car into gear and crawled across the bridge, turning back onto the state road that led past enormous plantation homes and the green one-story house of the girl he had raped and tormented. He slowed his car in the shadows across from the house and shifted the transmission into park. His head was spinning, either from his fear or the oil smoke rising through the floor. Then he had an idea. What if he wrote out the words he needed to say, and walked up to the door and knocked? In his mind, he saw Thelma Baylor and her father and mother answer his knock in unison, anxious for his apology, as though it were what they had waited for ever since the night she was taken into the hospital by paramedics.

Yeah, man, just read the statement and put the piece of paper in their hands and get in my grandmother's li'l car and rocket on down the road, he told himself.

He found a brown paper hand towel on the floor and a magazine on the seat. He flattened the hand towel on the magazine, propped the magazine on the steering wheel, and began to print with a ballpoint pen:

To Miss Thelma and the family of Miss Thelma,

I am sorrie for what I have did to her. I wasn't always that kind of person. Or maybe I was. I am not sure. But I want to make it right even tho I know it is not going to ever be right with her or anybody who was hurt like she been hurt.

He paused, his heart beating, and looked at what he had written. For some reason, the words made him feel better than he had felt in a long time. Behind him, he heard the sound of tires rumbling over the drawbridge and automatically he looked in the rearview mirror. A truck had just crossed the bridge and turned down the bayou, in the opposite direction from Bertrand. But it was not the truck that got his attention. The white man with the long head and indented face had parked a gleaming blue Mercury under shade trees in front of a historical plantation house on the corner. The man was standing on the shoulder, the driver's door open between him and Bertrand, his forearms propped on the car's roof, evidently admiring the huge white facade and stone columns of the building.

Definitely a weird-looking motherfucker, Bertrand thought.

He went back to his letter. Suddenly the front door of the Baylor home opened, and Thelma and a heavyset man and a blond, sun-browned woman stepped out into their yard, their faces turned up like flowers into the sunlight.

Bertrand was petrified. He had bathed last night in his grandmother's claw-footed tub, but a vinegary smell rose from his armpits. He wanted to get out of the car, to wave his unfinished letter at them, to make them listen to his offer of restitution. It couldn't be that hard. Just do it, he told himself.

Then the Baylor family backed out of the driveway, into the road, and drove away as though he were not there.

Bertrand opened his car door and spit on the ground. The wind blew in his face and puffed his shirt, but he knew that once again there would be no respite from his fear and that failure and self-loathing would lay claim to every moment of his day. He wanted to weep.

He got out of his car and wandered down the slope by the bayou, his legs almost caving. The man who had been studying the antebellum home under the oaks roared down the asphalt toward New Iberia, glancing once at Bertrand as he passed.

The man's face looked exactly like the back of a thumb, a pale white thumb, Bertrand thought. He could not remember ever seeing anyone who looked as strange. Then he sat down in the leaves and put his face in his hands.

WEDNESDAY AFTERNOON I drove to Bo Wiggins's office in the old Lafayette Oil Center. Actually it was more than an office. He had purchased the entire building and had placed a sign that read "James Boyd Wiggins Industries" over the front entrance. He was not there and neither was his statuesque secretary with the white-gold hair. The receptionist was talking on the phone. A magazine lay open on her lap and she kept looking down at it while she spoke, shifting her legs so the page wouldn't flip over and cause her to lose her place. After she hung up, I asked her where I might find Bo and his secretary. She bit on a nail and developed a faraway look in her eyes. "Houston?" she said.

"You're asking me?" I said.

"No, it's Miami. They went on his private jet. With some other guys."

"Which guys?"

"Some contractors."

"Which contractors?"

"The ones who're hauling all that storm junk out of New Orleans?"

She had turned a declarative sentence into a question again.

"When will they be back?" I asked.

"Tomorrow, I think."

I decided this was a conversation to exit as soon as possible. I gave her my business card and drove back to Lafayette in a downpour that left hailstones smoking on the highway.

THURSDAY MORNING Helen Soileau called me back into her office. "What I said to you yesterday about departmental resources was straight up. But that doesn't change the fact Bledsoe is a dangerous man and has no business in our parish."

I waited.

"Get him in the box. Let's see what he's made of," she said.

"On what grounds?"

"We want to interview and continue our exclusion of him as a suspect in the break-in at your house."

"I've been that route."

"Tell him the sheriff of Iberia Parish wants to meet him."

"What if he doesn't want to come?"

"If he is what you say he is, he'll come."

"Why's that?"

"Because he wants to show us he's smarter than we are."

Helen knew our clientele. Sociopaths and most mainline recidivists share certain characteristics. They are megalomaniacs, narcissists, and manipulators. No matter how ignorant and uneducated they are, they believe they are more intelligent than law-abiding people. They also believe they can intuit the thoughts of others. It's not coincidence they often wear a corner-of-the-mouth smirk. I've always suspected their behavior and general manner have something to do with the origin of the term "wiseguys."

I found Ronald Bledsoe sitting in a deck chair in front of his cottage, wearing Bermuda shorts, a short-sleeved shirt printed with green flowers, and dark glasses with big round white frames. He was drinking a glass of iced tea and reading the newspaper, one hairless pink leg crossed on his knee.

"Sheriff Soileau would like for you to come down and talk to her, Mr. Bledsoe," I said. "It's purely voluntary. By the way, sorry about that fracas the other night."

He folded his newspaper and tilted his head, his eyes unreadable behind his glasses. "I've heard a lot about your sheriff. I hear she's an interesting person. I think I'd be delighted to meet her. Can we go in your vehicle?"

I didn't overtly try to engage him in conversation on our way back to the department. He seemed to enjoy riding in a cruiser, and he kept asking questions about the various pieces of technology on the console and along the dashboard. Then he removed his glasses and I felt his eyes probing the side of my face.

"Know what the de facto definition of a criminal is, Mr. Robicheaux?" he said.

"No, sir, I don't."

"A man with a demonstrable record of criminality."

"Yeah, I guess that's hard to argue with."

"You appear to be an educated person, as your daughter does. You ever run across the term 'solipsism' in a philosophy course when you were in college?"

"I don't think I did." We were still on East Main, headed into the historical district. In less than five minutes we would be at the courthouse parking lot and in all probability Bledsoe would stop speaking on a personal level, something I didn't want to happen. "What is 'solipsism,' exactly?"

"The belief that reality exists only in ourselves and our own perceptions."

"That's a new one."

"Let me ask you the age-old puzzle: If a tree falls in the forest and no one hears it, has it really fallen? Tell me your opinion on that and I'll tell you mine."

"I'd say it had fallen."

He laughed to himself and watched the blocks of antebellum and Victorian and shotgun homes slip by the window.

"So what's your opinion?" I said.

"I've already told you. You just weren't paying attention." He punched me in the arm with one finger.

His eyes were merry, a liquid green under his thick, half-moon, Curious George eyebrows and jutting forehead. "Is it true your sheriff is a hermaphrodite?"

We went through the back door of the courthouse and I took him directly to the interview room. Several uniformed cops turned around and looked at us as we passed them in the hallway.

"I'll tell Sheriff Soileau you're here. How about some coffee and doughnuts?"

"I like doughnuts."

"Coming up," I said.

I left him in the interview room and asked Wally to take him some doughnuts and a cup of Community coffee, then I told Helen that he was here.

"How did he behave coming over?" she said.

"He asked me if I was familiar with solipsism."

"With what?"

"It's a philosophical view that the only reality is one our minds generate. Then he asked me the riddle about a tree falling in the forest."

"If no one hears it, does it really fall?" she said.

"I told him it falls, whether anyone hears it or not. He laughed."

"What do you think he was trying to say?"

"Earlier he had said something about the definition of a criminal being the physical record of the criminal. I think he was ridiculing us because we can't find evidence of any criminal activity in his life. I think he just gave us his whole MO. He's a sociopath who doesn't get caught. Like Bundy or BTK and probably thousands of others, they burrow into the woodwork and nobody knows they're there until the house falls down."

"How do you want to play it?" she asked.

"This guy is a sexual nightmare. I suspect he hates women, particularly female authority figures."

"Can you imagine that?" she replied.

We walked down to the interview room, a relatively small enclosure, with two oblong glassed slits in the wall that allowed someone in the hallway to look at the subject with a degree of invisibility.

"Check him out," I said.

Helen peered through the glass. "Jesus Christ," she said.

"Ready?"

"When you are," she replied.

I opened the door and we went inside. Wally had brought Bledsoe at least four custard-filled doughnuts and a king-size paper cup of Community coffee. He ate them as you would a hamburger, feeding the whole doughnut into his mouth, the yellow cream glistening on top of his nails.

"My name's Ronald. What's yours?" Bledsoe said to Helen. He partially rose from his chair and sat back down again.

"I'm Sheriff Soileau, Mr. Bledsoe. Appreciate you coming down." She closed the door behind us and glanced up at the video camera on the wall. "Since this is just an informal conversation, I had that camera turned off."

"I never noticed it."

There were two empty chairs at the table, but Helen and I remained standing.

"Let's get right to it," she said. "Somebody broke into Detective Robicheaux's home and vandalized his daughter's computer and pissed in the wastebasket. You gave us your DNA voluntarily and we appreciate that. But we have a larger concern. What the hell are you doing here in New Iberia?"

The shift in her tone caught him off guard. He lifted his eyes into hers. They were as bright and green as emeralds. "I'm a private investigator in the employ of several insurance carriers."

"Which carriers?"

"Confidentiality precludes my giving out their names."

"I see. Do you know what obstruction of justice is?"

"I do."

"You've factored yourself into a homicide investigation, Mr. Bledsoe. I'm talking about the shooting of two black men in front of Otis Baylor's house in New Orleans."

"Those men of color were looters. They stole from homes insured by my employers."

"Otis Baylor is going to help you recover stolen property?"

"I didn't say that."

"You know Sidney Kovick?"

"I know his name. Everyone in New Orleans does."

"Do you work for him?"

"No, I'm a bond agent and an insurance investigator, not unlike Mr. Purcel, Mr. Robicheaux's friend. Can you tell me why Mr. Purcel is not in custody, considering the amount of injury he did to Bobby Mack Rydel?"

"Our focus is on you, Mr. Bledsoe."

"Do you have any more napkins? These are messy."

"Is that what your mother told you? Don't have messy hands?"

"What was that?" he said.

Helen leaned down and propped her fists on the table, only inches away from him. A tube of muscle stood out in the back of each upper arm. Her hair hung on her cheeks. Her physical presence was palpable, her scent like a mixture of flowers and male body heat. Bledsoe's nostrils whitened around the edges. He shifted in his chair and placed his hands in front of him. His fingers were long and pale, as though they had been in water a long time.

"Who the fuck do you think you are?" Helen said.

He looked straight ahead and seemed to gather his body inside his clothes. "You don't have the legal right to touch my person."

"If I touched your person, Mr. Bledsoe, I would scrub my skin with peroxide and a wire brush. Is it true you get off scaring the hell out of working girls?"

He glanced up at the camera on the wall, clearly wondering if indeed it was turned off and if that was good or bad for him. "Does it seem logical that a man who hires prostitutes would want to scare off prostitutes?" he said.

"Yeah, if everything about him creeps them out," Helen said.

For the first time I saw a darkness sweep across his face. Helen leaned closer to him, her hip brushing again him, her face intersecting his line of vision. "What did your mother do to you when you were a kid?"

"She didn't do anything."

"When you wet the bed, did she make you sleep in your own stink? Did she wash out your mouth with soap when you sassed her? Did she tell you your underwear was inside out and that skid marks were on it, that you made her ashamed you were her son, that you disgusted her?"

He started to get up from the chair.

"Sit down. I'm not through talking to you," she said. "She did things to you in the dark, didn't she? Your father wasn't around and so you were the dildo. Did she ever hold your penis in her hand and then punish you for it later?"

The temperature in the room had grown warmer and I felt myself clearing my throat.

"You're making this up. You don't know me," Bledsoe said.

"You made a mistake coming to this parish. You're a sick man and you'll be treated as such. Detective Robicheaux, go get him another cup of coffee. I want to talk to Mr. Bledsoe a little more privately."

"I don't want any. I want to return to my cottage now."

"You know why you keep looking at that camera, Mr. Bledsoe?" she said. "It's because your identity is self-manufactured and you're nothing like the person you want the world to see. We know everything about you. You're genetically and psychologically defective. People like you and Richard Speck and John Wayne Gacy should have been flushed down the toilet with the afterbirth five minutes after y'all were born. Unfortunately your mommies didn't do that and instead raised up big titty babies that everyone else has to take care of."

I picked up his coffee cup from the table. "You want cream or sugar?"

His bottom lip trembled. Helen had delivered a cut that went to the bone.

"Answer him," she said.

He sat up in the chair, his eyes blinking and refocusing, like a man who had just undergone a violent decompression inside a bathysphere. Then he huffed air out his nostrils and straightened his shoulders. I suspected that behind that jutting forehead he was re-building his mental fortifications a block at a time, a process he had learned in an environment most of us can only guess at. He bit into a doughnut and pushed the custard inside his mouth with his fingers.

"It's been real nice y'all having me here," he said. "I won't hold your words against you. That's not my way. My mother was a lovely, kind woman and you don't have any idea of what you're talking about."

"You need to talk to us, Mr. Bledsoe," I said.

"No, sir, I surely don't. Very harsh things have been said here today." He got up from the chair and took his pair of dark glasses from his pocket, the ones with the round white frames, and fitted them on his face. "Looks is only skin deep, Ms. Soileau. If you're a Christian, maybe you should give more thought to the feelings of other people."

With that, he walked out of the room, down the hall, and out of the courthouse.

"Do you believe that?" Helen said.

"Want me to take him home?" I said.

"Screw him," she said. She walked in a circle, her hands on her hips. "Think he slipped the punch?"

"You took his skin off."

"And?"

"Bledsoe's a psychopath. He's incapable of accepting injury done to him by others, either real or imagined. He hates our guts and he'll get even in whatever way he can."

I think Helen had drawn on her own childhood experience when she turned the screws on Bledsoe. I also suspected some of the images she had used in her interrogation were of a kind she herself did not like to remember.

"Some fun, huh, bwana?" she said.

LATER THAT DAY Bertrand Melancon was sitting on the steps of his grandmother's gallery, wondering what he should do next, when a blue Mercury turned in to the Quarters and splashed through a puddle, fanning a muddy spray back across its immaculate surface. The driver sighted Bertrand and turned in to his grandmother's yard.

Another storm front had moved in and the sky overhead was blue-black and blooming with electricity. The driver of the Mercury got out and walked toward the gallery, avoiding the pools of rainwater, lifting his trouser cuffs above his two-tone shoes.

"Hi," he said.

"What's happenin'?" Bertrand replied.

"My name is Ronald. What's yours?"

"Same as it was this morning, when a guy wit' a face just like yours was following me down by the drawbridge in Jeanerette."

"You're smart. I bet you been to college."

"What you want, man?"

"Can I sit down?"

"No."

The man with the indented face opened a badge holder with a photo ID and an ornate gold and blue shield inside. "I'm an investigator for an insurance carrier. I'd like to pay you a recovery fee."

Was this one of the guys who had taken Eddy out of Our Lady of the Lake and stolen his mind? Bertrand wondered. Or lured Andre into a car outside the FEMA camp? No, those guys wouldn't drive up to his grandmother's house in daylight, in full view of the neighbors.

"Recovery of what?"

The man who had introduced himself as Ronald removed a big

envelope from his side pocket. It was thick and crimped tightly in the center with two double-wrapped rubber bands.

"Here, see what's inside," he said, holding it in front of Bertrand's face.

Bertrand folded his hands and pretended to look into the distance.

"Open it up," Ronald said. "A smart man always gets the information up front before he does his decision making. A smart man sees what's on the table, then makes an informed choice. You're a student of people, I can tell that. You a cautious, smart man. I know that, 'cause I'm a student of people, too."

The man named Ronald touched the edge of the envelope against the back of Bertrand's hand. "What you got to lose?" he said. "Think those rich people in those big houses down the road are worried about you and your grandmother?"

Bertrand looked down the street that was lined with shotgun houses and dirt yards in which the people parked their vehicles. Across the state road he could see a field full of green sugarcane and a thoroughbred horse farm bordered by white-painted railed iron fences and dotted with breeding barns that cost more than his grandmother's entire neighborhood, all of it backdropped by a sky that leaked thunder.

Bertrand reached out and took the envelope. It was heavy and solid and felt good in his hand, the way a stack of money packed into an envelope can feel solid and good.

"How much in here?" he said, his voice suddenly dry and speaking of its own accord, before he could even organize the words in an intelligible fashion.

"Forty thousand. But that's just for now. You get another forty thousand after we do the recovery. Go ahead. Stick your finger in there. Close your eyes and tell me what it feels like. Make you think of anything else?"

Bertrand cracked the glue on the seal with his thumb and looked at the sheaves of one-hundred-dollar bills inside. "How I know it ain't counterfeit?"

"Tomorrow morning I'll drive you to the bank. Or tonight we can go to the casino. We'll buy some chips with it and see what happens.

The people at the casino know counterfeit when they see it. You're a smart man, all right."

A camera lens opened in Bertrand's mind and he saw himself driving a convertible down an ocean highway, waves sliding up on the sand, big coral rocks hissing with foam. He saw girls in bikinis slapping a volleyball back and forth across a net. He heard music pounding from his stereo speakers and felt the salt spray in his face.

"Time to start a new life," Bledsoe said.

Next door a woman began shouting at her children. Bertrand heard her hit one of them, a bone-deep slap, the kind that sent a child to the floor.

"You right," he said.

"That's what I thought."

"That why I ain't interested. Besides, you got the wrong guy," Bertrand said.

He handed the envelope back to Bledsoe and knitted his fingers between his legs. Spots swam before his eyes. He could not believe the amount of money he had just held in his hand and returned to the man who had offered it to him. He spit between his knees and let his mind go empty.

"What you just said is not only illogical, it's untrue," Ronald said, mustering his most tolerant voice.

"What's that suppose to mean?"

"If you're the wrong guy, you wouldn't know enough to say you're not interested. Besides, you look just like your brother."

Bertrand could hear an electric rip in a cloud, a tearing sound at the bottom of the sky. "How you know what my brother looks like?" he asked.

Ronald's eyes retained their mirthful brightness, but a pause took place in them, a beat or a blink that was not a blink, a split-second inner recognition that he had made a slip.

"I got both y'all's mug shots. I got them from a friend at NOPD."

"Yeah, New Orleans cops that been wading in water up to their chins love to do that for guys who get their badges out of Cracker Jack boxes."

"I'm trying to be your friend, Bertrand. I want to make you rich. You're inches away from having the most beautiful women in the world."

"Hey, man, no hard feelings, but I don't think you know nothing about beautiful women."

Bertrand got up from the step and went back in the house. He wondered if he had managed to conceal the fact he had made Ronald as one of the men who had kidnapped Eddy. When he looked back through the screen, Ronald was turning his car around in the yard, one tire mashing over a tomato plant in his grandmother's garden. The shape of his head reminded Bertrand of a question mark. Then Ronald's eyes locked on Bertrand's. The expression on Ronald's face made Bertrand step back from the screen.

A FEW MINUTES LATER Bertrand drove down to the grocery store in Loreauville and bought a chocolate drink from the soda machine. He drank it in the car, in the parking lot, across from a Catholic church, and tried to think. This dude with a head and face that reminded him of the curved head of a long-reach toothbrush was lying. He was one of the dudes who had grabbed and tortured Eddy. Which meant he was one of the dudes working for Sidney Kovick. But why didn't they just grab Bertrand, too? They knew where he lived. They knew his movements. They knew who his grandmother was. Bertrand should have been dog food by now.

Because the guy was working his own deal? Because the guy was going to stiff Sidney Kovick?

That was it. Kovick's hired geek had got off his leash and was going to make his own score, at Kovick's expense.

Maybe it was time to mess with a couple of people's heads as well as set things straight with somebody who thinks it's all right to pop other people in the face, Bertrand thought.

He changed the last five dollars of the money his grandmother had given him into silver and used the pay phone on the front of the grocery store to call long-distance information. "Yeah, Kovick's Flowers in Algiers, that's it, you got it," he said. "Snap it up, too, okay? This is an emergency situation."

He looked at his watch. It was 4:56. Come on, come on, he thought. "Hey, ain't y'all heard of computers? What's the holdup?" He danced up and down on the balls of his feet. "All right, say it again." He wrote the number on the grocery store wall. "Tell your supervisor to give you a raise. Tell her Bertrand Melancon give her the green light on that."

He punched the number into the pay phone, his ulcers singing, his head light as a balloon with the adrenaline pumping through his system.

Be there, be there, be there, he prayed, because he knew if he didn't connect with Kovick now, his courage would wane and fail him later, as it always had.

After the eighth ring, Bertrand almost gave up. Then someone picked up the receiver and said, "Kovick's Flowers. Could I help you?"

The voice at the other end of the connection made Bertrand's bowels turn to water.

"Could I help you?" the voice repeated.

"No, you can help yourself, motherfucker."

There was a pause, more of fatigue than surprise. "Is this who I think it is?"

"Yeah, Bertrand Melancon, the brother of Eddy Melancon, if that name mean anything to you. Know a cracker drives a blue Merc, looks like somebody beat on his face wit' an ugly stick when he was a kid?"

"No."

"Think hard. Carries a PI badge. Thinks the niggers are gonna start tap-dancing and spitting watermelon seeds when he rolls the gold on them?"

"You seem to be a slow learner, kid. Why don't you drop by and let's have a talk?"

"No, this time you listen to me. Your man was here with a fat envelope full of dead presidents. Guess what he was doing. Cutting his own deal for them blood stones and selling your sorry ass down the drain. Maybe you ought to hire a higher class of circus freaks to do your dirty work."

"Where can I get in touch with this guy?"

"I don't know and I don't care. I called for another reason. Maybe I deserved what you done to me. Maybe I went there axing to get bitch-slapped and kicked in the ass in front of people. But I learned something there you ain't gonna understand. I learned I ain't no killer. I couldn't cap you, no matter what you done to me and Eddy. So I come out of this wit' something you didn't figure on. I know I ain't like you, a killer done cut off a man's legs, and that's worth more to me than them blood stones."

The line was silent.

"You there?" Bertrand said.

"Where are you?" the voice said.

"In your head, just like you been in mine. But not no more," Bertrand said, and hung up.

Wow, he thought, his skin tingling like he'd just walked out of an igloo.

CHAPTER
25

THE WHITE FLICKER of lightning in the trees surrounding her house made Melanie Baylor think of the summer storms she had known as a child growing up north of Chicago. The family had lived on Lake Michigan, in a neighborhood of hardwood trees and elevated lawns and sailboats tacking in the wind against a background of azure water that seemed as large as the sea. The storms could tear at the lake's surface and torment the trees, but the big two-story house she had lived in was a safe place, one where her father, a stockbroker, smoked a pipe in front of the fireplace and was always full of good cheer. Even during the winter, when the boathouse was locked up and the lake plated with ice, the house and the small town where they shopped were safe places, far from wars and urban unrest. Melanie knew she would marry and move away one day, perhaps to the East Coast, but she would always remain a midwesterner and her real home would always be located inside chestnut and beech and maple trees on the shores of Lake Michigan.

That was before her father had a massive coronary in the bed of his mistress in Naperville. That was before the Securities and Exchange Commission investigated his brokerage service. That was before his creditors sued the estate and took every cent the family had, including the home on Lake Michigan.

Melanie lifted the bottle of bourbon from the cupboard shelf and poured an inch into her glass. Then she poured again and got ice from the refrigerator and placed three cubes in the glass and added water. She could hear rain on the roof now and the trees in the backyard were wet and dark green when the lightning flickered in the clouds. Otis and Thelma were still at the grocery store in New Iberia. By Melanie's estimate, the combination of bad weather and driving distance and the amount of groceries they had to buy ensured they would be gone for at least an hour and a half. She would enjoy her bourbon and her solitude until then, and perhaps fix one strong drink just before they arrived back home, and that would be it for the evening.

She wasn't an alcoholic. That's what her first husband had been. One thing was for sure. She would never be like him. *That* was not up for debate.

Otis didn't take her to task because she had lost her abstemious ways, nor did he monitor the amount that was gone each day from the Chianti bottle in the pantry or the decanter of brandy in the dining room. Otis was a good man, she told herself with a degree of self-fondness, proud of the way she had come to accept him and his physical ways and the smell of testosterone his clothes sometimes carried.

She showered and washed her hair and dried herself in front of the mirror. She turned sideways and raised herself slightly on her toes and looked at the flatness of her stomach, the firmness of her breasts, the sun-browned, almost tallowlike smoothness of her skin. She felt an imperious sexual urge that made her wet her lips and tilt back her head, creating an erotic self-image in her mind that made her wonder if indeed she wasn't a narcissist. She bit down sensuously on her lower lip and removed a strand of hair from her eye. Then she slipped her feet into her sandals and, while she watched herself in the mirror, carefully blotted the drops of water off her cheeks and forehead.

She picked up her drink from the top of the toilet tank and drank. Otis thought he knew everything about her, but the reality was otherwise. Maybe she would give him a little lesson one of these nights. Her erotic power was far greater than he knew. The men who looked at her with an adventurous eye were never made to feel they were acting inappropriately. Maybe Otis should become a little more aware of the desire she could stir in others.

She put on her fluffy robe and wrapped her head with a towel and took her drink into the living room. She turned the stereo to the university's classical music station and opened a book on her knee and sipped from her glass. Outside, the rain was blowing in a vortex that looked like spun glass in the porch light. The two-lane road in front of the house was black and slick, and across the bayou she could see lights in a backyard and a Negro man on a ladder redistributing the bricks that held down the blue tarp and canvas that covered a hole in his roof left by Rita.

When would this bad weather end? When would all the problems wrought by the hurricanes just go away?

A car leaking oil smoke went by the house and turned around by the drawbridge. A moment later the car's headlights went out. Melanie set down her drink and book and went to the window, unconsciously closing her robe at the throat.

The car was barely discernible in the darkness created by the overhang of the trees. She strained her eyes but could not tell if the driver was still inside or not. In the background, up on the drawbridge, a vehicle she never expected to see in a rural area of southern Louisiana suddenly appeared in the glow of the bridge's overhead lights. A lavender Rolls-Royce clattered across the grid, turned by the plantation house next door, and headed down the bayou road, in the opposite direction from the parked car and the Baylor house.

She checked the lock and chain on the front door and lowered the blinds. Then she sat quietly in her chair and finished her drink. The bourbon went down into her stomach like an old friend, in a way that made her feel warm and confident and erotically empowered at the same time. Then it spread throughout her body and deadened all her nerve endings, like someone closing her eyes with his fingers, like someone whispering in her ear that the world was a safe and good place and that one's mistakes would be healed by the anodyne of time.

What better friend could one have?

• • •

BERTRAND MELANCON finished writing his letter of amends to the Baylor family and read through it one more time. He wondered if they would be bothered by the fact it was written on a paper towel. More important, he wondered if they would be repelled by his visitation at their home. But rain or shine, it was time to boogie down the bayou. He drank from the bottle of chocolate milk his grandmother had bought for his stomach, folded the paper towel with a neat crease, and stuck it inside his shirt.

Rain swept in sheets across the Loreauville Quarters and the cane fields and pecan trees and danced in a yellow mist on the bayou's surface. He ran through his grandmother's flooded yard and started her car, feeding it the gas, waiting for the spark plugs in all the cylinders to get hot enough to run in sync so the engine would stop backfiring and belching clouds of smoke out of the broken muffler.

He drove onto the state road and headed toward New Iberia, the rain beating so hard on his roof and windows, the rubber on his windshield wipers was coming off. As he turned onto Old Jeanerette Road and followed the bayou toward the Baylors' house, he discovered he had another problem as well: the brakes were not responding until the pedal was almost to the floor.

His grandmother had said something about low brake fluid earlier, but he had been working on his letter of amends and hadn't paid attention to her. Now he was in the midst of another rainstorm with a defective brake system and layers of oil smoke rising up his nose. How much else could go wrong?

He pumped the pedal and felt the resistance level firm up, but a moment later it went soft again and he almost drove through the stop sign at the four-corners in a rural slum by the bayou. There were self-serve gas pumps at the convenience store on the highway, across the bridge, but it was doubtful he could buy brake fluid there. So he pushed on toward Jeanerette and the Baylors' house, the rain sluicing down his windshield, his ulcers blaring like the Mormon Tabernacle Choir.

Finally he passed Alice Plantation and saw the lights of the Jean-erette drawbridge glowing in the mist. He passed the Baylors' house and made a U-turn at the bridge and parked in the shadows of trees. The rain had turned to fog and a soft drizzle that seemed to adhere to every surface in sight. The gallery light was on at the Baylor house, and so were the lights in the living room and the kitchen. Maybe the whole family was there. Briefly he saw a silhouette at a window, just before somebody dropped the blinds.

Bertrand had always wondered how paratroopers mustered the courage to jump out of airplanes. What kind of fool would leap out a door thousands of feet above the earth, hoping a bunch of cloth streaming out of his back didn't shred into rags, hoping he wasn't going to become a keyhole in a barn roof? In the St. John the Baptist jail he got the chance to ask a paratrooper just that question.

The paratrooper picked at his nails and said, "You just don't think about it before you do it and you don't think about it after it's over."

"That's it?"

"Yeah, more or less," the paratrooper replied.

Bertrand tried to use the paratrooper's words to muster the courage he needed to approach Thelma Baylor's home. But they were of no help to him and he wondered if in fact there were certain words you never adequately understood until you had earned the right to understand them.

He took a breath and headed for the Baylors' front door, his letter of amends still inside his shirt. Behind him, he heard a heavy vehicle clatter across the drawbridge's grid. He turned and saw a luxurious lavender automobile of a kind he had never seen before. The chrome radiator cap was on the outside of the hood. The bodywork was so smooth it looked like plastic that had been poured into a mold. Then the automobile disappeared down the back road toward the ragged outline of the old sugar mill.

Bertrand walked across the Baylors' front yard and mounted the steps. He hesitated a moment, then he pulled open the screen door and went inside.

• • •

MELANIE HEARD THE rain slacken, then become nothing more than a whisper of tree branches across the tin surface of her roof. The side yard was strung with fog, the sky still flickering with electricity that made no sound. She had poured her glass half full of bourbon and had added more ice but no water. When she drank from the glass, the bourbon was cold enough and strong enough to anesthetize everything it touched. It was particularly effective in preempting or editing images from the night Katrina had made landfall and changed her life forever.

She thought she felt a vibration caused by footsteps on the gallery. But the footsteps couldn't belong to Thelma or Otis, could they? Melanie would have seen the headlights in the driveway. Besides, Thelma and Otis always unloaded the groceries under the porte cochere and entered the house through the side door, just as they had in New Orleans.

She set down her book and listened. Then any doubts she had about the presence of someone on the gallery were removed by a sharp knock. She got up and approached the door at an angle, so she could see through one of the warped panes at the top without being seen by the person outside.

Suddenly she was looking at the profile of a black man. He was of medium height, unshaved, his hair uncut, his face beaded with moisture. He kept looking back at the road, where a vehicle's headlights were burning on the road's shoulder. Then the headlights went out and the young black man turned back toward the door.

Melanie stepped back quickly. The whiskey that had nestled in every corner of her system, warming and comforting her, seemed to evaporate like water on an overheated woodstove. Her hands trembled and her breath caught in her throat. She went to the kitchen and punched in 911, then realized there would not be time for the police to get there. She would have to deal with the black man herself, either by confronting or ignoring him.

But if she ignored him, he would assume no one was home and perhaps break in. She closed her eyes and thought she heard a gunshot, then realized the sound was not real, that the whiskey had betrayed her and was now re-creating and amplifying memories it was supposed to protect her from.

She heard the voice of a black woman speaking from the phone receiver: "What is the nature of your emergency?"

"What did you say?" Melanie asked.

"What is the nature of your emergency?"

"A man is at my door. Send someone out."

"Is he breaking in?"

"He's a black man. I don't know who he is. He has no business here."

"We'll send someone out, ma'am. Is there someone else at your house?"

"No, you won't send somebody out. You'll give priority to auto accidents. I know you people."

"What do you mean by 'you people,' ma'am? Do you need medical assistance? You sound like you've been drinking."

"No, I don't need medical assistance, you ignorant thing," Melanie said. She dropped the receiver on the table, rejecting the dispatcher but not breaking the connection.

She pulled a butcher knife from one of the slits in the wood block where she kept all her sharpest knives. Then she went back to the front door and flung it open, the butcher knife concealed behind her.

The black man stood in front of her, clutching a flattened brown paper towel in both hands, like someone who had come Christmas caroling.

"Are you Miz Baylor?" he asked.

"What do you want?" she said.

"Is Miss Thelma or Mr. Baylor here?"

"I asked you what you want."

"So I guess they ain't here. Let me read this to you, ma'am, then I'm gone."

He positioned himself so the overhead light fell on the paper towel.

"Are you crazy?" she said.

"'To Miss Thelma and the family of Miss Thelma,'" he read. "'I am sorry for what I have did to her. I wasn't always that kind of person. Or maybe I was. I am not sure. But I want to make it right even though I know it is not going to ever be right with her or anybody who was hurt like she been hurt.

"'Andre and my brother Eddy and me was the ones who attacked her by the Desire. We done the same thing to a young girl in the Lower Nine. I want to tell her I'm sorry, too, but I cain't find her. So if you know who she is, please tell her what I said.

"'The night of the storm I went in your garage and stole gas. We also stole what is called "blood stones" from a man who stole them from somebody else. I hid them where the map on the bottom shows. They are yours. They won't make up for what we done. But Eddy is ruined and Andre is dead and I think I have already lost my soul. So that's all I got to say, except I apologize for what we done.

"'Thank you, Bertrand Melancon.'"

She stared at him, stupefied. "You raped Thelma?" she said.

"Yes, ma'am."

"You piece of shit, you come to our house offering us blood diamonds? You goddamn piece of shit."

"I ain't meant to upset you."

The cream he used in his hair had started to run and she could smell it on his skin. It smelled like aloe and body grease and candle wax. In her mind, she saw a bullet punch through a black man's throat and, behind him, the skullcap of a teenage boy explode in a bloody spray. She thought she was going to be sick to her stomach but she wasn't sure why. One thing was clear, however. She viscerally hated the black man standing on her gallery.

"You've ruined our lives. You destroyed my husband's career. We're losing everything we own because of you. You ask for forgiveness? You have the arrogance to ask that from us?"

He saw the knife in her hand. The blade was short, deep at the hilt, tapering triangularly to a honed point. "I'm sorry I bothered y'all, ma'am. I t'ought it was the right thing to do. I ain't gonna do it again."

He tried to offer her the letter he had written on the paper towel.

he tore it from his hand and threw it in his face. He backed away from her, through the screen, then fell down the steps into the yard.

"Take this with you," she said. She picked up the paper towel from the gallery, crumpling it into a ball, and threw it at him. "Did you hear me? I hope you do go to Hell."

But Bertrand was already running for his grandmother's car, looking back over his shoulder, wondering if redemption would ever be his or if insanity was the rule in human beings and not the exception.

Then he saw the lavender automobile again, the one with the chrome radiator cap on the outside of the engine. The driver was standing by the front headlight, watching Bertrand, his polished, elongated head unmistakable against the glow of the drawbridge.

Just won't give it up, will you, motherfucker? Okay, let's see if you got a pair of peaches or a pair of acorns on you, Bertrand said to himself.

He fired up his grandmother's car, dropped the transmission clanking into reverse, and floored the accelerator. The tires spun a shower of mud and water into the air, and oil smoke bloomed in black clouds from under the hood as the car sped toward the front of the strange-looking vehicle with the radiator cap outside the engine.

Here I come, Toot'brush Face.

Bertrand was twisted all the way around in the seat as he steered, aiming through the back window at the man who called himself Ronald, the bald tires slick with mud, spinning serpentine lines on the asphalt and the shoulder. Ronald tried to hold his ground, but at the last moment he leaped aside and took cover behind the trunk of a live oak.

Figured you for gutless, Bertrand said to himself.

He took his foot off the accelerator and jammed on the brakes, expecting to slide within an inch of the lavender automobile with the outside radiator cap.

Instead, the brake pedal went all the way to the floor, as though it were totally disconnected from the rest of his grandmother's car. The rear bumper crashed into Ronald's restored Rolls-Royce, exploding the front end, scattering the asphalt with bits of headlight glass and wiring and pieces of chrome.

Oh shit.

Bertrand dropped the transmission into drive, floored the acceler
ator again, and spun back out on the road, taking pieces of Ronald's
collectible with him. When he looked in the mirror, he saw Ronald
staring in horror at the destruction that had just been done to his
vehicle.

Tough luck, Chuck. Sorry to skin your hide, Clyde. But you been
sacked, Jack. So adios, Toast.

Bertrand's mouth was wide with laughter as he roared down the
road. There was only one problem. He had left behind his grand
mother's bumper as well as her license tag.

CHAPTER
26

FRIDAY MORNING I called Bo Diddley's office in Lafayette. The receptionist answered, the same one who was a master at saying as little as possible.

"This is Detective Dave Robicheaux, with the Iberia Sheriff's Department. Has Mr. Wiggins returned from his business trip to Miami?"

"He's in a meeting right now," she replied.

"Is his secretary there, the lady with the white-gold hair?"

"She's on vacation."

"Put Mr. Wiggins on."

"I can't do that."

"Yes, you can. Go do it," I said.

I marked the time on my watch. Almost two minutes went by before Bo picked up. "What's the problem, Dave?"

"I have the feeling you don't want to see me."

"Where would you get an idea like that?"

"Did your receptionist tell you I was in your office Wednesday?"

"I probably didn't see the message slip. Don't take it out on her."

I waited a beat before I spoke again. "I'll be at your office in about forty minutes. If I were you, I'd be there. If you're not, we'll have you picked up by Lafayette PD."

"What in the hell are you talking about?"

I thought it was time for Bo to experience a little anxiety. "You're about to find out," I said, and hung up.

The traffic was thin and I made it to the Lafayette Oil Center in a half hour. Bo's office was spacious and full of windows that gave a sense of airiness to an environment that was purely utilitarian. He was standing at his desk behind his glass partition, talking on the phone. He peered at me over his reading glasses and gestured for me to come in, as though he were anxious to see me.

"You tie one on last night?" he said.

"Where's your secretary, the woman who was at the casino with Bobby Mack Rydel?"

"She's out sick."

"That's funny. Your receptionist said she's on vacation."

Bo made an exasperated expression, as though his newly acquired Christian charity were indeed being tested. "Why do you want to treat me like this, Dave? Something I did back in college? Maybe I punched you when I was drunk? I always got the sense you thought I was hard on black people, hard on folks that maybe had more than I did. Well, if that's how you felt, you were right. But I'm not like that today."

He grinned, his eyes on mine, waiting for me to respond. His modesty, his candor, his vulnerability were a study in manipulation. But to portray him as a hypocrite would not be fair. James Boyd Wiggins had learned his value system from the oligarchy that had created him. In Louisiana, as in the rest of the South, the issue was always power. Wealth did not buy it. Wealth came with it. Televangelist preachers and fundamentalist churches sold magic as a way of acquiring it. The measure of one's success was the degree to which he could exploit his fellow man or reward his friends or punish his enemies. In our state's history, a demagogue with holes in his shoes forced Standard Oil to kiss his ring. Bo Diddley might have valued money, but I suspected he would fling it into an incinerator a shovelful at a time rather than take down the name of James Boyd Wiggins from the entrance of his office building.

"Why you looking at me like that?" he said, a grin still on his mouth.

I shook my head. "How long has Bobby Mack Rydel been working for you?"

"A security guy?"

"Among other things."

"I retain a security service out of Baton Rouge for all my shipyards. They subcontract some of the work. I think Rydel might be a subcontractor for them, but I'm not sure. He's out of Morgan City, isn't he? Is this about the fight between him and your friend at the casino?"

As with all fearful people, Bo's agenda always remained the same: every action he took, every word he spoke, was an attempt to control the environment and the people around him. He filled the air with sound and answered questions with questions. Most disarming of all was his ability to include an element of truth in his ongoing deceptions.

"Rydel is a merc. He specializes in interrogation. That's a bureauratic term for 'torture,'" I said. "Ever seen a woman who's been suffocated with a plastic bag over her head?"

"No, get out of my face with this stuff."

Bo was wound up like a clock spring. It was time for the hangeup.

"You said you wanted to help me find a priest who went missing in the Lower Nine," I said. "I think your interest lay elsewhere. I think you're interested in blood diamonds that were looted from Sidney Kovick's house."

His eyes stayed locked on mine and never blinked.

"You know Sidney, don't you?" I said.

"This is Louisiana," he replied. "You don't do business in New Orleans without crossing trails with people like Sidney Kovick. Say that stuff about diamonds again?"

Don't let go of the thread, I told myself. "But you know Kovick personally." I didn't say it as a question.

"No, I don't associate with gangsters. Neither does my wife. You should come to our charity golf tournament sometime and find out who our friends are. You *know* me, Dave. I burn stringer-bead rods. Everything I got I earned with my own sweat."

His eyes had still not blinked. His facial skin was tight against the

bone, his forearms thick and vascular, his nostrils swelling with air.
knew he was lying.

"Bobby Mack Rydel hangs with a misogynist and degenerate by
the name of Ronald Bledsoe. I think they both serve the same employer. This man Bledsoe has done injury to my daughter. Before thi
is over, I'm going to square it."

"You want to hear what I found out about the priest?"

He caught me off guard. Bo knew my weakness. But I didn't care
I knew I wouldn't get anything else out of him. "Go ahead," I said.

"I sent people down into the Lower Nine. I sent people into th
shelters. They interviewed evacuees who knew your friend. They knew
where his church was. They were there when that wall of water came
right across the top of the parish. They didn't have any reason to lie."

"Get to it, Bo."

He looked genuinely inept, frustrated by his inability to speak
with confidence outside the confines of a locker room or welding
shop. "The guy didn't make it. Almost everybody in that church
attic drowned. I don't know why they didn't get out when they had
a chance. Hundreds of school buses was left parked in a lot till the
water was up to their windows. That's what happens when people
don't take care of themselves."

But my attention had faded. I don't know what I had hoped for
Supposedly ancient people placed heavy stones on the burial place
of the dead so their spirits would not roam. I believe there is another
explanation, too. When we can fasten the dead to the earth and keep
them safely in our midst, they cannot obligate us to search for them
in our sleep.

"Thanks for the information," I said.

But he wasn't finished. Why he made the addendum I will never
know. I have always suspected that born-again people such as Bo
Wiggins find themselves in a dilemma they do not wish to recognize
If they truly come to believe in the precepts they profess, they can no
longer remain who and what they are.

"A bunch of people say they saw lights under the water, like phos-
phorescent fish swimming around. That's not what happened. Jus
after the priest fell off the roof of the church or maybe got pushed

a Coast Guard chopper flew over. It was lit up like a Juárez whore-house. What those people saw was the reflection in the water and the downdraft of the chopper stirring up the reflection."

"If that's true, why didn't the chopper pick up the people who were drowning?"

"You'd have to ask them, son."

His face looked as vacuous as a scarecrow's.

THAT AFTERNOON, a black patrolwoman by the name of Catin Segura came into my office. She had started off at the department as a 911 dispatcher, then had gotten an associate degree in criminal justice at a community college in New Orleans. Like Helen Soileau, she had worked as a meter maid before becoming a patrolwoman in both Uptown and across the river in Gretna. When Helen decided to increase the number of black female deputies in the department, Catin was the first one she hired.

Catin was a short, compact woman, unassuming, a bit withdrawn, a single mother who lived with her two children in Jeanerette. She was one of those decent, ordinary people you could always depend upon. You gave her the assignment and then forgot about it. I always admired the grace and dignity that seemed to govern her life.

"What's the haps, Catin?" I said.

"I was on my way home last night and saw the aftermath of an accident by the Jeanerette drawbridge. It looked like a hit-and-run." She pulled a notebook from her shirt pocket and peeled back two pages. "A guy named Ronald Bledsoe claims he was parked on the shoulder using his cell phone when some maniac backed into him and took off. His radiator was split open and all the antifreeze was draining on the road surface. There was also debris from both vehicles all over the road. Bledsoe was driving a Rolls-Royce. You know this guy, Dave?"

"He's bad news. He may have broken into my house."

She gave me a look. "Anyway, he said he was waiting for a tow. But he never called nine-one-one. When I asked him why, he said he figured it was a waste of time. I told him his insurance company would want a police report. He said he hadn't thought of that. The guy looks like he escaped from a freak show."

"That's part of his charm."

"Here's where it gets weird. Otis Baylor came out in his yard and was watching me and Bledsoe. I asked him if he had seen the hit-and-run and he said he had not. I asked him if anybody in his house had. He said no. I thought he would just go back inside but he didn't."

"So what happened?"

"I got my push broom out of the trunk and starting sweeping all the glass and broken metal onto the shoulder. That's when I saw the license tag in the grass. Baylor must have seen it, too. When the tow truck came and was hooking up the Rolls, he walked out on the road and looked down at the tag. Then he walked back to his house. I could see him pretty clear in the porch lamp. I'd swear he took a pen out of his pocket and wrote something on his hand."

"The tag number?"

"You tell me. I just ran it. It's registered to an Elizabeth Crochet in Loreauville. Mean anything?"

"No, but give me the address."

She wrote it in her notebook, then tore the page out and handed it to me. "I know Baylor is out on bail, so I thought I should tell you about all this."

"You did the right thing."

"Baylor shot some black kids in Uptown?"

"That's what everybody says."

"It must be hard on his wife."

"How's that?"

"I knew her in New Orleans. She was in my Al-Anon group. Her first husband was a sado-porn addict. Call me if you need anything else," she said.

LATER, I CALLED Otis Baylor's house, but there was no answer. I also called the phone number of Elizabeth Crochet. No help there, either. Just before quitting time, Clete Purcel came by.

"I'm either experiencing delayed stress syndrome or having day-time nightmares," he said.

It was Friday afternoon and I didn't want to hear it. "What's going on?" I said.

"I saw Marco Scarlotti in the Winn-Dixie."

"Are you sure?"

"I followed him outside. It was Marco. Charlie Weiss was waiting for him in a car. They had two big sacks of groceries. I waved them down, but they kept going. What are Sidney Kovick's greaseballs doing in New Iberia?"

"You got me."

"I went to the Lafayette Oil Center this afternoon to check out this Bo Diddley Wiggins character. He told me to get lost. He also told me he gave you all the information he had on Bobby Mack Rydel."

"That's right."

Clete began unwrapping the foil from a stick of gum. "So you're factoring me out of the investigation?"

"I wouldn't say that."

He fed the stick of gum into his mouth and chewed it. I heard a bird thump into my window glass. "Bobby Mack Rydel checked out of the hospital today. I made a couple of calls to Morgan City. He's not at his home or office."

There was nothing for it. Clete was either going to work alongside me or work by himself. If the latter was the case, it would not be good for anyone, particularly Clete. "Want to have a bite to eat with us, then take a drive up to Loreauville?" I asked.

"What's cooking?"

"My guess is Bertrand Melancon, in a big iron pot," I replied.

IT RAINED right at sunset, then the sky cleared and the air was fresh and smelled of fish spawning and water dripping out of the trees. Alafair was going on a date and Molly was going to a meeting of Pax Christi at Grand Coteau. I opened all the windows to let in the wind and the cool autumnal fragrance of night-blooming flowers in our yard. Through the trees the clouds were purple- and rose-stippled in the west. Down at the foot of the slope, a blue heron stood among the lily pads, pecking at insects on its wing, its slender lines like a haiku inside feathers.

I didn't want to chase down Bertrand Melancon or leave this perfect moment inside our simple house on Bayou Teche. I didn't want to return to the world of violence and avarice that seems to define the era in which we live. As a police officer I was not supposed to hate. But in reality I despised those who manipulate and exploit our society, and I'm not talking about the pathetic collection of miscreants we spend most of our time and money locking up. But maybe the world has always been the way it is today. I can't say. Like Voltaire's protagonist Candide, I just wanted to retreat to a private garden and not deal with it anymore.

Unhappily, that's not the way it works.

Clete and I got into his convertible and, like a pair of 1950s lowriders, headed up the bayou to the Loreauville Quarters and the home of Elizabeth Crochet.

Decades ago, during the 1960s, a black minister in Oakland, California, addressed an open letter to the founders of the Black Panthers, young men he had known since childhood. His thesis was simple, namely, that the foundations of the black community had always rested in the church and the family. The family was matriarchal and the church was usually Southern Baptist.

The minister added that his young friends did not understand the atavistic nature of loyalty within the black family. Unlike whites who would call the Man on their own children, the matriarch would open her veins before she would dime a grandchild with Officer Chuck. Because the Panthers did not respect either the church or the traditional ethos of the family, their constituency would prove to be evanescent at best and their movement little more than a historical asterisk.

Elizabeth Crochet wore her gray hair in a bun and walked with a cane, her back terribly bent. When she pushed open the screen for us to enter, she could barely lift her head sufficiently to see our faces. Clete removed his porkpie hat, and I showed my badge and photo ID. Her living room was neat, the faded throw rugs broom-swept clean, the slipcover on the couch printed with a floral design. She sat in a hard chair and indicated the couch and the one stuffed chair were for us. Her blue eyes jittered when she tried to focus them on us.

"You say my li'l car been in an accident?"

"Down by the Jeanerette drawbridge," I said.

"News to me," she said.

"Where is your car now, Ms. Crochet?" I asked.

"It ain't out front?"

"No, ma'am," I said.

"Then I guess it ain't here, no."

Clete suppressed a yawn and looked out the door, knowing the drill from many years.

"Ms. Crochet, we've already spoken to a couple of your neighbors," I said. "I know your grandson is Bertrand Melancon. I know he's staying with you. I don't want to see him hurt. But some very bad men will do whatever it takes to get their hands on something they believe Bertrand has in his possession or at least has access to. I can't stress enough how dangerous these men are."

"He's in trouble again, huh?"

"Yes, he is."

"It started with their mama," she said.

"Pardon?"

"Their mama always liked a downtown man. She went off to New Orleans, wasn't gonna live in the Quarters like a field hand, she said. Eddy and Bertrand never had no real daddy."

For just a moment I thought our trip was not in vain. "Where's Bertrand right now, Ms. Crochet?"

"Don't know."

"Has a man named Otis Baylor tried to contact you?"

"Who's he?"

I wrote my home phone on the back of my business card and put the card on her coffee table. "Ask Bertrand to call me."

"I got the feeling I ain't gonna see him again, Mr. Robicheaux."

I was surprised she had remembered my name and I realized that her mind and intelligence were far less influenced by her age than her body was. "Why is that?"

"'Cause I always knowed he was gonna die young. He didn't talk till he was fo' years old. Know why? He was always scared. A li'l boy scared every day of his life. He always been that same li'l boy, trying to prove he ain't scared of nobody."

"Bertrand told me he had an auntie in the Lower Nine. Think he might be with her?" I smiled when I said it.

"From what I hear, ain't nobody left in the Lower Nine, lessen you count dead people."

I got up to go.

"Suh?" she said.

"Yes?"

"What's Bertrand done? He ain't killed nobody? He ain't done somet'ing like that, no?"

She made me think of a small bird looking up from the bottom of a nest.

CLETE AND I got back in his convertible and drove up the lane, to the end of the Quarters, on the outside chance Bertrand was at a neighbor's house. I could tell Clete was exasperated by the way the interview had gone. "Why didn't you tell her her grandson probably killed a Catholic priest?" he said.

"Because it wouldn't do any good. Because she's too old to handle that kind of weight."

"You didn't press her about the aunt, either."

"I can't chase him all over the state, Clete. I don't have the time or the resources. How about lightening up?"

The right-front tire hit a chuckhole and the frame slammed down on the spring, splashing water on the windshield.

"It's your case, but he's still my bail skip," Clete said. "And he's still the guy who ran me down with his automobile."

"That's right, it's my case. I'm glad we have that straight."

Clete clicked on the radio, then clicked it back off, the color climbing in his neck.

"Say it," I said.

"It's your case, handle it the way you want. But I think you cut these bastards too much slack."

I looked out the window and decided this time not to reply.

Clete turned onto another lane and drove slowly back toward the state road. The sky had darkened and lights were going on in the shotgun houses on either side of us. The boarded-up windows, the junker cars, the wash lines, and the open drainage ditches full of trash were like photos taken by Walker Evans during the Great Depression, as though seven decades had not passed. Who was responsible? I have trouble with the notion of collective guilt. But if I had to lay it at anyone's feet, I'd start with the White League, the Knights of the White Camellia, the Saturday-night nigger-knockers, and all the people who did everything in their power to keep their fellow human beings poor and uneducated and at one another's throats so they would remain a source of cheap labor.

"Did I piss you off?" Clete said.

"No," I said. "I think Bertrand Melancon was at Otis Baylor's house."

"He wants to square what he did to Baylor's daughter?"

"Yeah, but how?"

"He could give them the diamonds. But I don't think a pus head like Melancon has it in him."

I was tired and didn't want to think about it anymore. "I'll buy you a Dr Pepper up at Miller's Market."

"I can't wait. Life with you is—"

"What?"

"You're the best cop I ever knew. But you're nuts, Dave. You always have been," he said. "Life with you is like being around a guy who's got kryptonite for a brain."

THE CALL CAME in the middle of the night. Outside, the moon was white in the heavens and the wind buffeted the house and whipped leaves down the slope onto the surface of the bayou. I turned on the light in the kitchen and picked up the receiver. The caller ID indicated the caller was using a cell phone. "Mr. Dave?" the voice said.

"Listen, Bertrand—"

"Don't hang up, man. Somebody shot into my grandmother's house. I was standing by the window and the bullet come right t'rou the glass. I was packing my things and my grandmother axed me to get her a glass of water. If I ain't turned around just then, I'd be dead."

"Who shot at you?"

"I don't know. This guy Ronald was at my grandmother's house, pretending he's some kind of insurance cop, trying to bribe me into telling him where them stones is at. I think he works for Sidney Kovick, except maybe he decided to screw Kovick and put toget'er his own deal. So I called up Kovick and tole him that."

"You dimed Ronald Bledsoe with Kovick?"

"Yeah, you could put it that way. Hey, man, what worse trouble could I be in? I helped tear Kovick's house apart. I stole his diamonds and his counterfeit money and his blow and his thirty-eight out of the wall. We even tore the chandeliers out of the ceiling."

"Kovick had cocaine in his walls?"

"Just one bag. We took it wit' us. It had already been stepped on. It was his private stash."

That piece of information didn't fit, but I didn't pursue it. "Where are you, Bertrand?"

"Wit' my grandmother, in a safe place."

"Where?"

"Look, I tried to make it up to the Baylor family. But they wasn't interested. I cain't do no more than what I done. You been straight wit' me, man, so I t'ought I had to tell you these things. My grandmother didn't have nothing to do wit' any of it. She don't know about no crimes I committed, either, so don't be hanging an aiding-and-abetting on her."

"How did you try to make it up, Bertrand?"

"What difference do it make now?"

There was no point in trying to extract any more information from him. Maybe it was finally time to leave Bertrand Melancon to his fate, whatever it was. But I had one more question.

"When Father LeBlanc fell from his church roof and you saw lights under the water, did a Coast Guard helicopter fly by overhead?"

"There wasn't no helicopter. That's how come all them people drowned," he replied. "Who tole you there was a helicopter? I would have heard it. All I heard was them people yelling for help inside that attic. You don't never forget sounds like that."

CHAPTER
27

I COULDN'T SLEEP the rest of the night. In the morning I told Molly about the content of Bertrand's phone call. Alafair had stayed overnight at a girlfriend's house in Lafayette. It was 8:37 a.m.

"What time did Alafair say she was going to be home?" I said.

"She didn't. Why?" Molly said.

"Because I think Bledsoe is making a move. He tried to double-cross Kovick or whoever hired him by bribing Melancon, then he tried to clip Melancon to cover it up. I think he plans to blow Dodge, but not before he pays back Alafair for kicking his face in."

Molly was framed in the back door, Snuggs's bowl in one hand and a sack of dry food in the other. The sunlight seemed to form a red nimbus around her head. "Maybe Bledsoe won't do that."

"A guy like that doesn't make decisions. His choices are already hardwired into his head. He seeks pleasure for himself or he seeks revenge against his enemies. Often the two are the same."

"If you're trying to scare the hell out of me, you're succeeding."

I looked through the Rolodex and called the home of Alafair's friend in Lafayette. No one answered. I tried to think, but I was too tired, too used up to see anything straight.

"Something Melancon mentioned doesn't make sense," I said. "He told me he and the other looters took a bag of cocaine, a thirty-eight, some counterfeit money, and the blood diamonds from Kovick's wall. He said the coke had already been cut, which to Melancon meant it was probably Kovick's private stash. Except Sidney isn't a doper and neither is his wife. I think the coke and gun and counterfeit all belonged to the same people Sidney took the diamonds from."

"I'm not following you," Molly said.

"Maybe Sidney has no connection to Ronald Bledsoe. Maybe our enemy is Sidney's enemy."

Molly poured dry food into Snuggs's bowl and set it on the floor, then opened the back screen and let Tripod in. Tripod and Snuggs began eating nose-to-nose out of the same bowl, their tails stretched out behind them. Molly lit a burner on the stove and dragged a big iron skillet on top of it.

"Bledsoe is evil, Dave. I don't care who he works for. If he comes here with the intention of hurting any member of this family, I'll kill him. That's a promise. Now sit down while I fix us some eggs and coffee."

It must have been coincidence, but both Snuggs and Tripod stopped eating and looked up from their bowl.

I DROVE TO Helen Soileau's house in an old neighborhood close to the downtown area. Her house had a wide gallery and tall windows with ventilated shutters like my own. Almost every Saturday morning children came to her house ostensibly to help with the yard work, but the morning activities usually ended with homemade ice cream and hot dogs. On this particular morning four or five kids were helping her weed her flower beds. I parked my pickup at the curb and walked up on the lawn. She got up from her knees, brushing grains of dirt from her gloves. She looked at my face.

"You okay, Pops?" she said.

"We need to get Bledsoe into custody."

"What else is new?"

"He may have taken a shot at Bertrand Melancon last night. If that's the case, I suspect he's about to blow town. I think he might try to get even with a few other people before he does."

"You said 'if.'"

"Maybe it wasn't Bledsoe. Sidney Kovick's gumballs are in New Iberia. Maybe they'd like to take Melancon off at the neck, too. Plus, I think Otis Baylor may have found out Melancon was staying at his grandmother's in Loreauville."

"How does one black kid get half the planet on his case?"

"But the one certifiable psychopath in the mix is still Ronald Bledsoe. He also has the greatest motivation. He tried to cut his own deal with Melancon and Melancon dimed him with Kovick."

The day was cool, the sky a hard blue, the sunlight through the trees like gold coins on her face. She watched two children spraying charcoal lighter on the portable grill in the side yard. "You guys wait for me to do that," she said.

Then she looked back at me, her thumbs hooked in the sides of her jeans. "We rousted him once. It didn't work. We can't tell the guy 'We don't like you. Get out of town before sundown.'"

"How would you like him around these kids?"

"You want my job, run for office. In the meantime, don't lecture me, Streak."

I got back in my truck without saying good-bye and drove away. In my rearview mirror I saw her toe at the grass, her thumbs still hooked in her jeans, like a teenage girl who had just lost something of value.

ALAFAIR CAME HOME at noon, blowing out her breath as she came through the door, a drawstring bag slung over her shoulder. I wanted her to tell me her overnight stay in Lafayette had been uneventful, that somehow my concerns were inflated. But I knew better, even before she spoke.

"I think I saw Ronald Bledsoe this morning," she said. "We were eating breakfast in a café by the university. He was parked in a blue car under a tree. We went to the mall and I saw him again."

"Why didn't you call me, Alf?"

"Because I wasn't sure the man in the blue car was Bledsoe. At the mall I was. Are you going to arrest him because he goes to the same mall I do?"

"If there's a pattern, we can get a restraining order."

"With Bledsoe, that's like writing a traffic citation on the guys who flew planes into the Towers."

She was right. To make matters worse, we were now arguing among ourselves about a degenerate.

"Stay close today, will you, kiddo?"

"I'm not a child, Dave. Don't treat me like one," she replied.

Clete Purcel had always said "Bust them or dust them." But what do you do with those who have probably been looking for an executioner all their lives, perhaps ensuring their evil lives on in the rest of us long after they are gone? What do you do when those you love most become angry when you try to protect them?

Maybe there was another way to deal with Ronald Bledsoe.

I WENT TO CITY PARK and used my cell phone to call Sidney Kovick's flower shop. His wife answered the phone.

"It's Dave Robicheaux, Eunice. I need to talk to Sidney."

"He's not here."

"On Saturday?"

"No, he's not here," she repeated. But she didn't tell me where he was.

"This isn't a courtesy call. Marco Scarlotti and Charlie Weiss are in New Iberia. I think I know why they're here, too. Sidney needs to talk with me."

"Give me your number."

I gave her both my cell and home numbers. I thought the conversation was over, but it wasn't.

"Dave, you don't know what's going on. Years ago, Sidney committed a terrible deed. It never allowed him any peace. But he met Father Jude LeBlanc through Natalia Ramos, the El Salvadoran girl he hired to clean his office. You remember my mentioning her to you?"

"Yeah, I do," I replied, my attention starting to wane.

"Father Jude talked to Sidney about changing his life and making up for what he did. Sidney is trying hard to be the best man he can.

He's not always successful, but he's trying. Be patient with him, will you?"

Patient with Sidney Kovick? Sidney as victim was a hard act to buy into. "He's in New Iberia, isn't he?"

"I'm not sure."

Yeah, you are, Eunice, I thought. But I let it go. "I look forward to hearing from him," I said, and closed my cell phone.

Actually, at this point I wasn't sure whether I wanted to talk with Sidney or not. Was Sidney actually trying to change or just feeding Eunice's illusions? I was tempted to turn my cell phone off. But as I sat in the picnic shelter on the bayou's edge, I could look across the water and see the shadows in my backyard and the caladiums rippling around the trunks of the trees and the lighted kitchen where Molly and Alafair were preparing an early supper so we could go to Saturday afternoon Mass in Loreauville.

Somewhere out there in the larger world, William Blake's tiger waited to take it all from me.

Which was more important, protecting one's family or worrying about the redemption of a man who had put on a raincoat and rubber boots before entering a basement with a chain saw? In my mind's eye I saw his victim—in handcuffs, probably bound at the ankles, his mouth taped, his eyes popping with terror. What kind of human being could do something like that to his fellow man?

Just as I got to my truck, my cell phone vibrated in my pocket. I flipped it open and placed it against my ear. "Dave Robicheaux," I said.

"My wife says you want to talk with me," a voice said.

"You in town, Sidney?"

"Why did you call my shop?"

"I warned you a long time ago about Ronald Bledsoe, but you wouldn't listen. He's got his own deal going on those blood diamonds. I think he's planning to hurt my daughter as well. If that happens, you're going to have the worst fucking experience of your life."

"No, you're the one who doesn't listen, Robicheaux. Marco and Charlie and a few other guys from the Giacano family work for me.

ledsoe doesn't. You got that straight? I want my goods back. It's a
pretty simple concept."

"Then who does he work for?"

"Maybe the Fuller Brush Company. They hire a lot of bald-headed
uys."

There was still time for one more run at Sidney before he broke
he connection. "After the loss of your little boy, did you kidnap
our neighbor, Sidney? Did you take his legs off with a chain saw?"

"I'm going to give you a short answer here. Did I use a chain saw
n somebody? No. Did a guy in Jefferson Parish disappear? Yeah, he
lid. Is he coming back? No, he ain't. Tell Bertrand Melancon I'm the
nly person in this state who can keep him alive."

The line went dead.

HAT AFTERNOON we attended Mass in Loreauville, then returned
o the house. The wind was blowing hard out of the south, the sur-
ace of the bayou wrinkling like old skin. I went to an AA meeting
upstairs at the Methodist church on Main, but I couldn't shake my
onviction that Bledsoe or one of his associates was about to make
 move on us.

Bledsoe was the trigger, but the sense of angst I was experiencing
had been a problem in my life long before I met him. Psychologists
believe there is a form of long-term anxiety that is caused by turmoil in the natal home: the parents fighting, the child being shaken or
dropped, someone constantly bursting through the door in a drunken
age. I can't say where it comes from. For me it was not unlike seeing
 mortar round fall short of your position, followed by a second
ound that goes long. In that moment you know with absolute cer-
ainty you're registered and the next round is coming down the stack.
The feeling you experience is like someone stripping off your skin.

The truth is, I wanted to drink. Maybe not a lot, just a couple of
hots with a beer back, I told myself, just enough to turn down the
butane on the burner. Or I wanted to load up my cut-down twelve-
gauge pump or my AR-15 and kick it on up to some serious E-major
ock 'n' roll.

At dusk I looked out the front window just as a cruiser with a black uniformed female deputy behind the wheel pulled into the driveway. Catin Segura got out and gazed at the trees in the yard and the gold and red clusters of four-o'clock flowers opening in the shadows. "You have such a nice place here," she said.

"It is," I said.

"I was just going off shift and I thought I should mention something to you. I was patrolling the Loreauville Quarters and I saw Otis Baylor talking to a family on their gallery. The address was next door to the house rented by the owner of the hit-and-run tag I ran, Elizabeth Crochet. When I cruised the Quarters again, about ten minutes later, he was knocking on another door, one street over.

"I asked him if I could help him with anything. He said no, he was an insurance man and was just checking on a couple of clients. I told him I was the same sheriff's deputy who had investigated the hit-and-run in front of his house. I told him I thought he was there for other reasons."

"What did he say?"

"'Thanks for your offer of help.' Then he got in his car and drove away. What's he after, Dave?"

"A guy named Bertrand Melancon."

I used my cell phone in the yard to call the Baylor home. When Otis answered, I hung up. Molly and Alafair were going to the movies. I waited until they left, then I drove down Old Jeanerette Road and pulled into Otis's driveway. He walked out on the front steps, a napkin tucked inside the top of his shirt.

"Was that you who called about fifteen minutes ago?" he asked.

"Why would you think that?"

"Because you can't leave us alone."

"No, that's not the problem at all, Mr. Baylor. The problem is the fact you were in the Loreauville Quarters. You knew who was driving the hit-and-run vehicle and you used your insurance connections to run the tag number and get the address of the owner. You were in the Loreauville Quarters looking for Bertrand Melancon. Except he wasn't there, so you started questioning his neighbors."

"If you know all this, why bother telling me about it?"

"I wouldn't be clever, Mr. Baylor. What I don't understand is your motivation. Melancon has done irreparable damage to your daughter and family, but evidently he's tried to make amends. You still want to cancel the guy's ticket?"

"What do you mean, 'amends'?"

"I talked with Melancon. He said he tried to make it up to y'all. I don't think he was lying. He knows he'll probably end up as a contribution to landfill."

I don't think I have ever seen a man look as dumbfounded as Otis Baylor did in that moment. He stared at me for a long time. "Mr. Robicheaux, please don't be vague or misleading."

"What I've said to you is an accurate statement. For what it's worth, I think Melancon is sorry for what he did. I think he also knows it's a matter of time before he catches the bus. If he's lucky, somebody won't use a blowtorch on him first. That's not an exaggeration. Andre Rochon probably suffered the pains of the damned before he died."

"My God in heaven," he said in dismay, his face white.

"What have you done, sir?"

He shook his head, his eyes filming.

"Talk to me, Mr. Baylor. This is the time to do it."

"I haven't done anything," he said. "Please excuse me. We have to finish dinner. I have to help my wife with the dishes. I have to help my daughter with some of her schoolwork. Please excuse me, sir."

He went inside the house and I heard him snap the door bolt in place. But I didn't leave the yard. I stood a long time in the shadows, inside the sounds of birds gathering in the treetops and some kids in a pirogue out on the bayou. The wind rattled the shutters on his windows and sent leaves feathering off the eaves. The blinds were drawn, the window frames etched by yellow light from inside. Under other circumstances, the house might have been a picture of familial warmth against the coming of the night. But not a sound came from the house and my guess was that nothing aside from misery lived inside those walls.

• • •

SUNDAY MORNING I convinced Molly and Alafair to go with me to a camp I had rented on the levee by Henderson Swamp. It was a fine place, built of pine, partially set on pilings, the screen gallery facing a bay that was dotted with cypress trees and willow islands. The wind was down, the sac-a-lait had been biting, and I wanted to get out of town and away from concerns about Ronald Bledsoe, at least for a day. We hitched up the boat and trailer, packed food and cold drinks in the cooler, and stretched bungee cords across the rods and life preservers in the bottom of the boat. I glanced at the sky in the south and went back into the house for our raincoats. Alafair followed me inside.

"Dave, we don't have to do this," she said.

"Do what?"

"Run away from this guy."

"The perps all go down. Just wait them out and they go down."

"How long was Hitler killing people? Twelve years?" she said.

When we reached the swamp, the bays were dented with raindrops. The early-morning fishermen who had gone out for crappie, or what are called "sac-a-lait" in south Louisiana, were already coming back in. We drove along the top of the levee, past the boat-rental and bait shops and the restaurants that offer swamp tours in French and English. Then we entered a long stretch of verdant waterside terrain that was unmarked by litter or development or even weekend fish camps of the kind I had rented.

Alafair and I put the boat in the water and used the electric motor to fish along a chain of willow islands between the levee and the bay. We tried shiners and then jigs, both without success. The wind had come up and the water was cloudy and too high, the time of day wrong as well. But I didn't care. I just wanted to be with Alafair and Molly, away from town, away from the job, away from avarice and deceit and people scamming people and profiting from the desperation and hardship of their fellow Americans.

The change of the season was already in the air. The leaves of the cypress had turned gold and I could smell gas on the breeze.

The flooded woods along the shore were dark, the lily pads that had bloomed with yellow flowers in the summer now curling into brown husks along the edges. I could smell schools of fish under the water, like the seminal odor of birth, but I could see nothing below the darkness on the surface, as though part of a life cycle were being removed from my own life.

Up on the levee a skinned pickup truck loaded with a family bounced down the road toward a boat ramp. Then a kid on a motorbike went by, followed by a black Humvee with tinted windows rolled halfway up.

A solitary turkey buzzard turned slowly overhead, as though in anticipation of a death that had not yet occurred. Then it tilted against the sky and glided farther out on the bay, perhaps seeking carrion in another place, or perhaps indicating respite, I didn't know which. I did not like to dwell on the biblical allocation of threescore and ten. But at a certain age, consciousness of mortality is not an elective study.

"You worry too much about Molly and me," Alafair said out of nowhere.

"Think so?" I said, our boat drifting unanchored in the wind now.

"What happens, happens. We're not afraid. Why should you be?"

Because I live inside you, I thought. Because if you die, so do I.

"What did you say?" she asked.

"Nothing. I just talk to myself sometimes. It goes with the seventh-inning stretch."

"You're too much," she said.

Later, a shower passed over the swamp, then the air turned cool and the sky brightened and we went back down the levee for supper at a restaurant that was built over the water. It had been a fine day, even though we had caught no fish, and we began straightening up the camp, washing and putting away the dishes, locking all the windows. Out on the bay, behind a distant line of trees, the sun seemed to be sliding off the watery rim of the world. A determined fisherman in a straw hat had dropped anchor in the willow islands, inside the clouds of mosquitoes that always gathered in the trees just before sunset and usually brought the sac-a-lait up just before dark.

He kept wiping mosquitoes out of his face and jigging his pole, like an agitated man trying to impose magic on a fruitless pursuit. Then his line snagged in a tree and he stopped long enough to hose himself down with insect repellent before starting in again.

"Give me the truck keys, Dave, and I'll bring the trailer around," Alafair said.

"How about a piece of pecan pie before we go?" Molly said.

"I'd really like to get a little done on my novel tonight," Alafair replied.

I gave her the keys and through the back window watched her start the truck and drive toward the crushed brick ramp where we always put the boat in, the empty trailer bouncing behind her. I poured the last of the coffee from a pot on the stove, added a teaspoon of sugar, and drank from it. Through the front window I could see Alafair back the trailer down the ramp until the wheels were hubcap-deep and the taillights submerged. Then she put on a pair of rubber boots she had taken from the truck bed and began wading into the shallows.

I had thought she would wait for me. Normally when we loaded the boat back onto the trailer, one of us backed the trailer into the water while the other cranked up the outboard and powered the boat onto the rollers, allowing the driver to hook the winch onto the bow and hand-crank the boat snug.

Out among the flooded willows, I saw the solitary fisherman lean down in his boat and pick up something from the bottom. He knocked his hat off his head to give himself better vision and raised the rifle to his shoulder. I could not make out the features of his face, but the moon had started to rise and I saw the light gleam on his bald head inside the shadows.

I was already out the screen door and running down the slope when he let off the first round.

CHAPTER
28

PERHAPS A GUST of wind buffeted his boat or the sound of my bursting out the screen door startled him, but the bullet went wide by perhaps two inches and whanged off the housing on my outboard motor. The rifle looked to be a semi-automatic carbine, maybe a .223, with a suppressor on the muzzle. The second and third shots came out of the barrel with a flash and made the same sound as the first round, like someone spitting a dry object from his mouth. Alafair had run in a crouch on the near side of the boat, then had thrown herself to the ground behind the truck. The back half of the truck was parked deep enough in the water so that the shooter could not fire under it.

The shooter took one shot at me just as I ran for the inside of the cabin. The bullet notched a bright slice of wood out of the doorjamb and broke glass somewhere in the bedroom. I landed on the floor, on my face, and could see Molly crouching below the drain board, working her way toward me.

"Did he hit Alafair?" she said.

"No, she's behind the truck. He can't get to her unless he moves his boat."

Two more rounds blew glass and a potted plant out of the kitchen window, powdering Molly's head and shoulders.

I crawled on my hands and knees into the bedroom, where my rucksack lay in the corner. I reached inside the flap and felt my hand clasp the checkered grips of my .45. I unsnapped the holster strap and slung the holster aside, then found the extra magazine I kept in the rucksack and shoved it in my back pocket. I pulled back the slide and fed a brass-jacketed 230-grain hollow-point into the chamber.

I crawled back into the kitchen. Molly was crouched at the edge of the front door, trying to see where Alafair was, her cell phone in her hand. "I called the St. Martin Sheriff's Department. Is it Bledsoe?" she said.

"It must be. Look, the nine-one-one response time out here might be fifteen minutes. I'm going outside. Stay on the floor."

"I'm going out there with her."

"No, no, no," I said. "Don't do that. Please, stay here. Please don't argue about it."

"No, I'm not going to leave her there."

I started to speak, but I knew my words would be wasted and that I couldn't afford to lose any more time. Just then, the shooter opened up again, pocking holes in the truck and flattening a tire and drilling two holes in the icebox. I went out the door in a run, crouching low, my right arm extended in front of me, firing at the willow island.

I saw the flash of the shooter's muzzle again and realized the shooter had changed his angle of fire. I suspected he was using an auxiliary electric motor and had moved the boat closer to the edge of the willows so he would have easier access to the bay. I dropped to my knees next to Alafair.

Her face was cut under one eye, her clothes and forearms streaked with mud.

"Are you hurt, Alf?" I said.

"No, a piece of aluminum hit me, I think," she said. "I saw him. He's got a semi-automatic rifle."

"Is it Bledsoe?"

"I couldn't tell."

"I'm going to get this guy. Molly already put in the nine-one-one. Stay here until the St. Martin Parish guys arrive. Don't try to go to the cabin. There's no way the guy can get on land."

Hardly were the words out of my mouth when Molly ran from the cabin to the truck, bending low, her cell phone in one hand, a small first-aid kit in the other. She blew her hair out of her eyes and looked at me, her cheeks red. She placed her hand against the side of her neck and examined it. Then she touched her neck with the ends of her fingers. There was a stripe across the side of it, like a rope burn that had started to bleed.

I wanted to be mad at her for leaving the cabin and exposing herself to greater danger, but how do you become angry at someone who will risk her life to bring a first-aid kit to her loved ones?

I worked my way to the front of the truck and fired three more rounds at the shadowy outline of the willows, the ejected shells tinkling on the crushed brick. I heard one round knock into wood, another blow water into the air, and another bite into metal. My slide locked open on an empty chamber.

I let the magazine drop loose from the butt of the .45 and pulled the loaded magazine from my back pocket and jammed it into the butt. I released the slide, feeding a shell into the chamber. But before I could get off a shot, the shooter cranked his outboard and spun the hull of his boat into open water, plowing a trough across the bay.

I pushed my boat off the trailer, climbed in over the bow, and started the engine. My boat was only sixteen feet long and was utilitarian in construction and unremarkable in appearance. But the 115-horsepower Yamaha mounted on its stern gave it thrust and capability that were far beyond the expectations for a humble bass boat. I twisted the throttle open and mud and dead vegetation boiled under the propeller. The bow rose into the air and the bottom swerved sideways as I slid between two willow islands. In seconds the hull was slapping across the bay as fast as a speedboat.

Less than one hundred yards away, I could see the shooter heading for a grove of dead cypress by the levee. He was hunched low in the stern, glancing back over his shoulder as he entered a cove of dead water coated with algae. He swerved around a log, scraping against fluted cypress trunks, and went deeper into the cove, looking back again, his propeller probably miring in nests of hyacinth roots. He disappeared inside the cypress, but I could hear his engine whining, like a skill saw biting into a nail.

Above the cove, on the levee, I saw the lights of a vehicle go on and off and then remain off.

I went straight into the cove, sliding across the tops of downed trees, clanging against the hollow trunk of a tupelo gum. Up ahead, on the far side of the cypress, I could see the grassy slope of the levee and, on top, the square outline of a Humvee silhouetted against the sky.

The man in the boat was in trouble. He couldn't get through the trash in the water to the levee bank and I was now no more than twenty yards from him. Inside the gloom, I saw him pick up his rifle, catch hold of a tree limb, and jump over the side into the water, hoping to find a solid bottom.

Instead, he went chest-high into the water, his shoes sinking into silt and layers of rotted vegetation. He slogged through the flooded trees toward the bank, the back of his shaved head white in the moonglow. At the edge of the water was a half-sunken commercial boat of some kind, with a home-carpentered plywood cabin aft, the entire hull soft with decay and scrolled with the scales of morning glory vines, the flooded hold a home for gars and alligators.

If he thought his luck could not get worse, he was wrong. The Humvee on the levee came to life and drove away, leaving the shooter to his fate. He struggled through the water, trying to knock down tree branches with one hand and keep his rifle dry and in the air with the other. Then he went behind a tree trunk and I lost sight of him.

I cut my engine and climbed out of my boat onto a cypress knee, then lowered myself into the water. I pushed the boat away from me, across a clearing, and watched it slide through the film of algae on the water, then clank against a tree.

A solitary shot came from behind the pilothouse of the sunken boat.

I leveled my .45 across a tree branch with two hands and sighted on the pilothouse. I cannot say why the shooter took cover there. The wood was as soft as decayed cork, the protective properties of the structure an illusion. But I suspected the shooter did not have a lot of choices at this point in his life and looked upon a man-made construction as the natural place to seek refuge in an alluvial piece of geography where he never thought he would find himself trapped and alone.

I pulled the trigger. Flame flew into the darkness and the recoil brought my wrists up into the air. The second time I fired I heard him cry out. I had six rounds left in the .45. I fired a third round and saw wood explode out of the back of the pilothouse.

He started wading up the mudflat onto the levee, limping, the rifle still in his hand. I lowered the sight on the small of his back and pulled the trigger again, except this time I didn't stop firing until the magazine was empty and my ears were deaf from the explosions.

I waded through a deep spot in the cove, then felt my shoes touch a hard bottom. I fitted my hand on the back of the half-sunken boat and pulled myself up on the levee, still shaking from the pursuit and the exchange of gunfire. The shooter lay facedown in the grass, his arms spread out by his sides, like a man who had fallen from a high altitude and pancaked into the earth. I lay the .45 in the grass and turned him over on his back. The exit wounds in his chest were the size of quarters, the cloth around them torn outward.

At first I did not recognize the shooter because of the shaved head and the sutured injuries in his scalp and the look of astonishment that had frozen on his face.

Then I realized that Ronald Bledsoe had not only tried to kill my family but had also screwed his partner. I guess I should have felt pity for the man I had just killed, but I didn't. I also suspected he had invested most of his adult life in doing evil to others. In fact, I suspected he was one of those whose past consists of deeds we never want to learn about.

Looks like you got a shitty deal, Bobby Mack, I thought to myself. But who knows? Maybe not all is lost. Maybe they play Texas Hold 'Em down in Hell.

· · ·

OTIS BAYLOR did not consider himself proficient in many skills, but there was one element in his life he was certain about: He was a natural-born insurance man. He knew how to provide it from the cradle to the grave. He knew people and what they needed and how to talk to them. And he also knew how to find them and to find out anything about them, particularly when they filed claims.

In his visit to the Loreauville Quarters, it had not taken him long to discover through the neighbors that Bertrand Melancon had an auntie in the Ninth Ward. It took him even less time to find her name in a database shared by his former employer. She had filed a claim for damage done to her house by the floodwaters from Lake Pontchartrain, little knowing that in all probability the mention of floodwater virtually guaranteed she would receive nothing.

But Otis Baylor was not worrying about the misfortune of Bertrand Melancon's family members. Melancon had been to his house. The car tag left behind on the road was incontestable evidence he had been there. The purpose of his visit had remained unknown, but the fact he had been there was, in Otis's mind, justification for whatever Otis did next.

Then, while eating Saturday night supper with his family, a detective had knocked on his door and given him information that changed his entire perspective about his relationship to his wife, who had deceived him, and a rapist who had robbed his daughter of her soul.

He did not sleep Saturday night and he spent much of Sunday sorting out his bills, paying them selectively, so that his utility services were not turned off and he did not default on the mortgage for his house in New Orleans. By midafternoon he knew he would get no rest until he went to the source of all his grief.

He called a friend who worked as an adjuster for the company that carried the policy on the house in the Ninth Ward owned by Bertrand Melancon's aunt.

"Her name is Clemmie Melancon," Otis said. "I suspect she's long gone, but since she filed a claim, I figured you might have a mailing address or contact phone number for her."

"She evacuated to the Superdome, but she's back home now," the adjuster said.

"In the Ninth Ward?"

"She's not in the worst part of it, but, yeah, she's back home. She's got Parkinson's. I think all those people down there are going to get bulldozed eventually."

"How's her claim looking?"

"Forget it."

"Thanks for your help," Otis said, and started to hang up.

"It's true, you been teaching the claimants how to slide one by us?" the friend said.

"'Slide' is the wrong word. Think more in terms of 'wrecking ball,'" Otis said, this time hanging up.

It was 3:46 p.m. Outside, the sky was gray, the wind blowing, wet leaves plastering against the windows of his home office. Otis took his car keys from his pants pocket and spun them on his finger.

"Where you going, Daddy?" Thelma asked.

She stood in the doorway, one hip against the jamb, her expression inquisitive and innocent, the way it used to be before she and her date had gotten lost in a neighborhood that in minutes swallowed her alive.

"My father and my uncle were members of the Ku Klux Klan," he said. "They joined a hateful organization because they had been taught by others to resent themselves. My father was a good man, but he never understood who his real enemy was. It wasn't people of color. It was the dragon that lived inside him. You think maybe it's time you and I go look at the dragons?"

THE RAIN HAD STOPPED and the night sky had cleared when Otis Baylor and his daughter entered the Ninth Ward of Orleans Parish. The topography, the windowless houses, the layers of building debris and garbage and dried flotsam did not look real but instead resembled a movie set or perhaps scenes spliced together from World War II black-and-white footage of a bombed-out city, leached of color, the only light provided by cook fires wavering under sheets of corrugated tin the remaining residents had propped across cinder blocks or stacks of bricks.

Thelma had been silent for the last hour, and Otis wondered if he had asked too much of her, if indeed he had not made a choice for her that wasn't his to make. He steered around a section of the street that had caved into a canal.

"Daddy?" Thelma said.

"Yes?" he said.

"If he's there, what are you going to do?"

"I'm not sure. I'm not even sure I trust myself about that."

"Will you hurt him?"

"I can't say. But I might. I think I might like to do that. Until Mr. Robicheaux came to our house, I thought maybe I was going to kill him."

"You make me sad when you talk like that."

"Why?"

"Because it's not who you are."

Otis didn't reply and kept his thoughts to himself, lest his daughter see a side to his personality that even he feared.

He was amazed at how easy it was to find the house owned by Bertrand Melancon's aunt. Someone had propped up the mailbox in the front yard and raked the mud off the numbers, even though there would probably be no postal delivery in the Ninth Ward for months, if ever. The yard was stacked with virtually everything the house had once contained: cloth-covered chairs and a sofa, a refrigerator, mattresses, bedsprings, a television set, clothes, food, a chest of drawers with flower decals pasted all over it, stripped wallpaper and carpeting, all of it caked with a greenish-black sludge that had dried like plastic. The windows of the house were tacked over with plywood, a screen in place on the entrance. In the driveway, on the side of the house, a young black man and an older black woman in a dress that hung on her like a sack were sitting on hard chairs by a fire burning in a ventilated oil drum.

Neither one of them looked up when Otis approached them. Six slices of white bread, with pieces of cheese on them, were browning on a refrigerator grill above the fire.

"You know who I am?" Otis asked.

Bertrand raised his eyes and lowered them again. Then he looked at the car parked on the street and the young woman in the passenger seat. "Yes, suh, I ain't got no doubt who you are."

"Who are you, ma'am?" Otis asked the woman.

"Who are you, standing in my drive, axing questions?" she said. Her skin was as wrinkled as old putty, her breasts nothing more than dried dugs. Her movement was erratic, as though her motor control would not coordinate with itself. One of her eyelids drooped. Her hair was so thin it looked like duck down on her scalp.

"My name is Otis Baylor. The young woman in the car is my daughter. Her name is Thelma. I suspect you're Miss Clemmie, Bertrand's auntie."

The woman watched the cheese melt on the bread slices. She picked up a tin can from her lap, bent over, and spit snuff in it.

"Did Bertrand tell you what happened to my daughter, Miss Clemmie?"

"She ain't part of this, suh," Bertrand said.

"You're staying at her house. She's giving your refuge. That makes her part of it. Where's your grandmother?"

"Inside, resting. It's cool tonight. She t'ought she'd rest."

"Mr. Robicheaux says you came to my house and tried to make amends. How does a man like you make amends for what he did, Mr. Melancon?"

"I wanted to give y'all some diamonds I taken from a man who taken them from somebody else."

"That's an insult."

"Suh, I ain't mean to hurt y'all no more. I t'ought I was—" He stopped and widened his eyes, as though smoke were in them. "I ain't gonna say no more. Call the cops or do what you come here to do."

Otis wore a short-sleeved shirt that suddenly seemed too small for his chest and throat, so small and tight he couldn't breathe. "You wait here," he said.

He went inside the house without knocking. It was dark inside and he could hear the hum of mosquitoes in the rooms. The floor and walls seemed to be covered with the same greenish-black sludge or mold that he had seen on the debris piled in the yard. A woman lay on a cot in the hallway, breathing audibly, a pillow stuffed behind her head. "That you, Bertrand?" she said.

"No, my name is Otis Baylor."

There were bandages wrapped around the palms of both the woman's hands. "Where's Bertrand at?" she said.

"Outside, in the driveway," Otis said.

"You one of the men shot into my li'l house?"

"No."

"You a policeman?"

"No, I'm not."

"Then what you doing here?"

"I'm an insurance man."

"You come here about Clemmie's claim?"

"No, I didn't," he said.

"Would you help me up?"

Otis reached down to take her by the arm. Then he heard the screen door behind him. "That's all right, suh. I got it," Bertrand said. He held a small white bowl in one hand. "She burned herself on the grill. I got to help her with her soup."

"These women shouldn't be here," Otis said.

"Ain't no place to take them," Bertrand said.

Otis watched while Bertrand hand-fed his grandmother. Otis wiped the mosquitoes out of his face. When the wind changed and blew through the back door, the odor of feces struck his nostrils. "I want to talk to you," he said.

"I got to finish here," Bertrand said.

"No, you come outside and talk to me now."

Bertrand set the bowl down on the floor, next to the cot, and followed Otis outside.

"I feel like tearing you apart," Otis said.

"I guess you do."

"You go over to that car and you apologize."

"Suh?"

"You heard me. You look my daughter in the face and you apologize, you sonofabitch, before I do something awful."

Bertrand walked to Otis's car and stood in front of the passenger door, his back to Otis, blocking Otis's view of his daughter's face. While he spoke, Bertrand's arms were folded on his chest, his head turned to one side. In silhouette, his body looked like it had no arms, like a wood post painted on the air. On the far side of the street, a dog was trying to dig something loose from a pile of smoldering garbage.

Bertrand turned away from the car and walked past Otis toward the front door of the house. He was wiping his nose with the back of his wrist.

"You come here," Otis said.

"What for?"

"Did you hear me?" Otis said. He fitted his hand under Bertrand's arm, almost lifting him into the air.

"What you want from me? I done all I could do," Bertrand said. "If them men who killed Andre and tortured Eddy get their hands on my auntie and grandmother, what you think is gonna happen to them? You tell me that, Mr. Baylor."

The question Bertrand had asked was legitimate: What did Otis want? To somehow give new life to the spiritual cancer that had fed at his father's heart? To use his daughter's suffering to justify beating a man bloody with his fists?

"Daddy?" he heard Thelma say behind him.

He turned and stared into her face.

"Daddy, it's all right. Let him go," she said.

"Honey—" he began.

"I'm all right," she said. "Let's go home."

She took his big hand in both of hers and smiled at him. "Come on, Daddy, we're finished here," she said.

Bertrand Melancon remained stationary in the yard as they drove away. He was not sure what had happened between Otis Baylor and his daughter or what he should do next. In fact, he was not sure about anything. He wondered if his grandmother's soup had grown cold. He wondered if his auntie and grandmother had any idea of the crimes he had committed. He wondered if his mother was still alive someplace and if she ever thought about him or Eddy. He wondered why every event that had transpired in his life was not what he had planned.

How could that be? he asked himself. For just a moment, he wondered if the priest he had killed could give him an answer. That thought set his stomach on fire and caused him to spit blood in his auntie's yard.

CHAPTER
29

THE PROBLEM WITH an adrenaline high, unlike one driven by booze, is that you cannot sustain it. When the heart-thundering rush subsides, when the clean smell of ignited cordite is blown away by the wind, you find yourself in the same kind of dead zone that a drunkard lives in. You wake in the morning to white noise that is like a television set turned up full volume on an empty screen. The streets seem empty, the sky brittle, the air stained with industrial odors you do not associate with morning. The sun is white overhead, the way a flashbulb is white, and the trees offer neither birdsong nor shade. Whatever you touch has a sharp edge to it, and ineptitude and remorse seem to wrap themselves around all your thoughts. The world has become an unforgiving prison where the images from a mistaken moment have not disappeared with sleep and instead pursue you wherever you go. You spend your time rationalizing and justifying and eventually you take on the persona of someone you don't recognize. It's like stepping around a corner onto a street on which there are no other people. It's not an experience you come back from easily.

Monday morning Helen came into my office and sat down across from me. "You feeling okay, bwana?"

"Right as rain," I replied.

I could hear her chewing gum, her jaws working steadily.

"Why do you figure Bobby Mack Rydel came after you?"

"Bledsoe was behind it. He played Rydel just like he plays every-body."

"You're sure you didn't see Bledsoe in the Humvee up on the levee?"

I knew what she wanted me to say.

"I didn't see the guy in the Humvee," I said.

"Too bad. Look, you're supposed to be on the desk till IA clears the shoot, but we should have that out of the way by close of business. We need Bledsoe in a cage. I'm with you on this one, Streak. I don't care how we do it. This creep has spit on us again and again and gotten away with it. Let's run at it from a different angle."

"How?"

"Who was it who said, 'When people say this is not about money, it's about money'?"

"H. L. Mencken."

"This is about those blood stones or whatever. Put all the scorpions in a matchbox and shake it up."

"With Bledsoe it's personal. He enjoys it. If someone didn't pay him to hurt other people, he'd pay to do it."

"Start over again. Go after Otis Baylor," she said.

"Waste of time."

"Really? I wonder why he's downstairs," she replied.

I BUZZED WALLY and asked him to send Otis Baylor up. I expected Wally to make a wisecrack. But he surprised me. "Glad you and your family are okay, Dave. I'm glad you capped that dude, too. That was a righteous shoot. Everybody here knows that. You hearing me?"

"Yeah, I do, Wally. Thanks," I said.

Two minutes later Otis knocked on my glass pane and I waved him inside. He was wearing a navy blue suit and white shirt and tie, and his shoes were brushed to a soft luster. He put a piece of lined notebook paper on my desk. "That's Bertrand Melancon's address in the Ninth Ward. If you want him, he's yours."

"Sit down, Mr. Baylor."

He didn't argue. He took a chair in front of my desk and gazed around my office.

"I'll pass this information on to NOPD. I'll also pass it on to the FBI in Baton Rouge. Maybe they'll get around to picking him up one day, but I don't believe that's going to happen soon. I think others will get their hands on Bertrand first, and when they do, they'll boil the meat off his bones."

"Then it's on y'all. My family and I are finished with him."

"I have a feeling something happened since I last saw you. Want to tell me about it?"

He did just that, in detail, leaving nothing out, describing his temptation to tear Bertrand Melancon into pieces in front of his auntie and the act of intervention and mercy on his daughter's part.

"I admire what you've done, sir, but yesterday I shot and killed a man by the name of Bobby Mack Rydel. I killed him because he tried to kill my daughter, my wife, and me. He did this because Ronald Bledsoe put him up to it. Are you aware of all this? Because you don't seem to be."

"No, I wasn't aware. We got back from New Orleans late last night. I didn't watch the news or read the paper this morning. I came straight to your office. I'm sorry to hear about your trouble."

I thought it was time to use the information Deputy Catin Segura had given me regarding Otis Baylor's wife.

"You didn't shoot those looters, Mr. Baylor. I think your wife did. I think before you two met, she was sexually abused, probably by someone with sadistic tendencies, maybe someone addicted to sado-porn. I think she saw the looters approaching your house and got frightened and opened up on them."

He was quiet for a moment. "Who told you this stuff about Mrs. Baylor?"

"Who cares? Your wife picked up the Springfield and probably fired it out the front door. She was probably scared. Who wouldn't be? A jury should be able to understand that. I think it's pretty dumb to protect someone who perhaps doesn't need protecting."

His eyes stayed on mine and I knew he was thinking about the statement I had just made. I had said a jury "should understand." Like most intelligent people, Otis knew equivocation and nuance in language when he heard it. He also knew that a prosecutor would emphasize to the jury that the shooter had been deadly accurate and had managed to take down not just one but two looters with a single shot. It was obvious the shooter had not fired simply to frighten them away.

But right now I was no longer interested in whether or not Otis worked out his family problems.

"Bertrand told me he tried to make amends to you. I think he tried to give you part or all of the blood diamonds stolen from Sidney Kovick's house. I need to know where they are."

"We have nothing to do with that."

"Does you wife know where they are?"

"No."

I remained silent, turning a pencil in a circle on my blotter with my finger, leaving the burden of evidence on him.

"Look, Melancon brought a letter to the house," he said. "He had handwritten an apology to our family and tried to read it to her. He told my wife the location of the diamonds was on the bottom of the letter. But she threw it in his face. I found the letter in the yard. It was written on a paper hand towel. The ink had dissolved in the water. It's unreadable."

"Where is it now?"

"Probably still in the can I use for yard cleanup."

"With your permission, I'm going to send someone out there to pick it up," I said.

"Do whatever you want," he replied.

I got the exact location of the trash can from him and called the Acadiana Crime Lab. After I got off the phone, I looked at Otis for a long time. "I wish you had told me this before," I said. "Your lack of cooperation hasn't been good for any of us, Mr. Baylor, least of all for yourself. If I can share a little bit of police wisdom with you, it's a fool's errand to take other people's weight."

"I'm not up on police terminology. You want to rephrase that?"

"When we allow others to victimize us in order to prove our own worth, we invite a cancer into our lives."

"We through here, Mr. Robicheaux?"

I felt my old enemy, anger, flare in my chest. My daughter and wife had almost lost their lives the previous day and I had been forced to shoot and kill their assailant. Regardless of what he had suffered himself, I was tired of Otis Baylor's recalcitrant attitudes.

He was studying my face, perhaps finally aware that other people have their limits.

"No, we're not through. And it's Detective Robicheaux. Why do you think we came down on you with both feet?" I said.

"Bad luck?"

"Because your neighbor gave you up."

"Tom Claggart?"

"He said the night the looters were shot, you made a statement about 'hanging black ivory on the wall.' You remember saying that?"

"Yeah, I do. But I don't blame Tom for telling you that. He's a simpleminded man who wants to please authority. He went to the Virginia Military Institute or the Citadel or one of those military colleges. I don't see what this has to do with anything."

It has to do with the fact you're unteachable, sir, I thought. But I kept my feelings to myself.

MY GUESS WAS that Ronald Bledsoe had already left town. Wrong again. Two other detectives went to his motor court early Monday morning and were told by the manager that Mr. Bledsoe could be found at an assisted-care facility next door to Iberia General.

One of the detectives, Lukas Cormier, called me on his cell phone from the parking lot outside the facility. He had a bachelor's degree in business administration, with a minor in psychology, and was a good investigator. "You want to come over here?" he said.

"I'm supposed to be on the desk till IA cuts me loose," I said. "What's going on?"

"When we went inside, this guy who looks like he was squirted out of a toothpaste tube was reading a Harry Potter book aloud to a roomful of Alzheimer patients. He goes, 'Hi, my name is Ronald. What's yours?'"

"What's his alibi for yesterday?"

"He says he was in Barnes and Noble in Lafayette, buying books for his Alzheimer friends."

"Does he have any purchase receipts?"

"No, I asked him."

"How about the Humvee? You got anything on it?"

"Zip. We tried all the rentals and talked to a couple of dealerships. But without a tag number I don't think we're going to get anywhere on the vehicle. You want us to bring him in?"

"No, let him think he's slid one past us."

"He's got no sheet at all? Mental institutions, stuff like that?"

"None. Bledsoe is a blank. Not so much as a traffic violation."

There was a beat and I knew what was coming.

"Dave, I don't want to seem casual about your experience with this character, but are you sure we've got the right guy? I don't see this guy as New Iberia's answer to BTK. Guys who try to whack a cop and his family don't hang around. They also have histories. By your own admission, Bledsoe doesn't fit the job description."

"BTK had a university degree in criminal justice and worked as an animal control officer in Wichita, Kansas. He also installed security systems in people's homes. He was also an officer at his church. He also tortured people to death, including children, for twenty years. Happy motoring, Lukas."

I hung up, more angry than I should have been, I suppose. But when you are on the receiving end of a fist, you are less inclined to be sympathetic toward those who are disingenuous at your expense.

I called Sidney Kovick's flower shop. Eunice answered the phone.

"Is Sidney back from New Iberia?" I asked.

"I never said he was in New Iberia," she replied.

"Right, I forgot that. Since I talked to Sidney on Saturday, a friend of Ronald Bledsoe tried to kill my family and me. I tried to stoke up Sidney so he'd take down Bledsoe for me. But I want Bledsoe alive and I want the people he works for. Please ask your husband to call me."

It took a moment for my statement to sink in. "You tried to get Sidney to do your dirty work?"

"Not exactly. But I wouldn't have objected."

"Then shame on you."

I felt my face burning. "Will you pass on my message?"

"Sometimes you strike me as absolutely clueless. It's Sidney who needs your help. He just called. He's worried about Marco and Charlie. They went into the Atchafalaya Swamp Saturday and didn't come back to the motel. They don't answer their cell phones, either."

"What were they doing in the Atchafalaya Swamp, Eunice?"

"I'm not sure."

Right, I thought. "Maybe they got lost. Marco Scarlotti and Charlie Weiss probably couldn't find snow in Antarctica. You want to get straight with me or see Sidney in a box?" I said.

"They were following Ronald Bledsoe."

"I'm at the Iberia Sheriff's Department. Tell Sidney either to come in or call me. You're a reasonable person. I want you to think hard about the following question. Don't answer it, just think about it."

Eunice had grown up in the fiefdom of Plaquemines Parish and knew firsthand that justice is indeed blind, at least when it involves political corruption. I let the spring wind itself tight, then I used the interrogator's classic trick of posing a question that appears based on a premise. "When Bo Wiggins goes down, do you think he's going to take the bounce by himself? A guy with hundreds of millions of dollars in government contracts? When it comes to money and status, Bo Wiggins has the humanity of a feral pit bull. What do you think he's going to do to Sidney?"

"I don't know, Dave. I've never met the man. I'm not sure Sidney has, either. I'll ask him to call you. You don't need to call here again."

My time in the dead zone seemed open-ended.

BUT SIDNEY did not call and I began to believe that both he and Eunice were much more vulnerable than I had thought. As I mentioned before, I never quite understood Sidney. Historically the men who ran the Mafia rose to power through treachery, betrayal of friends, and assassination of their superiors. Their skill lay in their ability to manipulate others, particularly those who were good "soldiers" and had ferocious levels of physical courage that their leaders lacked.

This was not the case with Sidney. He wasn't afraid and I never saw him betray one of his own. Actually I think Sidney had a peculiar kind of secular theology at work in his life that was similar in many ways to those who conflate nationalism and religion and business. For Sidney, "sin" and "failure" and "poverty" were the unholy trinity. If there was a perdition, it was the home on North Villere Street where he had grown up.

Unfortunately for Sidney and the men who worked for him, evil sometimes comes in a package that has no label on it.

SIDNEY'S OPPOSITE WAS Clete Purcel, a man who was born and raised in the same privation as Sidney and, worse, exposed at an early age to his father's rejection and unnecessary cruelty. Why does one man turn out to be a gangster and the other a beer-soaked, blue-collar knight errant? I didn't know the answer. I was just glad that Clete was my friend.

As soon as Clete heard about the shoot-out, he had come to my house. He stayed until almost midnight, then, instead of leaving as he said he was, he pulled his Caddy into the driveway and went to sleep in the backseat, determined that Bledsoe wouldn't have another run at us. We had to argue with him in order to make up a bed for him on the couch.

He came to my office on Monday morning, shortly after I had talked to Eunice Kovick. "So Sidney hasn't called you, huh?" he said.

"He's not going to admit he's painted himself into a corner," I replied.

It was bright and cool outside, and I lowered the blinds to take the glare out of the office. When I closed my eyes, red rings seemed to recede into my brain and for just a second I thought I could see muzzle flashes from a semi-automatic rifle. I could feel Clete's eyes following me around the room.

"Stop it," I said.

"I didn't say a word."

"Sidney wants his goods. He probably thinks Bertrand Melancon is still in New Iberia or he thinks Bledsoe can lead him to Melancon."

"You don't think Bledsoe is working for him?"

"If he was, he isn't now."

"What do you figure is the deal on Bo Diddley Wiggins?"

"I think he's mixed up in it. But here's the rub. Bo Diddley is a businessman. Sidney fancies himself one. Ronald Bledsoe and Bobby Mack Rydel are cut out of different cloth. If I had to take a guess, I think Bo and Sidney probably stepped off a cliff and didn't know how to get back on it."

I could see Clete's irritation growing. "Guys like Bledsoe and Rydel don't operate in a vacuum. They do the jobs that guys like Kovick and Wiggins don't want to dirty their hands on. Like kidnapping and suffocating Courtney Degravelle to death. I got two regrets in all this, Streak. One, that I drug Courtney into it. Two, that it wasn't me who parked a couple of big ones in Rydel's brisket."

Fortunately my desk phone rang. It was Mack Bertrand, at the Acadiana Crime Lab. "We picked up the letter at Otis Baylor's place. It was in the trash can, like he said. The biggest problem is the note was printed on low-grade paper that's been sitting in water. It was almost mush when we lifted it out. Anyway, I've done a computer reconstruction of it. What are you looking for in particular?"

"Directions to some stolen property. How legible is it?"

"You ever eat alphabet soup when you were a kid?"

After I hung up, I looked at Clete, my palm still resting on the receiver, unsure what I should do next. Clete was not a welcome presence at the sheriff's department. At best he was tolerated because he and I were friends. At worst, he was still looked upon as a disgraced cop who hunted down street mutts for hire. "I need to go over to the Crime Lab," I said.

He waited.

"Want to come?" I said.

The Crime Lab was outside the city limits, in a quasi-rural area. On the way there, a small deer ran across the road. It sprang across a rain ditch and ran through a sodden field of sugarcane that had been ruined by flooding and high wind. We were in my truck, and Clete turned in the passenger seat and strained to see out the back window as the deer bounced over a fence into a grove of water oaks. Then he stared straight ahead at the road.

"What's on your mind?" I asked.

"I was just thinking about something you said. The reason this case doesn't hang together is because we've got a mixture of business types and greaseballs and sociopaths all in the same blender. It's the amateurs who stay under the radar. They're not predictable. They do business in Iran and get blow jobs in Nigeria, then take their families to First Baptist back in Big D. You think you're hunting down Charlie Manson and instead you end up dealing with Beaver Cleaver."

"What are you saying?"

"We don't have the juice to take these guys down. I'm glad you capped Rydel when you had the chance."

"He dealt it."

"That's not my point. The guy was protected. He was a killing machine for years and always had somebody with juice covering his butt."

"You think that's how Bledsoe has stayed off the computer?"

"No, that's where it doesn't make sense. Bledsoe is no mercenary. He's a serial predator, a guy who doesn't like to take orders. Maybe somebody brought him in for a short gig. That's all I can figure. This whole bunch should have been in soap dispensers a long time ago."

He was quiet the rest of the way to the Crime Lab.

TECHNICALLY I WAS still on the desk, but technically again my desk extended to the Lab. The head forensic technician there was Mack Bertrand. He was a slender, nice-looking family man, always well groomed, who carried his pipe in a leather case on his belt. Wherever he went, he trailed a fragrance of apple-spiked pipe tobacco. I could tell he wasn't entirely comfortable with Clete's presence inside the Lab. Clete sensed it, too, and went outside.

"Did I say something?" Mack asked.

"It's all right. What have you got?" I said.

Mack had created virtual images on a computer screen from the dissolved texture of the paper towel on which Bertrand Melancon had written his letter of amends. In our earlier conversation on the telephone, Mack had made use of a metaphor involving alphabet soup. The metaphor could not have been more appropriate.

I could make out several words in the body of the letter, but toward the bottom of the page, only a few letters, re-created from both the ink and the pressure of the ballpoint pen, were discernible:

Th dym   s un   the ri s on   e ot   ide of h   an.

"Does that help you?" Mack asked.

"Not right offhand. But maybe it'll make sense down the line."

"Tell Purcel I've got nothing against him. But it's supposed to be only authorized personnel. I always thought he was a pretty decent guy."

"It's my fault. I shouldn't have brought him in," I said.

"You okay from yesterday?"

"No problem."

"That's the way. When they deal it, we slam the door on it, case closed. Right? Don't think about it," he said, knowing a lie when he heard one, both mine and his.

THE NEXT DAY, in the Atchafalaya Basin, a black man was bobber-fishing with a cane pole inside a grove of flooded trees. It wasn't the abandoned rental car on the levee that caught his eye. It was the gray cloud of gnats that hovered above the boxlike remains of a cabin at the foot of the levee. The cabin had been built of plywood and tarpaper and had been blown or floated there years ago by a hurricane. On several occasions, during an electrical storm, the black man had taken shelter inside the cabin, and he knew it to be a dry, empty place that was clean of any dead animals or discarded food.

He paddled his pirogue through the trees, dropping his baited hook and cork bobber into the dark pools that were unruffled by the wind out on the channel. Then he heard flies buzzing and saw shadows swooping across the grassy slope of the levee. When he looked up into the sky, he saw three turkey buzzards gliding in a circle.

He turned his back toward the levee and lifted his pole in the air, swinging the line back toward the channel, dropping the worm next to a cypress trunk. The wind changed direction, blowing down the slope of the levee. An odor that made him gag struck his nostrils.

He rolled his line up on his pole and paddled through the flooded trees onto the mudflat, sufficiently upwind now. He dragged the pirogue onto the grass and climbed the levee, then descended again so the wind was firmly at his back. The door to the cabin hung partially open. He picked up a stick to open it the rest of the way, then felt foolish at his fearful behavior. He put his hand on the edge of the door and dragged it open, scraping the bottom across the ground.

"Oh Lord," he said under his breath.

WHEN HELEN SOILEAU and I arrived, the St. Mary Parish Sheriff's Department had already strung yellow crime scene tape from the flooded trees to the top of the levee, sealing off access to the cabin. The St. Mary sheriff was out of town and the investigation was being run by a lead detective named Lamar Fuselier. His blond hair was cut short and boxed on his neck, and he wore a blue windbreaker and starched khakis and spit-shined black shoes. I used to see him at Red's Gym sometimes in Lafayette, dead-lifting three hundred pounds on the bar. That's when he was taking courses in criminal justice at the university. That was where I also saw him pay a student in the locker room for an examination that had been stored in a fraternity file.

"What's the haps, Lamar?" I said.

He was writing on a clipboard, his brow furrowed with concentration. He looked up and away from me, then huffed air out his nose. "Smell it?" he said.

"Hard not to," I said.

"We're still waiting on the coroner. The old black guy over there called it in. How come y'all are down here?"

"We're looking for a couple of guys who might be missing," I said.

"If I had to bet, I'd say these guys had been at the casino. Maybe somebody followed them or got in their car and forced them to drive down the levee."

"To rob them?" I said.

"Yeah, they got no wallet or ID on them. We found four ejected twelve-gauge shells inside."

"What did you find in the rental?" I asked.

"Nothing. Somebody emptied the glove box. I thought that was strange. Why would the shooter take the paperwork out of the glove box?"

"Probably to make our jobs harder."

"If you see puke inside, that's from the old guy. He got sick when he went inside." He laughed under his breath.

"Mind if we take a look?" Helen said.

"Be my guest," he replied, finally taking notice of her. His eyes traveled up and down her person. "We got barf bags in one of our cruisers if you need one."

"Give mine to your wife," she said.

The door to the cabin had been pried back onto the levee's incline, allowing the sunlight inside. I took out a handkerchief and held it to my nose. The odor of decomposition was exacerbated by the nature of the wounds. Both men had been shot at close range, in the stomach and in the face. Their viscera were exposed, their facial features hardly recognizable. Their brain matter was splattered all over one wall. Both men wore sports coats, silk shirts, and expensive Italian shoes with tassels on them. Both of them lay on their side, the remnants of their eyes glistening.

I stepped back out in the sunlight and blew out my breath. Helen looked at me.

"I'm pretty sure it's Charlie Weiss and Marco Scarlotti," I said.

"Kovick's gumballs?"

"What's left of them."

"You see Bledsoe for this?"

"I see Ronald Bledsoe for anything," I replied.

Then I looked up on the levee and saw Clete Purcel watching us. He must have used his police radio scanner to find the location of the double homicide. Lamar Fusilier looked up and saw him, too.

"You got no business at this crime scene, Purcel. Haul your fat ass out of here," he said.

Clete lit a cigarette in the wind and flipped the dead match down the levee, never moving from his position, smoke leaking out of his mouth.

CHAPTER

30

IF YOU HAVE stacked a little time in the can, or beat your way across the country bucking bales and picking melons, or worked out of a Manpower Inc. day-labor office on skid row, you probably already know that human beings are infinitely complex and not subject to easy categorization. I'm always amazed at how the greatest complexity as well as personal courage is usually found in our most nondescript members. People who look as interesting as a mud wall have the personal histories of classical Greeks. I sometimes think that every person's experience, if translated into flame, would be enough to melt the flesh from his bones. I guess the word I'm looking for is "empathy." We find it in people who have none of the apparent characteristics of light-bearers.

I had gone directly home from the levee in St. Mary Parish, primarily because I feared what Ronald Bledsoe would do next. The lead detective at the crime scene would lift all the prints he could from the shotgun shells and the tarpaper shack, but I doubted if his investigation would come up with anything of value. In my opinion, Bledsoe had been the shooter and Bledsoe wasn't about to get nailed by a detective who had to pay for a copy of an examination in order to pass a criminal justice course.

At 4:41 p.m. Sidney and Eunice Kovick pulled into my driveway, Sidney behind the wheel, both of them looking like people who had just discovered the enormity of their own miscalculations. Sidney got out of his vehicle and rested one hand on the roof. "I heard two guys got it in the Atchafalaya," he said.

"That's right," I said.

"Who were they?"

"They didn't have any ID on them. I suspect by tonight or tomorrow the St. Mary Parish Sheriff's Department will have some definite information."

"I heard about it on the radio. I went by your office. Nobody would tell me anything. They said you were over here."

"I've told you what I know, Sidney," I said.

"*Dave,*" Eunice said softly. She was still belted in the passenger seat, her face turned up toward mine.

"These guys were driving a rental Avalon," I said.

"You saw the bodies?" Sidney said.

"The shooter used a twelve-gauge shotgun. The features were hard to recognize. But the victims looked like Charlie and Marco," I said.

Sidney clenched his fist on top of the roof. "Where's Ronald Bledsoe?"

"*I'm* supposed to know that? You've been jerking me around from the jump, Sidney. Maybe it's time you develop a little clarity in your life."

"You don't understand, Dave. You've never understood what's going on," Eunice said.

"How can I? You don't share information. Sidney believes the function of cops is to return property to him that he stole from somebody else."

"Here's your news bulletin of the day. I didn't steal anything from anybody. I made a deal to bring certain goods into the country. I paid for them. Then I found out these goods were being handled by some guys who wipe their ass on their bare hand. So I blew the deal out of the water and confiscated my goods and maybe left a couple of guys with some bad memories to take back to Crap-a-stan."

"Bo Wiggins was your partner in this?"

"Bo who?" he said.

"We're done here, Sidney. You want to make your bullshit a matter of record, come into the office tomorrow."

"You listen to me, Dave. Marco took a shank in the arm for me when we were kids in the project. Charlie Weiss's daddy fought on five-buck-a-pop fight cards with my old man during the Depression. Charlie did thirty-eight months on Camp J rather than give me up."

"Why were they following Bledsoe into the Atchafalaya Basin?" I asked.

"I don't know. They were following him all over. We wanted to find the black kid who looted my house. We figured Bledsoe had a lead on him. I feel to blame."

Sidney's face was covered with shadow, and leaves were drifting out of the trees onto the waxed surface of his car, further obscuring his expression. I believe his eyes were actually glistening.

THAT NIGHT I sat in the kitchen and tried to figure out combinations of letters that would give meaning to the illegible remnant of Bertrand Melancon's statement of amends to the Baylor family. In reality, I didn't care if anyone ever found the blood diamonds or not. My only interest in them at this point was to find out who had hired Ronald Bledsoe. I still believed he may have worked for Sidney. But if Sidney wasn't lying, that left only Bo Diddley Wiggins.

"What are you doing?" Alafair asked, looking over my shoulder.

"Probably wasting time," I replied.

"Is this part of the note you said was in the Baylors' yard?"

"That's right."

She picked up the yellow legal pad on which I had printed the disconnected letters. "Let me try a few combinations on the computer."

"How's that going to help?"

"If the words had been typed rather than hand-printed, it would be fairly easy. The problem with a hand-printed version is the absence of uniform spacing. So you have to be imaginative in order to compensate."

"Really?" I said.

"Lose the sardonic attitude," she said.

I walked down the slope of the yard to the bayou. The air was damp, the evening sky lit by the fire stacks at the sugar mill. I was more tired than I had ever been. Perhaps it was my imagination, but I could almost feel a great weight oppressing the land, a darkness stealing across its surface, a theft of light that seemed to have no origin. Was this just more of the world destruction fantasy that had invaded my childhood dreams and followed me to Vietnam and into bars all over the Orient? Or was William Blake's tiger much larger than we ever guessed, its time finally come round?

I called Clete on his cell phone. "Where are you?" I said.

"At the motor court."

"Any sign of Bledsoe?"

"No."

"Look, I don't want to leave the house. Come on over."

"What for?"

"Nothing. That's it. Nothing is up. And I'm powerless to do anything about any of it."

"Any of what?"

"I don't know. That's it, I don't know. Sunday, I blew a plug out of a guy's chest the size of a quarter. I enjoyed it. I had a fantasy about the guy going to Hell."

"So what?"

"We've got blood splatter all over us, Clete."

"The only time that's a problem is when it's ours and not theirs."

"Wrong," I said.

"Dangle loose. I'm going to motor on over."

I had advised Sidney Kovick to develop some clarity in his life. What a joke.

WEDNESDAY MORNING I experienced one of those instances when middle-class people walk into a law enforcement agency and in the next few minutes trustingly consign their lives to a bureaucratic system that operates with all the compassion of dice clattering out of a leather cup.

I happened to glance out the window just as Melanie and Otis and Thelma Baylor entered the building. I believed I knew the nature of their visit and I didn't want to be part of it. Contrary to popular belief, the lion's share of police work is administrative or clerical in nature. Occasionally we get to slam the door on people whose convictions represent only a small fraction of their crimes and you take a pleasure in separating them from the rest of us. But sometimes you are forced to sit down with offenders who are little different from yourself. They cannot believe the damage they have done to their lives. Even worse, they cannot deal with the institutional consequences that await them. I had come to believe the Baylors fell into this category and I did not want to aid them in their own dismemberment.

Sure enough, Wally buzzed me on my extension and told me the Baylors wanted to see me.

"Keep them down there," I said.

"I t'ought you liked Mr. Baylor. I already sent them up."

"It's okay, Wally. Don't worry about it," I said.

I met them at the door and stopped Otis before he could speak. "I think you need to talk to either the district attorney or Sheriff Soileau."

"No, we need to talk to you, Mr. Robicheaux. We've deceived you and we need to set things right," Otis said.

Of course, they had no attorney with them.

"I want you to understand this. The Iberia Sheriff's Department has no direct relationship to the prosecution of your case, Mr. Baylor. We're liaison people on lend-lease to other agencies. It's only because of Katrina that we were drawn into your case. Your issue is with the FBI and the Orleans Parish DA's office. Sir, use your head."

"Shut up, Mr. Robicheaux," Melanie Baylor said.

"Excuse me?"

"You're going to tell us to get a lawyer. We have a lawyer. I let you hound my husband and I have to account for that. I shot the two black men. My husband had nothing to do with it and neither did my stepdaughter."

There were circles under her eyes, and the smell of whiskey and cigarettes was deep in her lungs. I suspected that in her naïveté she believed her sudden admission of guilt would disarm and vanquish all those who had persecuted her and her family, that somehow culpability and accusation would be replaced by the healing balm of martyrdom.

"Would you like to sit down?" I said to her.

"What for?" she replied.

I took a yellow legal pad and a ballpoint pen from a shelf and dropped them on my desk. "So you can write out an account of what happened the night the two men were shot in front of your house," I said.

"I don't see why that's necessary. I just told you what happened," she said.

"You're under arrest, Mrs. Baylor. You can have a lawyer here if you wish. You do not have to talk to me, you do not have to write on that legal pad. Whatever you say here from this moment on can be used against you. You are now formally in custody and in all probability you will not return home today. But you came to my office of your own volition. I think that fact will have a strong influence on the disposition of your case. I wouldn't mar that gesture by obfuscation and recalcitrance now."

She looked at her husband and stepdaughter.

"Do what he says, Melanie," Otis said.

Then her face began to dissolve, just like papier-mâché held to a hot light.

Mrs. Baylor was not a likable woman. I believe she sighted on Eddy Melancon's throat with forethought and intentionally took his life. I also believe his death was entirely avoidable and that he and Kevin Rochon posed no threat to her safety. But in that moment, as she broke down in my office, who would choose to take on her burden by becoming her judge?

I handed her a box of Kleenex and watched the Sunset Limited wobble down the railway tracks while she wrote on my legal pad.

CLETE PICKED ME UP at noon and we drove toward my house in his Caddy, the top down. Molly was at work and Alafair was doing research for her novel at the university library in Lafayette. Ronald Bledsoe still had not returned to his cottage at the motor court. I told Clete about the confession of Melanie Baylor.

"How do you think it'll play out?" he said.

"Remember that Japanese exchange student who went up a driveway in Baton Rouge on Halloween evening? He asked at the side door for directions to a party?"

"The wife panicked and the husband shot and killed the kid with a forty-four Mag?" he said.

"Yeah, the shooter walked."

"That's because the Feds weren't in on that one. This time they are. Look, Dave, we've got one issue here and that's to bag the guys who tried to kill your family." He turned onto East Main, a net of light and shadow sliding across his face. "We've missed something, I just don't know what it is. I had a funny dream last night. I was walking in a woods and I could smell fall in the air. There were leaves and mushrooms all over the ground, and air vines were hanging from the trees. When I came out of the woods, you were standing on the edge of a stream with a suitcase by your foot, like you were about to go on a trip. You said, 'You walked over a grave, Clete. Didn't you see it?' Then you waded into the water."

The connotations of his dream made something drop in my chest, like a stone tumbling down a well.

"What do you think it means?" he said.

"Nothing," I said. "Dreams are just dreams."

"No, we missed something. I stepped on a grave and didn't see it. We've been chasing blood diamonds and street pukes and dealing with Dagwood and Blondie while Ronald Bledsoe wipes his ass on the drapes. Bledsoe is the key. How could a guy like that go this long without getting busted somewhere for something? There's another story to this, Streak."

We pulled into my driveway. I opened the front door of the house, then checked all the locks and the windows. I went into the backyard and checked on Snuggs and Tripod. I even squatted down and looked under the house for wires or a device or a package that didn't belong there. That's what the inculcation of fear does. Without leaving his home, your enemy makes you his prisoner and controls every minute of your day.

Clete was waiting for me in the kitchen when I came back into the house.

"When I told you about the dream? About you walking into the water? I saw a look on your face. Why'd you look like that, Dave?"

"I don't remember," I replied, avoiding his eyes. "Let's fix lunch. I have to get back to work."

THAT AFTERNOON Wally came up to my office, wheezing from the effort of climbing the stairs. He had a folded sheet of lined paper in his hand. "This come over from lockup. It's for you," he said.

I unfolded the letter and looked at the flowing calligraphy and the name at the bottom. "Thanks, Wally."

After he had gone, I sat down and read the letter. No one is exactly sure of the engines that drive the alcoholic. AA literature makes use of terms like "self-centered fear" and "self-will run riot" and "moral and psychological insanity." Some people consider it a deep-seated neurosis and personality disorder. But regardless of its origins, pride is high up on the list of its attributes.

> To Detective Robicheaux,
>
> I want to clarify my statement in your office earlier today. I shot into the darkness in order to dissuade the looters from entering our home. Now I must be accountable for that, even though I think one of the looters positioned himself in the path of the bullet, probably because of the self-destructive nature of his kind, although I cannot say that for certain.
>
> I confessed to my "crime" because you harassed my husband and daughter and would give our family no peace. I have been told by members of my aerobics class you have a history as a drunkard and your meddlesome ways are your means to avoid not being drunk all the time.
>
> If you want the truth about what happened that terrible night, I will now tell you and you can attach it to my earlier

statement. We were at the mercy of depraved animals. The next-door neighbor and his friends said they would protect us. But the next-door neighbor, with his supposed military training and background as a "Southern gentleman," is a poseur and a blowhard as well as a drunkard like yourself, and after my husband fell asleep from exhaustion, I had to take charge of things and fire blindly into the darkness before the looters who were also the ones who raped our daughter broke down our doors.

I forgive you for what you did. Your ineptitude and low intelligence are probably not your fault, but your alcoholic personality is. If I were you, I would do something about it, if not for your own sake, then for the sake of those who have to live around you.

> Sincerely,
> Melanie Baylor

I made a Xerox copy of the letter and sent the original to the district attorney's office, hoping I never heard the name of Melanie Baylor again.

CHAPTER
31

L<small>ATER,</small> I <small>CALLED</small> Betsy Mossbacher at the FBI office in Baton Rouge. I had left her a message after I had found out Bertrand Melancon was in the Ninth Ward. I had also called her after Bobby Mack Rydel had tried to kill my family. But she had not returned my calls. This time she picked up.

"Where have you been?" I asked.

"All over the state. What's this about?"

"I left you a message about Bertrand Melancon. Otis Baylor found him. Melancon is at his aunt's house in the Ninth Ward. I also left you a message about Bobby Mack Rydel."

"Yeah, I was sorry to hear about that. I'm glad you're okay."

I waited for her to go on, but she didn't.

"Y'all been pretty busy?" I said.

"Give me Melancon's address. I'll see what we can do."

I could feel my energies draining. We had been called into a jurisdiction not our own and asked to do scut work that was the responsibility of other agencies. Now I was getting the inference, I had become an annoyance. I gave her the address of Melancon's aunt in the Ninth Ward.

"Melanie Baylor confessed this morning to shooting the looters. Her husband was covering for her."

"Sheriff Soileau faxed us that info an hour ago."

"Melancon wrote a letter of amends to the Baylor family. He gave them directions to the blood diamonds. Except the letter got water-soaked and so far hasn't been of much value to us. In the meantime, two of Sidney Kovick's guys got whacked in the Atchafalaya Basin."

"Yeah, we got that."

"Betsy, I'm supposed to share information with you. If you don't want me to do that, tell me to get lost."

"We're buried alive in work. Maybe all this will get sorted out one day, but it's going to be a long time. Do you have any idea how many open homicide cases we have in New Orleans? The city is a giant repository for the dead. I'm not talking about gangbangers, I'm talking about patients who were allowed to drown in nursing homes. Do you realize how many complaints about unjustified police shootings we have to investigate? I can't even get information about our own people. I think some Navy SEALs took out some snipers we don't know about."

But I wasn't concerned with the FBI's problems. "I've got to get a net over Ronald Bledsoe. He's ruining our lives," I said.

I heard her breathe air out her nose. But I didn't allow her to speak and continued to bore in. "Sidney Kovick inasmuch as told me he took the diamonds off some guys from the Mideast. You told me yourself he fancied himself a patriot. Maybe these guys are al Qaeda. You have unlimited electronic access when it comes to Homeland Security matters. Bledsoe is the loose thread on the sweater. We just have to pull on it."

"Good try, no cigar."

"So long, Betsy. I think you're working for the right bunch," I said, and hung up, coming down hard with the receiver.

WEDNESDAY EVENING was exceptionally beautiful, as though the earth and the heavens had decided to join together and re-create South Louisiana the way it was before Katrina and Rita tore it apart. The sky was a hard blue, the evening star twinkling in the west, a big brown moon rising above the cane fields. The rains had turned the oaks a deeper green and had sent Bayou Teche over its banks, swirling along the edges of our yards. You could smell barbecue fires in the park and the tannic odor of chrysanthemums and a clean, bright odor that perhaps signaled the coming of winter, but not in a bad way. For no demonstrable reason, I felt a sense of peace, as though I had been invited to a war but at the last moment had decided not to attend.

Alafair was returning to the university library to finish the research for her novel and Molly was going to drive her. "You're sure you won't come?" Molly said from the doorway.

"I'll probably just read a bit and take a walk," I said.

"I think I almost have the words worked out on the bottom of the letter the black guy left at the Baylors'," Alafair said. "It's just a matter of finding the right combination, not the letters, but the words themselves, so they form a sensible statement."

I tried not to show my lack of enthusiasm. "That's good," I said.

"Would the word 'bricks' mean anything?" she said.

I thought about it. "Yeah, it could."

"I'll let you know what I come up with. Actually this is great material. I'd like to use it in my novel."

They said good-bye and started out the door. Alafair snapped her fingers in the air. "I forgot my purse. I don't have any money," she said. "I was going to pick up a dessert."

"Here," I said. I took twenty dollars from my wallet and handed it to her. "I'll put it on your tab."

"We won't be late," she said.

"I'll still be up," I replied, and gave her the thumbs-up sign, the one I had always given her when she was little.

A HALF HOUR LATER, I saw Clete's Caddy pull into the driveway. I went outside and waited for him on the gallery. He tore the tab on a can of beer and sat down on the steps, his porkpie hat slanted forward on his forehead. He stuck a cigarette in his mouth and lit it and blew smoke out into the yard. He still had not spoken except to comment negatively on the price of gasoline. I took the cigarette from his mouth, walked out to the curb, and dropped it into the storm drain.

"Dave, being around you is like being married. Will you lay off ?"

"What's on your mind, Cletus?"

"What's on my mind is I've either been living in my own thoughts o long or I've developed shit-for-brains syndrome."

I sat down next to him. The streetlights had gone on and the anopy of oaks that arched over the street ruffled when the wind lew.

"Remember when we were searching the Baylor property and the eighbor came out and asked us what we were doing?" he said.

"Yeah, his name is Tom Claggart."

"Remember I told you I thought I'd seen him somewhere?"

"Yeah, I do."

"Last year I took a gal for a boat ride out in the Basin. It was old as hell and I ran out of gas. There were some hunters in a camp p on an island, about three hundred yards from the Atchafalaya. walked up on them while they were dressing a deer. The deer was anging by its feet from a tree. There were guts and strips of hide all ver the ground. These guys looked pretty uncomfortable. Then I emembered deer season had closed two or three days earlier.

"One guy goes, 'We got this six-pointer last week, but it froze up n us.'

"I pretended I didn't know or care what he was talking about. They ave me two gallons of gas and wouldn't let me pay them for it. Just s I was leaving, a guy with a bullet head and thick mustache came to he door and looked at me. I think it was that Claggart guy."

"So maybe Claggart hunts deer or has a camp in the Basin," I aid.

"There was a laptop opened on the table behind him. I could see through the doorway. The image on the screen was a bunch of laying cards floating into a black hat, you know, the kind magi-ians use. I think it's one of those video games for gamblers. Bledsoe s always playing them."

I squeezed my eyes shut, then opened them. "No, he doesn't just lay them. He plays *that* one," I said.

"Say again?"

"I saw that program running on Bledsoe's laptop when I was in his cottage."

"Oh man, we walked right over it, didn't we? Where you going?"

"To apologize to the FBI."

I went into the kitchen and called Betsy Mossbacher's cell phone.

"Hello, Dave," she said.

"Can we deep-six that conversation we had this afternoon? I need your help," I said.

"You push me into corners, then you blow hot and cold. I never know who's coming out of the jack-in-the-box. It can be a drag, Dave."

Don't argue, don't contend, I heard a voice say.

"We've been looking in the wrong places for information on Ronald Bledsoe. We've been looking for a criminal record that doesn't exist and faulting ourselves for not finding it. The real story on a guy like Bledsoe is in the façade of normalcy."

"I don't follow."

"The reason guys like BTK and John Wayne Gacy and the Green River guy, what's-his-name, Gary Ridgway, can kill people for decades is they're protected. Their family members live in denial because they can't accept the fact they're related to a monster, or that they've slept with him or had children with him. How would you like to find out your father is Norman Bates?"

"I got the point. What do you need?"

"Everything I can get on a guy by the name of Tom Claggart. He has a house next door to Otis Baylor's place in New Orleans."

"What's his tie-in?"

"He's an export-import man. Baylor said Claggart attended either Virginia Military Institute or the Citadel. The Citadel is in South Carolina. That's where Bledsoe seems to be from."

"How soon do you need this?"

"Right now."

"I'll see what I can do."

"Betsy, Bledsoe sent Bobby Mack Rydel after my daughter. She came within inches of being killed. We've been square with you guys. You owe me."

There was a beat. "I think we do," she replied.

• • •

THE SKY HAD SOFTENED to a dark blue when Molly and Alafair parked their automobile next to Burke Hall, the old drama and arts building hard by a lake that was thick with flooded cypress. Molly had a guest-faculty sticker on her car and almost always used the same parking area when she visited the university because there were no evening classes in Burke Hall and the spot between the building and the lake was secluded and usually empty. She put her purse under the seat and locked the car, then she and Alafair walked across the campus to the library.

The grass in the quadrangle had just been mowed, and the air smelled like flowers blooming and wet hay, and leaves and pecan husks someone was burning in a damp pile. The roofed walkways that enclosed the quadrangle were full of students, the moss in the live oaks limned by the glow of the lighted windows in classroom buildings and student dorms. A sorority was conducting a bake sale in front of the library entrance, the girls wearing sweaters because of the chill, an aura of innocence about them that one would associate with a 1940s movie. The scene I describe is not one of nostalgia. It's one that existed. It's one in which we either believe or disbelieve. It represents I think to all of us the kind of moment that should be inviolate.

Unfortunately it is not.

After Molly and Alafair entered the building, a man in a raincoat paused at the bake-sale table and bought a pastry. He wore a rain hat that seemed too large for his head and cupped his ears, like an oversize bowler sitting on a manikin. He also wore a mustache with streaks of white in it. He seemed to be a nervous man, and he gave off a smell that was like a mixture of deodorant and moldy fabric or socks left in a gym locker.

He paid for the pastry with a five-dollar bill and wanted no change. When he pushed the pastry into his mouth, his eyes were fastened on the interior of the library. The coed who had sold him the pastry offered him a napkin. He took it from her and entered the building, wiping his mouth. In his right hand he still held the napkin the coed had given him and the cellophane the pastry had come wrapped in. A trash receptacle was less than three feet from him. But he balled the cellophane and napkin in his palm and shoved them in his coat pocket. Then he walked up the stairs to the second floor of the library, his face lifted, like a hunter glancing upward into the canopy of a forest.

I DIDN'T WAIT for Betsy Mossbacher to call me back with information about Tom Claggart. I used my cell phone, in case Betsy called on the landline, and talked to the state police in both Virginia and South Carolina, but the people on duty were all after-hours personnel and had the same problem I did, namely that all the state offices that could give answers about Tom Claggart were closed.

Then I used the most valuable and unlauded investigative resource in the United States, the lowly reference librarian. Their salaries are wretched and they receive credit for nothing. Their desks are usually tucked away in the stacks or in a remote corner where they have to shush noisy high school students or put up with street people blowing wine in their faces or snoring in the stuffed chairs. But their ability to find obscure information is remarkable and they persevere like Spartans.

The tidewater accent of the one I spoke with at the Citadel library in Charleston was a genuine pleasure to listen to. Her name was Iris Rosecrans and I had the feeling she could read aloud from the telephone directory and make it sound like a recitation of Shakespearean sonnets. I told her who I was and asked if she could find any record of a past student by the name of Tom Claggart.

"As you probably have already gathered, Mr. Robicheaux, the registrar's office is closed until tomorrow morning," she said. "However, that said, I think I can go back through some of the yearbooks and be of some service to you."

"Ms. Rosecrans, I need every bit of information I can get regarding this man. It's extremely urgent. I don't want to burden you with my situation or to seem melodramatic, but someone tried to kill my daughter and I think the man responsible is named Ronald Bledsoe. I think Ronald Bledsoe may have some relationship to Tom Claggart."

She paused a moment. "Spell 'Bledsoe' for me, please."

Twenty minutes later she called back. "Thomas S. Claggart was a freshman and sophomore student here in 1977 and '78. His hometown is listed as Camden. He's not included in the yearbooks after '78. Ronald Bledsoe appears never to have been a student here."

"Well, I appreciate your—"

I heard a piece of paper crinkle, like a sheet on a tablet being folded back. "I do have other information, Mr. Robicheaux," she said.

"Please, go ahead."

"I talked to the reference librarian in Camden. She checked the old telephone directories and found a T. S. Claggart listed during the years '76 to '79. I called the police station there, but no one had heard of a Claggart family. The officer I spoke with was kind enough to give me the number of the man who was police chief at the time. So I called him at his house. Would you like his name?"

"No, no, what did he tell you?"

"He remembered the senior Claggart quite well. He said he was a United States Army sergeant stationed at Fort Jackson. His wife had died several years earlier, but he had a son named Tom Junior, and perhaps a stepson. The stepson was named Ronald."

"Bledsoe?"

"The retired police chief wasn't sure of the last name. But it was not Claggart. He said the boy was peculiar-looking and strange in his behavior. He had the feeling the boy had been in foster homes or a place for disturbed children.

"That's all I was able to gather. We're about to close. Would you like for me to search a little bit more tomorrow? I don't mind."

"What I would like, Ms. Rosecrans, is to buy you an island in the Caribbean. Or perhaps to ask the Vatican to grant you early canonization."

"That's very nice of you," she said.

I told Clete what I had just learned from Ms. Rosecrans. He was eating a sandwich in the living room, watching the History Channel.

"You think Claggart has been covering Bledsoe's ass all these years?" he said.

"Probably. Or maybe they work as a team. You remember the Hillside Strangler case in California? The perps were cousins. Explain how one family can have two guys like that in it."

He started to reply, but I opened my cell phone and began punching in numbers.

"Who you calling?" he asked.

"Molly."

"Relax, they're at the university. I mean it, noble mon, you're giving me the shingles just watching you."

I got Molly's voice mail and realized she had probably left her cell phone in the automobile or turned it off when she entered the library. I tried Alafair's number and got the same result, then I remembered Alafair had left her purse at the house.

The phone rang in the kitchen.

ALAFAIR HAD SPREAD her note cards on a table that was not far from shelves of books that dealt with the flora and fauna of the American Northwest. She was writing down the names of trees and types of rock that characterized the escarpment along the Columbia River Gorge just south of Mount Hood. Then her eyes began to burn from the fatigue of the day and the sleepless nights she had experienced since Bobby Mack Rydel, a man she had never seen before, had tried to kill her.

In her earliest attempts at fiction, she had learned that there are many things a person can do well when he or she is tired, but imagining plots and creating dialogue and envisioning fictional characters and writing well are not among them.

She gathered up her note cards and placed them in her book bag, then took out the yellow legal pad on which I had written down the remnants of the words at the bottom of Bertrand Melancon's letter to the Baylor family.

In the stacks, a man with a raincoat over his arm and an oversize hat on his head was gazing curiously at the titles of the books arrayed along the shelf. He lifted a heavy volume off the shelf and seated himself on the opposite side of Alafair's table, three chairs down from her. He did not glance in her direction and seemed intent upon the content of his book, a collection of photographic plates of scenes in Colorado. Then, as an afterthought, he seemed to remember that he was still wearing his hat. He removed it and set it crown-down on the table. His scalp was bone-white under the freshly shaved roots of his hair.

"How do you do?" he said, and nodded.

"Fine, how are you?" Alafair replied.

He opened his book and began reading, his forehead knitted. Alafair went back to work on Bertrand Melancon's water-diluted directions to Sidney Kovick's diamonds. Molly returned from the restroom and looked over her shoulder. The original letters had been *Th dym   s un   the ri s on e ot ide of h   an.* Alafair had spaced them out ten times on ten lines, trying different combinations with them on each line. By the tenth line, she had created a statement that seemed to make syntactical and visual sense.

"You should have been a cryptographer," Molly said.

"Spelling is the challenge," Alafair said. "He probably spells most polysyllabic words phonetically. So if the first word is 'The' and we create 'dymines' out of 'dym,' we've got a running start on the whole sentence. If the third word doesn't agree in number with 'dymines' and we substitute 'is' for 'are,' it begins to come together pretty quickly."

The man with the mustache and shaved head paused in his reading, stifling a yawn, his head turning in the opposite direction from Molly and Alafair. His eyes scanned the high windows for a flicker of lightning in the sky. He watched a tall black kid in a basketball letter sweater walk by, then resumed reading.

"We turn 'un' into 'under' and let 'the' stand. Put a 'b' in front of 'ri' and add a 'k' and you get 'bricks.' 'On' stands by itself and 'ot' becomes 'other.' 'Of' stands alone and we turn 'h' into 'the.' So we've got 'The dymines is under the bricks on the other side of the . . .' It's the 'an' I haven't worked out."

Molly thought about it. "Put a 'c' in front and an 'e' behind."

"'Cane,' that's it. 'The dymines is under the bricks on the other side of the cane.' How about that?" Alafair said.

The man staring at alpine scenes in the large picture book he gripped by both covers, the spine resting on the table, looked at his watch and yawned again. He got up from the table and replaced his book on the shelf. Then he walked over to a periodicals rack and began thumbing through a magazine, occasionally glancing out the window at the darkness in the sky.

At 9:53 Molly and Alafair left the library and walked toward their automobile.

It was 9:12 p.m. when the phone rang in the kitchen. I hoped it was Molly. I looked at the caller ID and saw that the call was blocked. I picked up the receiver. "Hello?" I said.

"I had to cajole a couple of people, but this is what I found out," Betsy said. "Tom Claggart attended the Citadel in the late seventies. His father was stationed at Fort Jackson. The father was a widower and had only one child with the name Claggart. But at various times on his tax form he claimed two dependents besides himself, his son. Tom Junior, and a foster child by the name of Ronald Bledsoe."

"Yeah, I've already got that."

"You've got that? From where?" she said.

"A reference librarian at the Citadel."

"A reference librarian. Thanks for telling me that."

"Come on, Betsy, give me the rest of it."

"Dave, try to understand this. An agent in Columbia, South Carolina, drove to Camden, thirty miles away, and found people who remembered the Claggart family. He did this as a favor because we were in training together at Quantico. Be a little patient, all right?"

"I understand," I said, my scalp tightening.

"Claggart Senior was originally from Myrtle Beach. Evidently he had a child out of wedlock with a woman named Yvonne Bledsoe. She came from an old family that had fallen on bad times, and ran a day care center. Evidently she thought of herself as southern aristocracy who had been forced into a life beneath her social level. According to what my friend found out, a couple of parents accused her of molesting the children in her care. Tom Claggart, Junior, seemed to have lived with his father at several army bases around the country, but Ronald Bledsoe stayed with the mother until he was fifteen or sixteen."

"Where is she now?" I asked.

"She burned to death in a house fire, source of ignition unknown."

When I hung up, the side of my head felt numb. I called Molly's cell phone again but got no answer. Clete was looking at me, a strange expression on his face. "What is it?" he said.

"Let's take a ride," I said.

MOLLY AND ALAFAIR walked across a stretch of green lawn between two brick buildings covered with shadow, crossed the boulevard, and entered an unlit area by the side of Burke Hall. The wind was colder now, threading lines through the film of congealed algae in the lake. The vehicles that had been parked by Molly's car were gone, the windows in Burke Hall dark. Molly unlocked the driver's door, then got behind the wheel and leaned across the seat to unlock the passenger side. In a flicker of lightning, she thought she saw a man standing at the rear of the building, leaning against the bricks, his arms folded on his chest. When she refocused her eyes, he wasn't there.

Alafair got in on the passenger side and closed the door behind her. "I'm tired. How about we pass on picking up a dessert?" she said.

"Fine with me," Molly said.

Molly removed her purse from under the seat and set it beside her. She slipped the key into the ignition and turned it. But the starter made no sound, not even the dry click that would indicate a dead battery. Nor did the dash indicators come on, as though the battery were totally disconnected from the system.

"I bought a new battery at AutoZone only three weeks ago," she said.

"Let me have your cell phone. I'll call Dave," Alafair said.

A gust of wind and rain blew across the cypress trees in the lake and patterned the windshield. Suddenly the man who had been sitting across from Molly and Alafair in the library was standing outside Molly's window, wearing his raincoat, his oversize hat cupping his ears. He was smiling and making a circular motion for Molly to roll down her window. That's when she noticed there was a one-inch airspace at the top of the glass, one that she didn't remember leaving when she had exited the car.

She hand-cranked the window down another six inches. "Yes?" she said.

"I saw you upstairs at the library," the man said.

"I know. What is it you want?"

"It looks like you got car trouble. I can call Triple A for you or give you a ride."

"Why do you think we're having car trouble?" Molly said.

"Because your car won't start," the man replied, a half-smile on his face.

"But how would you know that? The engine made no sound," Molly said.

"I saw you twisting the key a couple of times, that's all."

"We're fine, here. Thanks for the offer," she said.

The man looked out into the darkness, toward the side of the building, holding his raincoat closed at the throat, his face filmed with the mist blowing out of the cypress trees. "It's nasty weather to be out. I think a storm is coming," he said.

Alafair gave Molly a look, then pulled Molly's purse toward her, easing it down by her foot.

The man who wore a hat that cupped his ears and whose mustache was streaked with white leaned closer to the window. "I got to tell you ladies something. I didn't choose this. I feel sorry for you. I'm not that kind of man."

"Take the mashed potatoes out of your mouth and say it, whatever it is," Molly said.

But before the man in the raincoat could answer, Alafair's window exploded in shards all over the interior of the car. Alafair's face jerked in shock, her hair and shirt flecked with glass. A hand holding a brick raked the glass down even with the window frame, grinding it into powder against the metal.

Alafair and Molly stared at the grinning face of Ronald Bledsoe. In his right hand he clutched the brick, in his left, a .25-caliber blue-black automatic. He fitted the muzzle under Alafair's chin and increased the pressure until she lifted her chin and shut her eyes.

"Pop the hood so Tom can reconnect your battery, Miz Robi-cheaux," he said. "Then lean over the backseat and open the door for me. We're going to take a drive. Y'all are going to be good the whole way, too." He leaned forward and smelled Alafair's hair. "Lordy, I like you, Miss Alafair. You're a darlin' young girl, and I know what I'm talking about, because I've had the best."

Molly hesitated.

"You want to see her brains on the dashboard, Miz Robicheaux?" Bledsoe said.

Molly pulled on the hood release, then leaned over the backseat and opened the rear door. Bledsoe slipped inside, closing the door as quickly as possible to turn off the interior light. Molly was still extended over the seat, and his face and eyes were only inches from hers. His silk shirt rippled like blue ice water. She could smell the dampness on his skin, the dried soap he had used in shaving his head, an odor like soiled kitty litter that rose from his armpits.

The man in the raincoat slammed down the hood.

"Start the car," Bledsoe said, clicking the switch on the interior light to the "off" position.

"I don't think I should do that," Molly said.

The man in the raincoat pulled open the back door and got inside. He struggled a minute with his raincoat before getting the door shut. He would not look directly at either Molly or Alafair.

"Want to be the cause of this little girl's death?" Bledsoe said. "Want to be the cause of your own, just because you decide to be stubborn? That doesn't sound like a nun to me. That sounds like pride talking."

Molly's hand started to shake as she turned the ignition. "My husband is going to hang you out to dry, buddy boy," she said.

"He'd like to. But so far, he hasn't done such a good job of it, has he?" Bledsoe said. He teased the muzzle of the .25 under Alafair's ear. "Pull onto the street, Miz Robicheaux."

Molly turned on the headlights and began backing up, craning her neck to see out the back window. The sidewalk and lawn area in front of Burke Hall were empty, the giant oak by the entrance obscuring the light from the intersection to the south.

"Miss Alafair, reach there into your book bag and give me that yellow tablet you were writing on," Bledsoe said. "That's right, reach in and hand it to me. You a good girl. You play your cards right, you cain't tell what might happen. You might come out of this just fine."

Bledsoe took the yellow legal pad from Alafair's hand and examined the top page, all the while holding the .25 against Alafair's head. "Miss Alafair, you just made a bunch of people very happy. Isn't that something, Tom? It was sitting in your backyard all the time, under that big generator, I bet. It took an educated young woman to figure this out for us. She's special is what she is. Hear that, darlin'? You special and that's how I'm gonna treat you. You'll like it when we get there."

He picked a piece of glass out of her hair and flicked it out the window. He did not say where "there" was.

They pulled out on the boulevard and drove past a women's dormitory to a stop sign on the edge of the campus. Then they turned onto University Avenue and headed toward the edge of town.

MOMENTS LATER, a few blocks up the avenue, between a Jewish cemetery that was covered with the deep shadows of cedar and oak trees, and an old icehouse that had been converted into a topless club, a jogger had to dodge a car that had plunged out of the traffic, across the median, and possibly had been hit by another car. The jogger could not see clearly inside the car because of the mist, but when he called 911, he told the dispatcher he had heard a sound like muffled firecrackers and he thought he had seen a series of flashes inside the windows.

• • •

I CLAMPED THE portable emergency flasher on the roof of my truck and let Clete drive. By the time Clete had driven us through the little town of Broussard, the highway was slick, the sky black, and traffic was backing up because of construction outside Lafayette. We went through a long section of urban sprawl that in my college days had been sugarcane fields and pecan orchards, threaded by a two-lane highway that had been lined on each side with live oaks. But that was all gone.

It was almost 10:00 p.m. I had called Molly's cell phone three times en route, getting her voice mail each time.

"You're worrying too much. They're probably headed home by now," Clete said.

"She always checks her voice mail. It's an obsession with her," I said.

"Think about it a minute, Dave. Nothing has changed since this afternoon, except for the fact we found out Claggart is Asswipe's half brother. That doesn't mean Molly and Alafair are in greater danger. You know what I think is bothering you?"

"I have a feeling you're going to tell me."

"You smoked Rydel and now you want to drink."

When I didn't speak, he said, "Remember when we did that bunch of Colombians? I've never been so scared in my life. I drank a dozen double Scotches that night and it didn't make a dent."

"Clete?"

"Yeah?"

"Will you shut up?"

He looked at me in the glow of the dash, then mashed on the accelerator, swerving across a double stripe to pass a tractor-trailer rig, rocking both of us against the doors.

I punched in 911 and got a Lafayette Parish dispatcher. "What's the nature of your emergency?" a black woman's voice said.

"This is Detective Dave Robicheaux, Iberia Parish Sheriff's Department," I said. "I'm on my way to the UL campus to find my wife and daughter. They usually park by Cypress Lake, next to Burke

Hall. They're not responding to my calls. I think they may be in jeopardy. Will you send a cruiser to the campus and check out their vehicle, please?"

I gave her the make and model of Molly's car.

"We have a five-car accident on University, but we'll get someone over to the campus as soon as possible," she said. "Do you want me to call Campus Security?"

"Yes, please."

"You didn't tell me the nature of the emergency."

"Some guys tried to kill my family on Sunday. They're still out there."

"Give me your number and I'll call you every ten minutes until we know they're safe."

"Thank you," I said.

As I said, it's the most humble members of the human family who remind us of the Orwellian admonition that people are always better than we think they are.

Clete hit a clear stretch of four-lane road and floored my truck. We went through a brightly lit shopping district, then entered the old part of Lafayette, where live oak trees hung with moss still form canopies over the streets. We turned left on University Avenue and passed the five-car pileup the 911 dispatcher had mentioned. The mist was gray, floating across the trees and shrubbery and hedges in the university district. A church bus passed us in the opposite direction, then a tanker truck and a stretch limo and a small car barely visible on the other side of the limo.

The roof of the car had the same rusty tint as Molly's. I turned around in the seat and looked through the back window, but I had lost sight of the car.

"Was that Molly and Alafair?" Clete said.

"I'm not sure."

"Want me to turn around?"

I thought about it. "No, check Burke Hall first," I said.

"You got it, noble mon," Clete said.

• • •

As THEY DROVE DOWN University Avenue past a five-car pileup, Ronald Bledsoe propped both his arms on the back of Alafair's seat to conceal the .25 automatic he had wedged against her spine. He smelled her hair again and ticked the back of her neck with his fingernail. When she tried to lean forward, he hooked his finger in her collar.

"Why'd you kick me in the park?" he asked.

"Where are we going?" Molly said.

"Straight ahead. I'll tell you what to do. You don't talk anymore until I tell you to," he replied. He nudged Alafair with the automatic. "You didn't answer my question, darlin'."

"I kicked you in the mouth because you asked for it," she said.

"I did no such thing. You shouldn't lie."

Alafair's face was growing more intense, her features sharpening. He put his lips on the nape of her neck, then mussed her hair with his free hand.

"Do you believe we let this sick fuck take over our car?" she said to Molly.

"Miss, don't talk like that to Ronald," Tom Claggart said. "You don't want to do that."

"What else can you do to us? You're going to kill us. Look at you, you're pathetic. You both have heads that look like foreskin. Who was your mother? She must have been inseminated by a yeast infection."

The effect of her words on the two men was different from what she had expected. Bledsoe cupped his hand under her chin and drew her head close to his mouth. Then he bit her hair. But it was Claggart who seemed to be losing control, as though he were witnessing a prelude to events he had seen before and did not want to see again. He became agitated, his eyes twitching. He rubbed his hands up and down on his thighs. Then he realized his raincoat was caught in the door. He began jerking at it, as though he were happy to have something to distract him.

"Pull over. My coat is caught," he said.

"There's a semi going fifty miles an hour on my bumper," Molly said.

"I don't care. Pull over right now. Make her pull over, Ronald," Claggart said.

Then Claggart opened the door while the car was still moving. Molly swerved the wheel and he lurched sideways. Bledsoe wasn't sure what was happening. In seconds, the environment he had imposed total control on was coming apart. He spit Alafair's hair out of his mouth and grabbed Claggart's arm, just as the open door was hit by a car traveling in the opposite direction.

Alafair reached down on the floor. All in one motion, she pulled Molly's .22 Ruger from her purse, worked the slide, and brought up the barrel into Ronald Bledsoe's face. His eyes were filled with disbelief. But his bigger problem was the fact he was twisted in the seat, his own brother fighting with him over a raincoat, his shoulder jammed against the seat so he couldn't get off a shot at Alafair. The next second was probably the longest in Ronald Bledsoe's life.

"Suck on this, you freak," Alafair said.

She pulled the trigger four times. The first round went into his mouth and punched through his cheek. The second embedded in his forearm when he lifted it in front of him, the third clipped off the end of a finger, and the fourth shattered his chin, slinging blood and saliva across the seat and the back window.

Molly's ears were deaf in the blowback of the Ruger. In the rearview mirror she saw Bledsoe staring back at her, his ruined mouth twisted like soft rubber, his concave face like a cartoon that was incapable of understanding the damage it had just incurred.

Molly's car struck the curb and came to a stop, cars swerving around her in the mist, their horns blowing. Alafair jumped from the car and pulled Bledsoe out the back door onto the concrete. She reached down and picked up his gun from the floor and threw it into the shrubbery on the edge of the cemetery. Tom Claggart sat frozen in the seat, his raincoat and shirt whipsawed with blood.

Bledsoe stared up at her from the gutter, waiting, his eyes genuinely puzzled, as a child might look up from its crib at the looming presence of its mother. Alafair extended the Ruger with both hands, aiming it into the center of his forehead.

"Alafair—" Molly said, almost in a whisper.

Alafair's knuckles whitened on the Ruger's grips.

"Hey, kiddo," Molly said.

"What?" Alafair said angrily.

"We never give them power."

"He'll be back."

"I doubt it. But if he does, we still don't give them power."

Alafair widened her eyes, releasing her breath, and stepped back-ward, clicking on the Ruger's safety with her thumb. She swallowed and looked at Molly, her eyes filming.

By the time Clete and I arrived at the scene, Alafair and Molly were sitting in the back of a cruiser, talking to a detective in the front seat. Tom Claggart was in handcuffs behind the wire-mesh grille of a second cruiser, and two paramedics were loading Ronald Bledsoe into an Acadiana ambulance.

Alafair got out of the cruiser when she saw me walking toward her from the truck. The detective had given her a roll of paper towels and she was scrubbing her hair with them, lifting her chin, flipping a strand out of her eyes. She looked absolutely beautiful, like a young girl emerging from a sun shower. "What's the haps, Streak?" she said.

"No haps, Alf," I said.

"Don't call me that stupid name," she said.

Molly leaned forward in the backseat of the cruiser, beaming. She gave me the thumbs-up sign with both hands. "What kept you?" she said.

EPILOGUE

I HAVE LONG SUBSCRIBED to the belief that the dead lay strong claim on the quick, that indeed their spirits wander and manifest themselves in the middle of our waking day and whisper to us when we least expect it. Many years ago, during a very bad time in my life, my murdered wife would talk to me out of the rain. Members of my platoon who I knew were KIA would call me up long-distance during an electric storm. Inside the static, I could hear their voices —cacophonous, sometimes frightened and nonsensical, sometimes breaking apart, like a walkie-talkie transmission when the sender is too far away.

A psychotherapist told me I was experiencing a psychotic episode. I didn't argue with him.

But if these experiences have ever happened to you, I'm sure you have come to the same conclusion about them as I. You know what you heard and you know what you saw, and you no more doubt the validity of your experience than you doubt the existence of the sunrise. A great change has occurred in you, and the change lies in the fact you no longer have to convince others about your vision of the world, not of this one or the next.

New Orleans was a song that went under the waves. Sometimes in my dreams I see a city beneath the sea. In it, green-painted iron streetcars made in the year 1910 still lumber down the neutral ground through the Garden District, past block upon block of Victorian and antebellum homes, past the windmill palms and the gigantic live oaks, past guesthouses and the outdoor cafés and art deco restaurants whose scrolled purple and pink and green neon burn in the mist like smoke from marker grenades.

Every hotel on Canal still features an orchestra on the roof, where people dance under the stars and convince one another that the mildness of the season is eternal and was created especially for them. In the distance, Lake Pontchartrain is wine-dark, flanged with palm trees, and pelicans skim above the chop, the rides at the waterside amusement park glowing whitely against the sky. Irving Fazola is playing at the Famous Door and Pete Fountain at his own joint off Bourbon. Jackson Square is a medieval plaza where jugglers, mimes, string bands, and unicyclists with umbrellas strapped on top of their heads perform in front of St. Louis Cathedral. No one is concerned with clocks. The city is as sybaritic as it is religious. Even death becomes an excuse for celebration.

Perhaps the city has found its permanence inside its own demise, like Atlantis, trapped forever under the waves, the sun never harsh, filtered through the green tint of the ocean so that neither rust nor moth nor decay ever touches its face.

That's the dream that I have. But the reality is otherwise. Category 5 hurricanes don't take prisoners and the sow that eats its farrow doesn't surrender self-interest in the cause of mercy.

New Orleans was systematically destroyed and that destruction began in the early 1980s with the deliberate reduction by half of federal funding to the city and the simultaneous introduction of crack cocaine into the welfare projects. The failure to repair the levees before Katrina and the abandonment of tens of thousands of people to their fate in the aftermath have causes that I'll let others sort out. But in my view the irrevocable fact remains that we saw an American city turned into Baghdad on the southern rim of the United States. If we have a precedent in our history for what happened in New Orleans, it's lost on me.

Ronald Bledsoe was sentenced to twenty years in Angola Prison for the abduction of my wife and daughter. I believe he and Bobby Mack Rydel and probably others murdered Andre Rochon and Courtney Degravelle and Sidney Kovick's hirelings, but Bledsoe gave nobody up.

I do not believe Bledsoe qualifies as a "solid" or "stand-up" con. Ronald Bledsoe belongs to that group who take their secrets to the grave. They never reveal the nature of their compulsion, their motivations, or the methods they use. Paradoxically, psychiatrists and prison administrators and journalists eventually create a composite explanation for sociopathic behavior that gives them a human personality and works in their interests. My own belief is that people like Bledsoe pose theological questions to us that psychologists cannot answer.

My only fear is that one day Ronald Bledsoe will be released from prison. If that happens, I'll be waiting for him. I would like to say the last statement brings me consolation. But it doesn't. Sometimes I have a disturbing dream about Bledsoe and I wake before dawn and go out into the yard and drink coffee at our redwood table until the darkness leaves the sky. Then the day takes on its ordinary shape and I go about doing all the ordinary things that ordinary people do.

Tom Claggart, Bledsoe's half brother, tried to implicate everyone he could, except himself. If he is to be believed, he unknowingly became involved with a diamond-smuggling operation in Buenos Aires, one fronted by Mideastern operatives, and raised capital through Sidney Kovick and Bo Diddley Wiggins. Sidney got hit with a bolt of patriotism and took the diamonds off a Mideastern courier, along with his dope and a pistol and thousands of dollars in counterfeit money. Sidney's patriotic fervor did not include turning the diamonds or the queer bills over to the Treasury Department, Homeland Security, or U.S. Customs.

The upshot?

Guess.

Tom Claggart is now hoeing soybeans for the State of Louisiana, and Sidney is running his flower store and Bo Diddley and his bovine wife are whocking golf balls with over-the-hill television celebrities at a Lafayette country club. I saw Bo three days ago, at a shopping center, his arms loaded with parcels. He shook my hand enthusiastically, his face full of warmth, his grip moist and firm. There wasn't a fleck of guilt or ill ease in his eyes. I probably should have simply eturned his greeting and walked away, but too much had happened and too many people had been hurt.

"Bo, the Degravelle woman was tortured to death," I said.

The skin under one eye seemed to wrinkle just a moment. "I don't know what you're getting at, but the way the Feds explained it to me, that woman was passing phony money or something."

"Have a good day, Bo. I probably won't be seeing you again, but I hope everything works out for you," I said. "If you see my daughter, you stay away from her."

He tried to get a firmer hold on his parcels, almost dropping one. "Yeah, sure, see you around," he said, unable to put together the implication of my words.

Melanie Baylor avoided manslaughter charges and got one year in a federal lockup on a civil rights beef. I receive postcards from her every two or three weeks, each one indicating ways I can improve my spirituality through various 12-step programs. My favorite included these lines: *Detective Robicheaux, there are those among us who are psychologically incapable of honesty. But there is hope even for these. Sir, don't give up. I and others here are praying for you.*

Otis Baylor has opened up an independent insurance agency as well as a grocery store he co-owns with a Laotian refugee who at one time was an opium grower and CIA mercenary. If there is a purgatory, I believe Our Lord will vouchsafe Otis's marriage to Melanie as payment in full for any debts he might owe.

Clete is still Clete. He seems to have accepted the destruction of the place where he was born, but he no longer refers to it as "the Big Sleazy." I wish he did, though, because that would mean the city under the sea I dream about is still alive. There was only one strange development about Clete in the aftermath of this story, one he will not talk about or explain.

I went back to the Ninth Ward to check on Bertrand Melancon's grandmother and aunt. I also wanted to check on Bertrand, because I thought Clete still intended to pick him up as a bail skip and return him to custody. But the house of Bertrand's aunt was empty, the yard piled to the eaves with debris from other teardowns on the block. When I asked the neighbors what had happened to the aunt and grandmother, they said a white man in a blue Cadillac convertible had brought some FEMA people to the house and the FEMA people had taken the two elderly women to a hospital in North Louisiana.

"Where did Bertrand go?" I asked.

No one seemed to know. But when I was about to leave, an old man whose back was terribly bowed and who walked with two canes made his way out to my truck. His skin was so black it looked like tar on his bones. "You gonna arrest that boy?" he asked.

"Maybe."

"Cain't say he don't deserve it, but I t'ink somet'ing bad already happened to him."

"How's that?" I asked.

"One night right after his auntie and grandmother left, he got a-holt of a rowboat and a trailer. I said to him, 'Where you t'ink you going wit' a rowboat?' He pointed to the sout' and said, 'Way on out yonder.'

"I said, 'There ain't nothing out there but water. All the trees, all the land, is tore up. Ain't nothing but water far as the eye can see. Ain't nothing but dead people in that water, either.'

"He said, 'It don't matter to me. That's where I'm going.'"

"He didn't say where, huh?" I asked.

"It don't matter where he go. Boy ain't never had peace. He ain't gonna have it now."

I thanked him and drove away. For a long time I could still see him in my rearview mirror, propped on his canes, dust drifting off my wheels into his face, surrounded by amounts of wreckage that perhaps no one can adequately describe.

I didn't like Bertrand Melancon or, better said, I didn't like the world he represented. But as I have to remind myself daily, many of the people I deal with did not get to choose the world in which they were born. Some try to escape it, some embrace it, most are overcome and buried by it. After his brother was shot, I think Bertrand tried to become the person he could have been if he'd had a better shake when he was a kid. But who knows? Like Clete says, going up or coming down, it's only rock 'n' roll. Bertrand was able to perform a couple of noble deeds before he disappeared. That's more than we expect from most men who started off life as he did.

Sometimes at twilight, when Clete and I are out on the salt and we can look northward at the vast green-gray misty rim of the Louisiana coastline, I have a fantasy about Bertrand Melancon and my old friend Father Jude LeBlanc, whose only trepidation in life was his fear that the uncontrollable shaking in his hands would cause him to drop the chalice while he was giving Communion.

In my fantasy, I see Bertrand far out on the water, pulling on the oars, his arms pumped with his task, the ruined city of New Orleans becoming smaller and smaller in the distance, a great darkness spreading across the sky just after sunset. The blisters on his hands turn into wounds that stain the wood of the oars with his blood. As the wind rises and the water becomes even blacker, he sees hundreds if not thousands of lights swimming below the surface. Then he realizes the lights are not lights at all. They have the shape of broken Communion wafers and the luminosity that radiates from them lies in the very fact they have been rejected and broken. But in a way he cannot understand, Bertrand knows that somehow all of them are safe now, including himself, inside a pewter vessel that is as big as the hand of God.